Bedroom Seductions

NICOLA MARSH
ANNE OLIVER
LUCY KING

Published in Great Britain 2014
by Mills & Boon, an imprint of Harlequin (UK) Limited,
Eton House, 18-24 Paradise Road, Richmond, Surrey, TW9 1SR

BEDROOM SEDUCTIONS © 2014 Harlequin Books S.A.

Two Weeks in the Magnate's Bed, Business in the Bedroom and *Bought: Damsel in Distress* were first published in Great Britain by Harlequin (UK) Limited.

Two Weeks in the Magnate's Bed © 2009 Nicola Marsh
Business in the Bedroom © 2008 Anne Oliver
Bought: Damsel in Distress © 2009 Lucy King

ISBN: 978 0 263 91168 8
eBook ISBN: 978 1 472 04463 1

05-0114

Harlequin (UK) Limited's policy is to use papers that are natural, renewable and recyclable products and made from wood grown in sustainable forests. The logging and manufacturing processes conform to the legal environmental regulations of the country of origin.

Printed and bound in Spain
by Blackprint CPI, Barcelona

TWO WEEKS IN THE MAGNATE'S BED

BY
NICOLA MARSH

Nicola Marsh has always had a passion for writing and reading. As a youngster, she devoured books when she should have been sleeping, and later she kept a diary, which could be an epic in itself! These days, when she's not enjoying life with her husband and son in her home city of Melbourne, she's at her computer doing her dream job: creating the romances she loves. Visit Nicola's website at www.nicolamarsh.com for the latest news of her books.

With thanks to fellow Harlequin Romance
author Claire Baxter, for helping me brainstorm
Zac in all his dynamic, enigmatic glory!

CHAPTER ONE

AS THE taxi screeched to a halt, Lana Walker flung open the door and scrambled for her bags.

'Hey, slow down. You haven't missed the boat.'

The deep groove in the driver's caterpillar mono-brow had been honed with years of practice if his glare was any indication.

The way she saw it, she might have arrived on time to board the *Ocean Queen*, but she'd missed the boat metaphorically in every other way that counted—which was exactly why she was taking this trip.

She rummaged for the fare and darted a curious glance at the ship, spotting several officers in white uniforms on deck.

Very impressive—and the ship wasn't half bad either.

A shadow loomed over the open passenger door as the driver held out his hand. 'Some people have all the luck. How about my fare, lady?'

Grouch. She resisted the urge to poke out her tongue as she handed him the money, picked up her luggage and headed for the escalators.

What would he know about luck? She'd worked hard for what she had—damn hard: five years as curator at Melbourne

Museum, and three years as head curator at Sydney Museum had been amazing, stimulating and stressful.

Sure, she had a stellar reputation in the industry, and a gorgeous apartment in the beachside suburb of Coogee, but that was about it.

She didn't have a life.

No time out, no socialising, no fun.

Over the next two weeks she planned to change all that.

Though luck had played a part in this trip; if she hadn't won the cruise she wouldn't have taken a holiday, sad workaholic that she was.

As thoughts of work crowded her head, namely how she'd recently missed out on the opportunity of a lifetime courtesy of her crippling shyness, she stumbled at the top of the escalator and pitched forward, silently cursing the three-inch heels her shoe-crazy cousin Beth had loaned her for the trip.

So much for the hope that the illusion of height would give her extra poise. It would be difficult to feign elegance when she landed on her butt.

Grabbing wildly at anything more stable than air, she exhaled on a relieved sigh as a strong pair of arms shot out, holding her in a vice-like grip.

'Whoa. These things are lethal if you don't concentrate. Too busy daydreaming about the *Love Boat,* huh?' The smooth voice, with more than a hint of amusement in its husky depths, sent an unexpected shiver down her spine as she looked up into her rescuer's face.

Wow.

Seeing good-looking guys on a daily basis was a perk of her job. The museum was a haven for sexily scruffy archaeological students, attractive teachers, even the odd university professor with a distinguished Sean Connery thing going on.

Yet this guy who now pinned her with arms displaying a great set of biceps was so much more than that. Striking was more appropriate. Even sex-on-legs, as brazen Beth would say.

Hypnotic eyes, a deep, cobalt blue, were fringed with long dark lashes any woman would have envied, and those baby blues were pinned on her, a teasing glint in their rich depths.

She inhaled sharply, unprepared for an intoxicating fresh citrus scent that left her head spinning—and not just from her near-fall.

As for his lips, curving with the hint of a smile, for the first time in her reclusive life she understood the label 'kissable'.

All too aware she was staring—gawking, more like it— she dropped her gaze. Only to be confronted by an equally intriguing sight: a broad expanse of tanned chest where the two top buttons of his shirt were undone.

Hotter than Indiana Jones, leapt to mind.

She had a major thing for Indiana—always had—and, lucky her, Indiana's double was holding on to her as if his life depended on it.

She'd wanted to gain confidence, step outside her comfort zone, experience new things on this cruise. To broaden her outlook to the extent she was never passed over for a work opportunity again. She had been thinking along the lines of dance lessons, lectures on exotic destinations, shore excursions, that sort of thing.

However, being held by this guy had her mind sailing down channels she'd never usually contemplate. Not a bad thing entirely, if taking this holiday had already affected her mindset. Maybe shy, geeky Lana—as she'd once overheard some colleagues call her—was already slipping into vacation mode.

Her heart thumping, whether in fear of her strangely errant thoughts or excitement at what they might urge her to do, she eased out of his grip.

He grinned and, typically, he had a sexy smile to match the rest of him. 'So, do I pass inspection?'

Great. He knew she'd been checking him out. Her skill at covert observation was on a par with her wardrobe: shabby at best.

'What makes you think I was inspecting anything? You were holding me so tight I had nowhere to move, let alone look.'

'Feisty. I like that.' His eyes gleamed, and the corners of his too-tempting-for-comfort mouth twitched in amusement.

Heat suffused her cheeks as she struggled to come up with a comeback. She hated how she always thought of a great retort ten minutes too late.

How was it she could answer any student's query in a second, but right now her brain—a whiz at cataloguing priceless artefacts, leading tour groups and calculating storage data—was totally befuddled?

'Thanks for breaking my fall.'

As replies went, it was pretty lame. Pathetic, in fact; it looked as if her comeback skills had sunk to the same level as her flirting expertise: below average bordering on non-existent.

More embarrassed than she cared to admit, she managed a tight smile, picked up her luggage and turned away, striding towards the ship though her knees wobbled like just-set jelly.

'Watch your step!' he called after her, his voice shaking with laughter.

She stiffened, but didn't break stride, determined not to look back, refusing to give him the satisfaction. Besides, she could feel his stare boring holes into her back.

Her skin prickled at the recollection of those incredibly blue eyes twinkling at her, laughing at her, and she shook her head in disgust. She was such a novice at this.

'Live a little, cuz. Let your hair down. Go crazy,' Beth had encouraged her. 'You've got two weeks to cut loose, to be someone you wouldn't dream of being on land. Make the most of it.'

Great advice, and it had sounded easy coming from her bubbly, confident cousin, who bounced through life with a perpetual smile on her face. And Beth sure knew what she was talking about, considering her positive attitude had landed her Aidan Voss, the dreamiest husband on the planet.

As for Beth's other advice—'dust off the cobwebs, get laid'—Lana blushed just thinking about it.

It was precisely three years, two months and five days since she'd last had sex. Not that she was counting or anything. Besides, she'd have to date to have sex—would have to get emotionally involved with the guy to contemplate it—and she didn't trust her emotions any more; not after what Jax the Jackass had done.

She tucked her old holdall under her arm tighter and headed for the gangway. Beth was right. While her professional life shone, her social life sucked. She had no confidence, no social skills, and no hope of being chosen for the museum's next overseas jaunt unless she learned to be more assertive, more outgoing, more *everything*.

Maybe this cruise would be just what a conservative curator needed?

Zac watched the petite brunette cut a path through the crowd, confused and intrigued.

Most of the holidaymakers he met were dressed to kill, and wearing enough make-up to sink a ship—no pun intended—yet she wore a simple navy suit bordering on severe, and barely a slick of lipgloss. And yet she had managed to capture his attention anyway.

He'd reached out to her in an instinctive reaction, but once she was in his arms his synapses had short-circuited and he'd found himself wanting to hold on way longer than necessary.

What was with that?

He'd lost any tender regard towards the fairer sex around the time Magda had done her chameleon act, and he hadn't let a woman get close enough to sink her talons in since.

Unwittingly, his gaze was drawn to the diminutive figure striding towards the ship, head up, shoulders squared, as if ready for battle. No simple walking for her. No, sirree. She had to sway her hips in a natural, tantalising rhythm in sync with her legs.

Running a hand across his eyes didn't help his quest to wipe her imprint from his retinas. Her sexy gait was replaced by an instant image of feline hazel eyes and a full, pouting mouth. Lord, that mouth. He could fantasise about it for ever. As for that innocent schoolgirl-channelling-schoolmarm expression she had down pat—he'd never seen anything like it.

When she'd stared at him with those striking burnt caramel eyes she'd appeared wide-eyed and ingenuous one second, and ready to give him a severe scolding the next.

Interesting. Very interesting. But he didn't have the time or the inclination to follow up on the first woman to pique his interest in a long time.

He had more important things on his mind—like doing a damn good job the next two weeks before he moved on to the next stage of his life. His uncle wanted him here. They'd noticed a pattern to the series of accidents that had plagued their cruise fleet, and the pattern suggested that the *Ocean Queen* was the next target. He planned for it to be the last.

After unpacking, Lana made her way to the promenade deck and wandered away from the crowds along the railings, finding a deserted spot with a clear view of the hustle and bustle below.

Circular Quay buzzed with activity, and people were waving as the ship pulled away from its berth, snapping the colourful streamers that bound it to shore. She had a great view from her vantage point: the Sydney Harbour Bridge on her left and the Opera House on her right as the ship sailed up the harbour. Both landmarks were imposing in the fading light.

The sound of low voices from somewhere on the deck above had her craning her head. If she had a great view from here, theirs must be amazing.

'Looks like loads of single women down there. Half are here for flings; the other half hope to find a husband. It's the same every cruise.'

'Your job is to pamper those women, not judge them.'

'Easy for you to say, buddy. If they see an unattached guy they're like piranhas circling their next meal.'

Despite her intentions to ignore the conversation, this harsh judgment captured Lana's attention, and realisation dawned as she looked up. Standing above her, silhouetted against the bridge, stood the stranger who'd saved her from falling earlier.

He wore a crisp white uniform that accentuated his tan—a larger than life Richard Gere in *An Officer and a Gentleman*—and she swallowed, disconcerted by how she'd compared him to two of her favourite movie stars in under an hour.

Deep furrows marred his brow as his gaze swept the crowd, and she shrank back, hoping she was hidden. She didn't want to be scrutinised by that disconcerting stare—not when she'd been eavesdropping, albeit unintentionally.

Mr Nautical's generalisations about women had her bristling enough to barge up there and give him a verbal spray, but if she had the guts to do that she'd be winging her way to Egypt right now, as the museum's spokesperson, not cowering under a deck hoping she wouldn't be spotted.

He was entitled to his opinion, and she to hers. And right now, as she darted a quick glance overhead, taking in those broad shoulders, deep blue eyes and the mop of unruly dark curls, her opinion screamed *Neanderthal*.

The band starting up drowned out the rest of his conversation, and she stood still for several minutes, waiting for the men above to move so she could make her escape without being seen. After a few extra minutes of shuffling her feet to kill time, she sidled along the deck, taking a few steps back towards an open door.

'Watch out!'

The owner of the low voice stood so close his warm breath caressed her ear, and she jumped and whirled around, her heart pounding as she stared into those familiar indigo eyes barely inches from her face.

'You startled me.' She glared, desperately trying to hide her embarrassment at being caught eavesdropping.

'Sorry. Maybe if you watched where you were going we'd stop bumping into each other like this? By the way—Zac McCoy.'

He stuck out his hand, seemingly unaware she'd heard every word of his damning conversation. She'd wanted to keep it that way, so couldn't be as rude as her first instinct prompted her to be.

'Lana Walker.'

She placed her hand in his, unprepared for the jolt that shot up her arm as his fingers closed over hers. She yanked back, flustered by the residual tingle buzzing from her fingertips to her shoulder.

His eyes widened as he stared down at her hand. Great. Now he thought she was bad-mannered as well as clumsy. Way to go with the first impressions. Not that she had any intention of impressing him after what she'd just heard—and as if she'd even contemplate impressing him if she hadn't, she thought derisively. Old clothes, minimal make-up and boring brown hair weren't exactly designed to impress any guy, let alone someone in Mr Tall, Dark and Nautical's league.

'I need to finish unpacking, so if you'll excuse me?'

As she pushed past him her bare arm brushed his. The strange buzzing was back with a vengeance, spreading upwards and outwards and confusing the heck out of her. She had no idea why her body was behaving like this.

Okay, so that was a lie. Jax the Jackass might have been her only boyfriend, the only guy she'd ever slept with, but once he'd dumped her and she'd fled to Sydney she'd had two less than memorable dates with co-workers. She still recognized that buzz.

Hormones. Her reaction to sailor boy had to be purely physical—no doubt intensified due to the fact she hadn't been this close to a guy in over three years.

'I'll leave you to it. Nice meeting you.'

She mumbled a non-committal answer and sent him a half-hearted wave, glancing over her shoulder as he walked away, her curious gaze lingering on parts it had no right scoping out.

She had a thing for guys in uniform. Always had.

Starting way back, when a young sailor had given her a flower after she'd dropped an ice cream cone and cried. A clumsy five-year-old who'd never forgotten her first crush. Her mum's warning at the time, to steer clear of men like that, hadn't meant much, considering she hadn't known what 'that' meant back then.

Now, seeing the white cotton outlining Zac McCoy's butt as he strode away, she knew exactly what *that* was, and it sent her scurrying for her cabin.

Banishing the encounter from her thoughts, she showered and dressed for dinner. Beth had crammed her case with designer dresses and shoes, but Lana would never have the self-confidence to wear half the sexy stuff her cousin did, so she settled for her one good dress: a plain black coat dress, cinched at the waist, set off with her cousin's sparkly jet Manolos.

Beth had pestered Lana to allow a complete makeover, but the thought of a radical haircut and new wardrobe was way too intimidating for a girl who equated the latest fashion with the occasional update of her tortoiseshell spectacle frames.

She'd settled for a sedate trim to her *blah*-brown hair and contacts. Beth had settled for giving her enough shoe castoffs to make the *Sex and the City* girls sit up and take notice.

As for the rest of Beth's advice on how to boost her selfconfidence? She'd take it one step at a time in these damn uncomfortable shoes.

She entered the Coral Dining Room and barely had time to notice the giant chandelier, the string quartet and the silver service place settings before the *maître d'* whisked her to a table where two seats remained vacant.

Sliding into one of them, she let the other occupants introduce themselves—a couple in their forties and two other women—hoping they wouldn't expect her to make small talk. She was lousy in social situations like this, preferring to sit and listen than participate in idle chit-chat.

She listened to their friendly banter while perusing the extensive menu. As the empty chair on her right was drawn back, her skin prickled disturbingly. A sensation she associated with the hives she'd been unfortunate enough to bear several times when a strawberry came within a whiff of her.

However, this prickle had nothing to do with fruit. This time something far more dangerous to her health—well, to her peace of mind—caused her skin to flush and tingle.

'Hi, everyone. I'm Zac McCoy, Public Relations Manager. I'm delighted you'll be joining me for meals at my table. On behalf of the ship's company, the Captain and the crew, we hope you enjoy your cruise.'

Fate liked to play jokes on her. Maybe she should take out a lottery ticket and be done with it.

Resisting the urge to surreptitiously scratch the flushed skin behind her ears, she tried to ignore her erratic pulse which had shifted into overdrive the minute he sat down. She toyed with the cutlery, pleated her napkin, and successfully avoided looking at him until the table introductions reached her.

'How are you, Lana?'

He flashed that killer smile, blue eyes glinting with amusement.

'Fine, thanks.'

That's it. Slay him with scintillating conversation. For a professional who gave presentations weekly—as painful as it was, speaking in front of her peers—she was doing a marvellous job appearing to be a brainless bimbo.

While the voluptuous blonde on his right distracted him,

she couldn't resist sneaking a peek. Smooth, suave and sexy. He was exactly the type of guy any sane woman would stay away from: a glib, good-looking charmer, with the body of Adonis and a face designed to turn heads. Way out of her league.

As dinner proceeded she remained silent, toying with her food, faking polite smiles. She'd never been a flirt, like Beth, and sitting next to a guy like Zac had her tongue-tied. Probably for the best, as she doubted he'd be interested in the latest marsupial display in the Australian Gallery, or in hearing her expound the virtues of digital cataloguing. Though her reticence was barely noticed as he maintained a steady flow of conversation, captivating everyone at the table.

During dessert—a light chocolate soufflé that melted in her mouth—he turned towards her.

'You're awfully quiet. Maybe we should get to know each other better?'

His bold stare scanned her face, focusing briefly on her mouth before returning to her eyes, and admiration tinged with something more—something that made her heart go pitter-patter—glittered in those blue depths.

'Maybe. Though I should warn you. I'm single, and probably hungrier than a piranha.'

His smile slipped as he dabbed at the corners of his mouth with a linen napkin, those vivid eyes never leaving hers for a second. She blinked to break the hypnotic contact.

'You overheard me earlier?'

'Yeah, and your opinion of women on cruises sucks.'

She silently applauded her bravado—fuelled by indignation—even while cringing at her outburst. Antagonising him wouldn't be conducive to remaining unnoticed, which was what she'd hoped for if she had to sit next to him every night for the next two weeks.

His eyes deepened to midnight, dark and challenging, as he leaned towards her.

'Care to change my mind?'

'And disillusion you because I'm not the man-hunter you think I am?' She eased back, needing some distance between them before she leaned into him and lapped up some of that delicious citrusy-sea-air scent he exuded. 'Where's the fun in that?'

'Oh, I think it could be fun,' he said.

His gaze dipped to her mouth again, lingered before sweeping back to her eyes. and she flicked her tongue out to moisten her lips, which tingled as if he'd physically touched her.

'And seeing as you think I'm a judgmental idiot, you would take a lot of convincing.' His voice dropped to a conspiratorial whisper. 'Which could equate to *a lot* of fun.'

'I didn't say you were an idiot.'

He chuckled—a rich, deep sound which washed over her in a warm wave. 'You didn't have to. You've got very expressive eyes.'

'Must be the contacts.'

Her dry response elicited more laughter.

'Look, I'd really like to clear the air between us. I honestly didn't mean anything by what you overheard. It was merely an observation from working on these tugs too long.'

She opened her mouth to respond and he held up a hand. 'Yes, it was a sweeping generalisation. And, yes, I'm suitably chastened and I apologise. But tell me, Lana Walker, which are you?'

He leaned closer. So close she couldn't breathe without imprinting his seductive scent on her receptors. 'Husband-hunter or fun fling girl?'

She reared back, knowing now was the time to clam up

as she usually did, before she scolded him like a tardy student. As she compressed her lips into an unimpressed line she noticed the teasing sparkle in his eyes, the cheeky smile playing about his mouth.

'You're trying to wind me up.'

'Is it working?'

'No.'

'So I could say anything and you'd be totally immune to me?'

Immune? She could have a hospital's worth of vaccinations against suave sailors and it still wouldn't give her guaranteed immunity—the type of immunity she needed more and more urgently the longer he stared at her with those twinkling eyes.

'That's right.'

'So I could say you intrigue me and you wouldn't react?'

'Nope.'

'What about if I tell you I think there's more to you than the obvious?'

She rolled her eyes. 'That's the same as intrigue, so you need to come up with a better line, sailor boy.'

'Sailor boy?'

A slow grin spread across his face as she mentally slapped a hand over her mouth.

Nicknames implied camaraderie. Nicknames implied fun. And there was no way she'd be foolish enough to *ever* contemplate having fun with him.

'Figure of speech.' She pleated her napkin, folding it over and over with origami-like precision, till he reached over and stilled her hand, setting her pulse rocketing as she tried not to flinch from his touch.

'What if I said I like you?'

Taking a great gulp of air to ease her constricted lungs,

she frowned. 'You're still trying to wind me up. And you're good. I'll give you that much.'

She extracted her hand on the pretext of picking up her wine glass, racking her brain for an easy way to end this conversation before she blurted out exactly how wound up she was by his teasing. The nape of her neck prickled. A colony of ants had taken up residence under her skin, and her blood flowed thick and sluggish, heating her from the inside out. Logically, she knew it was merely a physiological response— a simple chemical reaction to the first male to enter her personal space in a long time. But logic wouldn't untie her tongue or stop the rising blush from making her feel more gauche and awkward than ever in a social situation like this.

Smiling, he picked up his own wine glass and raised it in her direction.

'You do intrigue me. And I'm not trying to wind you up.' His smile widened. 'Well, not much. For some inexplicable reason I've taken an instant liking to you, despite your somewhat prickly exterior, and I've got two weeks to prove it to you.'

Prickly? The cheeky son of a—

He chuckled, and she knew he was winding her up again, trying to get a reaction.

She bit her tongue, mulling over what he'd said. He'd taken an instant liking to her, huh? As if. If she believed that she'd believe the ship would sail into the horizon and drop off the end of a flat earth.

Leaning forward, he murmured in her ear. 'Two very interesting weeks.'

She stiffened, unable to think when he was this close. What was the best response? Ignore him? Berate him? Wait the requisite ten minutes it would take to think up a scathing comeback and put him firmly back in his place?

'What? Nothing to say? Surprising, from a woman with such strong opinions about me.'

Sitting back, he fixed her with a smug smile—a smile that said he knew how flustered he made her, how she was struggling to come up with a suitable response.

She should have ignored him, pleaded a headache and left the table. That would have been her usual course of action—quietly slinking away, ruing her shyness. But his self-satisfied smile was too much, goading her into matching wits with him.

He assumed she couldn't come up with a quick answer? She'd show him.

So rather than pushing back her chair and making a run for it, she felt blood surge to her cheeks, and her head snapped up as she fixed him with a scathing glare.

'Go ahead, then, sailor boy. Prove it.'

CHAPTER TWO

LANA'S eyelids creaked open at the crack of dawn the next morning. A newly converted gym junkie, she usually bounced out of bed early and hit the nearest gym at six, when fitness fanatics liked to sweat through their first aerobics class of the day.

She'd never graced a gym, let alone tried an aerobics class, till eighteen months ago—all part of Operation Obliterate. Obliterate her memories of Jax, obliterate the embarrassment of how he'd used her; obliterate the fact that her first love had seen her as nothing more than a fling.

Now, not only was she hooked, she'd become a qualified instructor just for the fun of it. Madness? Probably. But for the hour she jumped around every morning she was just like the rest of the sweaty women around her, when no make-up and casual clothes weren't a big deal.

After a quick shower, she donned her favourite capri pants—in urgent need of replacing, considering the frayed cuffs—and a plain white T-shirt. She had a ton of them, as they went with everything. Then she slipped her feet into a pair of well-worn slingbacks.

Beth had shuddered when she'd seen her casual outfits, but, hey, she'd always been a comfort-over-style girl.

Besides, she didn't adhere to the old 'dress to impress' motto. She used her brain to get people to notice her. Discounting last night, when her intellect had gone AWOL.

Prove it, she'd dared Zac. All very brave in the heat of the moment, when she'd fired off the retort without thinking it through properly, but now, in the clear light of a perfect summer's day, her resolve wavered.

It was one thing setting out to build confidence by trying new things, but challenging a pro like Zac to flirt with her could only end in disaster.

He'd pushed her, taunted her till she'd snapped. He couldn't have known she'd react that way, for she still couldn't believe she'd done it herself. And while she now regretted her outburst, a small part of her was jumping up and down with joy at the unusual flash of bravado.

The old, sensible, conservative Lana would have ducked her head, pushed her ancient glasses up her nose and ignored him. She would have scuffed her well-worn sensible shoes under the table, tugged on the hem of her favourite shapeless sweatshirt and made a quick escape. She'd always taken the safe route, always done the right thing, always focussed on her career and nothing else.

She was the diligent employee, the dependable colleague, the model girlfriend, the reliable cousin. And where had it got her?

She'd been dumped, overlooked for a brilliant opportunity at work, and had come on this cruise for one reason and one reason only: to gain confidence socially and ensure she was never passed over at work again.

If she couldn't rely on her job, the one thing in this world she knew she was good at, what hope did she have?

Maybe standing up to brash sailors and proving she wasn't a push-over fell into the category of confidence-building?

With a shake of her head—as if that would dislodge the memory of making a fool of herself with that rash challenge—she headed for the lido deck, where continental breakfast was being served. She helped herself to a plate of mango, melon and pineapple, before finding a table next to the floor-to-ceiling glass overlooking the Pacific Ocean, stretching as far as she could see, its undulating swell infinitely soothing.

Her apartment in Coogee had an ocean view, though nothing as gorgeous as this. She'd deliberately chosen a sea view for its calming qualities and, boy, had she needed it when she'd first moved to Sydney from Melbourne, hell-bent on leaving her past behind.

'Enjoying the view this morning?'

She glanced up, her pulse-rate accelerating in an instant. Zac—in a navy polo shirt and matching shorts, his hair recently washed and slicked back, resident charming smile in place—rivalled the ocean in the stunning stakes.

She took a sip of water, trying to ease the dryness in her throat. 'Yes, it's spectacular.'

He wasn't looking at the view. Instead, that steady, captivating blue-eyed gaze remained riveted to her. 'Spectacular would describe it perfectly.'

She blushed and glanced down, toying with the fruit on her plate rather than face his intense scrutiny.

What made her think she could practise gaining confidence with this guy? He was a major player, and she'd barely graduated from Little League.

'You really should try some of that mango rather than playing with it. It's succulent this time of year.'

The way he said 'succulent' fascinated her; tripping from his lips, it almost sounded obscene.

'Shouldn't you be circulating amongst the passengers?'

She speared a piece of juicy mango and bit into it, trying to appear casual yet anxious to fob him off.

As if in slow motion he reached his index finger towards the corner of her mouth, where a rivulet of juice had started to run, and wiped it up.

Shaken to her core, she watched him lick the droplet of juice from his fingertip in a shockingly intimate gesture.

'Mmm—tasty.'

His smouldering gaze dropped to her lips before sweeping back to her eyes, triumphant blue clashing with shell-shocked hazel.

'You're right. I should get back to work. I can't have my time monopolized by one woman," he teased, before adding, 'Delectable as she may be.'

With a cocky smile, he gave her a half-salute and sauntered away.

The corner of her mouth was still quivering from his sensual touch. Great. If that was his first foray into *proving it* she was in trouble. Big trouble.

With a trembling hand she devoured the remainder of her breakfast, eager to escape. Whenever she looked up she caught a glimpse of him, moving among the tables, talking to various people. Their eyes met only once across the crowded room, and she looked away first, hating the blush staining her cheeks, hating her inadequacy at coping with light flirtation more.

It was hot in this room, way too hot. Pushing her plate away, she almost tripped in her haste to stand and dashed for the door, keeping her head down, unwilling to tempt fate further. After virtually falling into his arms, landing next to him at dinner, and then running into him first thing this morning, it looked as if fate was having a mighty big chuckle at her expense.

* * *

Zac watched Lana bolt, hiding a triumphant grin as he flipped the pages on his clipboard. He had her thoroughly rattled, if that stunned, wide-eyed gaze when he'd touched her lips was any indication.

Maybe he'd pushed the boundaries a tad there, but he hadn't been able to help it; he wanted to see if anything disturbed that cool-bordering-on-haughty mantle she wore like a fine fur.

He'd disconcerted her last night to the point where she'd thrown out that challenge. He was in little doubt she would never have been that brazen, that sassy, if she'd been thinking straight. After all, a woman who turned up to her first dinner on a luxurious cruise liner wearing a drab black dress with oversized buttons, a God-awful belt, and barely a slick of make-up, and who rarely spoke, wasn't exactly brimming with confidence.

Yet he'd wanted to push her buttons anyway.

Must be the pressure. He had a job to do, a saboteur to uncover, and some bad publicity to bring to a screaming halt. His uncle was relying on him, and he owed Jimmy big-time. He'd let him down once. Never again.

He needed to concentrate on business—needed to convince everyone he was just the new PR guy. The success of his plan depended on it. Even if he was actually the CEO of the whole damn company, and usually had bigger fish to fry.

And concentrating on business meant not giving Lana a hard time—challenge or not. Though there had been something about the spark in her eyes when she'd fired back at him last night, something about her wary yet indignant expression that had him wanting to delve beneath her prim surface to discover the hidden depths.

Maybe if he unnerved her enough, unsettled her enough, he'd get to see the real her?

An interesting proposition, but for now work came first. Work was reliable, dependable, and never let him down. It wasn't clouded by emotions and it didn't change when he least expected it. Work was the one constant in his life. The only constant.

Exactly the way he liked it.

Lana studied *Neptune's News,* the ship's daily planner, as she lounged around the lido pool, staggered by the array of activities on board: lectures on ports they were due to visit, wine-tasting, art auctions, dance lessons—the list went on for ever. She studiously avoided any activities with Zac's name pencilled next to them, and finally decided on ballroom dancing—something she'd always wanted to try but never had the guts to. Hopefully mastering a waltz or two might give her a quickstep in the right direction to boosting her self-confidence.

Finding her way to the ballroom proved easier said than done. Maps were clearly visible around the ship, but understanding the difference between port and starboard was the first hurdle to overcome in figuring out directions, and only after several botched attempts did she finally find the room. So much for her sure-fire navigational skills; apparently they only applied to the maze of one-way streets around Sydney and to convoluted museum corridors.

Several women stood to one side of the ballroom, while a few men loitered on the outskirts of the dance floor. She learned from Mavis, the woman standing next to her, that the men were hosts, hired by the ship's company for single women who needed a dance partner.

'This is my seventh cruise, dear. Why do you think I

keep coming back? Though I'm seventy, these dance hosts make me feel twenty-one again, whisking me all over the dance floor. Not to mention their youthful good-looks.'

Lana smothered a smile as the youngest host appeared to be a greying fifty-five. She observed that the men were skilled at mingling with the women, and soon everyone had paired off. Predictably, she had no partner. Story of her life, really.

'Don't worry, love, you'll be the lucky one paired with the instructor.'

Mavis, veteran cruiser, obviously knew how these things worked.

'I hope he's good.'

Because she was a dervish out there on the dance floor? Yeah, right. She moved her feet to an imaginary samba rhythm and almost took a tumble.

'I'm better than good. Let's just hope you can keep up.'

Her nerve-endings snapped to attention as the deep voice rippled over her, and she didn't have to turn around to know who it belonged to. Fickle fate dealing her a bum hand yet again.

'Okay, class, let's get to work. As you can see, I'm not Rafe, our illustrious dance instructor. He was called away to a last-minute rehearsal for tonight's extravaganza, so you're stuck with me instead. For those who don't know me, I'm Zac McCoy, the PR manager. Though I'm not a professional entertainer, I can safely say I don't have two left feet, and I've managed to learn a thing or two during my years working with the entertainment staff. So, how about a waltz to start with?'

'Anything you want, handsome. Oh, if only I was thirty years younger.' Mavis fanned her face, a twinkle in her eyes.

'If only I'd decided on taking the chess class,' Lana muttered, wondering if she could feign a sprained ankle.

'Did you say something?'

She had two choices. Duck and run, as she usually would in an uncomfortable situation like this, or ignore the blush burning her cheeks, discount the fact she'd never done this before, and suck it up and see if she could get through this awkward encounter without making a fool of herself.

She shook her head, managing a tight smile resembling a grimace. 'No.'

'Right, then. Shall we dance?'

Zac grinned and held out his hand, leaving her no option but to take it. She tried to relax, she really did, but as he pulled her closer, his body grazing hers, she inadvertently stiffened.

His knowing smile didn't help. 'See—a perfect fit.'

'I thought we were doing a waltz. The way you're holding me seems more like the Lambada.'

'Fancy a bit of dirty dancing, do you?'

'Don't flatter yourself. You certainly don't hold a candle to Patrick Swayze.'

A glint of hidden excitement lit his extraordinary eyes.

'And here I was thinking you were falling under my spell. You disappoint me.'

She averted her gaze, focussing on anything other than those all-seeing eyes, wishing her heart would stop racing. 'Don't you ever stop flirting?'

His grin widened. 'I'm sure Fred did his fair share of flirting while he whisked Ginger around. I'm just taking my role seriously.'

'Your role as the resident Casanova, you mean?'

The naughty glint in his eyes alerted her to the fact she hadn't insulted him. Moreover, he was enjoying their sparring way too much.

'We're both adults here. There's nothing wrong with a bit of harmless flirtation. Besides, you dared me—remember?'

More fool her.

'Look, this is silly. You were taunting me last night. I bit back. Let's just forget it, okay?

The naughty glint didn't let up. If anything it intensified as his lips kicked up into an all too sexy grin.

'Unfortunately for you I have a very good memory, so I can't forget it. But I'm willing to concentrate on our dance steps for now.' And with that he spun her outwards, at arm's length.

'If that's your way of changing the subject, I'm not buying it.'

He reeled her in with a slight tug on her hand. 'Who said anything about needing to change the subject? I enjoy flirting. You're the one with the problem.'

If he only knew.

She didn't know how to flirt—had absolutely no experience at it. Jax had targeted her, played her, said all the right things—done all the right things to get her to fall for him. Flirting hadn't entered into it. As for her other two dates, they'd been stilted, awkward, rushed dinners, with limited small talk and frequent glances at watches on both sides.

It wasn't so much having a problem with flirting, she just didn't have a clue how to do it.

She stumbled, winced, trod on his toes, and wished the parquet floor would open up and swallow her.

'Easy, Ginger. Just follow my lead.'

If he'd smiled or smirked or had the faintest amused twinkle in his eyes she would have slammed her heel on his foot—well, she would have thought about it—and made a run for it.

Instead, he tightened his hold on her hand, gently increased the pressure with the other in the small of her back, and counted softly under his breath as he led her around the dance floor.

The counting was for her benefit, but it didn't help. Clumsy, stiff and awkward didn't begin to describe how she felt in his arms—like a mannequin given an airing before being dumped in a shopfront in only her knickers.

Thinking of knickers while in his arms had her trampling his toes again, and she bit her lip, silently cursing her ineptness.

'Sorry.'

Her gaze fixed on his chest, heat scorching her cheeks.

He stopped twirling her about, placed a finger under her chin and tilted it up so she had no option but to look at him.

'Don't apologise. This class is about learning, and you're doing great for a beginner.'

His understanding smile sent a tremor through her. Why couldn't he be condescending and obnoxious so she could dislike him, rather than considerate and kind?

She mumbled a noncommittal answer, wishing he'd stop staring at her like a pet project. Though it could be worse; he could be looking down on her as a charity case with pity in his eyes.

'Just feel the music. Let the beat take you.'

Easy for Fred Astaire Junior to say.

Her dubious expression had him chuckling as he pulled her closer again. 'Come on. You'll enjoy it.'

To her surprise, he was right. As soon as she stopped focussing on her feet not stomping on his, and ignored the fact he was holding her close, she started to relax.

The music filtered over her, soft and ethereal, a classical hit from a bygone era, and she found herself humming softly, swept away in the magic of the moment.

She closed her eyes, remembered a dancing show she'd

once seen on TV, and imagined herself in a red chiffon dress with a fitted bodice held up by will-power alone, with handkerchief layers cascading from her waist to her ankles. She imagined snazzy red shoes to match, sequinned, with impossibly high heels, that floated across the dance floor of their own volition.

With immaculate hair and make-up, and the smile of a ballroom dancing champion, she lived the fantasy, let the music infuse her body, her senses, and allowed Zac to whisk her around and around, her feet finally falling into step with his as an exhilaration she'd never known rushed through her.

She'd never felt so light, so graceful, so unselfconscious. If this was what ballroom dancing could do for her, she'd sign up for a year's worth of classes as soon as she got back.

But there was more to it than perfecting a waltz and she knew it.

Zac had given her this gift—had given her the confidence to let go of her reservations and enjoy the moment. He'd empowered her to believe that for a precious few minutes she could be agile and lithe and elegant, rather than a shy, clumsy klutz.

When the music died her eyelids fluttered open, but rather than feeling let down by reality, the gleam of appreciation in his deep blue eyes had her craving to do it all over again.

'You're good.'

His admiration made her want to perform a few extra twirls for good measure.

She flushed with pleasure. 'Thanks. So are you.'

'You up for a cha-cha?'

Ignoring the usual flicker of nerves at the thought of trying something new, she nodded. 'Sure. Let's give it a try.'

Not only did she try a cha-cha, Zac showed her the finer

points of a foxtrot too. While the class danced around them, she matched him step for step, exhilarated by his fancy manoeuvres, thrilled by her increasing confidence to try more complicated steps.

At the end of the hour she collapsed into a nearby chair, her face flushed, her feet aching and her imagination still tripping the light fantastic.

He crouched next to her as she puffed at the damp hair strands falling over her face, knowing she must look a hot, rumpled mess. Yet a small part of her was still feeling like that dance champion she'd imagined.

'You're just full of surprises, aren't you, Ginger?'

'Why? Because I only managed to break all the toes on your right foot and not your left?'

He laughed. 'You'll be pleased to know my toes are just fine. Better than fine, considering I had to do some fancy footwork out there to keep up with you once you got going.'

There was a reason he was in PR. He probably laid it on this thick for countless other gullible females every cruise.

'Yeah, well, I told you I was good at the start.' His eyebrows shot up as he clearly relived every clumsy stumble she'd made initially and she smiled. 'And you're not such a bad teacher, once you concentrate on the task at hand and put a zip on the banter.'

'Thanks. I think.' He stood, stretched, and she quickly averted her gaze from the window of tanned, flat stomach poking between his polo shirt and shorts. 'See you tonight at dinner?'

His smile was pure invitation. If he'd asked her a few hours ago she would have sent him a short, sharp RSVP in the negative, but after the enlivening hour she'd just spent, thanks to him, she found herself nodding.

'Uh-huh.'

'Right-o. See you then.'

She fanned her cheeks as he walked away, wondering if it was the exercise, the exhilaration of feeling graceful for the first time in her life, or being wrapped in his muscular arms that had made her hot and bothered?

In reality she should be happy—ecstatic, even. She'd tried something new today and had given her flagging confidence a much-needed lift. Her sense of achievement was immense, and she owed it to one guy.

And now she'd experienced the rush of feeling graceful for the first time in her life she wondered how much further he could boost her confidence—if she didn't try so hard to fend him off.

CHAPTER THREE

WHILE Zac had impressed her with his sensitivity during dance class yesterday, he had ruined it by slipping into full flirting mode over dinner last night. Her fledgling confidence hadn't lasted and she'd clammed up, grunted monosyllabic answers, and done her best to ignore the persistent attentions of a suave sailor boy with smooth moves and slick words.

She hated the fact it was a game to him, a response to the challenge she'd thrown down in a fit of pique. Her inherent shyness was a bane she lived with every day, it affected her professionally, socially and romantically, yet he seemed to view it as something she could shrug off if he teased her enough.

He was really starting to get to her, but thankfully the ship had docked at Noumea today, and she wouldn't waste another minute thinking about him. Instead, she explored the French-inspired capital of New Caledonia, with its tree-lined boulevards flanked by trendy boutiques and cafés, enjoying every minute.

She savoured the aroma of freshly brewed coffee wafting on the light tropical breeze, she scoffed melt-in-the-mouth flaky croissants, and she scoured the shops—something she never did back home. When she shopped it was for necessity rather than a burning need for retail therapy—no matter how many times Beth dragged her from one boutique to another trying to make her see otherwise.

Yet here, with the balmy breeze ruffling her ponytail and the tempting shopfronts laid out like bright, sparkling jewels in the sun, she couldn't help but browse.

Entering a small boutique, she meandered through aisles crammed with enough hangers and clothes to outfit the entire cast of *South Pacific*. Her hands drifted over soft silky sarongs, short strappy summer dresses, before lingering over the swimwear. The only bathers she'd brought on this trip were an old black one-piece cut high in the front—the ones she used if she swam at home as part of a workout.

So why was she picking up a cerise bikini, its hot pink colour the exact shade her cheeks would be if she ever had the guts to wear something so revealing?

She put it down and trailed her hand over some straw hats, before her gaze settled on the bikini again, drawn to it, mesmerised by its newness, its brightness and its blinding contrast to everything else in her wardrobe.

Glancing down at her worn black flip-flops, khaki Bermuda shorts and well-washed grey T-shirt, she hovered over the bikini, sorely tempted. Just looking at it gave her the same buzz she'd had when floating around the dance floor in Zac's arms—the feeling she could be more assertive if she set her mind to it.

Spurred on by an eagerness to recreate that feeling, she snatched it up and headed for the counter before she changed her mind.

After thrusting the bikini at the young Melanesian guy behind the counter, she ducked her head on the pretext of searching for her purse in her straw carryall, hating how her cheeks burned when making what was a simple, every-day purchase for most women.

She rummaged around, waiting for him to ring it up, and was unprepared for the small puff of perfume in the vicinity of her right ear.

'This fragrance will be perfect for *mademoiselle*.'

She shook her head, ready to tell him she wasn't inter-ested, when an intoxicating blend of light floral tones mingling with subtle vanilla drifted over her. She inhaled, savouring the heady scent, feeling surprisingly feminine after one small squirt.

She never wore perfume, had never owned a bottle in her life, but when the young guy stared at her with soulful choco-late-brown eyes and insisted again that it was perfect for her, in a divine French accent, she found herself handing over her credit card and being handed back a duty-free bag with two purchases she'd never dreamed of making, let alone using.

But for those few minutes when she'd watched him wrap the bikini and the perfume she'd stood a little taller, felt a little braver—as if she could be the type of woman who *wasn't* passed over for an amazing trip to Egypt as the museum's spokesperson just because she wasn't articulate or outgoing enough.

However, her flash of spirit didn't last as she strolled back to the ship. The perfume box banged against her leg, a constant reminder of its presence, and she couldn't help but feel a fool.

Since when did she wear perfume? Let alone go for something so…so…out there? Seductive, feminine items were for girls not short on confidence—girls who'd have the guts to live up to the perfume's promise; girls who'd have the spirit to match wits with sailor boys. Girls abso-lutely nothing like her.

Impulse buying a stupid perfume with a naughty name wouldn't give her the confidence boost she needed. Nothing would. And she'd be better off remembering that rather than entertaining foolish dreams of showing everyone, Zac included, that she wasn't the shy nerd they'd labelled her.

When she got back to her cabin, she flung the duty-free bag into the wardrobe and slammed the door shut.

Ruing the waste of money—as if she'd *ever* have the chutzpah to wear that bikini—she wriggled into her trusty one-piece and headed for the Dolphin Deck pool. She dumped her towel and sarong on a deckchair before plunging into the water, eager to wash away memories of her recent foolishness.

Closing her eyes, she flipped over, floating blissfully until a dark shadow passed over her. When it didn't move, she opened her eyes.

And promptly sank.

Torn between the natural urge to fight her way to the surface for air or stay submerged, safely away from charming sailor boys, she eventually floundered her way to the surface, spluttering and coughing and ruining her Esther Williams impersonation.

'Need a hand?'

She glared at his outstretched hand and shook her head, deriving some satisfaction as water droplets sprayed his immaculate uniform.

'No, thanks.'

His lips curved into a deliciously tempting smile. 'You sure? Not tempted to try and pull me in?'

The thought hadn't crossed her mind, but now he mentioned it maybe a good dunking would cool him off.

'Not really. And I'm quite capable of hoisting myself out of the pool—if you'd move out of my way?'

'I like a strong woman.'

She rolled her eyes. 'You like women, period.'

'What's wrong with that? I'm a healthy red-blooded male.'

Her gaze drifted across his broad shoulders of its own volition, and lower, before snapping back to meet his all too sure of himself stare.

'I'll take your word for it.'

She pushed away from the side of the pool, treading water, floundering out of her depth physically and literally. Ever since she'd been silly enough to dare him that first night he'd been teasing her, pushing her for a reaction.

'As much as I'm enjoying your mermaid impersonation, why don't you come a little closer so we can have a proper chat?'

'About…?'

'Tonight. You and me.'

How did he do that? Infuse every word with mystery and mayhem and untold promise? As if his sexy smile and come-get-me eyes weren't enough.

For the second time in as many minutes she went under, cursing her inability to be anything other than clumsy and inept in his presence. He unnerved her to the point of bumbling, and it was high time she got over this funk he had her in with his constant teasing. Either that or jump ship.

She breaststroked underwater to the side, and hauled herself up the pool ladder. 'Don't say a word. Just hand me that towel, please.'

He was smart as well as good-looking, for he didn't speak as he passed her the towel. Then again, he didn't need to. His smug smile said it all.

He had her squirming, wanting to match wits with him, wishing she could, but scared of the consequences. Her heart was slamming against her ribcage at the thought of what they might entail.

For some strange reason he'd fixated his charms on her this cruise. Her—the last woman who'd reciprocate, the last woman to put up with his nonsense, the last woman to dally with if that was his intention.

She wasn't a dallying type of girl, yet with him staring at her with a twinkle in those deep blue eyes it was hard not to wish she was.

'Aren't you at all interested to hear what I have in mind for you and me tonight?'

Oh, she was interested all right—interested to the point she'd almost drowned when he'd strung the words *you, me and tonight* into the same sentence.

Tying her sarong around her waist, having quickly patted herself dry, she aimed for casual. 'I'm sure you'll tell me.'

He chuckled. 'Nice to see you this wound up. It must mean I'm getting somewhere in my quest to prove how much I like you.'

'I'm not wound up.'

She finished tying the knot at her waist with an extra hard yank, almost cutting off her circulation in the process.

'No?'

He sent a pointed stare at the twisted mess she'd made of her sarong, and she stopped fiddling with it, crossing her arms instead.

Bad move, considering the wicked gleam in his eyes as he dragged them away from her cleavage.

'I just wanted to make sure you're coming to the Island Banquet. You won't want to miss it.'

'That good, huh?'

'Better.'

His lowered tone indicated he wasn't just talking about

the banquet. See, this was where she struggled. She had no idea if he was being clever or flirty or deliberately naughty—no idea how to respond without sounding repressed and uptight or foolishly naïve.

'Well, then, I look forward to seeing your prowess at organising events.'

'I'm sure you won't be disappointed with my *prowess*.'

He took a step towards her and ran his hand lightly down her arm. She shivered, tiny goosebumps crawling across her skin as she belatedly realised she'd given him the upper hand yet again.

'That's a promise.'

Oh, he was good—too good. She should just hoist her white flag up the main pole now in surrender.

He'd won. He'd bombarded her with enough smooth moves and clever words to prove he liked her. Though it was just a game to him, and she knew it. Then why the urge to ignore her head, the logical part of her that she always listened to, the part telling her to jump ship now before she was sucked into believing any of this was real?

'See you tonight.' His husky tone washed over her like a warm wave, soft, soothing, seductive, and he grazed her arm in a fleeting touch before walking away, leaving her helpless and yearning and cursing her inexperience with men more than ever.

Lana needed a shot of confidence, and in the absence of a ballroom dancing class she settled for a squirt of that frivolous perfume.

Considering her hand still shook as she pulled a brush through her hair it hadn't worked and she contemplated staying in and ordering Room Service rather than face another inevitable encounter with Zac.

Her nerves were shredded. She couldn't pretend to be someone she wasn't, and standing up to his incessant beguiling barrage could wear her down eventually. She couldn't handle that.

As she strolled towards the huge marquee about a mile from the ship, where the banquet was being held, the warm trade winds ruffled the hair at the nape of her neck. She knew wearing a new perfume and hoping it would give her poise while under duress was wishful thinking.

Fear settled in the pit of her stomach. Pep-talks to herself, telling her to stay cool and not let him rattle her, were fine in the confines of her cabin, but how would she stand up under pressure from his persistent charm?

Smoothing her old formal dress with nervous hands, she entered the marquee, where suspended fairy lights created a magical effect as they reflected in the water. Tables lined the outskirts, heavily laden with local seafood delicacies, salads and decadent desserts, and she tried not to drool. Easy, considering a certain sailor boy was nowhere in sight.

Mavis, resplendent in a floral dress with an orange hibiscus tucked behind her right ear, sidled up to her, beaming as usual. 'Aloha, dear.'

Lana didn't have the heart to tell her the Hawaiian greeting wasn't used here. 'You're looking very tropical.'

'Yes, well, we've got to get into the island spirit, haven't we? By the way, where's your beau? I haven't seen him.'

'My beau?'

Mavis tut-tutted. 'Don't play coy with me, my girl. I saw the way that sailor looked at you yesterday in dance class. I may be old, but I'm far from senile, and if my eyes didn't deceive me I think you liked the attention.'

'No way—'

'Why don't you live a little? Have some fun, dear.

You're only young once. Now, in order to do that you need to keep mingling and stop wasting your time talking to an old chook like me.' She patted Lana's cheek. 'Say hello to that gorgeous boy for me,' she said and waddled away, chuckling under her breath

Have some fun. You're only young once.

She wanted to, she really did, but ignoring the habits of a lifetime was tough. Even if she knew how to flirt, would Zac be satisfied with that? She doubted it. If she responded he'd take it as a signal that she was interested in more, would probably expect more, and she couldn't give it to him.

She was anti-casual-sex for a reason, a damn good one, and casting off her inhibitions along with her reservations would be near impossible.

Unless she had great motivation?

Maybe she did—all wrapped up in six-foot-plus of sexy sailor. Was Zac incentive enough for her to drop her guard and see where it led?

The thought had her bolting from the marquee for the safety of the deserted beach, where she could quash daft thoughts like that before they blossomed and encouraged her to indulge in all kinds of crazy, uncharacteristic actions.

Zac made small talk with a couple from Alabama while his gaze was riveted on Lana as she left the marquee.

He was an expert at multi-tasking—his job, his *real* job, demanded it—so he had no trouble nodding and laughing and responding even while hiding a grimace at yet another hideous dress, this one in a drab brown, and at the way it hid her curves.

And she had them—man, did she have them. He'd seen them on full display this afternoon, despite that neck-to-knee ensemble. Okay, it hadn't been that bad, but those boring bathers were gruesome just the same, and she no doubt thought they hid the curves that could give a guy ideas of how far he'd like to push this challenge, despite his every intention not to.

She'd come to the banquet. He'd had his doubts after the way he'd taunted her at the pool earlier. She was still nervous around him—something he couldn't figure out, considering she'd come alive in his arms in that dance class after she'd loosened up, and the way she'd started smiling at some of his jokes over dinner.

Socialising didn't come naturally to her. He saw it in the fiddling fingers, the tense shoulders, the lowered gaze whenever his flirting got too heated. He should feel sorry for her, should leave her alone.

An image of her in that wet, clinging, black one-piece sprang to mind again, instantly obliterating his good intentions to keep his distance. The bathing suit hadn't been remotely sexy, but the woman in it—now, that was another story.

All afternoon he'd mentally rehearsed the reasons he shouldn't push this: the 'employees don't fraternise with passengers' policy he'd devised himself; the importance of focussing on the quest to catch their saboteur; the debt he owed Uncle Jimmy. All perfectly legitimate reasons to keep his distance and stop toying with her—not to mention the fact she hadn't returned his interest in the slightest.

But he couldn't get her out of his head. He'd never met anyone like her: fragile, shy, clumsy and yet infinitely endearing. Quite simply, she captivated him.

It couldn't be purely physical, not with the dreadful clothes she wore—old-fashioned clothes that hid her body rather than enhancing it. And she rarely wore make-up, she tied her hair in a ponytail most of the time, and she wore no jewellery.

But that was what intrigued him the most: her apparent lack of artifice, which allowed the natural intelligent sparkle of her expressive eyes to shine through, and her genuine smile on the rare occasion one of his funny barbs hit its mark with her.

Her acerbic wit attracted him—the guarantee she wouldn't put up with any of his crap. He liked that enough to know more, a lot more, and now, with curiosity egging him on, he bade goodbye to the couple and followed her.

The soft sand silenced his footsteps, and he pulled up as she stopped at the ocean's edge, rubbing her arms before wrapping them around her middle. It was a vulnerable gesture that had him wondering who or what had put the wary expression in her eyes that he'd glimpsed on more than one occasion.

For someone her age—he'd pegged her as mid to late twenties—she was too serious, too withdrawn, and each time he'd seen caution creep into her striking hazel eyes he'd wanted to slay whatever demon had put it there.

Crazy, considering his demon-slaying days for any woman were long gone. Magda had seen to that.

Her posture screamed *hands-off* so what was he doing here, disturbing her solitude? Up for another bout of flirting? Another bout of teasing her when he knew it couldn't lead anywhere? She'd made that pretty clear.

He needed to leave her the hell alone. But before he could take a step the breeze picked up, and a waft of fragrance assailed his nostrils. He inhaled, savouring the tantalising scent of frangipani with a hint of vanilla. Pure ambrosia, piquant and addictive. He shook his head to clear it.

He must have made a noise, for she turned, pale moonlight casting alluring shadows over a face otherwise bathed in luminosity, her eyes wide and incandescent.

He'd never seen anything so stunning. The impact of her simple beauty hit him like a blow to the solar plexus, and for an oxygen-starved moment all he could do was stare.

'Sneaking up on me again?'

The slight curve of her lips belied the hint of annoyance in her voice.

'You look like you could do with some company.'

'Maybe.'

'Really?'

'Don't sound so surprised. You're not too bad for a persistent pain in the butt.'

He laughed, surprised she'd instigated a bit of light-hearted wordplay for the first time.

'Be careful. That almost sounded like a compliment, and it might go straight to my head.'

'Which part? The persistent pain part or the part where I actually admitted you're not too bad?'

'Take a guess.'

She smiled, and the effect was breathtaking. 'I'm sure you're well aware of your attributes, so anything I say isn't going to surprise you too much.'

'My attributes, huh?' He flexed his biceps, straightened his shoulders. 'Nice to know you noticed.'

She rolled her eyes. 'See? I knew it'd go to your head.'

He chuckled and closed the short distance between them, ducking his head towards her neck. 'What's that perfume, by the way? It's entrapment for any male who gets within five feet of you. Look at me; I'm putty in your hands at the moment.'

'It's called Seduction. Stupid name, but it smells okay. I bought it today in a fit of madness.'

She'd stiffened imperceptibly at his nearness, meaning he should probably leave her alone.

But he couldn't.

Not when the word Seduction tripped from her lips like a saucy invitation. Not when the word conjured up all sorts of wicked images in his over-heated imagination. Not when she smelt and looked divine under a star-studded sky just made for romance and frivolity and getting swept away in the moment.

'Seduction, huh?'

Her small nod brought her ear within nibbling range, and he gritted his teeth, straightening, removing delectable necks and ears out of temptation's way—only to catch the flicker of awareness warring with indecision in her unwavering stare.

'I couldn't resist it.'

'Like I can't resist this.'

He lowered his lips towards her as her eyelids fluttered shut, the faint pink staining her cheeks adding a natural glow.

He half expected her to push him away, and her tentative acceptance of his kiss surprised him, pleased him, considering her usual reticence for anything beyond the mildest flirtation.

He'd wanted to do this for days, yet the anticipation of her lips touching his didn't compare to the reality.

As he rested his hands on her waist, spanning it, she combusted.

There was no other description for her reaction as she wrapped her arms around him, tugging him closer, her hands frantic as they bunched his shirt, stroked his back, raking it while pushing against him, eager and spontaneous and incredibly responsive.

He deepened the kiss, demanding a compliance she was

more than willing to give, and her total abandonment fired his libido better than any aphrodisiac as she parted her lips, allowing his tongue to slide into her mouth, where it wound around hers in an erotic, sensual dance he didn't want to end.

Blistering heat scorched straight to his groin and he groaned, threading his hands through her silky soft hair, loose and cascading over her shoulders for once, angling her head for better access to the warm delights of her mouth, wanting more, wanting it all.

He knew he shouldn't be doing this. It defied logic, defied all reason. But her tongue touching his blasted every last shred of common sense out of his mind.

As her breasts pressed against his chest and her hands skimmed the waistband of his trousers sanity fled, and he tore his mouth away, blazing a trail of hot, moist kisses down her throat.

Her head fell back, giving him full access to her neck and her deliciously delicate skin, so soft, so enticing, so tempting.

He couldn't get enough, cupping her butt, pulling her against his arousal, wishing their damn clothes would disappear along with her inhibitions.

Lana gasped, her eyes flying open as the enormity of what they were doing hit her like a ten-ton anchor.

What the hell was she thinking?

Trying to hold her own with his flirting was one thing— but this? This mind-blowing madness where she'd responded to him like a nympho?

The heat that had pooled in her belly crept upwards, causing her neck to itch uncontrollably and her cheeks to light a beacon for the ship.

How could she have been so…so…stupid? So wanton? So reckless?

She shoved her hair out of the way, dragged air into her lungs and stepped away, desperate for physical distance where a moment ago she couldn't get close enough.

His mouth kicked up into a rueful smile. 'Guess that perfume almost lived up to its name.'

Soft moonlight reflected in his eyes, and while she couldn't fathom their expression, she knew hers was horrified.

'In your dreams, lover-boy.'

She blinked, wondering where that rapid retort had come from. The quick comeback had shocked her almost as much as her eager response to his kiss.

To her amazement he chuckled—a deep, rich sound that had no right warming her. 'I guess here's where I should say it was my fault and that the kiss was way out of line.'

Her head snapped up, her stare accusing.

'You're right on both counts—but you're not going to apologise, are you? You've been charming the pants off me ever since I issued that stupid dare, so the way your warped mind works you probably think of it as all part of the game.'

'Charming the pants off you, huh?'

He dropped his gaze to her dress, and she blushed before jabbing a finger at him.

'You're incorrigible, you know that?'

'So I've been told.'

He grabbed her finger, lowered it, taking the opportunity to hold her hand, strumming the back of it with his thumb, soothing her anger just when she was getting worked up. Anger was good. Anger was distracting. Much better than focussing on the other emotions whirling through her: wonder and awe and a soul-deep yearning to feel half as good now as she had for those brief seconds in his arms.

'What do you want to hear? That I've wanted to kiss you for days? Damn straight. Do I want a repeat? Hell, yeah.'

A few of Jax's parting shots echoed through her head: *frigid, frosty, aloof, cold.* How could she be any of those things when a kiss from Zac set her alight and he wanted a repeat performance?

But it couldn't happen again. Not when Jax's other comments still resonated: how their relationship had been a bit of fun, nothing serious, a fling. She'd given him her heart; he'd given her a case of dating stage-fright for the next three years. There was no way she'd ever get involved with a guy again without having the relationship parameters spelled out at the start.

As if a transient sailor boy who lived his life at sea would be interested in anything more than a fling.

She yanked her hand out of his, folded her arms. 'A repeat is not an option.' She frowned for good measure, her old prickly exterior firmly back in place. 'It was a mistake. Just forget it.'

He shook his head, the hint of a smile curving those incredible lips she'd never forget. 'Impossible.'

Great. Was he referring to not repeating the kiss or forgetting it? No way was she asking for clarification.

With her head a riotous confusion of thoughts and her heart a frightening jumble of emotions, she knew she had to escape. Fast.

Her usual shyness wasn't justification for this desperate need to run. This had more to do with the growing horror that she'd totally embarrassed herself by kissing him like a sex-starved Playboy Bunny, and the deep, unshakeable fear she'd like to do it again.

'I have to go.'

She didn't wait for a response. Kicking off her shoes,

scooping them up with trembling hands, she made a mad dash across the sand, wishing she could flee the memories of her insane response to his kiss as easily.

CHAPTER FOUR

LANA tossed and turned all night, haunted by a tall, dark sailor with piercing blue eyes who commanded her dreams in explicit erotic detail.

Sleep-deprived and grumpy, she rolled out of bed at six, needing an aerobics class more than ever to work off some of her pent-up frustration. It worked back home, when she had to unwind after dealing with missing freight or junior staff with non-existent people skills, so why not here?

Zac had kissed her.

And she'd let him.

Worse, she'd responded, lost control for an insane moment in time, dropping her guard for a pair of persuasive blue eyes and a dashing smile.

She never dropped her guard—not since discovering Jax's deception, not since he'd dumped her and trampled her hopes for a future in the process.

It was why she didn't go in for fancy clothes or make-up, or snazzy highlights in her hair. She was comfortable in her own skin, secure in using her bland appearance as a protective mechanism to ward off guys after more than she could give.

But Zac didn't seem to care. It was as if he saw past her

dreary dresses and sloppy T-shirts, as if he saw the real her: a woman with needs, a woman who wanted to break free of her conservative mould but was too damn scared to try.

How ironic. He'd caught her off-guard and she'd given in to temptation, her burgeoning confidence courtesy of the dance class and the perfume purchase retreating faster than the First Fleet under siege.

Now she had to deal with the aftermath of that scorching kiss and her cringe-worthy sex-starved reaction. Ensure she forgot it and make damn sure it never happened again.

Once dressed, she headed for the gym. Exercising was familiar, exercising was cathartic, and exercising would surely burn off the energy buzzing through her body since she'd lip-locked Zac McCoy.

She needed to stop dwelling, stop replaying it in her head. It had happened; she couldn't take it back. Now she needed to move on, protective armour firmly in place again.

Determined to stop brooding, she strode into the small gym, crammed with about twenty ladies of varying shape, age and attire warming up on exercise bikes and treadmills.

Some of her tension dissipated in an instant at the comforting familiarity, and she found a space, dropped her towel and started stretching. She was midway through a hamstring stretch, her leg resting on a bar with her head almost touching her knee, when the instructor entered.

She froze, her hamstring giving a nasty twang as her leg slipped from the bar when Zac strode past, barely breaking stride.

Oh, no. Seeing him now was too soon, too awkward, too much.

He faced the room and twenty women sighed in unison. She didn't—she was supposed to be forgetting last night—but she couldn't blame them. Not with him standing there looking decidedly sigh-worthy in navy shorts, white polo shirt, his ever-present charming smile in place.

'Good morning, ladies. I can see you're all keen to start working out if you're up this early. Unfortunately Shelley had an accident ashore last night, and has a severely sprained ankle. So I'm sorry, but these classes will be cancelled for the remainder of the cruise.'

Loud groans echoed through the room as Lana bit back a grin. Sailor boy didn't have a clue how desperate a bunch of women out for their daily endorphin fix could be, and if he thought a simple apology would cut it, he was in for a big surprise.

Zac was speaking again. 'However, she'll be able to check your gym programs from tomorrow. She'll be here between ten and three, though purely in a supervisory role. Thanks for your understanding.'

His thanks were pre-emptive. No sooner had he finished speaking than angry women besieged him.

'You've got to be joking. I've saved for five years to take this cruise and that's it? No aerobic classes? I must do my classes every day.'

'When I pay for service I damn well expect it!'

'The ship's company will be hearing about this when I get off this ship.'

'Isn't there anyone else to take over?'

He held up his hands, the smile long gone in the face of this terry-towelling tirade. 'Ladies, please. If you'll give me a chance to—'

'Now, listen here, mister. This is my tenth cruise, and I've cruised with different shipping lines all over the world. So far the service on this ship stinks.'

A large woman crowbarred into a purple leotard stood toe to toe with Zac, hands planted on ample hips.

'Ever since I set foot on this tub things have gone wrong. The air-conditioning in my cabin didn't work, the balcony door jammed, the incompetent waiters mixed up my dinner, the dance instructor was called away at the last minute only to be replaced by the likes of *you*, and now this. What next?'

Another woman stepped forward, her rake-thin body clad in designer gear—the type you don't sweat in—her coiffed blonde hair far too perfect for such an early hour of the morning.

'I'm surprised, Mr McCoy. In my day a PR man knew how to handle life's little dramas such as this. In fact, he was paid to promote the delights of cruising. You, on the other hand, don't seem to be earning your wage at all. I would even say you're rather incompetent.'

Oh-oh. The situation had turned from tense to downright ugly in the space of two minutes, and Lana felt sorry for him, wanting to help but unwilling to interfere.

Before he could utter a word, the designer dame jabbed an accusatory finger in his direction. 'I presume you know who I am, Mr McCoy?'

He nodded, his lips set in a grim line but his confident aura firmly in place. Lana had glimpsed the same unflappable Zac last night, after the kiss, when she'd slammed her barriers back in place and taken her anger out on him.

'Not only do Mr Rock and I contribute handsomely to this particular shipping line, our personal recommendations go a long way to securing promotions for staff onboard. Personally, I'm having a hard time finding *any* worthy staff on this ship.'

She punctuated the air with short, sharp jabs of her hand, lending weight to every word.

'And, furthermore, I recommend you rectify this farce as soon as possible.'

She spun around and sailed out of the room like the *Queen Mary,* majestic, impressive, unstoppable.

Nobody deserved to be publicly berated like that and, taking in Zac's tense posture and clenched jaw, Lana felt for him.

She knew what it was like to be on the receiving end of criticism like that—had faced it eight weeks earlier, when she'd appealed to the museum's CEO to let her be the spokesperson on the Egypt trip.

The result? If her self-confidence hadn't been much to start with, it had been non-existent after that meeting, when he'd told her in no uncertain terms she wasn't 'the face the museum is looking for'.

Apparently she was too reserved, too serious, too conservative. All perfectly legitimate qualities in a head curator, but not good enough to front TV cameras and reporters at the digs of their newest discovery. That honour had gone to her trainee, a woman with a bigger mouth, bigger boobs and a bigger wardrobe than her.

It had hurt. A lot. A whole damn lot.

She was brilliant at her job; it was the one thing that made her feel good about herself. Little wonder her limited self-esteem had plummeted as a result, and she needed this trip to give it a boost in the right direction.

Battling the sting of bitter tears threatening to complete her humiliation that day in the CEO's office, she'd vowed to gain confidence and never be overlooked for a work opportunity again.

After that kiss last night she'd taken a huge backward step, retreat being her best form of defence.

But now she possessed skills to help Zac out. Maybe she could take another baby step forward? What better way than taking a class she'd been trained to do?

She taught at the museum all the time, instructed students and peers alike, and it was the only time she never felt self-conscious in front of a group. She enjoyed teaching, enjoyed imparting skills to others, so why not here, now?

Clenching and unclenching her hands several times, she shook them out, wishing she could shake off her nerves as easily.

Tension clawed at her tumbling tummy, and she inhaled in and out, long, slow breaths, to clear her head and give her clarity of thought.

Maybe not such a good idea, as the more she thought about it the more she wanted to bolt for the safety of her cabin. But hiding away wouldn't improve her confidence.

It was now or never.

With a last deep indrawn breath, she marched towards Zac. 'Could I have a word with you?'

He rubbed at the bridge of his nose as a low rumbling resumed through the gym. It was the first time he'd appeared faintly rattled. 'Now isn't the time.'

'I can help. I'm a qualified fitness instructor. I can take this class right now, if you want me to.'

'*You're* a fitness instructor?'

He made it sound as if she was a space cadet, and his assessing gaze swept over her. Yeah, as if her outfit made any difference to her credentials.

'You really want to do this?'

'I wouldn't have offered otherwise.'

Relief eased the tension in his face, his lips kicking into a mischievous grin. 'Does it mean I'll owe you?'

She almost ran at that point, the memory of that sexy smile seconds before he'd kissed her all too fresh as she focussed on his lips.

'You won't owe me a thing.'

'Oh, but I will.'

Heck, how had this turned from her doing him a favour to having him in her debt?

With that beguiling smile and heat smouldering in his eyes, she was floundering out of her depth more than ever.

'Look, just forget it—'

'Go ahead and take the class. Once you're done, drop by my office.'

He straightened, brisk and businesslike, and she wondered if she'd imagined the loaded exchange a moment ago.

'Okay.'

As she turned away he laid a hand on her arm. Her skin burned despite the innocuous touch.

'One more thing.'

'What's that?'

'Just so you know—I always pay my debts.' He paused, his disarming smile capable of tempting a saint. 'And I fully intend making good with you.'

While her tongue glued itself to the roof of her mouth, his eyes glittered with clear intent before he released her and walked away.

Lana tucked strands of frizz into her bristling ponytail, all too aware she was fighting a losing battle as she stared at her flushed face covered in a perspiration sheen. The polished brass nameplate on the door to Zac's office was as highly effective as a mirror—too effective—and she belatedly realised she should've ducked down to her cabin before presenting herself here.

When he'd said he'd see her after the class he wouldn't have anticipated a bedraggled, scraggly mess arriving at his office. Then again, it wasn't as if she was trying to impress him. The opposite, in fact. The sooner he realised he couldn't charm her like every other woman on the planet, the easier her life would be. Even if a small part of her would miss his banter.

She knocked and waited for a 'come in' before pushing the door open. The sight that greeted her snatched the breath from her lungs.

She'd seen his many faces—sailor Zac, resplendent in uniform, dancing Zac, dinner companion Zac—yet the sight of him behind a desk, scrawling across a daily planner with one hand, tapping a keyboard with the other, issuing instructions into a hands-free phone all the while, had her grabbing the door to steady her wobbly knees.

Here was a guy in control—a guy who could do anything he set his mind to. He made multi-tasking look easy, and when he glanced up and smiled a welcome she had to steel her resolve, for executive Zac was as appealing as the rest. More so, considering she understood work, thrived on work, her life was *all* work.

'I'll get back to you. In the meantime, make sure those timetables are correct to within a second.'

He stabbed at the disconnect button on the phone, threw his pen down and leaned back in his chair, hands clasped behind his head.

'Well, well—if it isn't our very own Jane Fonda.'

With a shrug, she crossed the room and plopped into a chair opposite him. 'Jane Fonda? Aren't you showing your age? Her exercise videos are years old.'

He laughed. 'So how did it go? Bet those women didn't give *you* a hard time.'

'Why would they? Besides, I think they took out all their frustrations on you.'

'Did they ever.'

He dropped his hands and stood, his sudden proximity

making her rethink her choice of seat. The wide, stuffy leather chair in front of his desk had seemed perfect while he was seated, but now, with him towering over her, it wasn't so appealing.

'Thanks for stepping in and saving my butt.'

Oh, no. She wouldn't think about his butt…wouldn't go there…wouldn't remember how she'd made a grab for it last night in that fit of insanity.

Grateful she could blame her flaming cheeks on exercise rather than embarrassment, she cleared her throat. 'You're welcome.'

'Now that you're here, it's time we had a chat.'

'About?'

His eyes bored into hers, challenging, determined, as he gestured towards a document on his desk.

'Your employment contract, of course.'

CHAPTER FIVE

'PARDON?'

She tapped her ear, just to make sure she'd heard correctly.

He picked up the document and offered it to her. 'Take a look. It's your employment contract.'

'You're kidding, right?'

She stared at the document as if it was her marching orders to walk the plank. 'I'm on holiday. A well-earned holiday, I might add. I helped you out of a tight spot back there, but that's it.'

He threw the contract back on the desk and perched on the desk in front of her—way too close for comfort.

'I understand how you feel, but I need your help. You'd only have to take two classes a day. In return, you'll be well paid, and it won't interfere with your holiday at all. You love your job, don't you?'

'My job?'

A puzzled frown knit his brow. 'You said you're a qualified fitness instructor?'

'I am.'

But that wasn't her job. Her job entailed wearing boring business suits, cataloguing boring artefacts and devising boring staff rosters.

Okay, so she did love her job, and it wasn't always dull, but after she'd been passed over for the Egypt trip she'd started craving more, needing more, and—strangely—the opportunity now came from the most unlikely source. She stared straight at him.

Right then, it hit her like a meteor from Mars.

She needed to build her confidence this trip, and wanted to try new things in order to do so, but still she felt stifled by her conservative nature.

So what if she stepped into a new role? Became the type of person she'd like to be if she had more nerve? Besides, it wasn't as if she was lying. She *was* a qualified aerobics instructor. She just didn't do it for a living.

And who knew? Maybe doing this would give her the ability to form a coherent answer without wanting to duck her head in embarrassment every time he smiled her way?

'Let me take a look at that.'

Trying to hide a triumphant grin and failing, he handed her the contract.

'I took the liberty of contacting Madigan Shipping, the company that owns the *Ocean Queen*. I explained the circumstances and they approved a temporary employment contract—particularly when they heard the Rocks were onboard. They're influential people in shipping circles.'

'Do you always organise other people's lives, or will I actually have a say in your grand plan?'

His grin broadened. 'You're here, aren't you? And I'm giving you the option to sign on or not.'

'Yeah, right.'

Skimming the contract, she nearly fainted when she spied the remuneration—on a par with her monthly salary.

For taking two lousy classes a day? Too easy. And there was that new futon she'd coveted for the spare bedroom in her flat. Not to mention the slight shoe fetish she'd developed thanks to Beth's cast-offs. This extra cash would come in mighty handy for a pair or two of her own.

'What do you think?'

'I think I'm nuts, but why not?'

She picked up the pen he'd discarded earlier and signed the contract. 'There.'

'Don't forget I owe you.'

His eyes glowed, magnetic and enticing, and she suppressed a shiver at what her payment might entail.

'Don't worry about it.' She tugged at her ponytail, twisting the ends around her finger in a nervous habit she'd had since childhood. 'This is turning into some holiday. The ship's amazing, the ports are interesting, and that kiss last night—'

She bit her tongue and mentally slapped herself for running off at the mouth and thinking out loud. That kiss was history, remember? Forgotten. Never happened.

His gaze focused on her mouth, and her lips tingled as his blistering stare remained riveted. Surreptitiously she scratched behind her ear, where her skin prickled the most.

What had happened to the woman who'd just instructed an aerobics class for the first time and nailed it? What had happened to her newfound bravado? It looked as if it had deserted her, along with her common sense. Imagine thinking she could sign on as an employee and keep her distance from Zac.

She fidgeted, shifting her weight from one foot to the other, then rubbed the nape of her neck, wound her hair around her finger.

His gaze finally lifted from her mouth, only to lock onto her eyes, and all that endless blue was enticing and intense. She looked away first and gestured to the desk.

'Don't you have work to do?'

'It can wait.'

She couldn't stand all this tension, the air practically crackling between them, and she backed towards the door. 'Well, I need a shower, so I'd better go.'

He stalked towards her, like a powerful alpha wolf shadowing a helpless, quivering rabbit.

'But what about working out what I owe you?'

She waved her hand, fluttering. It was ineffectual at keeping him at bay. 'The payment's all there in the contract. Clearly spelled out in black and white.'

Stopping less than a foot in front of her, he leaned forward and she gasped.

'Nothing's ever that clear. There are many shades of grey here I think we need to figure out.'

Her breath caught as his head lowered, her heart pounding as if she'd just taken ten aerobics classes back to back.

'Like?'

It came out a squeak, and she darted a glance to the door handle a few inches from her hand. She should grab it, twist it, make a run for it. But she couldn't, was trapped beneath that disconcerting stare, overpowered by his sheer masculinity as he towered over her.

For one insane second she almost wished he'd kiss her again and get it over with, but instead he straightened, ran a hand through his hair and gestured towards his desk.

'Like a stack of paperwork, tax forms and so on that you need to fill out. How about you go take that shower and meet me back here in half an hour?'

She almost collapsed against the door in relief—or was that disappointment?

Buoyed by the fact she'd just had a lucky escape, she saluted. 'Aye-aye, sir.'

With her hand on the door handle, she couldn't resist a parting shot, considering he'd had the upper hand ever since she'd set foot in here.

'You know something? I'm looking forward to being your colleague. You might actually let up on me if we're co-workers.'

She closed the door as Zac sank into his chair and stared at the contract she'd signed, the fine print blurring.

Colleague.

Co-worker.

Lana Walker, the woman who was slowly but surely driving him crazy, was now his colleague, his co-worker, neatly circumventing his golden rule of never getting involved with a passenger.

Hell.

He leaned back and closed his eyes. It didn't help, as an instant image of pert breasts, narrow waist, toned abs and slim legs covered in Lycra haunted him. She wasn't tall, yet her perfect proportions gave the illusion of height—and he ached to touch her, every tempting inch.

Dammit, why couldn't she have stayed hidden behind those loose dresses and revolting pants she wore? First the wet one-piece and now this: tight candy-striped Lycra bike shorts, and a T-shirt fitted enough to highlight the curves he'd love to run his hands over.

He'd snuck back to the gym, watched the last few minutes of her class. And he had been blown away.

In a whirl of high kicks, arm twirls and jiggling breasts, she'd morphed from shy innocent to action goddess, and no matter how hard he tried he couldn't wipe her from his mind.

This teasing was getting out of hand. It had been fun at the start, amusing to get a smile out of that prim mouth, a rare fiery flash from those sombre hazel eyes. But somewhere along the way the lines had blurred, and what had started out as a bit of harmless fun to get a subdued woman to lighten up had morphed into his wanting her.

Seriously wanting her. His thoughts consumed by her day and night.

That kiss on the beach last night had changed everything.

He'd given in to temptation unprepared for the ferocity of her response—a response that had kept him up all night wishing he hadn't let her flee.

First her astounding response. Now her metamorphosis from shy and nervous to bouncy and brilliant.

If he hadn't been intrigued enough before, he sure as hell was now, and despite the importance of keeping his mind on the job this cruise, he had to know more.

What was it about her that had him coiled tighter than an anchor chain?

He rubbed the bridge of his nose, but it did little to erase the beginnings of a headache building behind his eyes.

She was forthright and tetchy—not his type at all. Yet she was so delightfully unaffected, with an underlying hint of vulnerability that tugged at his heartstrings no matter how hard he tried to ignore the fact he still had a heart.

But he couldn't get involved. At least not emotionally. Not now.

Besides, how would she feel if she knew he'd conned her? He hadn't placed any call to head office. He didn't have to. One of the perks of being the boss.

Speaking of which, he needed to get back to work. He was close, so close, to discovering the saboteur who was plaguing the company.

While Shelley's fall might well have been an accident, there had been a couple of other incidents that weren't as easily dismissed. His uncle's suspicions that the *Ocean*

Queen would be the next target had been well-founded. And the sooner he found the person who hadn't disclosed a reckless disregard for everyone's safety and comfort when boarding, the easier things would be for his uncle.

He owed Jimmy and, as he'd told Lana, he always paid his debts.

What would she think of the purely carnal payback system he'd like to instigate with her?

Lana stood under the shower, cool water sluicing down her body. She closed her eyes and tilted her head back, enjoying the spray peppering her face, though it did little to wash away the memory of that damn kiss.

She was determined to forget it, to relegate it to the back of her mind alongside other horrific moments, like the time she had walked in on one of her students with the museum taxidermist in a decidedly unstuffy moment in the archive room, or the time she'd bawled when she'd got her first promotion.

Truly shuddery, forgettable moments—just like her response to that kiss last night.

So why couldn't she wipe the memory, however hard she tried?

As she tipped her head forward and tied a towel turban-style around her dripping hair, she had a vision of Zac's hungry stare as she'd left his office. Not that she'd wanted to provoke him—far from it. But he delighted in rattling her, in teasing her, and she'd wanted to get one back.

It hadn't worked. The desire in his gaze had been real, potent, and oh-so-scary for a novice like her. Old Lana would have jumped ship and swum back to shore before he could wink. But she wasn't the old Lana any more.

The old Lana wanted a husband, a family, a house in the

suburbs to come home to every night after another satis-fying day at the museum.

The new Lana still wanted all those things, but for the first time in her life she was experiencing the flicker of ex-citement that came with self-assurance—the heady rush of having a guy like Zac pay attention to a geek like her.

She'd never had that. Jax had faked a few compliments, fuelled her need to be noticed by a guy—any guy—and had reeled her in as part of his plan. He had used her before saying she was frigid when she couldn't deliver what he'd wanted. His disdain haunted her to this day.

She knew his accusation was why she didn't date very often, why she froze when a guy got physically close.

So why had she combusted in Zac's arms during that kiss?

Subconsciously she knew.

She wanted to feel alive, wanted to tap into the passion simmering deep inside, wanted to be bold and brazen and beautiful rather than a mousy, boring workaholic.

Zac had a way of looking at her as if she was the only woman in the world, and when he did the small, wistful part of her that wanted to be that confident woman dared to hope.

She made it back to his office with a minute to spare.

'Come on in. I've got the forms for you.'

'Great.'

As she stepped into the office he briefly touched her elbow, bending lower on the pretext of closing the door. 'What? No perfume?'

Her gaze snapped to his, only to catch a fleeting glimpse of a cheeky grin before he turned away. Her scowl was wasted.

'Why don't I take them away with me, fill them out, and drop them at the front desk when I'm done?'

She might be feeling braver after breezing through the class, but there was something about him now—the way he looked at her, as if seeing her in a new light. While she should be happy, her inner introvert trembled at what he might do if he sensed the change in her.

He tapped the stack on his desk, beckoned her over. 'Believe me, when you take a look at these you'll be thanking me for filling them out here. I've helped employees through the rigmarole before; we'll get it done in half the time.'

Okay, so he was being helpful. Then why did it feel like the Big Bad Wolf lending Red Riding Hood a hand before gobbling her up?

'Right—let's get to work, then.'

She plopped on the chair opposite his, drew the forms towards her.

He stilled her hand by placing his on top, setting her pulse racing as she stifled the urge to yank her hand away.

'Not much intimidates you, does it?'

She raised an eyebrow. If he had any idea how her heart thumped, her lungs seized and her insides quaked at his simple touch, he'd withdraw that statement.

'I can usually handle stuff.'

Professionally, that was. Anything else and she was about as poised as a toddler on ice-skates.

'Think you can handle me?'

His voice had dropped seductively low, and the smouldering flame in his eyes warmed her, warning her that she was in way over her head with this one if she thought for one second a small boost in confidence could cope with the likes of him at his tempting best.

'I'm sure it wouldn't be too hard.'

She almost bit her tongue in frustration, unwittingly adding to the wordplay. Heat suffused her cheeks, and she wished she had the guts to toss her hair over her shoulder, not duck her head like the blushing virgin she almost was.

His grin had tension strumming her taut muscles. 'You're very assured when you want to be.'

Only when he needled her enough that she forgot her shyness.

'Mainly when putting guys like you back in your place.'

He leaned forward, close enough to whisper in her ear. 'Guys like me?'

Resisting the urge to jerk back from his proximity, she settled for a subtle slide of her hand out from under his instead.

'Over-confident. Smooth. Charming. Used to getting your own way.'

Rather than being offended, he laughed. 'Guilty as charged.'

He leaned into her personal space again, crowding her, overwhelming her, confusing her.

'So, is it working?'

'What?'

'My charm.'

'Not a bit.'

She crossed her fingers behind her back at the little white lie. 'Now, if there's nothing else, let's get these forms done so I can enjoy my holiday.'

'Actually, there was something else. You know I owe you?'

'Uh-huh.'

The instant wariness in Lana's eyes made Zac chuckle.

'How about a tour when we dock in Suva? I've got the day off, so I could show you the sights. What do you think?'

Her eyes lost their cautious edge as her lips curved into a smile—the type of genuinely happy smile that could easily tempt a man to want more, a lot more.

'Sounds good. Know any hot spots?'

Yeah. Just below her ear, above her collarbone, and dead on her soft lips...

'Several.'

His tone must have alerted her to his thoughts, for her eyes widened, glowed with understanding, till he could distinguish the tiniest green flecks in the molten caramel before the shutters quickly descended.

'A tour sounds great.'

She dropped her gaze in record time, her tongue darting out to moisten her top lip. The nervous action did little to dissipate his growing interest in discovering what really made this tantalising woman tick.

Considering how much he wanted to get to know her, perhaps he should rethink Suva—especially his idea about taking her to his favourite secluded beach. If he could barely keep his hands off her here, what hope did he have in blissful isolation on the most spectacular stretch of pristine sand he'd ever seen?

'Right, it's a plan.'

He'd almost said a date, but dates implied more of that physical stuff he was afraid would scare her off. No matter how hard he tried, he couldn't wipe a vivid fantasy of the two of them splashing in the lagoon, him play-wrestling her, her wrapping her legs around him, her wet skin plastered to his, no clothes...

She stood abruptly, the chair almost toppling. 'Look, I really appreciate the offer to help, but I'll be fine with these forms. I'll holler if I need anything.'

Judging by her shaky voice she knew exactly what he was thinking, and she reacted the way she usually did: by erecting verbal barriers and making a run for it.

She scooped up the papers and made a dash for the door

in an awful fluorescent flurry of floral ankle-length skirt the colour of a lifejacket. Her hurried departure left him shaking his head as she slammed the door.

After she'd left, he sank into his chair and wiped a hand over his face. No—didn't help. He could still see her wide-eyed guarded expression, the hint of suspicion in those hazel depths, the wary curve of her lips.

She didn't trust him—didn't accept his interest as real. Not that he blamed her. He'd given her no indication to the contrary, playing the flirt, keeping things light-hearted, seeing how far he could push her before she reacted.

Someone or something had destroyed her belief in her attractiveness, and he'd hazard a guess that some jerk had done a number on her. It would explain her naivety, her lack of artifice when it came to playing coy or flirting back. Which meant he should give her a wide berth. Instead, he wanted her with a staggering fierceness, and the depth of his need was obliterating every common sense reason why he shouldn't do this.

He didn't need the distraction. He had a job to do. But if his head kept spinning like a compass needle his concentration would be shot anyway so maybe he should spend a bit of time getting to know her—the real her, not the cagey woman who hid her mistrust behind lowered eyes and fiddling hands.

Muttering a few curses which wouldn't make many of his colleagues blush, he picked up the phone and placed his daily call to Jimmy.

The phone rang three times precisely—the same number every day—which proved his uncle waited by the phone, despite his protests to the contrary that he totally trusted him that the company was in safe hands.

'Hey, Uncle Jimmy, it's me.'

'Zachary, my boy. How's things?'

Where should he start? With the part where he still felt like a fraud, running the company from behind the scenes until their culprit was caught, or the part where he was crazy for a woman who bolted every time he got close?

'Fine. I'm making progress.'

He didn't need to spell it out. His uncle had been the first to notice the ever-increasing number of 'accidents', the first to see the bad publicity begin to affect sales, and the one to notice the pattern of the incidents and predict the *Ocean Queen* would be next.

And, though he'd never admit it, the ensuing stress hadn't helped his battle with the illness that was slowly but surely killing him.

'Good. Because once you sort out the Australian side of things, there's that Mediterranean problem that needs attention.'

'All under control.'

He'd decided to run things from the London office for a year. More to do with the old man needing him there rather than with business. Not that Jimmy wanted to be mollycoddled. He'd made that perfectly clear. But under all that gruffness was a scared man fighting to stay alive, and Zac would be damned if he left the only father he'd ever known alone at a time like this.

He wanted to ask Jimmy how he was feeling, how the treatment was going, but knew he'd get the usual brush-off.

'So how's things in London?'

'All good here.'

He heard the strain beneath the forced upbeat tone.

'And you? How're *you* feeling?'

A slight pause followed by a grim throat-clearing. 'Can't complain.'

James Madigan wouldn't. He hadn't complained when Zac had left him in the lurch for a year, after he'd run off to marry Magda, hadn't complained when he'd had a near-fatal heart attack as a result of the stress from his increased workload—picking up the slack because of Zac's selfishness—and hadn't complained when Zac had outlined his plans for a future in direct opposition to his.

He was that sort of man: rock-solid, steadfast. And he was the man Zac owed everything to—the type of man he aspired to be.

'Your PR stint working out okay?'

'Yeah, the staff are buying it, and I'm getting the info I need, so that's the main thing.'

Jimmy coughed—an ear-splitting, hacking cough that chilled Zac's blood. Aware that his uncle hated appearing weak in any way, he quickly tried to distract him.

'Get this. I had Helena Rock on my case this morning, going berserk. Can't tell you how close I was to telling her I actually run the company now. That would've put the old battle-axe back in her place.'

Jimmy chuckled—something Zac wished he could hear more often. 'Lucky you didn't. Otherwise you'd have had a mutiny on your hands. Imagine if everyone knew I'd made you head honcho and hadn't announced it officially yet? You wouldn't get to catch the bastard hurting our ships, for a start.'

'You're right. But I hate lying. The staff respect and trust me as a fellow employee. I feel like I'm using them.'

'Don't be ridiculous. This is business. Cruise lines are becoming more competitive every day. We can't afford to let this stuff continue or it'll really start to hurt us. It's your company now.' He paused, the rattle in his throat indicating another cough coming on. 'I'd do the job if I could.

Unfortunately, I'm just an old sea dog who has to live vicariously through you these days, so make sure you do a damn good job.'

Zac searched for words to reassure him, to explain he couldn't be prouder that Jimmy was leaving him the company he'd built from scratch. Though he was glad to get a chance to feel the salt air in his face one last time.

As if reading his mind, Jimmy said the right thing—as usual.

'I wouldn't have placed you in charge of my empire unless I thought you were capable, Zachary.'

'Yeah—a regular shipping magnate, that's me.'

He'd wondered why his uncle had pushed him into shipping after he finished his commerce degree, not twigging that the crafty codger was grooming him till a year into his first contract. By then he'd been hooked—addicted to the shifting deck under his feet and the tang of salt air in his lungs.

He was proud to be in charge of the Madigan Shipping conglomerate, and would do whatever it took to make it the best damn shipping line in the world. He had big shoes to fill. He owed Jimmy. Now more than ever.

'You're doing a fine job, my boy. Now, you better get back to work. Just because you're the boss now, doesn't mean you can slack off.'

Zac laughed, half raising his hand in a salute just as he'd used to when he was a little boy, before dropping it uselessly, all too aware he wouldn't have much time left to share a joke with his uncle.

'You look after yourself.'

He only just heard a mumbled, 'You're as bad as these damn nurses,' before Jimmy hung up.

Life was short. Seeing a strong, vibrant man like Jimmy

fade away reinforced that, and he'd be damned if he sat here and let Lana disembark next week without fully exploring this unrelenting attraction driving him to seek her out almost every second of the day.

He didn't want to look back on this time and regret it—didn't want to be left with memories of a kiss and little else.

She could run but she couldn't hide, and tonight he'd make sure she knew exactly how much he wanted her.

A woman like Lana needed to be wooed, deserved to be treated right—starting with a romantic first date designed to bring a smile to her face and banish her doubts that he was anything other than genuine—in his pursuit of her, at least.

CHAPTER SIX

SHE was lousy at this.

Zac had flirted with her over starter, main course and dessert, showering her with flattery, teasing her, making her laugh. By the time she'd finished a divine lime tart smothered in lashings of double cream her sides and her cheeks ached, and he'd well and truly slipped under her guard despite logic telling her he was playing a game.

'Fancy having coffee in one of the lounges?'

He leaned towards her, immediately creating an intimacy excluding the rest of the people at their table. It set her pulse racing, throwing her off balance quicker than the two-metre swells buffeting the ship.

'Only if you let up with the compliments.'

'Why?'

His eyes darkened like storm clouds scudding across a midnight sky.

'It's overkill.'

'But all true.'

She raised an eyebrow and sent a pointed look at her un-adorned navy shift dress. 'You think I look good in this?'

His gaze dipped to her dress, lifted to focus on her lips, before his curved into a roguish smile.

'What you wear is irrelevant. You're beautiful.'

She exhaled on a soft sigh, wishing for one incredible moment she could be seduced into believing him, giving in to his low voice, his hypnotic eyes, his sincere expression. But she wasn't beautiful, far from it, and falling under a suave sailor's spell was beyond foolish.

'Now that you've exercised all those smooth sailor boy lines for the evening, maybe I will have that coffee. I'm in need of a caffeine hit to wake me from the stupor you've got me in after all that stuff you've been shovelling.'

He laughed. 'It's a date. Just let me drop by the office to check on a fax, and I'll meet you in the Crow's Nest Lounge in ten minutes?'

'Make it five?'

'Can't bear to be away from me for long?'

'Actually, I was thinking more of the fact I need to be up early for my first official aerobics class, so I don't want to be out too late.'

'Spoilsport. I thought you might be pumping up my ego for a delusional moment there.'

'Like you need it.'

Tapping her watch face, she sent him a saccharine-sweet smile. 'Four minutes and counting. If you want that coffee you'd better get a move on.'

He held up three fingers. 'Bet I beat you there.'

'You're on.'

She made a dash for the Ladies' on the way, unable to resist touching up her lipstick. Woeful behaviour for a girl who rarely wore anything but a slick of moisturiser back home, but considering he kept studying her as if she was a priceless painting she had no choice. That sort of scrutiny put a girl under pressure—especially one who didn't feel beautiful, let alone believe she deserved compliments—and she needed all the help she could get.

As she strolled into the Crow's Nest with ten seconds to spare, her stomach somersaulted as she caught sight of Zac at a cosy table for two in the farthest corner, beckoning her over with a smug smile.

'What did you do? Sprint the whole way?'

He pulled out a seat for her and she sank into it before her knees gave the telltale wobble they had whenever he got too close.

'The fax hadn't arrived. I ducked my head in the door, had a quick look, and headed straight here. What about you? Have a quick dip overboard before you joined me?'

She tilted her nose in the air and sent him a withering stare. 'First I'm beautiful; now I look like a drowned rat. You need to work on your charm.'

'That's what you're here for.' He trailed a fingertip down her forearm and her breath caught. 'I need the practice. Now, fancy a coffee? Drink?'

'Make mine a double,' she muttered, snatching her arm away and sending him a disapproving glare that did little to curb his sexy smile.

'Really?'

She waved him away. 'No, just order me something sweet and yummy.'

'You've already got it. But I'll get you a drink too.'

Poking her tongue out in response to his corny comeback, she waited till he'd headed for the bar before grabbing a coaster and fanning her face.

Every second she spent in his company was confusing her further. The closest she'd come to feeling like this before was watching *Ocean's Eleven*. What hope did a girl have with George Clooney, Brad Pitt and Matt Damon on screen simultaneously?

She'd only agreed to Zac's invitation because she didn't want to head back to her tiny cabin just yet—didn't want to be alone.

Tonight was the anniversary of Jax spitting the truth at her—the anniversary of the night he'd dumped her in no uncertain terms. And while she'd made a new life, moved to a new city, taken up new activities, she couldn't forget the devastation, the embarrassment that she'd made such a monumental error in judgment.

It wasn't a night to be alone. It was a night to be distracted with funny quips and compliments, no matter how meaningless, a night to erase the memories of how naïve she'd once been.

'You okay?'

Her heart sank as he dumped their drinks on the table and pulled his chair next to hers, concern creasing his brow.

Blinking rapidly, she pointed to her contact lens. 'Still not used to these darn things. Wish I'd brought my glasses this trip.'

His eyes narrowed as they locked onto hers, probing, yet compassionate. 'I'd believe you if I hadn't seen your expression.' He jerked his thumb over his shoulder towards the bar. 'From over there you looked like someone had died. Then I get back here and you're almost crying—'

'I'm not!'

She sniffed as a lone tear chose that moment to squeeze out of her eye and roll down her cheek, plopping on the back of her hand clenched in her lap.

'The hell you're not.' He brushed a thumb under her eye, so tenderly she almost burst into tears on the spot. 'Now why don't you tell me what's really going on?'

She shook her head, mortified he'd seen her like this, frantically racking her brain for something halfway plausible to tell him—anything other than the truth.

Placing his hand over hers, he gave it an encouraging squeeze. 'Tell me.'

She opened her mouth, closed it, then repeated her goldfish impersonation. Her mind was blank apart from the glaring truth: that it had been over three years since Jax had dumped her, and the memory still had the power to make her blubber.

'It's a guy, isn't it? What did the jerk do?'

Her gaze focussed on his, her tears rapidly drying under all that fierce, fiery blue. He almost looked possessive, protective, and she found herself wanting to tell him. A small part of her was thrilled he actually seemed to care.

'Tonight's an anniversary of sorts.'

She stared down at his hand covering hers: tanned, strong, oh, so comforting. Some of that strength transferred to her as she took a deep breath and kept talking.

'I loved this guy—thought he was the one. He said all the right things, did all the right things, but turned out he was only after…one thing.'

She'd almost blurted the truth—that Jax had only been schmoozing her for what she could do for him at the museum. He'd wanted insider info on items for his private collection. But she couldn't tell Zac about any of that, considering he thought she was a fitness instructor.

'We didn't really click, so he dumped me.' She shrugged, hating the lance of pain still lodged deep in her heart. 'Said I was just a fling, a bit of fun.'

She hiccupped, a pathetic half-sob, angry at the sting of yet more tears, angry at herself more for being such a gullible fool.

'He laughed at me for getting so involved, for being old-fashioned and taking our relationship seriously.'

Zac cursed under his breath, turning his hand over to intertwine his fingers with hers. 'You listen to me. That piece of slime didn't deserve you. He isn't worth anything let alone you giving him a second thought.'

'I know.'

She sighed, enjoying the secure feeling of her fingers intertwined with his way too much. Holding her hand was a fleeting, comforting gesture—something a guy like him would do for any woman. But for one tiny moment it made her feel beyond special, as if he really cared.

'Come with me.'

He leaped to his feet, practically dragging her with him.

'But what about our drinks?'

'Forget them. Let's go.'

'Where?'

She had to almost run to keep up with him. His long strides were determined.

'Somewhere I should've taken you first, rather than easing into this date with a drink.'

Her jaw hit the deck as he pushed through a heavy glass door and led her out onto the open promenade. 'Date?'

'Yeah, date. You know—that thing two people do when they want to get to know each other better, when they like each other even if one of them doesn't want to admit it.'

If her mind had spun with memories of Jax, it was positively reeling now with Zac's little announcement.

They reached the railing and he finally released her hand, leaned forward, his gaze fixed on the undulating ocean. 'I've gone about this all wrong. I didn't want to scare you off by calling this a date tonight, but I'd planned on bringing you up here, talking a little, getting to know

each other, before catching a movie or maybe going dancing—or whatever you wanted to do.'

'Oh.'

She couldn't speak, the pain of memories of Jax anni-
hilated by the unbelievable joy unfurling in her heart.

He turned to face her, reached over and stroked her
cheek, soft, beguiling. She held her breath, stunned by his
intimate touch, and by her craving for more.

'I wanted tonight to be romantic, to show you I'm not
just toying with you.'

He stepped closer, took hold of her arms, and she looked
up, gasped, captivated by the moonlight glinting off his
dark curls and the striking shadows it created as it played
across his face.

He slid his hands up and down her arms, the rhythmic
contact depriving her of all rational thought as he gazed at
her with hunger and greed and passion.

'I don't know what to say—'

'Then don't say anything at all.'

He tugged her close a second before crushing her lips
beneath his. The scorching kiss, a sensual assault, left
her reeling.

If their first kiss on the beach in Noumea had rocked her
world, this kiss blew it into the stratosphere.

As she tilted, along with the deck beneath her shaky
feet, she realised she'd never been kissed like this—ever.

She clung to him as his tongue coaxed its way into her
mouth, teasing her to match him. She moaned, a guttural
sound deep in her throat, and the noise inflamed him. He
leaned into her, pressing her back against the rail as his
arousal strained against her, creating an answering
response in her core, setting her wildest desires alight.

She should stop this madness, re-erect the barriers that

had come crashing down the first instant his lips had touched hers.

But it felt so good to be desired, so good to have the attention of a man, so good to eradicate any lingering memories of what had happened on this night three years ago.

His hands tangled in her hair, angling her head, and he slid his lips repeatedly across hers as he tried to pull her closer.

Stunned by the ferocity of his need, she inadvertently rotated her hips against his pelvis as his hand strayed to her breast, cupping and kneading, sending her resistance spiralling dangerously out of control. His thumb circled her nipple through the thick cotton of her dress, the torturous rubbing firing electric shocks through her body.

The sound of a slamming door broke the erotic spell and they tore apart. Her breathing was ragged as he ran a hand through his mussed curls, his expression dazed.

She'd lost control in his arms—and she never, ever lost control. She was the epitome of control at work.

Christmas parties? She'd be the sober one, tidying up after everyone left.

Farewelling staff? She'd do the collection and choose the perfect gift.

Organising holiday rosters? All over it.

All over Zac, more like it. Her famed control was washed away on the tide.

He laid a tentative hand on her shoulder. 'Lana?'

'Hmm?'

She didn't know what to say, didn't know where to look. Focussing on Beth's indigo pumps with the gold wedge heel seemed a good start.

He tipped her chin up, leaving her no option but to meet his gaze. 'I have absolutely no control around you.'

She laughed—a brittle sound whipped away by the wind. 'I was just thinking about control.'

His hand hesitated, his thumb brushing her jaw before he dropped it. 'My lack of it?'

'Mine, actually.'

She hadn't wanted him to kiss her, hadn't wanted him to remind her of how good it had been the first time, but since he had, she was glad. Glad he'd made her feel desirable and womanly and special for an all too brief moment.

'You don't have to say anything. You were trying to cheer me up. I get it.'

He let another expletive rip. 'If you think that was a pity kiss, you're out of your mind.'

Out of her mind, all right. Out of her mind with wanting him to do it again and again and again.

'It wasn't?'

Shaking his head, he cradled her face, forcing her to look him in the eyes. 'You have no idea what you do to me.'

Flicking her tongue out to dampen her swollen lips, she said, 'I think I have some idea.'

Her wry response garnered a smile. 'I thought you were immune to my charm?'

'There's no vaccination strong enough against you, it seems.'

They grinned at each other like a couple of starstruck adolescents, the brisk ocean breeze buffeting them, pushing her towards him in an act from the heavens.

She'd usually flee—find a quiet place and dwell on why he kept chasing her when she wasn't remotely chaseworthy.

Though she didn't run at work; there she solved problems, enjoyed the challenge. Just ask her colleagues where she could be found: at the museum at all hours, tracking down the newest discovery, ensuring the latest display was eye-catching, cataloguing the backlog no one else wanted to do.

Thinking of the museum did it: she wasn't some *femme fatale* who went around inviting kisses from charming sailors on a moonlit night. She was career-focussed, with an aim to reach the top of her field with a little more confidence. She should know better than to read anything into a few casual kisses and his wanting to *date* her—whatever that meant.

She might be inexperienced with men, but she was old enough to understand the purely chemical reaction when two people remotely attracted to each other flirted a little and that flirtation got out of hand.

'You're driving me to distraction.' He ran a hand through his hair for the second time in as many minutes, more rattled than she'd ever seen him. 'And, considering the job I have to do this trip, I can't afford any distraction.'

'And you're telling me this because…?'

He leaned forward, wound a strand of her hair around his forefinger and tugged gently. 'Because, despite every logical reason why I shouldn't do this, I'm struggling to keep my hands off you.'

'Oh.'

The wine she'd consumed at dinner sloshed around her stomach, rocking and rolling in time with her pounding heart as he tugged harder, bringing her lips centimetres from his before brushing a soft, barely-there kiss across her mouth. It was a tender kiss, at complete odds with the passionate exploding kisses they'd previously shared, a heart-rending kiss that reached down to her soul despite her intentions to ward it off.

When they broke apart she couldn't fathom the expression on his face, the shifting shadows in his eyes.

'I have to go check on that fax.'

'Right.'

'Stay out of trouble.'

With a brief touch on her cheek he was gone, leaving her thoroughly confused.

Within the space of an hour he'd comforted her, kissed her, and apparently dated her.

And what was that 'trouble' crack about? She'd never been in trouble in her life: the model student who studied hard and didn't party, the diligent worker first in of a morning, last to lock up at night. Good old dependable Lana. Reliable, steadfast, earnest Lana. Which was exactly why she was here, trying to build her self-esteem and convince herself a sexy sailor could just be the way to go about it.

He'd been nothing but honest about wanting her, so why the sudden scram? One minute his kiss had been warm and gentle and caring, the next he'd made a run for it.

Ironic, considering she hadn't run for once. She'd embraced her newfound bravery and stayed, even after that scintillating kiss that normally would have sent her scurrying for cover.

But she was done with running.

If she couldn't handle a healthy dose of honesty— something he'd just given her, even if the truth of how much he wanted her scared the hell out of her—how could she hope to become the poised, confident woman she needed to be at work?

She mightn't be able to give him what he wanted—would probably disappoint him if she did—but that didn't mean she couldn't lighten up a bit and actually enjoy his attention.

If she was really brave, she might even have a little fun along the way.

CHAPTER SEVEN

LANA spied Zac at the end of the gangway and sighed in relief. After he'd run out on her last night she'd had her doubts about him showing up today. Crazy, considering she was the one who'd usually contemplate a no-show rather than worrying about him doing it.

Beyond impressive in uniform, today he was casually cool in black board shorts, a funky printed T-shirt and a peaked cap, with aviator sunglasses shading his eyes. She wished she could see those eyes, read them, get a feel for his mood after last night.

She hadn't heard from him, hadn't seen him this morning, and while she was relieved, a small part of her couldn't help but wonder what he had planned for today.

If last night's 'date' hadn't exactly happened, maybe he had other ideas today?

Taking a deep breath, she headed down the gangway, half of her looking forward to the tour of Suva, the other half looking forward to seeing how far her confidence extended.

'I thought you'd stood me up.'

Tipping her head forward, she looked at him over the top of her sunglasses. 'Why would I do that? I've been looking forward to your tour.'

'I'm very good, you know.'

'Ever heard the phrase "self-praise is no praise"?'

He grinned and gestured to a small four-wheel drive parked nearby. 'Come on, I have a car waiting for us.' He bowed low. 'Your chariot awaits, madam.' He pulled off his cap with a flourish.

'*You're* going to drive?'

She glanced at the chaotic scene on the dock, where cars darted between pedestrians and street vendors, and horns honked constantly as people jumped out of the way of moving vehicles in haphazard fashion.

He laughed at her horrified, sceptical expression. 'Don't worry, I've done this before. The car belongs to Raj, a friend of mine. He often lends it to me if I want to tour around. Once we leave the docks and head out of town the roads quieten considerably.'

Her doubt must have shown, for his grin widened. 'Don't you trust me?'

She quirked an eyebrow. 'Your driving skills? Maybe. As for the rest? Not on your life.'

He clutched his heart. 'You're a hard woman. Now, come on—get in the car before I change my mind.'

She laughed, surprisingly relaxed as they headed out of town and he pointed out interesting landmarks.

She'd expected some awkwardness, but he kept up a steady flow of casual chatter as they wound around the island. Content to sit back and watch the stunning scenery, she admired the sapphire ocean lapping at pearly sands, the beaches fringed by swaying palm trees. After half an hour, they stopped at a roadside café.

'Do you like Indian food?'

'Love it. The hotter the better.'

'Good. Raj put me on to this place years ago, and I

always drop in if I have time. They make the best chicken tikka this side of India.'

'What are we waiting for? I'm ravenous.'

As they entered the open-air café the proprietor, a tall Sikh wearing a maroon turban, rushed over. 'Hello, Mr Zac. Welcome back.' He pumped Zac's hand so vigorously Lana feared the action might dislodge his turban. 'Aah, you have brought a beautiful friend. Welcome to Sujit's Place, miss.'

Zac smiled. 'Sujit, meet Lana.'

He bowed over her hand. 'Welcome. Now, what can I get you?'

She deferred to Zac. 'You order. You'd know the specialities.'

'How about the usual, Sujit?'

Sujit bowed again. 'Most definitely, my friend. Coming right away.'

She looked around, surprised by how clean the place was, considering it was open to the elements. As for the sand floor—it would be a breeze for clean-ups.

'Adds to the island ambience, huh?'

She nodded, surprised he could read her thoughts so easily, and secretly pleased. 'What's with the lack of table settings?'

'Wait and see.'

'Very mysterious.'

His mouth kicked up into a cheeky grin. 'All will be revealed shortly.'

'I bet.'

He chuckled at her laconic response and gestured to a nearby table, where she plonked her straw carryall next to a chair and sat, savouring the spicy aromas coming from the nearby kitchen.

'Smells divine.'

Zac slid his aviators off, the impact of all that dazzling

blue rivalling the sky for vibrancy. 'The last ship I was on used to dock here every week. I put on six pounds as a result. See?'

He lifted his shirt and patted his washboard stomach. Her mouth went dry. Those were some abs.

Before she had time to comment Sujit arrived, bearing platters of food: naan bread, chicken tikka, dahl and lamb korma were placed in a tantalising array in front of them, and the dryness disappeared as the delicious aromas made her mouth water.

'Thanks, Sujit. This looks superb, as always.'

Sujit nodded, his hands held together in a prayer-like pose. 'Enjoy your meal.'

Zac glanced at her, a smile playing about his lips. 'Well, what are you waiting for?'

Confused, she pointed at the table. 'Plates would be handy?'

'See those large green leaves Sujit put in front of us? They're not placemats; that's your plate. Indian food here is served on a banana leaf. Usually, only vegetarian fare is served on leaves, but here it saves on the washing up. You just roll them up once you've finished and throw them out. As for cutlery—you're looking at it.'

He waved his fingers at her, and she couldn't help but notice how long, elegant and strong they were.

'I can cope with using my hands to eat as long as I clean up first. Is that sink over there for washing?'

He nodded. 'Follow me.'

As they soaped and scrubbed his hand brushed hers and she jumped, the innocuous touch raising an awareness she'd determinedly subdued since last night.

He stared at her, an eyebrow raised, and she managed a weak smile. 'I think our food's getting cold.'

First to break the stare, she turned away, feeling hot and clammy and out of her depth. He'd moved the boundaries with those kisses, had changed everything with his admission of how much he wanted her, and no matter how hard she pretended she could handle it, she couldn't cast off all her reservations at once.

With her head urging her to take a chance for once, and her heart scared of the consequences if she did, she headed back to the table.

This was going to be a long day.

Zac followed Lana back to the table, loving how she moved, all fluid lines and sinuous elegance.

Her long turquoise dress, surely a reject from the seventies, flowed from her shoulders to mid-calf, skimming curves along the way. He could see the straps of a bright pink bikini poking through, and he hardened immediately at the thought of seeing her in it. If the vision of her hot little bod in that dreadful neck-to-toe one-piece had been haunting his dreams, he could hardly wait to see her curves revealed in a bikini.

She'd pulled her curly hair back in a loose ponytail, and he longed to reach out and wrap the tendrils that curled at the base of her neck around his fingers. He loved her hair, loved watching it bounce against her shoulders as she walked.

A vivid image of that hair draped over his torso popped into his mind and he almost stumbled. This would be one hell of a tour if he walked around with a hard-on all day.

Determined to ignore his libido, he sat and pushed a platter of naan towards her. 'Let's eat.'

'Everything looks delicious.'

'Wait till you try it.'

He ladled a serving of dahl and korma onto her leaf, then

reached for a naan. Her fingertips brushed his as he reached for the same piece and he clenched his jaw in frustration.

It wasn't deliberate—one look at her shy gaze firmly fixed on her banana leaf told him that—and he needed to get a grip before he made a mess of things, as he had last night.

He broke off a piece of the soft, doughy bread, dipped it into the pungent curry sauce and stuffed it into his mouth before he said something he'd regret, like, *Let's get out of here and get naked.'*

'Mmm, divine.'

Her tongue flicked out to capture a drip of sauce and he stifled a groan, focusing on the unique blend of spices hitting his tastebuds rather than how much he'd like to lick away that spillage.

He needed to talk, to draw attention away from how much he wanted her, to focus on anything other than the driving, obsessive need to get her naked and moaning his name while he plunged into her.

'Sujit whips up the best Indian food I've ever had. It rivals some of the feasts I've had in Singapore and India for authenticity.'

'You've been around, haven't you?'

'Yeah—definitely a perk of the job. I've travelled almost everywhere.'

'Any favourites?'

He'd steered the conversation onto safe ground only to be diverted by the small moans of pleasure she made between mouthfuls, and he gulped his entire glass of water before answering.

'Probably Alaska, for its glaciers. I've cruised the Inside Passage from Vancouver, and the ship usually spends a day in Glacier Bay. It's amazing that ships like ours, which weigh around seventy thousand tons, can sail to within a mile of those monsters. I've even seen huge chunks of ice sliding off the face.'

Maybe he should focus on that ice, focus on all that cold—anything to dampen the urge to leap across the table and drag her into his arms as she stared at him with wide-eyed awe.

'I also love the Mediterranean. Especially Italy. Capri is great, with its ancient cobbled streets and home-made pastas.'

He could have regaled her with tales of his travels all day, particularly as her wide, luminous eyes were fixed on him, her expression fascinated, but the longer she stared at him the harder it was to forget every sane reason why he couldn't push their involvement—no matter how much he wanted to.

He'd seen the devastation in her eyes last night, the lingering hurt from the jerk who had screwed her around, and her desolation at having their relationship labelled a fling.

He'd planned on backing away then, but once he'd taken her on deck, once he'd kissed her, his plans to leave her alone had drifted away on the night air.

He wouldn't hurt her by having a fling. But he couldn't offer her anything else, considering where he'd be for the next year. So where the hell did that leave them?

For now, he'd keep things light. He'd promised her a tour today—the least he could do after she'd come through for him with the exercise classes—and he'd make it a fun day for her if it killed him.

'You know, the South Pacific islands are growing in my favourite places ranking all the time.' He leaned forward and crooked a finger at her. 'I think the present company has a lot to do with that.'

She blinked, as if startled by his compliment, and he wished he could wring her ex's neck for battering her self-esteem to the point where she couldn't accept a compliment without embarrassment.

'You mean Sujit? I totally agree. His food is to die for. I haven't been to those other places, but I'd definitely put Fiji first on my list.'

He grinned at her clever sidestep, but he wasn't done yet. 'What about Noumea? How high should New Caledonia rate? I hear their moonlit beaches are magical.'

The recollection of their first kiss stained her cheeks pink. Her eyes dipped to her banana leaf as he belatedly remembered he was trying to cool down, not get more wound up.

She waved towards the food. 'You'll give me indigestion, flirting on an empty stomach. At least let me put a dent in this feast before you turn on the charm.'

He laughed, more relaxed than he'd been in years despite his desperate yearning for her. It had been that long since he'd enjoyed a woman's company enough to spend more than a few hours with her, and while he'd dated infrequently, he'd never experienced such a connection on so many levels with any woman. Not even Magda— and he'd married her.

'Let's finish up and hit the road. I can't wait to show you the island's best beach. It's isolated, so tourists haven't wrecked it.'

She mumbled an acknowledgement and focussed on her food. He wondered what he'd said. She'd been cool one moment, and perspiration covering her skin in a delectable sheen the next. A sheen that had him envisaging all sorts of erotic ways he could clean it off.

If he were prone to flights of fantasy he'd almost say she was hot and bothered about his mention of being on an isolated beach together. Yeah, and of course she wanted to rip his clothes off too. Definitely wishful thinking.

'Is the food too spicy for you?'

Her guarded gaze snapped to his, as if trying to read something into his innocuous question. 'No, it's fine. It's just a little hot today.'

Hot? It was positively burning—though the weather had little to do with it.

He gestured towards the kitchen, indicating drinks, and Sujit bustled out shortly after, bearing two tall, icy glasses and a pitcher.

'Ever had lassi before?'

'No.'

'It's made from yogurt. Very refreshing. It should cool you down a tad.'

While he'd need to dunk in a vat of the stuff to remotely cool down.

She took a tentative sip, before gulping the cold, sweet liquid and running the frosted glass across her forehead. Her eyelids fluttered shut as a relieved smile curved her lips. 'That was good.'

Okay, maybe the lassi had done the trick for her, but he was about to explode—and as she opened her eyes he bit back a groan.

'You've got a milk moustache. Here—let me.' He reached out before thinking better of touching her and pointed at her top lip, his words strangled.

She laughed and wiped her lip. 'Thanks. Not a good look.'

He smiled and stuffed another piece of naan into his mouth, concentrating on his food as he mopped up the last of his curry with the bread—anything to take his mind off how much he wanted her.

He topped up her glass and she drank again. He had the strongest urge to reach over, pull her head towards him and lick the lassi off her top lip.

Instead, he had to sit there and watch her do it, her

tongue flicking out to caress her lip in a slow sweep, and he almost bolted from the table.

'Finished? I'll take care of the bill and meet you at the car.'

She nodded, the loose strands of hair around her face floating in the breeze. The urge to brush them away made his gut clench all over again.

'Thanks for lunch. It was delicious. Sujit's a great cook.'

As he pulled out her chair, his hand brushed her bare arm, and he gritted his teeth at the feel of her silky, soft skin. At this rate he wouldn't be able to walk.

'See you at the car.'

Her open expression told him she had no idea how much he was struggling with his libido, and he turned away and called out to Sujit, who appeared from the kitchen in an instant.

'Mr Zac, your friend is special.' Sujit's singsong lilting accent held a wistful note. 'You have known her long, yes?'

'Not long. Though I agree she's special.'

So special he'd given up a valuable day to be with her. After last night he'd almost reneged on their tour; he could have spent the day catching up on paperwork and following up that fax pointing to their suspected saboteur.

But his wanting to cancel had been more than business; not only had that jerk of an ex done a number on her for sex, he'd lied to her—and the second Zac had heard that he'd known he shouldn't get involved.

He was lying to her too.

Every moment he let her believe he was a PR manager at sea he was being dishonest, and while catching the saboteur demanded duplicity—and ultimately making good on his promise to his uncle—it didn't stop him hating every second of his deceit.

So he'd told her a partial truth to compensate for his

guilt—told her how badly he wanted her, expecting her to run at the mention of a date let alone anything else.

Instead, her response to his kiss had shaken him as much as the fact that she'd stood her ground and hadn't run. And even while he'd planned on begging off the tour today the memories of her fiery reaction had kept him up all night and drawn him here.

'It must be serious. You have never brought a woman to Sujit's humble café before. Are you going to marry her?'

Zac laughed. Life was so simple in some cultures. You met a girl, you liked her, you married her. Either that or your parents chose a bride for you.

'No.' A strange tingle ran up his spine, causing the hairs on the back of his neck to stand on end. 'I'm just showing her around your lovely island today. She'll be leaving the ship in a week.'

'Ah, she lives in Australia. Why should that stop you from marrying? You also live there, yes?'

'Yeah, but she's a friend, and I'm not remotely interested in marrying her or anybody else for that matter.'

Been there, done that, never forgotten the folly.

Sujit grinned, his teeth stained an ugly brown from years of chewing betel nut. 'Whatever you say. Though trust old Sujit—he has a feeling in his bones about this one.'

'You're an old degenerate.' Zac settled the bill and shook his hand. 'See you next time.'

'Maybe you'll both visit on your honeymoon?'

Zac chuckled, amused by the restaurant owner's one-track mind.

Marriage again? Not for him.

As he caught sight of Lana, casually leaning against the Jeep, the wind whipping her hair away from her face while plastering the dated dress against her shapely body, the faintest niggle of doubt entered his mind.

She was dynamite, packing a stronger punch than TNT and C4 combined. She blew his mind and short-circuited the rest of his body every moment he spent with her, till all he could focus on was how much he wanted her.

He'd been attracted to her mentally at the start, but how quickly that had all changed. Now he wanted her so badly he ached.

Yet for all her surprising bravado last night she was still inherently shy, retreating when he pushed too far, still hiding her sensational body behind those repulsive clothes.

So if they couldn't have a fling, what the hell should he do? Back off?

'Mr Zac, I've never seen you like this.'

He tore his gaze away from Lana, focussed on Sujit. 'Like what?'

'Distracted.' Sujit pointed to his forehead, imitated a frown. 'So very serious.'

That's because his growing feelings for Lana were serious. Even the fact he was using the word 'feelings' scared the hell out of him.

Sujit shook his head, his benevolent grin bordering on condescending. 'I can see you're making this more complicated than it is. You like this woman, yes?'

He nodded, his gaze inadvertently drawn to her again. Crushing need swamped him, blindsiding him faster than a swinging mast.

'Well, then, do not over-analyse. Do not worry about the future and what it may hold. Live for the moment. See where the winds of change take you.'

He stared at Sujit as if seeing him for the first time, his words echoing through his head.

Could it really be that simple?

Was he over-analysing, thinking too far ahead, allowing his fears from the past to destroy a possible future with a wonderful woman?

His conscience yelled a resounding *Hell, yeah!* and just like that a mighty weight lifted from his shoulders and floated away into a cloudless Fijian sky.

'Thanks, my friend, you're a genius.' He pumped Sujit's hand, his attention still firmly focussed on the woman who'd captured his heart without trying.

Sujit's grin widened as he placed his palms together and bowed. 'I know. Now, go.'

He didn't need to be told twice, and as he headed for the car, refraining from breaking into a run, he knew the decision he'd just made had the potential to change his life. For the better.

Lana squinted into the sunshine, watching Zac stride towards the car. He'd been in a strange mood over lunch and the odd times she'd caught him staring at her it had looked as if he fancied her as dessert.

It had made her uncomfortable, and she'd had no idea how to handle the attention, so she'd focussed on her meal, steered the conversation onto factual topics and muddled through the best she could. She just hoped things weren't as tension-fraught at the beach.

'Ready to go?'

'Sure.'

As he drove along a winding coastal road she focused on the picturesque scenery and replayed their lunch conversation in her head.

There was so much more to him than smooth words and a charming smile. He was well-travelled, articulate and self-assured, with charisma that captured her interest and engaged her mind. It only added to his appeal. But she'd be better off remembering most of what he said was designed to tease her, that words were cheap.

She'd fallen for slick words before. These days a guy's actions were the only thing that would let him anywhere near her bruised heart.

'Wait till you check out this beach. I've seen a few, but I think this is better than some of the Caribbean beaches— not to mention Queensland's hot spots.'

'I love any beach. My apartment's in Coogee, so you can safely say I'm a bit of a beach babe.'

'Well, you're right about one thing. You're definitely a babe.'

Her measly ego inflated momentarily, before she shot him a disapproving stare. 'Oh, yeah, I'm sure my designer wardrobe elevates me to babe status.'

He paused, as if searching for the right words. 'Don't take this the wrong way, but your wardrobe is a little…'

'Boring?'

Her sour interruption had him darting a worried glance in her direction before refocusing on the road.

'I was thinking more along the lines of sedate for someone your age.'

'Which is?'

'Hell, I'm digging myself in deeper, aren't I?'

She chuckled. 'Quit while you're behind, sailor boy.'

She liked her clothes. They might be old but they were safe, familiar, like snuggling into a favourite quilt on a cold winter's day.

She'd tried a new wardrobe once before, a new look, going the whole way with risqué lingerie. But none of it had made any difference with Jax. He'd hurt her just the same, designer dresses or not. Much safer to stay true to herself, to find a man who wanted her for the real her, not because of how she looked or what she could do for him.

'Actually, I like what you're wearing today. That blue brings out the green flecks in your eyes.'

'My weird eyes change colour according to what I wear.'

'Not weird. How about alluring?'

She snorted. 'You could bottle that charm and sell it.' His bashful smile made her laugh. 'And I see what you mean. I'm so *alluring* I have *hundreds* of men falling at my feet, and it's all because of my eyes.'

'You have one.'

'Who?'

'I'm a male, in case you hadn't noticed.'

Oh, she'd noticed, all right—was noticing more by the minute, despite all attempts to the contrary.

Fortunately she was saved from replying as he slowed the car and turned into a narrow dirt track. The Jeep bumped and lurched over rough terrain, the ground scattered with large potholes, and thick foliage slapped against the doors.

Just as her bones started to warn her they'd been rattled once too often the vegetation thinned, and he pulled over into a clearing which overlooked an inviting stretch of white sand, with an aquamarine ocean that stretched as far as she could see.

'Wow—amazing.'

Zac's blue-eyed gaze fixed on her, bold, challenging. 'Sure is.'

He wasn't looking at the view, and she squirmed under his searing stare.

'Come with me.'

She stared at his outstretched hand, wanting to take it, but nervous he'd read too much into it.

He took the decision out of her hands by grabbing hers on the pretext of helping her from the car, and she sent him a tremulous smile, wondering if he had any idea what a big deal it was for her to hold hands with a gorgeous guy as they strolled towards a secluded beach.

Holding hands implied trust, implied dependence, implied she believed in him enough to lower her barriers— much more than responding to his impulsive kisses inspired by chemistry and the length of time since she'd last been kissed, and the soul-deep yearning to be wanted by another person.

As her feet sank into the soft sand, and he gripped her hand that little bit tighter, she knew her resistance to this charming man was slipping dangerously.

A loud 'caw' captured her attention, and she glanced to her right, at a huge bird perched on top of a towering cliff ending at the lagoon's edge.

That was exactly how she felt—as if she was standing on the edge of a very steep cliff, torn between wanting to jump into the warm, welcoming ocean below and experiencing the thrill of a lifetime, or letting her feet back her up to the predictable safety of solid ground.

With Zac tugging gently on her hand she had no option but to follow, heading into the unknown with a man who had the power to unnerve her, when every self-preservation instinct screamed at her to dig her heels in the sand.

CHAPTER EIGHT

'WELCOME to paradise.'

They stopped beneath a coconut tree, the air fragrant with frangipani, the view picture-perfect.

'How did you find this place?' she whispered, reluctant to break the tranquility as they strolled towards the beach.

'Raj brought me here with his family. We had a picnic, swam in the lagoon, lazed around. It's great being able to relax away from the tourists swarming the island. I come back every chance I get, though I'm usually alone.'

'So you haven't brought a horde of women here before me?'

Though she kept her tone light, she knew some of her enjoyment would dissipate if he had brought countless others here.

He squeezed her hand. 'You're the first. I wouldn't share this place with just anyone.'

Oh-oh—there he went with more of that defence-shattering charm. With a nervous smile, she slipped her hand from his.

'More flattery. Aren't I the lucky one?'

He laughed. 'Come on, let's go for a swim.' He pointed to a row of palm trees. 'Let's dump our stuff over there. You get changed, I'll test the water.'

A great suggestion, as getting undressed in front of him would have made her beyond uncomfortable. Crazy, as he'd already seen her in bathers, but disrobing in front of someone implied intimacy. Besides, she'd taken another step down the confidence road today and worn the new bikini she'd bought in Noumea, and if the way he'd been staring at her over lunch was any indication, she'd be blushing from head to foot the entire time.

She dropped her bag on the sand and whipped her dress over her head, kicked off her sandals and rummaged in her bag for sunscreen. Just as she started to rub the lotion on her arm, he touched her hand.

'I can do that for you.'

She squeezed the tube so tight lotion spurted out in a noisy raspberry. 'I'm fine. You go ahead. I'll meet you out there shortly.'

He didn't budge, and held out his hand for the tube. 'Unless you're a contortionist I doubt you'll be able to reach your back. This sun can burn you in less than ten seconds flat, so let me help.'

He was right, but the thought of him rubbing any part of her body was already causing the skin behind her ears to prickle in that annoying way only he and strawberries could elicit.

'Really, I'm fine—'

'Damn, you're a stubborn woman.'

He snatched the lotion out of her hand and squeezed a healthy blob into his palm, raising an eyebrow when she frowned. 'Now why don't you play nice and lie face-down on your towel?'

With an exaggerated huff, she plopped on the towel, rested her forehead on her hands and braced herself for the first cold dollop of lotion.

'I suppose you want me to thank you?'

'Oh, you will.'

He thoughtfully warmed the lotion between his hands, though his first touch was as shocking, as electrifying, as if he'd squeezed the entire tube onto her back.

She gritted her teeth and tried to relax under his hands, while her skin tingled everywhere he touched.

She'd never been touched by a man like this before. Jax hadn't been touchy-feely, and his version of foreplay extended to a kiss and wandering hands.

She'd never experienced the luxury of a man's warm, firm touch gliding over her skin, and as platonic as this was, she couldn't help but enjoy it.

'You're very tense.'

'Must be the extra aerobic classes.' *As if.*

He didn't let up the pressure, his hands stroking her back in long sweeps designed to be impersonal yet driving her just a little bit mad with the sheer pleasure of it.

'Try to relax.'

How could she relax when he was stroking her flesh, his strong hands splaying over her back, her defences unravelling as fast as her muscles unwound?

His fingers kept snagging the tie of her bikini bra, though she didn't dare suggest he undo it. That would be *her* final undoing. She might be immune to his charms, but her body, long neglected, was enjoying this way too much.

'Why don't you turn over, and I'll do your front too?'

Just like that, her muscles twanged back to tense. The thought of him rubbing her stomach sent heat surging to her cheeks.

'Not a good idea.'

She flipped onto her back and held out her hand for the tube.

'Why not?'

'Because I'm perfectly capable of rubbing lotion onto my tummy.'

His eyes glittered and she shivered at their taunting glint. 'But where's the fun in that?'

Her skin prickled some more and she itched behind her ear.

'Give me the tube.'

He held it overhead and waved it around. 'Only if you ask nicely.'

Clenching her jaw, she stuck her hand under his nose. 'Please.'

He chuckled, and dropped the tube into her palm. 'Actually, it'll probably be just as much fun watching you do it.'

'Pervert.'

'Just interested. But you already know that.'

His low, suggestive tone had her squeezing way too much lotion into her palm, and rather than taking her time to ensure she didn't miss any spots she slapped the stuff onto her belly and made a few half-hearted circles before leaping from the sand.

'Right. Hope that water's warm.'

'It's perfect.'

His heated gaze slid over her before meeting hers and she bit the inside of her lip to stop it quivering. He totally unnerved her, from his roguish smile to the devilish glint in his eyes.

He was toying with her, she knew it, but with every compliment she let her guard down just that little bit more.

She wanted to believe him, wanted to believe he thought she was perfect. But she wasn't a fool. Not anymore. Objectively, how could he find her less-than-a-handful breasts—another Jax-ism she hated—no waist to speak of, and thighs with the first hint of dimples perfect?

'Oh-oh, you've got that serious look on your face. Come on—race you there!'

He flung the words over his shoulder and took off, tearing across the hot sand before she could move. By the time she'd caught up he'd dived into the water.

'Not fair. You've got longer legs.'

'Nothing wrong with your legs, from what I can see.'

Rolling her eyes, she waded into the cerulean lagoon, sighing at the blissful feel of the water.

'Now, if you hold off on the flirting for just a few minutes, I might actually enjoy this swim.'

He pushed her head under water in response.

She spluttered and spat salt water as she surfaced, clawing at him, trying to return the favour, only to have him slip out of her grip.

'You're in trouble, sailor boy.'

They tumbled in the water for the next few minutes, arms and legs flailing wildly, laughing so hard she got a cramp.

She couldn't remember the last time she'd had this much fun. Her long work hours weren't conducive to play, and when she went to the beach at the weekend it was to swim for exercise rather than leisure.

When they finally emerged, she clutched her side. 'You've given me a stitch.'

'Good. I've never seen you laugh like that.'

He touched her cheek, a brief, fleeting glance that had her fingers digging painfully into her side to stop herself reaching up and touching the skin he just had.

'That's because you're not that funny.'

'Ouch.'

He laid both hands over his heart and she chuckled.

'The day I wound that enormous ego of yours is the day I'll go skinny-dipping in the Pacific Ocean.'

'I'm wounded! I'm wounded!'

He fell to the sand in a pathetic heap, writhing as if he'd just been stung by a lethal jellyfish, and she laughed.

'I'm going to dry off. When you've finished with the theatrics, I'll see you up there.'

She pointed to the palm trees and headed off, ignoring his call of, 'You're no fun.'

She knew he'd meant it as a joke, a fly-away comment, but the words echoed as she towelled off.

She wasn't fun—didn't know how to have fun. Not when she'd spent her whole life trying to do the right thing.

Beth had once called her a nerd, and she'd shrugged, pushed her tortoiseshell glasses up her nose and scuffed her sensible shoes, agreeing with the assessment but hurt all the same.

Everyone saw her the same way: no fun. People at work, her cousin, even Zac—and while his opinion shouldn't matter, considering she wouldn't see him after the end of next week, it did. As he joined her, and she watched water droplets run in rivulets down his muscular torso as he bent to pick up his towel, she really, really wished her newfound confidence extended to having a little fun.

'I'm just going to dry off in the sun for a while,' she said. And blink away the sudden sting of tears for feeling inadequate and inexperienced and inept.

'Don't be too long. These UVs can seriously burn.'

She grabbed her towel and laid it on the sand a few feet away—an ill-chosen spot, considering she had a clear view of him stretched flat on his back—his long, lean body, his abdominals composed of ridges of hard muscle…

She squeezed her eyes shut to blot out the tempting

image, and must have dozed, for it seemed like an eternity later when his voice roused her.

'Excuse me, sun goddess, you should come into the shade now.'

Her eyes fluttered open and she stretched, feeling rested and composed and completely tear-free.

'Nice of you to be so concerned.'

She picked up her towel and flung it next to his, putting enough space between them to ensure no accidental contact.

'I'll admit my concern is altruistic. I don't want to rub lotion on you again.'

'Why's that?'

'I enjoyed it way too much.'

His gaze trailed over her body, lingering on every area he'd rubbed earlier and everywhere in between, and darn it if that prickly itch didn't start up again.

She quirked an eyebrow. 'If you enjoyed something as mundane as rubbing suntan lotion on my back, you must get out even less than I do.'

He leaned forward, too close, too masculine—too everything. 'Go on—admit it.'

She bit her lip, inched back. 'Admit what?'

'You enjoyed it too.'

His grin was pure temptation, and she waved her hand in front of her face as if swatting away a particularly bothersome fly.

'The only thing I'll admit is finding your incessant flirting extremely tiresome.'

His smile faded at the same moment the sun ducked behind a cloud. Both left her slightly chilled.

'Do you really feel that way?' he asked.

Her heart stuttered as she searched for a suitable answer. What could she say? That she didn't believe his compliments? That her self-confidence was so shot by a guy who'd used slick words before that she couldn't trust easily? That she wished she could believe one tenth of his attention was real and not just his natural instinct to charm? That she hid behind sharp retorts, using them as a barrier against her insecurities?

She settled for semi-truth, feeling a tad guilty her barb had tarnished what had been an enjoyable day.

'Honestly? I'm not used to the attention.'

He couldn't have looked more surprised if she'd stripped off in front of him.

'You said things ended with your ex three years ago, but you date, right?'

Heck, look what she'd got herself into now. She could lie, but she'd always been lousy at it. Beth said her mouth had pursed into a strange prune shape the few times she'd tried it, and she already had him staring at her as if she was nuts.

'My last date was with George Clooney, Brad Pitt and Matt Damon.'

He smiled. '*Ocean's Eleven* fan, huh?'

'Oh, yeah.'

He reached out, touched her hand. She flinched, silently cursing her reaction.

'Hell, Lana, I'm not some kind of monster. I like you. I want to get to know you better.'

She shook her head, using her hair as a shield to hide her face. 'What's the point? I'm off the ship next week, so why get to know each other?'

'Because it could be fun.'

Her gaze snapped to his. She was surprised by the serious glint in those deep blue eyes. She'd seen him cheeky, teasing, even wicked, but it was the first time she'd seen this solemn expression fixing her with concern.

'Fun? The only fun a guy like you would be interested in over the next week is a fling. And I'm not that kind of girl.'

His eyes darkened to midnight, disappointment flickering in their depths. 'You don't have a very high opinion of me, do you?'

She shrugged, hating that they were having this conversation, hating that she'd put a dampener on what had been a lovely day.

'You're a guy. You're a sailor. You meet women all the time. You're a master at flirting. The only reason you're paying me any attention is because of that stupid challenge I threw down the first night on the spur of the moment, because I couldn't think of anything else quick enough to get rid of you.' She took a deep breath, a steadying breath, clenching her hands to stop them from shaking. 'It's nothing personal. I understand that. You see me as some sort of challenge because I'm not falling at your feet like the rest of the female population probably does. You—'

'You're wrong. Dead wrong.'

He leaped from his towel and started pacing the sand with long, angry strides that showed he was wrestling with something. The truth, perhaps?

'Am I?'

Her almost-whisper stopped him dead and he swivelled to face her, dropping down on his knees in front of her.

'Damn straight. Want to know why you're here with me today, on my one day off a week?'

She waved her hand. 'Go ahead. I'm sure you'll tell me anyway.'

His hands shot out, cradling her face in their warm, firm grip before she could blink.

'Because I like you. *You.* Not your clothes, or your willingness to help me out, or because I want you to sleep with me. You. You're funny and smart and you make me laugh.'

'So now I'm a clown—'

'Shut up.'

He kissed her—a soft, tender kiss that reached down to her soul, shattering her defences along the way, scaring her beyond belief.

'Now, it's time to head back. And I don't want to hear another word.' She opened her mouth and he pressed his finger to it. 'Not one word. Not another character assassination. Not another assumption. Not one word unless you agree to play nice. Got it?'

Her lips twitched, and his answering smile made her heart sing.

He wasn't asking for anything, didn't expect her to sleep with him, and hadn't belittled her when he'd heard the sorry truth about her inexperience with men.

So what should she do? Spend some more time with him? Get to know him better? With the aim to do what?

He had his life on the sea. She had a great apartment in Sydney, a few colleagues she could call friends at a pinch, and a good job at the museum. They didn't have a future, no matter how well they got to know each other.

'Come on. Stop thinking so much.'

He held out his hand, and for the second time in as many hours she silenced her voice of reason and took hold of it.

'How about we go with the flow, see what happens over the next week? How much trouble can we get into in seven days?'

She raised an eyebrow, and he grinned as a scary thought flitted through her mind.

Plenty.

CHAPTER NINE

THOUGH she would have preferred silence, they made desultory small talk on the drive back to the ship, as a multitude of thoughts swirled through her mind—most of them focussed on the man sitting next to her.

She'd never met anyone like him.

Confident and charming, yet astute enough to look beyond the surface and home in on exactly what she wanted: a guy to recognise she had a brain, a sense of humour, and a yearning not to be taken for granted.

She couldn't believe he'd said all that stuff, had seriously cracked the protective shield around her heart with his sincerity.

So what now? She wouldn't have the guts for a fling, no matter how far her confidence soared. She couldn't do something like that unless she was emotionally involved. And while Zac said he liked her, *like* didn't equate to what she craved: a lifelong love from an incredible man who'd put her first.

Completely moronic, completely delusional, completely crazy, but she'd been dreaming of her own happily-ever-after for so long she'd somehow taken his genuine niceness and tangled him up in her fantasy.

She cast a sideways glance at his profile and sighed, her heart hoping for a minor miracle while her head shouted, *Wake up and smell the sea air.*

'What are you thinking?'

'Not much.' He really, really didn't want to know.

'I can hear your mind ticking from here.'

'If you're that perceptive, you tell me.'

'I think you're mulling over what I said back at the cove. Close?'

There he went again, being way too perceptive.

'Don't give up your day job. You'd make a lousy mind-reader.'

'So?'

'So you told me not to say anything unless it was nice, and I'm having a hard time coming up with anything.'

His chuckles warmed her better than the sun's rays. 'See—that's why I like you. Every prickly, cynical, blunt inch of you.'

'Yeah, well, I can't help it if you've been spending too long in this tropical heat.'

He slowed the Jeep and turned onto the dock. 'You know, you can hide behind that smart mouth of yours all you like, but I'm going to get to know you better whether you like it or not.'

'Yeah?'

He stopped the engine and turned to her, his slow, sexy smile sending a shiver through her. 'Yeah. Don't say I didn't warn you.'

Charming sailor boy she could handle. Single-minded sailor boy with a determined glint in his too-blue eyes had her plans to hold him off sinking faster than the *Titanic*.

Hoping her voice didn't quiver, she aimed for flippant. 'I stand duly warned. Thanks for the tour.'

'My pleasure. Hope it lived up to your expectations.'

If she'd had any he'd blown them clean out of the water with his shrewd observations back at the cove. She didn't want to get involved with a guy like him. But what if it was too late?

'Uh-huh.'

'Great. I better get this Jeep back to Raj. See you at dinner?'

She nodded, the thought of spending more time with him after the day they'd just had sending a tiny helix of joy interwoven with doubt spiralling through her.

He winked, sent her a jaunty half-salute, and drove away, leaving her mind spinning and her tummy tossing with nerves at the many possible ways he could 'get to know her' over the next few days.

Zac pulled up at the front of Raj's and switched off the engine, wishing he could switch off his thoughts as easily.

Things were out of control. Or, more to the point, things with Lana were out of control.

After lunch and his chat with Sujit he'd been all gung-ho, determined to explore the possibility of a relationship with her. Then they'd talked at the cove and things had rushed downhill from there.

He'd known she was inexperienced—but not even dating? Hell, did that mean she was a virgin too? No way. She'd had that moronic ex—not that that meant much—and there was the way she'd responded to his kisses, the way she had that funny gleam in her eyes at times. But what did that mean? That she had a bit of sass lurking beneath her prudish front?

He didn't dally with virgins. In fact he didn't dally with women, period, considering it took all his concentration these days to perpetrate his plan.

But he wasn't fooling around with Lana. Had known that the instant she'd made her true opinion of him clear.

He'd kissed her to shut her up, to demonstrate what she really meant to him—a gentle, soft kiss, when he'd been hankering to devour her all day.

He wasn't toying with her. He wasn't just after a fling. So what could he do to prove it to her?

He got out of the car and headed for the house. Considering Raj's happy marriage and five kids, maybe he could give him a pointer or two.

As he reached the veranda of the whitewashed bungalow, Raj stepped out. 'Hello, my friend. Had a good day?'

'Yeah. Thanks for the Jeep. I had a great time down at the cove.'

'I'm sure you did. Sujit phoned me and said you had a beautiful lady companion with you today.'

He groaned. 'I can't believe you two old gossips.'

Raj's grin broadened. 'He also said you were so ga-ga over this woman you could hardly finish your dahl. Must be serious. Care to tell me more?'

'Maybe. Though I'd kill for a cold beer first.'

Raj clapped both hands to his head. 'Where are my manners? Come in.'

As Zac sank into a comfortable cane chair with a beer in his hand, Raj raised an eyebrow.

'So my friend. Time to tell all.'

He had two choices: stay silent and listen to the hum of the ceiling fan, or get an objective perspective on a situation that was complicated at best.

'Lana's different from anyone I've ever met. I want to get to know her better, but I only have a week before I head to Europe. Not enough time to really get involved.'

Especially when the likelihood of her retreating back

into her shell was high. He'd seen her growing confidence—the perfume, staying on after the kiss last night, the hot new bikini today—but small changes didn't mean she wouldn't retreat at the first sign of an over-eager sailor laying a possible future relationship on her after knowing her for a week.

He took a long slug of beer, savouring the icy brew sliding down his throat. 'That's the short version.'

'Do you have to return to Europe?'

He nodded. He'd let his uncle down once before. Not this time. He'd make sure of it.

'Jimmy's sick again. The cancer's back and it's spread.'

Raj's bleak expression mirrored his. 'I'm sorry. Is it—?'

'Terminal? Yeah.' He downed most of his beer in one gulp, hating the injustice of this disease that had no cure and robbed a man of his health, his dignity, his life.

'How much time?'

He shrugged. 'He's seen all the best docs in London and had varying opinions. Some say six months; some say a year, max.'

Raj shook his head and clicked his tongue. 'Very sad.'

'He says he wants to be left alone, but I know the stubborn old coot better than I know myself. That's why I'm moving head office to London for the next year. So I can visit him whether he damn well likes it or not.'

'Ah…' Raj nodded like a wise old guru. 'So this is the problem with your woman. She lives in Australia and you'll be based in London for at least the next twelve months?'

Zac leaned forward, rested his head in his hands. 'It's more complex than that.'

'Matters of the heart often are.'

He leaped out of his chair and started pacing, wishing

he hadn't mentioned Lana to his friend. 'Why are we even having this conversation?'

'Because you have fallen, and fallen hard.'

He pulled up short. 'You know the biggest problem? I've lied to her, and she's a straightforward, no-nonsense person. She's been lied to before and it cut her up badly. How the hell am I going to tell her the truth now, when she barely trusts me as it is?'

Raj's eyebrows shot heavenward. 'She doesn't know your true profession?'

'No. You know secrecy's been paramount, to give me a chance to catch our saboteur. And I only met her a week ago.'

'For a woman you only met a week ago, you're sure doing a lot of soul-searching.'

Zac picked up his beer and slugged the rest, desperate to ease the dryness in his throat. 'Crazy, isn't it? Happily single for years, then I take one look at this quirky, captivating woman and can't get her out of my mind.'

'If she cares for you, she'll forgive you. Besides, it's only a little white lie. You have worked on ships as a public relations manager. You just also happen to manage the entire fleet.' Raj chuckled, doing little to soothe Zac's nerves.

'I'm glad you find this situation amusing.'

'You're really in a bind, aren't you?'

'I feel so much better after talking with you.'

'Sarcasm won't help, my friend. I suggest you go back to your ship and think long and hard about your dilemma of the heart.'

'Very poetic,' Zac muttered, knowing all the soul-searching in the world wouldn't get him out of this quandary. The way he saw it, there was only one solution: tell her the truth, start a relationship with her now and pray she'd be interested in continuing it.

Though he'd never been a fan of long-distance relationships, had seen them consistently fall apart around him over the many years he'd worked on ships, the thought of keeping in touch with her till he returned to Sydney, maybe seeing her on the odd flying visit, sent a thrill of hope through him.

'You know, between you and Sujit you two old reprobates could start your own relationship counselling service.'

Raj laughed, picked up the car keys and slapped him on the back. 'Come on, I'll drop you off. Everything will work out for the best.'

He grunted in response and hoped to God his friend was right.

Lana finished her aerobics class still feeling stressed, despite rave reviews from the participants. How could she keep her mind on the job when flashes of her afternoon with Zac kept popping into her mind at the most inopportune moments?

Take the rowing machine: it reminded her of boats, which reminded her of water, which reminded her of beaches and ultimately Zac.

The treadmill wasn't much better: walking hand in hand to the pristine lagoon, with Zac.

As for her towel, slung casually over a set of free weights, she wouldn't even go there, considering her skin prickled at the mere thought of his hands stroking her back while she'd been lying on that towel.

Thankfully, she made it back to her cabin without any more flashbacks, though once she set foot in the small space and closed the door she slumped against it.

Of all the fish in the sea, she had to get hooked by a sailor.

She smiled at the pun, though there was nothing funny

about the situation. She was falling for him. There was only so much a girl could take, and with that non-stop charm chipping away at her defences almost twenty-four-seven what hope did she have?

Considering he was a sailor and she was merely a land-lubber, they had little hope of making a relationship work. Especially the type of relationship she wanted: husband, kids, noisy Sunday afternoons in her very own backyard, rolling in autumn leaves with her brood, face-painting, playing tag, scoffing sticky toffee apples. The kind of childhood she'd never had. The kind of childhood she'd yearned for.

Beth understood. She'd wanted the same thing: they'd role-played happy families countless times as lonely six-year-olds, when their mums had died in the same car crash.

Beth had found her happily-ever-after, and while Lana was pleased for her cousin there wasn't a day that passed when she didn't secretly crave the same for herself.

Taking this cruise had been a first. Well, chalk up another—it was also the first time she'd met a guy who saw beneath her prissy veneer; the first time since Jax that she'd trusted a guy enough to get to know him better; the first time she'd felt real passion, if his kisses were anything to go by, and she knew without a doubt that if the last of her defences totally crumbled it would be the first time she'd fallen in love.

A knock on the door made her jump, and she opened it to find the man intruding on her thoughts filling the doorway, looking incredible as usual in full uniform, the gold embroidery on his epaulettes catching the light.

'Hey, there.'

'Hi.'

Why was it that every time he caught her unawares

her ability to respond coherently vanished as fast as her resistance?

She dropped her gaze, taking in his polished dress shoes, his long legs in formal black trousers and the white jacket ending just below his waist. She usually laughed at men wearing monkey jackets, yet on Zac it accentuated his butt.

'How did the class go?'

'Great.'

If she discounted her obsessing over inanimate fitness equipment and how it reminded her of him.

'Just wanted to let you know I won't make dinner tonight. Business calls, but maybe we can catch up later? The ship sails at ten, and it's a magical sight as we pull away from dock, so how about we meet under the bridge then?'

She hesitated. Was this wise? Spending more time with him when he'd said he wanted to get to know her better despite her resistance? Giving him the opportunity to chip away at her emotional barriers even more, to the point where they might disintegrate once and for all?

Maybe it was the wariness he glimpsed in her eyes, maybe the hint of uncertainty tugging at her mouth, but he stepped forward and touched her hand.

'Come on, you know you'll miss me at dinner. This way I'm just trying to make up for lost time.'

She laughed, as he'd intended, his charismatic smile disarming her quicker than she could say land ahoy.

'Okay. I need to sharpen up a few barbs.'

He squeezed her hand before releasing it. 'Great. I'll see you there just before ten.'

For the second time in as many minutes she leaned against the closed door, her head filled with Zac, her heart filled with foreboding.

* * *

'Hello, sailor.'

Zac straightened from where he'd been leaning on a railing, a poster boy for the gorgeous nautical male, silhouetted against the bridge, an appreciative gleam in his eyes. A misplaced gleam, considering she wore a boring black calf-length skirt and an olive top which had seen better days.

'Glad you made it.'

'Didn't think I would, huh?'

'I had my doubts, considering it's probably past your bedtime.'

She chuckled and waved a finger back and forth in front of him. 'Hey, I'm supposed to be the one practising barbs, not you.'

'Maybe we can practise together?'

His voice dropped lower and he wiggled his eyebrows suggestively. She shook her head, unable to keep a smile off her face.

'You're hopeless.'

'Your fault.' He sniffed the air like a hound, coming closer, too close, almost nuzzling her neck. 'You're wearing that damn perfume again. Any wonder I'm a broken man? Didn't I warn you that stuff was dangerous?'

'It's the only perfume I own.'

Maybe she could blame the perfume for her gradual melting towards him? Ever since she'd worn it her resistance had slowly but surely unravelled.

His low, sexy chuckle had her clutching the rail for support, all too aware that her collapsing resolve had little to do with the fragrance and more to do with the man staring at her with desire in his eyes.

'Well, if you keep wearing it you're definitely heading for a whole lot of trouble.'

Heat flushed her cheeks and she gripped the rail so hard her knuckles stood out. 'Oooh, I'm scared.'

'You should be.'

And for one crazy, loaded second as he leaned towards her she almost welcomed the danger of having a guy like him interested in her.

Clearing her throat, she deliberately relaxed her fingers and straightened. 'So, where's this magical sight you promised me?'

'Be careful what you wish for.'

His deep voice rippled over her like a silken caress, and her knees almost buckled right then and there.

As if on cue, the ship's horn blasted as the massive vessel pulled away from the dock. Suva's lights twinkled like a fairyland as the ship sailed up the channel, and a gentle breeze fanned her face—a welcome relief for her fiery cheeks.

She was no good at this. Even with him being so nice this afternoon, even with her defences lowered, she still couldn't throw herself into flirting unreservedly.

Hiding away was a habit of a lifetime. She'd done it as a child, leaving her dad to work through his grief, and she'd done it as a teenager, flying under the radar of her father's countless girlfriends who had waltzed in and out of a revolving door.

No prizes for guessing where her abhorrence of casual sex came from. Her folks had had the perfect relationship, with their love for each other radiating out to include her. They'd been the epitome of the happy family before that car accident had ripped their lives apart.

Her dad had always assured her she'd come first in his life and she had. He'd mourned her mum for seven long years before dating again. But she had never understood the women who could jump into bed so quickly when her dad made it perfectly clear he wasn't interested in a relationship—never understood what motivated them to be so free and easy with something she considered a gift.

'Well, what do you think?'

Her gaze swept the horizon, the sea. Eventually she raised her eyes to meet his, which were firmly fixed on her rather than the view. 'You're right. It's magical.'

His eyes glittered in the moonlight, a sexy smile curved his lips, and the skin behind her ears gave an alarming prickle.

'You're not looking at the view,' she said.

'I prefer this one.'

She tensed as he lowered his head, barely grazing her lips, and the feather-light kiss sabotaged her initial determination to pull away, rendering her resolve to keep her distance useless.

He kissed her again and again and again, gently increasing the pressure with each kiss as a languorous heat stole from her lips to her fingertips—a heat she'd never experienced, a heat that stole through her body and into her heart.

He hadn't laid a hand on her, yet every inch of her skin tingled as if he'd caressed it, and their lack of contact only served to increase the pleasure of their lips locked together, tasting, sampling, searching in an endless quest for satisfaction.

But she couldn't give him satisfaction—at least not the kind a virile man like him wanted, deserved. She pulled away, wishing she was another type of woman, wishing she had the courage to let go of her reservations all at once, throw caution to the wind and see what happened.

'Definitely magical.' He touched her lips, still quivering from the impact of his kisses, with a reverent fingertip, gently tracing the contours, undoing her one little stroke at a time.

She needed to reassemble her wits, to say something, but her mind wouldn't co-operate while her body was still in shock.

'I take it this is part of your plan to get to know me better?'

As if she'd tripped a silent trigger, the shutters descended over his eyes and his smile faded. 'Plan?'

She shrugged and wrapped her arms around her middle, suddenly chilled despite the balmy breeze. She had to say this—had to be bluntly honest. It was the only way she knew. 'You're trying to seduce me.'

'Am I?'

His sombre expression, the way his voice tightened, the distance he'd established between them by taking a step back, all indicated one thing: she'd insulted him.

Tugging on the end of her ponytail, matted by the wind, she met his bitter gaze head-on.

'Come on—level with me. I may be some naïve recluse who hasn't been on a date in far too long, but I'm not stupid. You said you like me. A guy like you has needs. So what I want to know is this. Why are you going through this game of charming me, kissing me, when there isn't a hope in hell I'll sleep with you?'

There—she'd said it. And while her gut churned with trepidation, her hands were surprisingly steady as she folded them in front of her, before realising she probably looked like a prim and proper nun and promptly released them.

A vein pulsed at his temple as he raked a hand through his hair, dishevelled and spiked and thoroughly tempting. Then he met her gaze, his clouded with disappointment, hers wary yet relieved that she'd asked what had been bugging her since that afternoon.

She'd had the guts to speak her mind, and he had no idea what a big deal that was.

'This isn't just about sex.'

'Oh, really?'

He jammed his hands in his pockets, shoulders squared, back rigid. 'I meant what I said this afternoon. I want to spend time with you, get to know you. But I'll be damned if I stand here and lie about wanting to drag you back to my cabin right this very minute and have amazing sex with you all night long.'

Her mouth dropped open, a squeaky 'oh' escaping before she shut it.

His eyes flashed blue fire as he fixed her with a steely gaze. 'There. Is that what you wanted to hear? Do I want to have sex with you? Hell, yeah. But I'm not going to push you. If you want me half as much as I want you, you'll have to show me.'

She bit her tongue, biding her time, trying to unscramble her brain long enough to answer, to give him a response halfway decipherable that didn't consist of another scintillating 'oh'.

Her hands trembled and her belly rolled in time with the ship as it headed out to the open sea. She searched for the words to make him understand half of what she was feeling: confused, scared, excited, a mish-mash of emotions that terrified her as much as falling for this incredible man who pulled no punches and spoke the truth without flinching.

Honesty was all-important to her—one of her top criteria in her perfect man, courtesy of the elaborate lies Jax had told to manipulate her. She'd never trust a liar again, and here was a guy who was dead-set honest about what he wanted. She admired him for it, even though the blunt truth of exactly what he wanted from her scared her beyond belief.

After a drawn-out silence, he reached out and she let him take her hand.

'Look, I'm sorry for laying all that on you. But you have to know you're driving me crazy.'

'Totally unintentional, I can assure you.'

His mouth kicked up at her wry answer and hers twitched in response.

'Do you want me to back off? Slow down? Just say the word.'

Oh-oh. It was like being given a choice between a decadent double choc fudge sundae—something wickedly indulgent she knew she'd end up regretting later—and a single scoop of vanilla—plain, boring. She knew exactly what she'd get if she took the safe option.

Did she want him to back off? Really?

Her head said it was the logical thing to do, considering she'd be off the ship shortly, but her heart was giving strange little twangs it never had before, quietly urging her to take a risk for once in her sedate life.

Maybe it was her turn for a dose of healthy reality? If he ran, it wasn't meant to be. If he didn't… Well, she'd face that frightening prospect if it arose.

Taking a deep breath, she went for broke. 'I can't get physical with a guy unless I'm emotionally involved. That's just me. And I hate to break it to you, but I wouldn't have let you kiss me just now unless I wasn't already starting to invest some emotion in us.'

Understanding, stark and pure, splintered in his eyes before coalescing into a bright, hard blue.

'I've kissed you before.'

She waved away his comment. 'Impulse kisses. You turning on the charm.'

'And tonight?'

After the time they'd spent together, after she'd grown to trust him through his actions—he hadn't pushed her for sex once, despite his admission just now of how much he wanted it—emotion had more than clouded her judgment. It had taken over to the point she didn't know why she was holding him at bay any more.

She raised her eyes to his, silently imploring him to understand. 'Tonight I've realised you've crept under my guard. And I'm starting to like it.'

The first flicker of awareness in his steady gaze made her want to execute a perfect swan dive into the ocean.

'How much?'

Drawing on her meagre reserve of resolve, she placed a tentative hand on his chest. 'A lot.'

He caressed her cheek softly, lingering for an exquisite moment. 'Then where do we go from here?'

Damned if she knew.

After Zac had walked Lana back to her cabin, he headed for the place he did his best thinking: the bridge.

Ever since he'd joined the fleet as a young, eager sailor he'd loved this control centre of a ship, the hub that drove these monstrous vessels. He loved the quiet efficiency of the staff going about their business, he loved the view, and—like any guy—he loved the gadgets. Hundreds of them, that beeped and lit up and made his fingers itch to touch them.

He usually popped up here on the pretext of consulting with the Captain over something, when in reality he loved the buzz, the feeling of control. He now owned this baby, and the decisions he made could drive her and the rest of the fleet further than the company had ever been before.

Ironic, considering he had no control over his situation

with Lana. Or, more precisely, control over his burgeoning feelings.

He couldn't believe what she'd just told him. Sure, he'd caught the odd gleam in her eyes that said she was thawing towards him in the attraction stakes—not to mention her genuine responses to his kisses—but to say she was emotionally involved?

Hell. It blew him away.

It was exactly what he wanted—what he'd hoped for to lead into a full-blown long-distance relationship, whatever that might entail.

The kicker was she'd given him the perfect opportunity to say he was emotionally involved too, but he'd held back.

For, no matter how long he stewed over this, hashing out scenarios, it all came back to Uncle Jimmy and the fact he couldn't let him down—couldn't let the man who'd given him everything die alone.

Which meant he'd be on the other side of the world for a year, a whole three hundred and sixty-five days, and he'd be damned if he expected her to wait for him for that length of time. She deserved more.

Besides, he'd travelled down this road before, with Magda waiting at home for him, and it had killed his marriage. She'd changed while he'd been away, irrevocably, and there'd been no going back.

But Lana wasn't Magda, and he owed it to her—to himself—to let her make the decision.

Rubbing a hand across the back of his neck, he sank into the nearest chair, leaned back and focussed on the control panel in front of him.

He had to give her the option—had to know he'd tried his damnedest to make it work with this quick-witted, infuriatingly shy, naturally beautiful woman. She was worth it—every unaffected inch of her.

He just hoped she cared enough to take the risk.

CHAPTER TEN

FEELING like a pawn in a romantic game of her own making, the last thing Lana wanted to do several mornings later was play chess, but she had a game scheduled with Mavis and she hated to let her down.

She plopped into a comfy armchair and ordered a double espresso from a waiter, hoping the after-affects of yet another sleepless night didn't show. She'd had to use concealer to hide the dark rings under her eyes for the first time ever. Beth would be proud she even knew what the stuff was for.

'Guess what arrived at my door this morning?'

Lana screwed her eyes tight, pretending to think. 'Let me guess. One of those dance hosts you're so fond of?'

Mavis roared with laughter. 'Bad girl. Next best thing, though: an invitation to the Captain's cocktail party tonight. I'm sure there'll be a few eligible men there to bat my eye-lashes at.'

'You're supposed to be setting me a good example.'

'Hah!' Mavis snorted. 'I think it's too late for you, my girl. You don't need any lessons, if that happy glow is any indication. I take it your tour went well the other day?'

The tour? It seemed like a lifetime ago, considering what had happened since. The chat they'd had the night the ship had left Suva had been replayed at will, over and over, till she wondered if she was going crazy. Luckily Zac had been tied up with work since, and she'd barely seen him. Maybe telling him she felt emotionally involved with him had been a good thing? Perhaps it had driven him away once and for all?

Indecision tore at her. She wanted to tell her friend everything, but was still trying to understand it herself, so she gave her a brief version of events instead. Mavis nodded in all the right spots, waiting till she'd finished.

'Have you fallen in love?'

Lana sighed, resigned to the truth. 'He's a sailor, married to his job. What hope have I got?'

'Have you told him how you feel?'

'Sort of.'

She'd told him she had feelings—of a kind. Invested emotion meant the same thing, right?

But they hadn't resolved anything that night. After she'd dropped her little 'emotion' bombshell they'd talked around it, he'd made one of his charming comments, she'd fired back a quick retort, and he'd walked her back to her cabin—*sans* kiss.

Besides, nothing would happen unless she wanted it to. He'd made that pretty darn clear.

'What does "sort of" mean?' Mavis touched a pawn, moved it forward by keeping her finger on it, frowned in concentration before moving it back. 'Some newfangled term you young people have for chickening out?'

Lana chuckled. 'Yeah, something like that.'

Mavis glanced up and fixed her with a stern glare. 'So what are you going to do, missy? You need to show him how you feel. Take a risk. See what happens.'

She had to *show* him. He'd said the same thing.

Would she have the courage to make a play for the man she'd fallen for?

As she watched Mavis toy with the pawn again, a glimmer of an idea shimmered through her consciousness, slowly coalescing into a plan that had her tummy clenching with nerves.

Did she have the gumption to pull it off?

'Listen to your heart, dear. It's the only way.'

Listening to her heart was what had got her to this point: confused, elated, petrified, yet buzzing with anticipation. Ironic, as she'd always listened to her head until now, had been the perfect curator, the perfect cousin, the perfect girlfriend.

She had a well-ordered, perfectly sensible life back in Sydney. So why was she looking to turn it topsy-turvy by getting involved with a guy like Zac?

She gestured at the chessboard. 'Your move. Then I might tell you my plan.'

'What plan?' Mavis's eyes gleamed with delight at the hint of subterfuge.

Lana chuckled. 'What time do you think you'll be ready tonight?'

'Well, there's a lot more of me to nip, tuck, polish, exfoliate, moisturise and pluck than you, so around six?'

Lana smiled and moved a bishop. 'That's fine. If you could meet me at my cabin shortly after, that'd be great.'

Mavis frowned. 'But what's the plan?'

She leaned forward and crooked her finger, dropping her voice to a conspiratorial whisper. 'I need your help.'

'How about this one?'

Lana glanced at the skimpy, thigh-skimming crimson silk dress and shook her head. 'I couldn't wear that.'

Mavis shrugged, flung it on the ever-growing pile on her bed, and picked another dress off a hanger from the quickly emptying wardrobe. 'What about this?'

Lana took one look at the skin-tight tangerine tube dress and wrinkled her nose. 'No way.'

Mavis sighed and added it to the pile. 'This cousin of yours sure has an interesting dress sense.'

'Way out, more like it.'

Beth had packed enough designer dresses to last Lana a month, but every one she'd contemplated wearing tonight had ended up on the discard pile. And, considering she'd have to make a decision shortly or do a Lady Godiva, her chances of finding anything suitable were rapidly dwindling.

'This one?' Mavis held a mulberry mini at arm's length, screwing up her eyes with a thoughtful look on her face. 'The colour's gorgeous.'

As was the dress. The fabric shimmered like the finest claret as Mavis turned it this way and that. But the dress was super-short, redefining the term 'mini', and she'd never be able to pull off something like that without tugging self-consciously at the hem all night.

She wanted to make a statement, to show Zac what she wanted—not show him what *he* apparently wanted!

'Here, let me hold it up to you.'

The second Mavis held it up in front of her and she glanced down and saw where the dress ended she shook her head vigorously. 'Next.'

Mavis tut-tutted as she reached into the wardrobe again. 'There are only a few left.'

Her heart sank. She'd seen what was left. She'd examined every single dress in there at least ten times since she'd made her decision this morning to go all out tonight and prove to Zac she was ready to take the next step.

She always came back to the same dress: a stunning floor-length formal gown in the richest shot-silk jade, its strapless bodice embroidered with tiny emerald crystals designed to capture the light and draw attention to the bust.

The gown was a stand-out—the type of dress to make a statement, the type of dress fit for a princess, the type of dress to turn an ugly duckling like her into a rare swan.

But she'd balked at trying it on, a small part of her terrified she wouldn't live up to a dress like that no matter how far she'd come in the confidence stakes.

She heard Mavis flicking hangers at a rapid pace, and knew the exact moment she caught sight of *the* dress.

'Oh, my.'

Mavis clasped her heart, drew out the jade sheath with reverence. 'I swear, if you say no to this one I'm marching out of this cabin right now.'

Lana gnawed on her bottom lip, twisted one of the few curls left hanging from the elaborate do Mavis had managed with a few bobby pins and a squirt of hairspray.

'Well?'

'I like it, but—'

'No buts. This is the one.' Mavis held it up to her and sighed. 'Perfect. You should see what this colour does to your eyes. That young man of yours won't know what's hit him when he sees you in this.'

That was all that mattered, really. What Zac thought. And the anticipation of seeing his expression when he caught sight of her all dolled up and wearing this dress was incentive enough to make her reach for it with gentle hands and slide it off the hanger.

Mavis smiled her approval as she unzipped it with fumbling fingers, stepped into it and turned around. 'Help me with this, please? I'm all thumbs, and the last thing I need is to ruin the zip on the one dress I like.'

As the metal teeth slid into place, she took a deep breath and glanced down, her eyes widening at her rather impressive newly created cleavage, courtesy of the in-built bustier. If that didn't make a statement, nothing would.

'Right, my girl, turn around. Let's have a look at you.'

When she turned, she caught sight of her reflection in the mirror behind Mavis a second after her friend's mouth formed a perfect *O*.

'You're beautiful!'

'Don't sound so surprised.'

Mavis reddened. 'I didn't mean it like that. It's just I've never seen you look—I mean, you don't usually wear—Uh—'

'It's okay.' She patted Mavis's arm. 'I'm not a clothes horse—never have been—and I never wear make-up because I can't be bothered.'

Mavis puffed up, nodding emphatically. 'Well, you're lovely without it.'

Lana stepped closer to the mirror, turning her head side to side. 'Though I have to admit you've worked a minor miracle.'

The glittering moss-green eyeshadow and dark khol elongated her eyes to exotic proportions, the foundation created the illusion of perfect skin, and the whisk of bronzing powder gave her razor-sharp cheekbones a healthy glow. As for her lips, she'd gone for a neutral nude pink. Nothing too over the top, considering whatever colour she wore wouldn't last long if she had any say in it…

'The make-up has only enhanced what the good Lord gave you.' Mavis held out a pair of shoes. 'Now, put these on and let's get going, before us Cinderellas turn into pumpkins before the night has begun.'

Lana laughed at the mixed metaphor and slipped on a pair of Beth's fabulous sky-high stilettos in a matching jade, took a final look in the mirror and did a little twirl for good measure.

The emerald shot-silk sheath fitted her like a second skin, the rich colour bringing out the green flecks in her eyes, and for a girl who'd never felt beautiful in her life, nothing came close to describing how she felt right at that moment.

'You're going to knock his socks off, my girl. Just you wait and see.'

It wasn't just his socks she wanted to knock off, but Lana wisely kept that gem to herself—though by Mavis's knowing look, she'd read her coy smile pretty well.

In this dress she was a woman with grit and determination; a woman ready to show her man how far she was willing to go; a woman with more than flirting on her mind; a woman willing to take a chance on an incredible man.

'Ready?'

Mavis held out a clutch bag and Lana smiled her thanks, slipping the sparkly bag into her hand, straightening her shoulders and following her out through the door, knowing she was as ready as she'd ever be.

Lana hovered near the entrance to the ballroom, watching the women in their designer dresses beguile their dates, sip champagne and laugh, clearly without a care in the world.

She wanted to be like that: sophisticated and flirtatious and carefree, the type of woman a guy like Zac would want in his life hopefully for more than just a couple of weeks.

But she wouldn't think about that now. Tonight was about showing him she wanted him as much as he wanted her. Tonight was a night for romance, for magic, for a shy girl to spread her metaphorical wings, preen and fluff out her feathers, demonstrate there was more to her than shapeless dresses and baggy shorts.

With her heart beating in rhythm with the jazz ballad playing softly in the background, she took a deep breath, squared her shoulders and entered the ballroom.

Her fingers convulsed around her clutch the exact moment Zac caught sight of her.

He was deep in conversation with another officer when he glanced up and stopped, shock etched across his handsome face, before he mumbled something and strode towards her. His gob-smacked expression was vindication that her make-over had made a statement—though, by the reproof shadowing those cobalt blue depths, definitely not the kind of statement she'd wanted.

When he reached her he stopped dead, his greedy gaze roaming over her before reproach, even censure, crept into his steely eyes. 'What's all this?'

At that precise moment her world crumbled.

She'd imagined this magical moment all day, had built it up in her head to be picture-perfect, with Zac taking her hand, twirling her at arm's length, before pulling her close and whispering how incredible she looked.

She'd imagined he'd take one look at her dress, her hair, her make-up, and know she'd done all this for him, to drive him mad with lust, to prove she felt the same way.

She'd imagined him so crazy for her he wouldn't be able to keep his hands off her, to the point where he'd drag her out of the party and straight to his cabin, where she'd finally shrug off the last of her insecurities and show him what a little confidence did for a woman.

Never in her wildest dreams—or nightmares—had she

imagined the cutting criticism underlying his question, or the disapproval creasing his brow.

While her first instinct was to hitch up her skirt and flee, she wouldn't give him the satisfaction of knowing how deeply he'd hurt her, how she'd trusted him enough to do this and how he'd rejected her anyway.

'By *this* you mean the dress?'

His frown intensified as he glanced at her hair, her face. 'And the rest.'

She bit down on the inside of her lip so hard she drew blood. The pain of his disparagement was slicing her heart in two.

Drawing on the last of her inner resolve, she concentrated on keeping her tone flat, unemotional. 'The invitation said formal, so I made an effort.'

'I see.'

Like hell he did.

For all his cheap words about getting to know her, admiring her intelligence and the real her, he didn't have a clue.

She had to get out of here—had to leave before her humiliation was complete and she broke down. 'You know something? I don't think you do.'

His eyes narrowed, the electrifying blue brought into sharp focus. With his midnight curls slicked back, and a tux accentuating his broad shoulders, he was breathtakingly handsome—a rakish pirate who'd stolen her heart and plundered her emotions without thought or feeling.

She didn't wait for a response before she rushed out of the room, her head swivelling both ways before she made a dash for the heavy glass door leading to the main deck.

She ran as fast as three-inch stilettos would allow, ignoring the heavy footsteps racing after her and the wind whipping her dress against her legs as her feet flew across the deck.

She reached the main deck as he shouted, 'Lana—wait.'

As if. She reached a dead end, swivelled to the right—and her heel jammed. She pitched forward.

Before she could hit the deck he'd caught her, his saving grip an instant reminder of how all this had started. Considering how it was about to end, she would have been better off sprawling on her butt that first day.

'You're making a habit of this.'

Stiffening, she silently cursed her clumsiness, straightened instantly, and was irrationally disappointed when he released her. 'Was there something you wanted?'

You, she wanted this seafaring charmer to say. As if that would happen, after his reaction to her make-over.

'Why did you leave in such a hurry?'

Her disbelieving look could have created an iceberg. 'Why do you think?'

Her clipped response didn't alter his guarded expression. This was a waste of time, and the sooner she made it to the sanctity of her cabin, ripped off this dress and slipped into her comfy cotton PJs, the happier she'd be.

He dragged a hand through his hair, muttered an expletive. 'I've made a mess of this.'

Too right. And while every self-preservation mechanism told her to make a run for it *now,* she couldn't help but wonder why he'd reacted that way.

'What's going on? I knew there was something wrong the second you saw me.'

His remorseful grimace didn't quell the rolling, rollicking waves swelling in her belly, making her nauseous when the three-metre swells buffeting the ship didn't.

'I overreacted. Your transformation took me by surprise.'

Glancing down at her dress, remembering the shock of seeing her expertly made-up face in the mirror after Mavis had worked her magic, she shook her head. 'There has to be more to it.'

'There isn't.'

He shrugged, his shoulders impossibly broad in the tux he wore as well as he did his uniform. 'Don't you get it? I *like* the fact you don't go for all the artificial stuff most women do.'

'You mean I'm a plain Jane?'

Ironic—she'd never felt so beautiful, so transformed, and he preferred simple old Lana.

Tipping up her chin, he searched her face. For…what? Proof his opinion mattered to her? A telltale sign that what he said had cut deep?

Whatever he was looking for, he wouldn't find it. She'd become an expert at hiding her feelings from a young age—had fooled her dad into believing she didn't care about his string of women, had convinced Beth she was happy being a frumpy nerd, when in fact she longed to be as gorgeous and confident and outgoing as her cousin.

'I mean I prefer the real you—the woman who captured my attention the first second she fell at my feet.'

'Oh, really?' Her mouth twitched at the memory of their first meeting.

"Yes, really." He trailed a finger down her cheek—soft, sensitive. 'So what's with the war paint?'

'Don't you know?'

Surely her dramatic eyes, her shaded cheeks and her pearly pink lips along with the sexy dress were enough of a clue?

Confusion creased his brow. 'Know what?'

'I did all this for *you*.' She gestured towards her dress,

her hair, her face. 'To show you there's more to me than just a brain and a smart mouth.'

His frown deepened. 'But I already know there's more to you. You're a gym instructor, for starters.'

She had to tell him. All of it. Now that she'd fallen for him, hoped for a future with him, he had to know.

Besides, it wasn't as if she'd deliberately lied to him. She'd just let him assume she was a boppy, trendy fitness freak, rather than a boring, conservative curator.

'Actually, I'm not a gym instructor.'

'What do you mean?'

'I don't work at a gym. I'm just a member.'

His jaw clenched. 'Then where *do* you work?'

'At the Sydney Museum. I'm head curator there.'

His muttered expletive had her repressing a smile.

'Tell me you're a qualified aerobics instructor and I haven't hired someone liable to send my insurance premiums to the bottom of the ocean?'

'Don't worry. I'm qualified. It's a hobby.'

He shook his head, as if trying to fathom what sort of a crazy person would work in a museum all day, then become a gym instructor for kicks.

Propping her elbows on the railing, she leaned back. This might take a while, and when she'd bored him sense-less he'd probably jump overboard.

'I'll give you the abbreviated version. I was raised in Melbourne. You know about my botched relationship. When it soured, I moved to Sydney. Not just because of Jax, but to get away from myself, start afresh. I wanted to try new things, do stuff outside my comfort zone, so I joined a gym.'

She'd never forget her first step class, when she'd slunk in wearing a faded T-shirt and baggy tracksuit pants and been confronted by twenty Lycra-clad fitness fanatics in fancy joggers.

'I made a sloth look good, so joining a gym was huge for me. The bizarre thing was I got hooked to the point where I took an instructor's course. Not that I'll ever do anything with it—' he raised an eyebrow '—after this cruise, that is. But it was something I needed to do—something to build my confidence, to chalk up in my quest to try new things.'

Something shifted in his eyes. Wariness? Hurt? She belatedly realised he'd probably add himself to that list.

'Curator, huh?'

'Yeah.' She flicked her hair over her shoulder, not used to wearing it softly curled with tendrils tickling her.

'I guess it fits.'

His eyes hadn't lost their brooding expression, and her heart sank further. She'd hoped that by telling him the truth he might soften a little, understand where she was coming from. By the look of his compressed mouth and the deep groove between his brows he didn't.

'Fits?'

'Your image…before this.'

He waved towards her in a vague gesture, and acute disillusionment made her want to rip the designer dress off and fling it overboard.

'Before looking like a woman who wants to impress a man?'

He shook his head, thrust his hands into his pockets. 'You don't need to go in for all this fake stuff to impress me.'

'But you said—' She bit her tongue, wishing she had more experience with men, wishing she had half a clue where to go from here.

She'd tried to show him she wanted him by changing her appearance but he didn't get it. Worse—he didn't like it.

So what was her next move? Tell him outright? Yeah, like she'd have the guts to do that.

'What did I say?'

'Nothing, Popeye.'

'Popeye?'

At last she'd made him smile—albeit by a slip of the tongue.

She held up her hand. 'Don't you dare make a wisecrack about your muscles!'

She expected him to laugh, but instead he held her gaze a moment longer, his eyes gleaming with desire before it faded as fast as his smile.

Shaking his head, he raked a hand through his hair. 'I'm sorry, but I really have to go. We've got a PR disaster in the making on our hands, and I need to deal with it.'

'And?'

There was more: she could see it in the clenched jaw, the rigid shoulders.

'Add to that the fact my work schedule triples in the final two days of a cruise.'

He was dumping her, in no uncertain terms, before they'd even properly started.

She hadn't expected this, couldn't have braced herself for it, seeing how he'd been acting towards her before tonight, and nothing could stop the sharp, stabbing pain cleaving her in two.

Mustering the limited reserve that had got her through the confrontation with her CEO when he'd told her she wasn't 'assertive' enough to go on the Egypt jaunt, she effectively blanked her expression.

'I understand.'

He reached out to her, but her infinitesimal move back had him dropping his hand uselessly to his side. 'It's business.'

'Business. Right.'

The first prickle behind her eyes had her frantically searching for the nearest escape. She couldn't cry, wouldn't cry, and she'd be damned if she showed him he had the power to make her do so.

'You better get to it, then.'

She turned on her heel and walked away, head held high, though her impulse was to hike up her skirt and make a run for the welcome seclusion of her cabin.

This was what happened when she stepped out of her comfort zone, when she tried to be someone she wasn't: an awful, unmitigated disaster that would take her a lifetime to recover from.

She'd tried to make a big statement. Well, she'd done that all right. Pity Zac wasn't interested in reading the signs or hearing what she had to say or anything else.

She bit her top lip to stop the sobs bubbling up from deep inside. She hated the taste of the lipstick, wishing she could swipe a forearm across her mouth and wipe it off. But she was already drawing curious glances from the odd passer-by strolling on deck, and she had a reputation to uphold even though her instructor contract would be fulfilled tomorrow.

Even here, now, she couldn't shrug off her responsible work ethic, and at the thought of returning to the museum next week, with sadness in her heart and no charming smiles from a suave sailor to brighten her days, a lone tear seeped from the corner of her eye and ran down her cheek.

Picking up the pace, she ran for her cabin, wishing she could run from the mess she'd made with Zac as easily.

Zac clenched his fists and shoved them deep into his pockets, torn between wanting to chase after Lana and jumping overboard.

Both options held the same danger: he'd be floundering way over his head.

He'd deliberately driven her away.

He'd seen the hurt in her eyes, in the tremble of her lip, and he'd felt lower than pond scum. But what choice did he have?

He'd planned on telling her the truth tonight, about exploring their relationship further after this cruise, but he couldn't do it now. Her little bombshell had put paid to that.

As if the dramatic change in her appearance hadn't already set him on his guard, the truth behind her move to Sydney sealed it.

She was a woman seeking change, a woman dissatisfied with her current life, a woman searching for something new.

A woman like Magda.

He'd survived losing Magda, had lived through the pain of seeing her change before his very eyes, had hidden the devastation when she'd walked out on him in search of more than he could give.

It had taken him years to figure out they never would have worked, even if he hadn't gone back to shipping. Magda had been needy, demanding all his attention, wanting to be the focus of his world. Their initial attraction had been powerful, all-consuming, and he'd mistaken it for love. He had given up his career for her temporarily, would have done anything she asked in those heady honeymoon months.

But his folly had cost him dearly—had nearly killed his uncle. Which was exactly why he couldn't let him down now.

Though maybe he was being a tad harsh? Lana was nothing like Magda. She didn't demand to be noticed; in fact the opposite. It had been her lack of artifice that had first drawn him to her; her natural vivacity had been a refreshing change.

Everything in his life was fake, all about 'show' for the passengers, yet she was real—so real he could hardly believe it. He felt good when he was with her, felt as if his life wasn't a sham, especially with the current subterfuge driving him to distraction.

He wanted to feel that good all the time. Wanted to cement their relationship and take it as far as it could possibly go.

And he'd just learned she had a fulfilling career of her own—a job that would need her attention during those long months when he wasn't around if he took a chance on a long-distance relationship.

But should he? After tonight's metamorphosis, after what he'd learned, he'd be a fool ten times over to contemplate taking their relationship further. She was hell-bent on trying new things, on boosting her confidence. What if he was just part of her quest?

She'd seemed so natural, so unaffected, so real. But did he really know her at all?

Unexpected pain, deep and raw, gnawed his gut at the thought of not seeing her every day, not hearing her quick comebacks or her gentle teasing.

He'd grown to love the way her eyes lit up when she saw him, the way her lips curled up at the corners when she was thinking, the way she blushed when his teasing hit too close to the mark.

Grown to love?

Hell, no! He couldn't love her.

He wanted to test the waters with her, see if they could have a long-distance relationship without the complications of love and need and expectation.

Love complicated everything. Love tugged at his loyalties, making him choose between an uncle he couldn't abandon and a woman who'd stolen his heart without trying.

But what if it was too late?

He loved her.

And he'd hurt the woman he loved. He hated what he'd done to her tonight, all in an act of self-preservation.

She was too special. She didn't deserve to be treated that way. He needed to make amends.

Starting tomorrow, when he'd wrestled this irrepressible, overwhelming, surprising emotion into some semblance of control.

CHAPTER ELEVEN

WHEN the ship docked at Vila the next morning, Lana almost bolted down the gangway. Anything to escape a possible encounter with the man she could happily strangle with her bare hands.

She'd pegged him for a smart guy. Well, he couldn't be too smart if he hadn't read the signs last night—the biggest, most glaring sign of all being her dressed to the hilt.

Not that she'd be wearing that dress again. It now lay in a rumpled, crushed heap on the floor of her cabin, after she'd ripped it off and flung it into the corner the minute she'd got back last night.

She felt like her old self today—well, almost, if she discounted a broken heart—in long baggy cut-offs, a loose tank top and comfy leather sandals.

As for trying to get enigmatic sailors to believe she was willing to put her heart on the line for them—never again.

She planned on having Room Service for the last dinner tonight, and on skulking from deck to deck to avoid Zac. Irrational, as he could easily find her by waiting outside the gym at the end of her aerobics classes, but she'd face that particular scenario if and when it happened.

Though after last night she seriously doubted he'd be seeking her out again. He'd made that more than clear.

Touring Vila, the lovely capital of Vanuatu, proved to be a good distraction for a few hours, but once she reboarded the jitters started again, and she slunk from the staircase to her cabin, darting quick glances up the corridors in the hope of avoiding him. She needed to get past this—get a grip.

With a muttered curse that rarely slipped past her lips, she fumbled her key before jamming it in the lock.

'I thought I'd find you here eventually.'

She jumped, her heart sinking as Zac's deep voice rippled over her, still holding the power to set her pulse racing.

Determined to play it cool, she turned. 'Was there something you wanted?'

'You know damn well what I want.'

He had the audacity to try a roguish smile after what had happened last night?

Her eyes narrowed as she tried her best death glare—the one that got co-workers to do her bidding without a word.

'Actually, I don't. I have no idea what's going on in that big head of yours.'

'Big head? Now, that's the woman I know and love.'

Her heart skipped a beat, several beats, before she realised it was a figure of speech.

'I'm tired.'

His smile faded when he reached for her hand and she snatched it away. 'We need to talk.'

'I don't think so. You made it pretty clear how you feel last night.'

'That's what I want to talk about.' He rubbed the back of his neck as if he had a pain there; probably her. 'All I'm asking for is a chance to explain.'

She should send him on his way. She should ignore the

tiny flicker of hope kindling deep inside. Instead, her stance softened under the hint of vulnerability in his eyes, at his earnest, almost pleading expression.

She held up a finger. 'You get one chance.'

His ecstatic grin had the corners of her mouth twitching in response. 'I finally figured it out.'

'What?'

'What you were trying to show me last night.'

She bit back the words *about bloody time*. The confidence her make-over had inspired was a crumpled heap, along with the dress. She couldn't have this conversation now—not in the corridor outside her cabin. She could invite him in… A thought she contemplated for all of two seconds before discarding it as quickly as her make-up last night.

'When I told you how much I wanted you the other night I said I'd back off until you showed me you wanted me as much.'

Her skin started prickling as she shuffled from foot to foot. She *soooo* didn't want to talk about this now, but with his intense gaze fixed on her she had nowhere to hide.

Reaching out, he touched her cheek softly, a brief, tender touch that conveyed more than words ever could. 'I think you were trying to show me last night, but I was too hung up on irrelevant things to really notice.'

His eyes searched hers for confirmation, and all she could do was stand there like a dummy, racking her brain for a quick comeback, a brush-off, anything coherent, and coming up empty.

Leaning forward, he brushed her ear with his lips. 'I'm as emotionally involved in all this as you are. Maybe more. And I want to show you how much.'

His warm breath fanning her neck sent a shudder of

yearning through her. His declaration left her in little doubt what he meant.

Heck, she'd always thought actions spoke louder than words, and if they'd made a mess of things trying to articulate how they felt maybe she should go for broke and let him *show* her?

Taking a deep breath, and hoping her voice wouldn't quiver as much as her insides were at that moment, she said, 'Last night was a big deal for me. I was trying to make a statement, to show you I'm not just some mousy geek.'

His hand rested on her hip, caressed her, gently tugged her closer. His molten gaze, an incandescent blue like the hottest flame in a fire, was riveted to her lips.

'Mousy geek? More like sex goddess.' He dipped his head, stole a kiss, tempting her, confusing her. 'And you want to know what else I think?'

He cradled her chin, tipped it up so she had no option but to meet his blazing gaze head-on.

'I think you hide behind those old clothes of yours when inside is a passionate, exciting woman struggling to break free. A woman wanting to express herself. A woman who is driving me crazy with how much I want her.'

With her heart thundering in her chest, filling her ears with its pounding, she could pretend it had drowned out his words. But it hadn't. She'd heard every single word. All of them true.

She *did* want to break free, to express the passion bubbling away beneath the surface, locked away where no man had untapped it.

Here was a man who could do it, a man who'd captured her imagination closely followed by her heart from the first moment she'd met him, despite all protests to the contrary.

Here was a man who could give her what she'd craved since his first scintillating kiss: fulfillment.

Mustering every ounce of courage she possessed, she stepped into his personal space. 'My showing you last night didn't work quite as I intended, so how about I show you like this?'

She stood on tiptoe, brushed her lips against his, initiating a kiss for the first time in her life. And it felt great. Liberating. Incredible.

Zac moaned and grabbed her hand. 'Come with me.'

She clung to his hand, almost tripping in her haste to keep up with his long strides as they followed several staircases marked 'CREW ONLY'.

Wouldn't Beth have a field-day with this? Her conservative cousin being dragged off to a sailor's cabin! Oh, yeah, there'd be at least a year's worth of gossip out of this!

She muffled a snort and he slowed. 'Going too fast for you?'

'It's taken us this long to get to this point. What do you think?'

His answering grin held wicked promises she intended on holding him to as he picked up the pace, guiding her through a host of warren-like corridors before stopping in front of D21 and inserting a key.

'I know we could've used your cabin, but this way you have the option of leaving any time you like,' he said, stepping aside to let her in. 'Because if it'd been the other way around I wouldn't leave your side till you booted me out the door.'

Her heart soared, and she wondered how she could have ever doubted him? To understand her enough to know this was a big deal, to know she might want to flee to the privacy of her cabin later if things got too much—simply, he was incredible.

Reality hit as she entered the tiny cabin and her gaze riveted on the bed. She and Zac were about to make love— unreserved, unashamed, undeniably hot, sizzling, exhilarating love.

He paced the confined space like a caged leopard, raking a hand through his hair and looking just as dangerous.

'Zac?'

He swivelled towards her, his expression torn while his hungry gaze roamed her body. 'You're sure about this?'

Heck no!

What if she was lousy in bed? Frigid, just like Jax had said? What if she disappointed him? Or, worse, what if they were cataclysmically brilliant together and she fell further for him?

She fiddled with the neckline of her top, surprised by the flicker of irrepressible desire in the glittering blue depths of his eyes. If this daggy old top turned him on, he really must like her.

'Nothing in life is a surety. We've got tonight. Let's not waste it.'

His lips curved into a deliciously dangerous smile as he held a hand out to her. 'Didn't anyone ever warn you about sailors?'

Showing more bravado than she felt now the moment of truth had arrived, she placed her hand in his. 'Oh, yeah. Luckily I gave up listening a long time ago.'

He tugged gently on her hand till she stood less than a foot away. 'You're one hell of a woman.' He traced a line along her jaw, tilting her chin upwards. 'And I intend to make this a night we'll never forget.'

Her heart slammed against her ribs and her pulse tripped in anticipation.

'Show me.'

Their gazes locked, the wild yearning in his sending a jolt of answering desire through her body.

Her breasts tingled, her stomach dropped and her knees quivered as he stepped away, his stare bold, assessing, as it raked her body, strongly seductive yet soft as a caress.

'Let me look at you.'

Her breath hitched as he tugged her top over her head and dispensed with her bra with a deft flick. His sure hands making light work of the side zip on her pants too.

'I feel naked,' she breathed on a sigh, as his fingertips skated around her knickers—practical white cotton, unfortunately. Being seduced by the man of her dreams had been the last thing she'd expected today. He toyed with the elastic, making excitement ripple through her.

'Almost…'

His sizzling glance from beneath lowered lids sent her self-consciousness about her plain panties evaporating, along with the last of her nerves.

Zac wanted her. *Her.* All of her—her comfy clothes, boring knickers and quick brain—and she'd never felt so special. If she'd needed a confidence boost, the adoration in his eyes as he scanned her body was it.

The air whooshed out of her lungs as he kissed his way down her body, slow, soft kisses trailing a path to her abdomen and lower, where she throbbed with uncharacteristic fervour.

She'd never felt remotely like this, had barely registered much pleasure at all during sex with Jax, yet Zac's lips, followed by his fingertips skating across her skin with infinite precision, had her wanting to fist her hands in his hair and shove him where she burned the most.

'Ooh…'

Her pelvis bucked as he slipped one finger, another, under the elastic of her panties, caressing her folds, teasing her, pleasing her with a few simple strokes.

'May I?'

He raised his head and she nodded, biting on her bottom lip to stop from crying out with the pleasure of it all.

With torturous patience he peeled her panties down, his hands stroking her legs all the way to her toes while easing her back onto the bed.

She squeezed her eyes shut against the sight of herself lying open for him, naked, and tried to ignore the inevitable doubts that accompanied being this exposed.

She didn't have a supermodel body, or big breasts, or long legs. Instead she had a hint of cellulite on the tops of her thighs and breasts that wouldn't win any wet T-shirt competitions.

She'd always felt inadequate naked, had never felt sexy, and Jax had reinforced her insecurities.

'You're beautiful.'

At that moment, with his gaze travelling over her, drinking in every flawed detail before looking her in the eyes with reverence in his, she almost believed him.

Her breath caught as he grazed her clitoris, once, twice, and she almost came before he lowered his head again.

She tensed as his hot breath fanned her. Her hand stilled him.

'I've never done this before.'

His head snapped up. His shocked expression would almost have been comical if she didn't feel such a novice.

'What I mean is I've had sex, but—not this.'

She waved towards her nether regions, heat flushing her cheeks as a gratified glint turned his eyes electric blue.

'Then I'm proud to be your first.'

With the first sweep of his tongue any lingering resistance evaporated.

With the second she clenched her hands to stop herself from digging them into his shoulders to hold him down.

With the third her thighs fell open all the way, and her eyes drifted shut as she savoured the mind-blowing sensation sparking through her body.

This was all too much, yet too little, as he kissed her intimately, swirling his tongue, nibbling, varying the pressure and the rhythm till she exploded on a loud cry, sobbing with the sheer, mindless rush of it all.

'Hell, are you okay?'

He wiped her tears away with the pad of his thumb, so gently, so tenderly, she wept harder.

'Lana, talk to me.'

As he cradled her close she clung to him, burying her face in his chest, where her tears quickly gave way to chuckles.

He stilled. 'Are you laughing or crying?'

'Both,' she mumbled, inhaling, savouring the addictive scent of sea air and Zac imprinted on his skin.

He pulled away and stared down at her in confusion. 'You know, those are two reactions guaranteed to make a guy feel mighty insecure after what just happened.'

She reached up and cradled his cheek. 'Sorry, I'm just overwhelmed.'

How could she articulate what she felt? The gift he'd just given her?

He covered her hand with his and planted a soft kiss on her mouth. 'You don't have to say anything.'

Smiling, she turned her hand over, intertwined her fingers with his, hoping he could read half of what she was feeling in her eyes.

'I want to… What you just did for me…'

'My pleasure.'

His wicked grin made her laugh, defusing the tension and giving her the courage she needed to tell him the rest.

'I'm guessing by my reaction to you that I'm not frigid?'

He swore and squeezed her hand. 'Who told you that?'

'My ex. The only guy I've ever had sex with.'

Realisation dawned, and his expression was thunderous. 'So not only is the jerk lousy in bed, he blames his partner? Nice.'

'I always thought the problem was me.'

So the old adage of sailors swearing was true, she thought, as the expletives tripping from his tongue at a rate of knots made her blush.

He cupped her face and stared into her eyes—direct, compelling.

'Listen to me. You're a vibrant, responsive woman and you drive me crazy. Promise me you'll forget everything that jerk said.'

She wanted to believe him, she really did, but how did he know, considering they hadn't technically had sex?

'But we haven't—you know—done anything.'

His lips curved into a delicious smile, a smile of promise. 'The way you just responded to me, sweetheart, we've done enough.'

No, they hadn't. If he made her feel this good with his mouth, imagine how exciting the rest would be.

Trying a coy smile, she met his darkened gaze. 'I want you.'

His eyes burned, hot and hungry, and his answering smile was pure devilry. 'The feeling's mutual.'

More emboldened than she'd ever thought possible, she slipped a hand between them, stroking his erection through his trousers, enjoying the shocked widening of his eyes.

Stilling her hand, he said, 'We'll take things slow.'

She didn't want slow. Slow would give her time to think and analyse, let a few of those old insecurities creep up. She didn't want to think—not now. She wanted to feel and savour and enjoy.

'Actually, I'm thinking fast.'

She blushed at her audacity, her nipples hardening as she leaned forward and rubbed against the crisp cotton of his shirt, desperate to feel skin on skin, to feel all of him.

'We'll go slow later.'

'Whatever you want.'

Her fingers were frantic as they fumbled buttons, tripped over ties and snagged on zips, but the end result—a gloriously semi-naked Zac—was well worth it.

Her bravado halted at his tight black boxers, her fingers trembling.

'Here. Let me.'

He shucked them, and her eyes widened.

'Can I touch you?'

He nodded, his beautiful blue eyes heavy-lidded with passion, his gaze smouldering.

Her hand shook as she enclosed him, hard velvet pulsing in her palm. She stroked him to the tip and back, easing down and up again, empowered, emboldened, decidedly wanton.

'You're driving me crazy.'

His voice cracked and, high on her newfound sexual power, she knelt before him, eager to taste him, to give him half the pleasure he'd given her.

Before she could take him in her mouth he dropped to his knees and reached for her.

'As much as I appreciate the sentiment, I want you so badly I'm not going to last five seconds if you do that.'

She raised an eyebrow, delighting in his tortured expression as her tongue flicked out to moisten her bottom lip and his gaze riveted to it.

'Do what?'

With a growl, he swept her into his arms and tumbled her onto the bed, where her laughter quickly petered out as he lay beside her, the heat of his body igniting hers as he cradled her head and plundered her mouth.

Sensation rocketed through her as his tongue duelled with hers, firing her blood, her imagination, and everywhere in between.

She whimpered as his hand slipped between her legs, her body throbbing and eager and yearning for release as his fingers worked their magic.

'I want you inside me,' she gritted out as she arched into him, clutching at his shoulders as the tension within grew and expanded and finally detonated on a shattering explosion into ecstasy.

He slanted a searing kiss across her quivering lips. 'You can have me.'

She should have been thinking about protection, thinking about the consequences of not using any, but with her body humming, floating on a plane it had never reached once before, let alone twice, all logic had fled.

Thankfully he rolled a condom on before rolling her on top of him, and his gaze was adoring as he gently pushed her up into a sitting position till she straddled him.

'You're incredible.'

His hands skimmed her waist, drifting slowly upwards to cup her breasts, teasing her nipples with the barest brush of his thumbs, sending aftershocks through her.

The faintest of spasms shuddered through her. The tension was building again, coiling tighter and tighter, ready to send her into orbit this time.

She sucked in her breath as his hands spanned her hips, lifted her as he surged upwards, thrusting into her till she cried out.

'You okay?'

'Never been better.'

She clenched her internal muscles—her scarcely used internal muscles—to show him exactly how much better she was with him inside her, and was thrilled by the flicker of shock in those endless blue eyes.

'You wanted fast, right?'

He thrust into her again, harder, deeper, and she gasped, her thighs quivering as he spread her a tad more.

'Fast is good,' she managed to say, as he drove in again and again, each thrust sending her closer to the brink, each thrust a lesson in exquisite pleasure, each thrust showing her exactly how great sex could be with the right person.

Though this was more than sex, and she knew it.

But she wouldn't think about that now—wouldn't think beyond the earth-shattering spasms building, climbing, snaking their way through her pelvis and spreading outwards till she could barely feel anything beyond the torturously exquisite tremors rendering her mindless.

Finding a natural rhythm, she picked up the tempo, glorying in his ragged breathing, his glazed gaze, his straining muscles as he pushed them both towards a climax big enough to cause a tidal wave to swamp the ship.

'Jeez.'

She collapsed on top of him, stunned and sated and satisfied—very, very satisfied—savouring his strong arms as he cuddled her close.

'Lana?'

'Hmm?'

She snuggled deeper into his chest, knowing she could happily stay there for ever.

And now they'd made love and proved what she already knew—she'd fallen in love with him—well, things were about to get interesting.

He ran a finger down her bare arm, from shoulder to elbow, dipping briefly into the hollow before continuing to her wrist, where her pulse beat frantically.

'You're not frigid. And I intend to prove it. Over and over again. All night.'

She whimpered, a low, desperate, needy sound, and she clutched at his shoulders, hanging on as he flipped her onto her back and propped over her.

'What do you think about that?'

She smiled, slid her hands down his chest, savouring the rasp of hair against her palms. 'What are you waiting for?'

Zac didn't need to be asked twice.

He growled, nuzzled her neck, and smiled when she giggled, a pure, uninhibited sound of joy.

She was incredible. The sex he'd been fantasising about had far surpassed his wildest dreams. To think some stupid bastard had called her frigid, dented her self-esteem, kicked her confidence. Little wonder she'd used to look at him as if he was some kind of monster at times.

But not now.

Now she gazed at him from beneath half-lowered heavy lids, her molten caramel eyes glowing with satisfaction, the green flecks glittering with excitement. She wanted him as much as he wanted her, and he'd make damn sure he obliterated any last lingering doubts that she was anything other than pure sex goddess.

'I'm going to do this all night.'

Her breath caught as he licked a slow trail from the tip of her shoulder to her earlobe, where he lingered and nibbled.

She moaned, and he tensed. He'd never heard anything so sexy, and he could scarcely believe he'd only just had mind-blowing sex, considering his straining erection.

'Can I explore you?'

Her hesitant question had him wanting to sweep her into his arms and cradle her close. The hint of vulnerability beneath her soft tone was enough to fell the strongest man. Considering he'd already fallen for her, all she had to do was glance in his direction and he was all hers.

'Go ahead.'

Thrilled by her eagerness, he lay back and folded his hands behind his head, watching her.

Lust rocketed through him as she placed a soft, open-mouthed kiss on his neck, another one above his collarbone, before flicking her tongue out to lick him, a tentative flick that had him twitching.

He groaned as she nipped the sensitive areola, flicking a nipple with her tongue.

'Do you like that too?'

Her tongue traced lazy circles around it, and her voice held more than a hint of wonder at his response.

'Like it? You're driving me wild.'

She stopped, raised her head, and sent him a smile that could have tempted Neptune. 'Good.'

'Is that right?'

He surged upwards, his mouth seeking hers hungrily. Needing her more than she'd ever know.

Her head fell back and her lips parted on a whimper as his tongue plunged inside, teasing and stroking, almost ravishing her in a deep, devouring kiss, while his hands took on a life of their own, roaming and exploring her curves.

'You're so soft,' he murmured against her lips, praying he'd have the control to make this last all night, just as he'd promised.

For, come morning, he had another promise to discuss with her—one he hoped she'd go for in a big way.

He slid his palms up her ribcage to her breasts, feeling the nipples pebble as her heart thudded beneath his touch. He knew his own matched her beat, the rapid staccato rhythm sending blood pumping to every inch of his body. She moaned as he skimmed his palms repeatedly over her nipples and she arched up to meet him.

'Zac, you're killing me.'

He smiled, reached over the bedhead and grabbed a condom. 'Not yet—but the night is young.'

She smiled, gnawed on her bottom lip before holding out her hand.

'Here, let me do that.'

Surprised at her willingness to take care of the essentials, he handed it over, watched her rip the foil open and finger the rubber as if it was priceless parchment. For all her limited experience, she sure knew how to drive a man crazy. Sweat broke out across his upper lip as desperate need tore through him at her first tentative touch.

'How's that?'

She unrolled the rubber slowly, every minute movement a lesson in exquisite torture.

He groaned and stilled her hand, on the brink of losing control. Again. 'Perfect.'

'Good.'

She caressed his cheek, hooked a leg over his hip and rose to meet him in an erotic invitation he was powerless to refuse.

Sliding forward, he entered her inch by inch till they were locked tight. He'd never known such a feeling of completeness, of being totally one with another person, and if he'd had any doubts that a long-distance relationship was the way to go, the realisation she could be his soul-mate dispelled them in an instant.

But for now they had tonight and he intended to show her exactly how much she meant to him, how much he hoped for the future, by making love to her with every inch of his body.

'That feels amazing.'

She arched into him, torching his body, rousing it to fever-pitch as he pumped into her, his thrusts setting her breasts jiggling, his excitement ratcheting up to an unbearable level as he watched them.

She threw her head back and, listening to her soft, urgent moans, he knew she was close as with each practised stroke he took her to the brink.

He wanted to wait, to make it last, but with his own climax hovering she screamed out his name and bucked into him, sending him over the edge. Spasms ripped through him, a galaxy of shooting stars exploding in his head as he shot to the moon and back.

How had he ever fooled himself into believing this was just about a light flirtation at the beginning?

The connection he shared with this funny, smart, quirky woman was real, was unique, and was so damn perfect he'd be a fool to let her do anything but agree to his plans tomorrow.

'You're incredible.' He brushed a kiss across her lips as she snuggled closer, stunned by the ferocity of his love for her.

Damn, he needed space—a few minutes to reassemble his wits before he blurted his feelings in the heat of the moment and scared her.

'Just going to the bathroom for a sec, okay? Don't move an inch.'

Lana watched Zac, her gaze greedily roving his naked back, his butt, not in the least embarrassed.

After what had just happened, what they'd just shared, her insecurities had been well and truly blasted sky-high. But it was more than physical, more than cataclysmic sex and the exhilaration of being one.

Something had shifted between them.

She'd seen it in his eyes—a depth of caring that lifted her heart and transported her to a place of hope and dreams and beyond.

But she wouldn't dwell on emotions now. She had a whole night of snuggling in his arms to look forward to—and several repeat performances of the magic they conjured together.

Unable to wipe the self-satisfied grin from her face, she slipped out of bed to turn off the lamp on the desk, stubbing her toe on the way.

'Ouch!' She grabbed her foot and hopped around, stumbling against the desk and knocking a stack of papers to the floor.

Managing a wry smile—it looked as if her clumsy gene kicked in even when he wasn't around—she scooped up the papers, and several photos that had fallen out of an envelope.

Her heart stilled as she glanced at the photos. Every one depicted Zac: in front of Sydney's newest high-rise business centre in a designer suit, shaking hands with the Prime Minister, behind a huge conference table filled with international delegates, standing behind an older man with a hand on his shoulder and the name plaque 'CEO, Madigan Shipping' in front of him.

She stared at the photos, confused, a million questions buzzing through her brain.

Who *was* the guy she'd just made love to, had given her heart to?

He stepped out of the bathroom at that moment, a lazy grin on his face as he glanced towards the bed. His grin faltered as he looked towards the desk, at what she held in her hands, and the colour draining from his face.

'I guess you have some questions—'

'Who *are* you?'

She hated the uncertainty, the accusation in her voice. She shouldn't have pried, should have shoved the photos back where they belonged, but now she'd seen them she needed answers.

Running a hand through his mussed hair, he padded over to join her. 'I own this shipping company.'

'You *own* it?'

He nodded, managing to appear proud and bashful and ashamed all at the same time. 'I'm actually the new CEO of Madigan Shipping. My uncle used to run the company, but he recently handed over the reins to me. We haven't formally announced it yet.'

She didn't get this. Why would a CEO be working on one of the ships he ran?

'So what's the PR stint all about? Trying to keep a tight leash on your employees?'

'Nothing like that.'

He took a robe from a wardrobe hook and offered it to her. Mustering as much dignity as an indignant naked woman could, she shrugged into it like a queen into royal robes, grateful when he slipped his shirt and trousers back on. She could do without distraction while they had this cosy little chat, though by the sense of foreboding clawing its way to consciousness she knew they'd never be cosy again once they'd finished talking.

Indicating she take a seat, he perched on the edge of the bed. 'The company's being targeted by a saboteur. Small things at first—dangerous levels of chlorine in the pools, things we could catch before they did any real damage— but the incidents have been growing in severity. Now I need to find the culprit and put a stop to it.'

He paused, looking suitably shamefaced.

'To collect the evidence I need, I had to go undercover. This ship was the most likely to be attacked next, and no one knows who I am. As far as they know James Madigan is still CEO—a distant figurehead they'd never connect with me.'

She couldn't fault Zac for being dedicated to his job, for wanting to protect the company he owned. She of all people understood what it was like to be driven to be the best in her field. But if he didn't work on ships anymore, if he was now stuck behind that great big desk she'd glimpsed in the photos…

'Where are you based?'

The instant he looked away she knew.

He *wasn't* married to his precious job aboard ships.

He *wasn't* so enamoured of the sea he'd never leave it for her.

He wasn't interested in her, period.

At least not enough to have a real relationship beyond this—this fling, or whatever it was they'd had.

'Where?'

Her voice had risen, and his gaze locked on hers, regret mingling with apology in those endless blue depths.

'Sydney.'

'Right.'

'Look, Lana, I was going to tell you—'

'Save it.'

Turning her back on him, she slipped off the robe and yanked on her old clothes, lying in a sad heap on the floor. A bit like her pathetic dreams of happily-ever-after.

She stalked to the door without a backward glance—had her hand on the handle before he crossed the small space and slammed his palm on the door.

'You need to hear me out.'

Holding her breath, determined not to breathe in and let his heady scent, his proximity, undermine her resolve to walk out of here with what little dignity she had left, she turned to face him.

'Actually, I don't.'

He didn't budge. 'I didn't tell you because I'm not going to be based in Sydney for the next year.'

She wouldn't ask him where he was going—wouldn't give him the satisfaction of showing a small part of her was curious, a small part of her still cared.

'I'll be based in London.'

'How nice for you.'

Her sarcasm fell on deaf ears as he fixed her with that steady, unwavering stare. So what if he appeared honest now? She couldn't trust one word falling from his mouth. Not when he'd been lying to her the entire time.

She hated liars.

Jax had lied to her, had feigned interest in her to get the inside scoop on some precious artefacts he wanted to add to his private collection, had belittled her. He'd ruined what little self-confidence she'd ever had. But she hadn't really loved Jax as she loved Zac. So what the heck would she do this time around to cope with the devastation of being lied to by another rich guy playing games to suit his own ends?

He dragged his free hand through his hair, his expression crushed. 'My uncle's dying. He has a year to live, max. He's my only family and he's in London. I owe him. I have to be there for him.'

Her anger fractured. A tiny crack that allowed a modicum of sympathy to seep in.

But why was he telling her this? It was irrelevant. He'd still lied to her, had always known there'd be nothing between them beyond this fortnight.

'I was going to tell you. I was hoping we could try a long-distance relationship.'

Her tummy trembled as for one brief moment she contemplated what it would be like being involved with a guy like him for more than two weeks: to call him her boyfriend, to cross off days on a calendar, counting down the minutes till she saw the love of her life again.

But she couldn't do it.

If she couldn't trust him to tell her the truth when they were together, what hope would she have with him on the other side of the world for three hundred and sixty-five long, interminable days?

She needed honesty. She needed trust.

By his actions, Zac could give her neither.

With a shake of her head she placed a hand on his arm barring her escape and pushed.

'I'm not interested.'

She didn't have to push hard, as the second the words left her mouth an icy, impassive mask slid into place. His eyes were a cold, hard blue as his arm dropped and he stepped out of her way.

'Well, I guess I was just one of those new experiences you were so hell-bent on trying this trip.'

With soul-deep sadness clawing at her insides, robbing her of breath, she scrambled for the door handle.

'Hell. Lana, wait—'

She flung open the door so hard it almost fell off its hinges, then slammed it behind her and didn't look back.

CHAPTER TWELVE

ZAC sank onto the bed and dropped his head in his hands, the echo of the slamming door reverberating in his ears.

He'd stuffed up—made a major mess of things.

He should be hurt by Lana's refusal to contemplate a long-distance relationship, should be smarting.

But he wasn't. He knew the score.

He'd seen the devastation in her eyes when she'd learned the truth, and he knew it wouldn't have hurt that much if she didn't love him as much as he loved her.

Every one of her responses had been genuine, from the first moment he'd met her until now, so there was no mistaking the depth of feeling simmering below the surface, the raw pain he'd seen in her eyes.

He'd hated hurting her, however inadvertently, had wished he'd told her everything from the start. But it was too late for wishful thinking.

A part of him wanted to give her space, a year's worth of it, before coming back and trying again. He'd learned through his experience with Magda that if you loved someone enough you needed to give them space to grow and change. She hadn't wanted that space, but Lana would. She'd said as much in her quest for new things. Maybe he should give her a year to do what she had to do, then re-enter her life and start afresh?

As pain rocketed through him he knew he couldn't do it. He couldn't leave her that long. He loved her too much.

He was a man of action—prided himself on it. Business plans, mission statements, corporate policies—he could take a plan and turn it into reality. And that was exactly what he would do here.

He loved Lana, and he would prove it to her whatever it took.

And as much as he wanted to chase after her now, sweep her into his arms, cradle her close and tell her everything would be okay, he wasn't that stupid.

She needed time to calm down, time to evaluate, *really* evaluate what had happened here tonight. Before the photos, before the accusations, before the truth.

Simply, they were meant to be, and he had every intention of making that happen.

She'd been summoned to the bridge by the Captain for him to thank her for taking the classes. Great—just what she needed. Instead of disembarking as fast as she could, she'd have to go through the final rigmarole of playing the dutiful employee.

What a crock. This whole trip had been a crock, from start to finish, and she wished she'd never won the darn thing.

Knocking at the door, she grimaced at her reflection in the glass. Lucky things had ended with Zac last night, for if she'd been a plain Jane before and he'd still been attracted to her he'd swim a mile regardless if he saw the frightful mess she looked today.

Placing both hands against the glass, she peered into the massive room, glimpsed a flash of uniform on the other side.

All those gadgets probably made noise and had muffled her knock, so she opened the door, stepped into the huge control centre.

'Captain?'

She heard a footfall, sensed a presence behind her, and her skin prickled as if she'd eaten a crate of strawberries.

Oh-oh—a ship's captain she'd never met wouldn't have that effect on her. Only one man did. The same man she never wanted to see again as long as she lived.

'I needed to see you. The Captain was kind enough to do my dirty work.'

'That'd be right.'

Her voice quivered as she turned, faced him, hating the fact that after all the heartache the sight of him could still reduce her to this—a nervous wreck.

'I need to know if I've missed the boat.'

She stared at him as if he'd taken leave of his senses, glancing out of the huge windows at Circular Quay on her left, the Opera House on her right, and the ship firmly berthed at its moorings.

He gazed directly into her eyes. 'Have I?'

In an instant she knew he wasn't referring to the ship. 'What's this about?'

He tugged on his tie—totally skewed, she noticed. He didn't appear the consummate professional for once, with dark stubble covering his chin and bleary eyes surrounded by dark rings. He looked as bad as she felt.

'I've been going out of my mind since last night.'

She shrugged, unprepared for the swift stab of pain at the recollection of what they'd shared and lost last night. 'You should've thought of that before you lied to me.'

'Please, let me finish.'

He sounded like a little boy asking for the last toy boat

for his bathtub, and though her head told her to run, her heart told her to hold her ground.

'You shouldn't have discovered the truth by those photos. I—'

'It wasn't about the photos, damn it!'

She took a steadying breath, as surprised by her outburst as him. She never shouted or lost control. Well, not unless she counted the times when he'd made agonisingly sweet love to her last night.

He opened his mouth to respond and she held up a hand. 'It's the fact you're based in Sydney, the fact you're mega-rich, the fact we could've had more than two weeks if you hadn't let me believe—'

Let her believe he was a sailor. Let her believe his precious job was all-important. Let her believe for one, tiny speck in time she might actually mean more to him than a handy lay.

'Believe this.'

He swept her into his arms and kissed her—a divine, devastating kiss that demanded more than she was willing to give.

For all of two seconds.

Powerless to resist, she responded by softening her lips, allowing him access to her mouth. The logic of pushing him away was shattered by the hunger of his kiss.

Her eager response shocked her more than the kiss itself and she broke away, dragging in breaths to clear her fuzzy head.

'Damn it, I didn't mean for that to happen.'

He raked a hand through his hair, adding to his rumpled state, and she clenched her hands, shaken by how much she wanted to reach out and smooth it for him.

Shrugging, she wrapped her arms around her middle to ward him off. 'I guess it always came down to that for us, didn't it? A chemical reaction. Nothing more.'

'You're wrong.'

Grabbing hold of her arms, he left her no option but to look up—and what she glimpsed in his eyes sent a shiver of sorrow through her.

Pain. A soul laid bare. A soul lost and confused and reaching out. Just like hers.

'I didn't want to fall for you. I didn't want to get emotionally involved. But I did.'

'Just not enough?'

His declaration should have had her running outside, vaulting the rail and doing a perfect dive into the water, but it merely served to widen the gap. Too little, too late. She could never trust him now.

'It happened to me once before. In my early days while I was still working the ships. I fell for a passenger.' His mouth twisted into a grimace. 'I fell so hard I ended up marrying her.'

Shock speared her, and she tightened her arms around her belly to ward off the pain.

'I gave up my job for her—left the ships for a year. I gave the marriage everything, paid her the attention she demanded, but it wasn't enough. She couldn't handle my career when I went back to it, my absences. She changed. Her appearance, her outlook, her needs, her lover—'

Her gaze snapped to his. She was not surprised by the hard, unyielding blue, or the sadness underlying his bitterness.

'That's why I overreacted that night you had the makeover. Another woman I loved changing before my eyes. Stupid, I know.'

Her befuddled brain backed up a sentence or two, wondering if she'd heard him correctly.

He must have seen the confusion clouding her eyes, for he took advantage of her bewilderment by caressing her arms before his hands slid up to cradle her face.

'That's right. I love you. Whether you're a fitness instructor or a curator or dressed to the nines or in nothing at all. I love you.'

Her heart leapt at the sincerity in his voice, the tenderness in his eyes. She wanted to fling her reservations to the wind and leap into his arms.

But she couldn't. It looked as if her fortnight of being frivolous had ended when the ship docked, and now she was back in Sydney she couldn't shake her conservative ways.

'I appreciate you telling me. But what about the rest? Why didn't you come after me last night? Explain all this then?'

Instead she'd spent a sleepless night, alternating between cursing him, herself, and the great cosmos that had brought them together in the first place.

'Because I had to tie up loose ends.'

'Loose ends?'

Her heart sank. She *knew* his declaration of love was too good to be true.

'As you know, I'm the new CEO of Madigan Shipping. When I ditched my job for a year to be with Magda I didn't know my uncle was about to hand over the corporation to me. I let him down, and because of ongoing job stress he had a heart attack.'

She touched his arm, sorry for his genuine sadness.

'Uncle Jimmy raised me, funded my education. He has been like a father to me, and I owe him. And now he's dying…' He shrugged, pain pinching his mouth. 'I've discovered our saboteur. Turns out to be a disgruntled employee who we suspect may be mentally unstable. The authorities are waiting to take him into custody. But I still need to prove to my uncle I can do this—prove I'm trustworthy, prove I can make his legacy the best in the business, make this difficult time for him the least stressful as possible.'

'So you'll be based in London for a year?'

He nodded. 'I'm afraid that's the non-negotiable part of the deal.'

Perhaps her head still spun from his kiss and his declaration, because she didn't quite get what he was saying.

'What deal?'

He caressed her cheek, his hand slipping to cradle her head, his fingers winding deliciously through her hair. 'The deal where you and I give this relationship everything we've got, long-distance or not. The deal where you use your annual leave to board the company jet and come visit your desperate boyfriend. The deal where I spend a fortune on teleconferencing and e-mails and every other newfangled way on the planet to keep in contact with the woman I'm crazy about. The deal where you can try as many new things as you want as long as you don't forget about your boyfriend pining for you on the other side of the world.'

Gently angling her head, he slanted a slow, sensual kiss across her lips—a kiss that reached deep down and soothed the parts of her soul that had ached when she'd thought she'd lost him for good.

'That's the deal.'

He broke the kiss, rested his forehead against hers. 'And, being the incredibly successful magnate I am, I won't take no for an answer.'

'You have to know this trip wasn't just about trying new things for me. I needed to build my confidence, and thanks to you I have. But what if we try the long-distance thing and it doesn't work?'

She had to ask. Logic demanded it. But she was almost afraid of his answer as her heart dared to hope. If she took a chance on him, on them, and it didn't work, her confidence would take another dive, and she'd hate that after how far she'd come. Not to mention how she'd handle a shattered heart.

'It'll work. I won't settle for anything less.'

Her breath caught as he cradled her face, stared directly into her eyes.

'I love you. I'll always love you. All the oceans in the world can't keep us apart.'

Her heart expanded till she thought it would burst, and her legs joined her hands in the shaking stakes.

'I don't know what to say…' She blinked back tears as his thumb skated across her lips, grazed her cheek.

'I think you do.'

His lips brushed hers, slow, thoughtful, in a soul-reaching kiss that coaxed her into believing this was happening and this was real.

'I love you too,' she breathed on a sigh, clinging to him, powerless to do anything other than love this incredibly impressive man.

As he let out a jubilant whoop, louder than the ship's horn, she kissed him with all the passion, love and adoration she'd been storing away for days now—ever since she'd realised the terrifying truth: that she loved this man, would never love another as much as she loved him.

'I love you so much, sweetheart. Don't you ever run out on me again. Last night was the longest, loneliest night of my life.'

'Same here.' Snuggling into him, she breathed in his sinfully addictive scent, stunned she'd get to savour it for the rest of her life.

He nuzzled her neck and she squealed as he nipped her, his lips searing a trail towards her mouth as heat flooded her body, having a predictable response as she swayed towards him.

It had been like this right from the start. Her body had always known on some instinctual level that he was the man for her, while her head had taken a while to process the idea.

Zac loved her. This powerful, commanding, sexy guy loved her.

Life couldn't get any better.

'You know, I could always see if any of the London museums are interested in a top-notch curator on secondment.'

He pulled away, shock widening his eyes to endless blue proportions. 'You'd do that for me?'

'Only if you're good.'

With the same wicked smile he'd used to charm her from day one, he wrapped his arms around her, stroked her back, set her body ablaze.

'Oh, I'm better than good. I'm brilliant.'

'That's a pretty high recommendation to live up to, sailor boy.'

'Care to help me try?'

'Aye-aye,' she murmured, and his lips lowered to hers.

* * * * *

BUSINESS IN THE BEDROOM

BY
ANNE OLIVER

When not teaching or writing, **Anne Oliver** loves nothing more than escaping into a book. She keeps a box of tissues handy—her favorite stories are intense, passionate, against-all-odds romances. Eight years ago she began creating her own characters in paranormal and time-travel adventures, before turning to contemporary romance. Other interests include quilting, astronomy, all things Scottish and eating anything she doesn't have to cook. Sharing her characters' journeys with readers all over the world is a privilege…and a dream come true. Anne lives in Adelaide, South Australia, and has two adult children. Visit her website at www.anne-oliver. com. She loves to hear from readers. E-mail her at anne@anne-oliver.com.

For my sister, Helen, who now enjoys
Queensland's climate and lifestyle year-round.

With thanks to my editor, Meg Sleightholme.

CHAPTER ONE

ACCORDING to her horoscope, this was Abigail Seymour's lucky day. And with a house named 'Capricorn,' she'd figured she couldn't go wrong.

Wrong.

She stared up at the run-down house from the base of the stairs, comparing it to the photograph in her hand. The weathered board on the veranda trim pronouncing that this was indeed 'Capricorn' hung at a dejected angle and swayed on rusted hinges in the sultry breeze.

In the photograph, the classic Queenslander home stood on stilts for air circulation, enclosed with open lattice-work. Wooden stairs led to a shady wrap-around veranda, which would catch the sea air and provide stunning views of the coastline. Tropical plants added a lush green aspect.

With several coats of paint, some time and energy—correction: a lot of time and energy—it could be that enchanting dwelling once again. She'd be having a few choice words with the agent about false advertising.

Which reminded her—where was he? They'd arranged to meet here this morning. She checked the e-mail printout in her hand, then her watch. A bad feeling cranked up her spine. A very bad feeling. This Gold Coast house was supposed to have been the premises for her new business, Good Vibrations.

At the moment the only vibrations seemed to be coming from somewhere within. And they weren't good. They were the hammering-and-drill-and-not-ready kind. And since she hadn't organised any interior renovations yet... She closed her eyes and took a deep breath. *Think blue, Abby, and calm down.*

Right now it didn't help.

'What the heck's going on?' she muttered. She climbed the stairs, found the front door unlocked and pushed it open.

And stopped in the middle of what looked distressingly like a demolition site. Her fingers clenched around the lease. The signed and dated lease that stated this place was hers from tomorrow.

Wood shavings and lengths of wiring littered the floor. Strips of faded wallpaper hung from one wall above where a large mirror might have hung once upon a time. Dust motes swirled in a thin beam of sunlight and over a wide plank supported by stocky A-frame trestles and covered in tools.

Worse, the place smelled of new wood and old mould, so not the way a massage and aromatherapy centre should smell. Everything was brown and beige and grey.

The usually cheerful jingle of her anklet and beaded sandals sounded out of place on the bare floorboards as she crossed the room. 'Hello?'

No reply. Just the high-pitched whine of a drill.

Picking her way over assorted debris, she skirted the plank table and headed for a door at the back. In the next room a ladder was propped open in a corner near another trestle table. The tinny sound of a transistor radio drifted through the manhole above.

She'd have to settle for grilling the workman. She rapped on the wall. 'Excuse me…?'

The drill reverberated to life again, drowning her voice. Okay, forget the fact that she didn't like heights and that she was trying for a bit of professional decorum here. Setting her bag and papers on the floor, she slipped off her sandals and hitched one side of her skirt under her panty strap.

The loud curse that rolled through the hole was followed by the overhead thump of heavy footsteps. One very bare, well-muscled masculine calf stepped onto the ladder. Then another. Tanned and liberally covered with dark hair. The thighs were no less impressive, and went up and up…until they disappeared beneath brief—and loose-bottomed—denim shorts.

Oh…my. Abby swallowed as those legs descended, followed by one firm, taut backside. She glimpsed a thick ridge of scarring on the back of one thigh disappearing beneath his shorts, then more bare skin, more shifting muscle as his back and a pair of plaster-showered shoulders came into view.

She took an involuntary step back—onto her discarded shoes. The movement caught his attention and the hunk swivelled his head and looked down at her.

Piercing blue eyes met hers. The kind of eyes that looked straight through a woman's clothing and saw her naked. Except this man's eyes never left her face. Still, she had the sensation that he knew exactly what she was wearing right down to her red lace panties.

'Can I help you?' His whisky and sandpaper voice shimmied down Abby's spine like the slow sweep of an exfoliating glove.

She shifted her shoulders inside her T-shirt to ease the tingle. Wiggled her toes back into her sandals. Tugged at her hitched-up skirt and smoothed it down her thigh. She was here on business. He, on the other hand, with his impressive sweat-sheened body and bulging biceps, looked more into brawn than business. More like…a personal trainer?

Her pulse did a little bump. *Blue, blue, blue. Ice-blue. Sky-blue. Lake-blue…like his eyes. Oh, for heaven's sake, get on with it.* 'I'm looking for the owner of this…' She swept an encompassing hand over the clutter.

Lips that were full and sensual and wasted on a man stretched into a smile, creasing his cheeks in a way that made her want to trace the grooves with a finger.

'You found him,' he said, descending the ladder two rungs at a time.

'You?' Mr Tall, Dark and Delicious? She belatedly covered the crack in her voice with a throat-clearing as he approached. Amazing—even at five feet eleven she still had to look up. Early thirties, dark hair, chiselled cheekbones. His slightly off-centre nose was part of the charm.

She wasn't here to be charmed.

Shaking herself into business mode, she retrieved her papers from the floor, straightened her shoulders. 'Mr…'

'Zachary Forrester.' He offered a hand along with another one of those stunning smiles.

Like everything about him, his grip was firm…and tantalisingly brief. But not brief enough for her to miss the sensation of hard, calloused palm against hers. The sparkle of awareness that tingled up her arm.

'Abigail Seymour. Abby. Mr Forrester, I'm…' She trailed off, frowning down at the paper in her hand. Zachary Forrester *wasn't* the name on the lease. She fought a sudden spike of nausea as he grabbed a towel slung on the ladder, swiped it over his sweat-damp hair.

'If you're the insurance rep…' His brow creased as he glanced at her attire.

'Do I look like an insurance rep?' She blew out a breath. 'I'm your new tenant.' She tapped her thigh with the document that proclaimed that fact. 'What's the deal here, Mr Forrester? Because I'm confused.'

His cute dimples winked out and his gaze narrowed. 'That makes two of us. You sure you have the correct address?'

'It says so on that rusted excuse for a mailbox. "Capricorn."' Stepping forward, she shoved the document at his chest—his broad, hairy chest—and caught a whiff of honest-to-goodness male sweat and dust. 'I have a lease for business purposes, starting tomorrow.'

Still frowning, he tossed the towel and reached into the pocket of his shorts, drawing her attention to the way the faded denim… *Keep your eyes above the belt, Abby.* Except he didn't have a belt, and the view above was just as dangerous. Neat little navel, tempting tanned skin… She looked up quickly and saw him slip on a pair of reading glasses.

As he skimmed the paper he raised an eyebrow and one corner of his mouth kicked up. *'Good Vibrations.'*

Abby drew herself up to her full height. Just like a man to take it the wrong way. 'Do you find this funny, Mr Forrester? I assure you, I do not.'

He regarded her over his spectacles, all trace of humour gone. 'Nor do I. This building is a private residence. What kind of business is it exactly…it's *Miss* Seymour, I presume?'

'Yes.' Her hand moved towards her throat as a flush of heat crept up her neck, thanks to the redheads' Curse. 'What are you implying, *exactly*, Mr Forrester? My application was accepted. I have a signed lease to prove it.'

'Not signed by me,' he said over his specs.

'Oh…' She closed her eyes as the lump in her stomach rose to her throat. Was she really standing here letting a sexy stranger witness her business inexpertise?

When she opened them again she was still here and he was still watching her, only now he'd added sympathy and curiosity to the mix.

'I'm sorry, Miss Seymour, but you've been conned.' He tapped the signature with one large blunt finger. 'Not mine. This isn't worth spit. It's not even a legal document.'

If he'd used his hammer, the words couldn't have hit harder. *Not legal.* Her throat constricted. Where had the money for the bond and first three months' hard-earned rent gone? Anger pushed through the emotions swirling through her. 'I signed it in good faith, I *need* this place, and I need it now.'

'How did you find this property?' he said, his attention still focused on the paper in his hand.

'On the Internet. We handled most of the details by e-mail. I had no idea—'

'Obviously.'

She bristled at the know-it-all tone. *Obviously* Zachary Forrester was a lawyer, as well as a handyman. Which had her wondering…how much did lawyers charge?

She wished he'd just hand the paper back and let her go. But, no, he was still reading the fine print. *She* hadn't read the fine print. Who put fine print on an illegal lease anyhow?

Her fingers flexed and curled against her chest. She'd executed the whole deal on her own, not even asked for legal advice. *Stupid.* Aurora would have told her to check it out before putting down her hard-earned cash, and she'd have been right, but she'd wanted to surprise the woman who'd been mother, mentor and friend for the past ten years.

Since her stroke Aurora had been frail, and Abby was

determined to find a place away from rural Victoria's cold, damp climate where she could live out her days in peace. And she'd fallen in love with the picture of the little house…

Now here she was in tropical Surfers Paradise with a phoney lease, a second-hand van of supplies and barely enough money to live on. Talk about Paradise Lost. The deal was also supposed to have included a small self-contained living area so she was now officially homeless, as well.

'Tell me you didn't hand over any money,' Zachary Forrester said, setting his glasses on the trestle.

She bit her lip.

He sighed. A long-drawn-out hiss between his teeth that underscored her own stupidity.

She tried to take the paper but he held it firm, the same way those eyes held hers. 'How much did you give him?' He shook his head. 'We might be able to trace the cheque, I suppose.'

'Um. I paid in cash. In Melbourne. He offered a discount for cash, said he was an agent…'

'Can you describe him? You'll need it when you report the matter to the police.'

'I think so…' Bearded. Blond? Mr Average. She lifted her chin. 'I'm sorry I bothered you, Mr Forrester.'

'Hang on, are you just going to leave it at that and walk away?' He shook his head, incredulous azure eyes searching hers.

'Of course not.' She tugged until the paper slid from his grasp, broke that unnerving eye contact and bent to pick up her bag all in one hurried movement. 'I have your name and address. Count on it, I'll be in touch.'

'What are you going to do?'

'I'm going to report it, then take some time and consider

my options.' *Without you watching,* she thought, sliding the useless document into her bag.

The universe was still out there, she just had to find her place in it. And that place was Queensland's Gold Coast until she sorted out the mess she'd made. Just the thought had her mouth turning as dry as the sand on the nearby shore.

'What options?' His mobile buzzed. He unclipped it from his waistband. 'Forrester. Hi, Tina, honey.' Genuine affection brightened his voice. 'Something came up.' His luscious-looking mouth curved at something Tina Honey said, then he glanced at Abby and it instantly flat-lined as the sparkle in his eyes dimmed. 'No. Nothing like that.' Pause. 'Plenty of time. Yeah. Soon.'

Disconnecting, he clipped the phone in place and said, 'You're not a local, then?'

'No, I arrived from Victoria this morning.' She licked her dried lips, flapped a hand when she saw him frown. 'I'll be fine. My mistake, my problem.'

'Looks like you could do with a drink.' The sandpaper was back in his voice. 'I have a bottle of water in the cooler, or a carton of iced coffee if you prefer.'

Tempting, since she hadn't had anything since her muesli-bar breakfast. But she had more urgent problems than quenching her thirst with an attractive man. This mess wasn't his fault and she'd not involve him any more than she had to. She hitched her bag onto her shoulder. 'Thanks, that's not necessary. And Tina Honey's expecting you.'

A corner of his mouth twitched. 'She's a worrier. It's her son's christening in a couple of hours and I'm the kid's godfather.'

'Congratulations. I'll let you get on with it.'

'Miss Seymour... Abby, we need to discuss this further—'

As he spoke she turned, the sole of her shoe skidded on something, twisting her ankle and sending a shard of pain through her foot. She struggled for balance, her arms pinwheeled and—

'Whoa there.'

Two hard hands were suddenly supporting her elbows from behind. Embarrassment was stronger than pain as she raised her throbbing foot and glared at the small drill bit on the floor that had caused such an undignified exit. 'This place is a health hazard,' she muttered.

'I'm sorry. I'm renovating on my own—Are you okay?'

As he spoke his breath stirred the hair at her nape, his body heat radiated over her back. And all she could smell was male. Healthy, sweaty male that just begged her female hormones to come out and play. 'It's nothing, I'm fine.' Or she would be if he'd just step away and let her *breathe*.

'Let's take a look.'

'N—'

'Just to be sure.' He cut off her protest as he slid an arm beneath her knees and deposited her on the trestle.

Her feet dangled off the floor—an absolute first. She scoffed to herself. Swept off her feet, the clichéd damsel in distress. Then, with a shifting of shoulder muscles, he hunkered down in front of her and she nearly did the unappealing swooning bit. Which made her stiffen and straighten up.

'Which foot?' His voice had lowered fractionally.

'It's just a strain. It'll be okay in a couple of minutes—'

'Which foot?' he demanded again.

'Right.'

He slipped off her sandal and cupped her bare foot in one rock-steady hand. Heat spread up her calf as his fingers probed for swelling. The man had the most marvellous touch. Up close, his bent head showed threads of grey amongst the brown.

Of course, he chose that moment to look up. His eyes looked languid, almost silver, but they darkened perceptibly as they met hers.

She looked away. It didn't make a speck of difference. Awareness pumped through her body. Awareness of his hard palm against her heel, his calloused fingertips as they skimmed once over the exquisitely sensitive inside of her ankle.

In the sudden stillness, she could hear her own heart hammering against her breast, the distant sounds of the radio and the waves on the nearby beach. She was having her first—and only—Cinderella moment.

'A gel pack,' he said abruptly. 'There's one in the cooler.'

His clipped no-nonsense voice snapped her back to reality. Time was wasting. Bare-chested hunks masquerading as princes were not on her timetable. 'No, really—'

'Yes, really. I keep it handy just in case.'

He rose, treating her to an eyeful of male crotch. She instantly studied the wall in front of her while he moved to the cooler in the corner.

As a trained remedial massage therapist, she should be used to the sight of the human body. But she wasn't used to the sight of *this* human body. Nor the way it affected her. She felt giddy, breathless, and she straightened her posture again, kept her gaze pinned to the wall.

'Here you go.' He wrapped a cold gel pack around her ankle and held it in place. Thankfully this time his hands didn't stray from the pack.

'Thanks.' She concentrated on visualising a peach-coloured mist around the site of the pain, imagined its healing energies seeping through skin and muscle. But her concentration was shot. Those deft fingers with assorted tiny nicks and scars… Well, they were simply more interesting. She straightened her spine in defiance. *Close your eyes, Abigail Seymour.*

Zak felt like a damn Prince Charming. Except that after a brief but necessary probe for swelling—he didn't need a lawsuit on his hands—this prince was keeping his fingers well away from that feminine ankle with its erotic silver anklet.

Abigail Seymour was *not* his ideal princess.

She'd knocked him off-beam when he'd first laid eyes on her only because he hadn't expected to see a spectacularly tall, red-haired female ogling his backside when he descended the ladder.

His gaze flicked to her face. Now she seemed to be locked in some sort of introspection. He already knew behind those closed lids her eyes were a misty grey. Like the ocean when a storm rolled in.

He wondered how they'd look glazed with passion.

And why had that particular image popped into his head? Because he hadn't indulged in that pastime in a long while, that was why. He knew the old saying: all work and no play…

He shook his head and rocked back on his heels, careful to keep his fingers at a constant pressure so as not to disturb her internal focus…and—turnabout was fair play—ogled her back.

She dressed like a seventies cast-off, and this morning's colour scheme seemed to be all about intensity—purple-on-magenta skirt and crimson top. She'd made some attempt to tame her red hair, which was pulled into a tight knot at her nape, but a few strands had worked loose and

the whole lot looked as if it might rebel given the least opportunity.

Freckles dotted her nose and cheeks. Minimal make-up,
a hint of soap overlaid by something more exotic. Some
sort of mysterious floral essence? Incense? She wore a trio
of silver rings on the fingers of her right hand. An aquamarine was suspended on a chain around her neck.

As if she felt his scrutiny, she opened her eyes. 'That'll do.'

She jerked her foot but he held it firm, his fingers
briefly straying beyond the pack. 'Better safe than sorry.
A couple more minutes. Isn't Victoria a long way to come
to start a business?'

'When you want something, my motto is go out and get
it… I guess it's not always as easy as you think it's going
to be.' She shrugged a shoulder, giving him a peek of red
lace bra strap.

The sight had his blood pumping a little faster through
his veins. He almost laughed aloud. He'd definitely been
out of circulation a long time if a bra strap turned him on.

What *did* she want? Just a business? She could do that
in Melbourne. A tropical lifestyle, then? A sea change?

Or a torrid affair.

He cleared a sudden tightness from his throat. 'So, you
owned a business in Melbourne?'

'Not exactly.' She shifted uneasily on the trestle. 'Mr
Forrester—'

'Zak. What's that supposed to mean: "not exactly"?'

'I was involved in someone else's business. Don't worry, I know what I'm doing.'

Debatable, he thought as she pulled her foot from his
grasp as if she couldn't wait to get away.

'You'll be late for Tina and I need to be going.'

'We're not finished…but it'll have to wait,' he said,

glancing at his watch. He set the pack on the trestle, slipped her sandal on.

As he closed his hands around the slender curve of her waist to deposit her on the floor a wariness flashed into her eyes and she raised both palms. 'I can manage, thanks.'

Her body remained as stiff as a patio post but her hands rose unwillingly to his shoulders as she slid off the trestle. He swore he felt each finger, a pressure point of what he refused to call pleasure. Pleasure was something he had no business feeling. Ever again.

The moment her feet hit the floor he stepped back. 'Where are you staying?' He heard the brusqueness in his voice. 'I need to be able to contact you. In case any information comes to light.'

Which it wouldn't. The low-life responsible had stolen her money and disappeared into cyber space long ago. It made Zak angry. Especially when he saw the spark of hope in her eyes as she gazed up at him.

'You think it might?'

'No.' He felt sorry for it, but that was the bare truth. 'And I want a photocopy of that lease.'

'Why?'

'You don't think I should have a copy of something involving my own property?'

She blinked as if the logic had just occurred to her. 'Of course you should.' She dug into her bag and pulled out a fancy feminine-looking pad and pen. She scribbled something, ripped off the sheet. 'My mobile number. You can contact me on that.'

Keeping his eyes focused on hers, he ripped off the bottom half. 'Don't you want mine?' He took her pen, warm from her fingers, wrote his number and handed both back. Then he pulled his wallet from his back pocket and withdrew a couple of business cards. 'In case you have any problems.' A foregone conclusion.

She glanced at the cards. '"Forrester Building Restorations" and "Capricorn Centre"?' Her eyes twinkled as she smiled at him for the first time. 'You're a busy boy, Mr Forrester. Do you make any time in your schedule for fun?'

His jaw tightened. He preferred it when she wasn't smiling. Fun with Abigail Seymour conjured disturbingly uncomfortable images. 'If my mobile's not switched on you can contact me through the centre's office.'

'O-kay.' She tucked them in her bag while he filed her info in his pocket.

He saw her wince on that first step as she accompanied him through the front room and out into the balmy ocean air. Beyond the fence he saw the beat-up van with Victorian licence plates and shook his head in disbelief. 'You drove all the way in that? Alone?'

She dug out her keys with a jumble of colourful crystals and whatnots attached to the ring. 'You wouldn't?'

'Not a chance.'

'Some of us don't have the luxury of that choice. Scrappy here's good for a few thousand ks yet.'

While he stared, still shaking his head, she patted it fondly, then climbed in.

He refused to acknowledge whatever the hell it was that hummed through his body as her exotic fragrance wound its way through his senses, at the sound of her anklet tinkling as she swung her legs beneath the steering column. As her eyes met his through the car's open window.

'I'll call you,' Zak heard himself say, and was suddenly conscious of his choice of words. 'Later,' he added. 'Contact me if you need anything in the meantime.'

He shut the door and watched the car chug off in a cloud of fumes. *Some of us don't have a choice.* She didn't deserve the low blow she'd been dealt. Brought about by her own carelessness, he reminded himself. He rolled his eyes to the tropical blue sky. How naïve could the woman be? To put down money without checking first—a more cynical guy might say she deserved what had happened to her. She wouldn't be so quick and trusting the next time.

He walked back inside and immediately headed for the cooler. Opened a bottle of water, gulped it down, then looked at the mess. He didn't even know what kind of business she'd wanted to set up—she'd sneakily let that question slide.

It wasn't his fault. *Don't get involved.* But, damn it, he *was* involved—it was his property after all—which meant giving her a call later, as he'd told her he would. See if he could help. Get a photocopy of her document.

He reached into his pocket and pulled out the piece of paper she'd given him. Her scent wafted to his nose as he unfolded it. A bold, flourishing *A* for Abby. One of those smiley faces at the bottom, and an *X*. His brow lifted. Presumably she ended all her correspondence in that carefree upbeat manner.

Would she make love the same way? With a snarl he shoved away thoughts and images that crept into his brain and edged dangerously close to desire. She was nothing like his kind of woman. Nothing like Diane. So there was *nothing* to worry about.

CHAPTER TWO

'WHERE have you been?' Tina Hammond demanded at the church door. 'And smelling…' Her classic patrician nose wrinkled as if she couldn't decide, then she arched her brows. 'Mmm. Exotic. What *is* that scent?'

Ignoring her scrutiny, Zak bent to kiss her forehead. 'Careful, you're starting to sound like a wife.'

She grinned, patted his cheek. 'Just trying it on for practice. Not long now.'

'You do realise you guys have the ceremonies back to front, don't you?'

'It just worked out that way.' Tina's blue silk dress rustled as she reached up to adjust his tie. The familiar feminine gesture and fussy sound she made as she smoothed his lapel was something he'd not been subjected to in a long while.

'We want to say our "I do's" on that island, even if we've had to wait a year for the booking.' Her dark eyes zeroed in on his with unsettling directness. 'Are you bringing the wearer of that perfume to the wedding?'

'Good grief, no.'

She cocked that little blond head of hers to one side, her eyes soft with sympathy and understanding. 'You haven't asked anyone, have you? I told you, I can arrange for a partner—'

'Not necessary.' Zak squeezed her hands briefly before setting her away and buttoned his suit jacket. He forced himself to put aside his misgivings about being surrounded by so many well-meaning friends when he'd prefer solitude and took a deep breath. 'Now, where's that godson of mine?'

'Nick's got him.' Tucking her arm in Zak's, she towed him down the aisle to her soon-to-be husband and the wide-eyed Daniel nestled in his arms.

Zak exchanged greetings, spoke briefly to the grandparents, skimmed a hand over the eight-month-old's silky head, then took his place alongside the family.

As the minister led the brief service Zak couldn't stop the memories of that day six years ago when he'd stood here in the emerald and sapphire and gold light filtering through that stained glass and made his marriage vows.

Tina was so similar to Diane, both petite blondes, well educated and fashion savvy. The three of them had been inseparable right through school, but it had been Diane who'd won his heart as childhood matured into adolescence and adulthood.

Tina worked four days a week in Zak's new office but Zak knew that these days her greatest love was being a mother. And now Diane had gone, that instinctive mothering seemed to extend to Zak.

He shifted restlessly in the pew as the minister droned on about family. He dreaded these social gatherings. The awkward silences. The consoling hand on his, the dinner invites. But this was one gathering he couldn't avoid.

Almost the entire assembled congregation knew him. Had known his wife. They knew he'd nearly lost his own life alongside her.

They didn't know of his nightmares, or the guilt that stalked him at every turn.

Because they didn't know the whole story…

'You weren't alone in that Singapore hotel room,' he accused Diane the moment he saw her an hour after she'd flown in on that last buying trip to Asia. He hadn't waited until they had privacy; no, he'd had to confront her at their friend's birthday bash. Mistake number one.

She'd only just turned up and they were by the front gate, the night cool and awash with purple shadows and bougainvillea.

'Nor did you tell me your flight arrival time,' he continued. 'Did he fly in with you? Is he a local? Do I know him?'

'You're being paranoid,' she said. But her eyes skittered away and she flitted past him, already smelling of booze.

'No. I'm not.' He grabbed her arm. 'I'm taking you home. We need to sort this out.'

'Let me go.'

'Okay, since you're so insistent.' But he hesitated, his fingers pressing into her flesh. 'If you're not going to come clean, this marriage is over.' The silence in that brief hiatus as the meaning sank in, for both of them, sounded like a gunshot. 'But I'm still taking you home.'

'I didn't tell you my flight because I didn't want you to miss the party.'

'Yeah, right.'

Her face was pale in the dimness, her eyes huge and moist. 'You've got it wrong. It was the TV you could hear…'

Right now all he could hear was his own heart pounding with fear. His gut cramped, his facial muscles twitched with strain. 'I'm not a fool.'

Mistake number two was letting go of her to dig in his pocket for his car keys, then dropping them in the low broad-leafed bushes that edged the lawn.

When he reached the kerb she was already gone, her car fishtailing as it veered left onto the main road.

He caught up with her a kilometre away and stayed with her for twenty minutes as she headed west towards the hinterland, cursing her, cursing himself a hundred times over. Then they reached the bridge…

Too late to listen to her side, to find out if he'd been wrong. God forbid, horribly wrong. Too damn late.

'Zak?' Nudging him out of his past, Tina whispered into his ear, 'You're supposed to stand now.'

He nodded, rose, rolled the kinks from his shoulders all in one movement. 'Sorry.' And hoped he'd make a better godfather than he had a husband.

'So, how are the renovations coming?' Nick Langotti asked, jostling his son on his hip. The christening was being followed by a lavish afternoon tea on Nick and Tina's palm-shaded patio.

Until a few weeks ago Zak had been occupying a room in the apartment building he'd bought soon after Diane's death last year while Forrester Building Restorations oversaw the renovations to turn it into a tourist and conference centre.

Zak popped the top on a can of beer. 'Kitchen's looking good and I've finished the two bedrooms and *en suite* bathroom. The rest of the place is still a war zone.' He selected a few slices of salami and cheese and put them on his plate. 'It's taking a backseat until Capricorn Centre's more established. And I still have that empty retail space to rent out there.'

'You still going with that ad campaign the agency suggested?'

'If I can find a suitable model.' The Face of Capricorn. Someone able to project the image of a professional who could have fun when lectures were finished for the day. 'I've got an appointment at a photographic model agency tomorrow to look through their books,' Zak said.

Nick's eyebrows jiggled. 'You want me to come with you and help check them out?'

'Help check who out?' With the unerring sense that wives—even soon-to-be ones—seemed to develop whenever a topic specific to the female gender came up, Tina materialised at Nick's side. She was licking cream from her index finger and eyeing Zak with that look he'd come to recognise as some sort of futile hope. 'Anyone I know?'

Time to leave, Zak decided, before anyone else got it into their head to offer him tea and sympathy.

And the thirty-minute walk home would clear his head. It was also the best way to avoid chauffeuring any of Tina's girl-friends who just happened to need a lift home.

'Had a few too many vinos, Te-e-na, I'm over the limit,' he told her with an exaggerated drawl before leaving his car in their driveway to pick up later.

Desperate for some fresh sea air and solitude, he headed straight for the esplanade. He tugged off his tie, slipped it in his pocket and undid the top couple of buttons of his shirt.

Being surrounded by all that family—its noise and laughter and love—reminded him of what he didn't have. His place didn't have cosmetics strewn over the vanity, a jar of home-made cookies on the kitchen bench, diapers airing under the veranda. Not that Diane had been the domestic sort. She'd worked long hours to get ahead in her job, which had left little time for anything else.

At present his kitchen table was home to assorted hardware rather than fresh flowers and the only cookies were store-bought and eaten straight from the packet, usually a month after the use-by date.

He realised he'd reached the esplanade and was standing on the beach—in his formals, for crying out loud. He watched the sky, lavender with early twilight, listened to the sound of the waves, a rhythmic shushing on the sand.

Then everything inside him stilled and tensed as his eyes focused on the view directly in front of him.

And what a view it was. Not the white sand or the turquoise water turning cobalt as the sun dropped below the high-rise apartment blocks behind him.

The woman. The don't-give-a-damn-who's-watching, living-life-and-loving-it woman.

A silver-spangled violet and blue skirt flared around her bare feet, revealing that she was indeed human and not a mermaid. The beaded turquoise top and the long rainbow scarf tied around her slim waist were pure gypsy.

Then she glanced over her shoulder, an innocently seductive movement that had Zak freezing to the spot, his breath backing up in his lungs.

Abigail Seymour.

She'd let her hair down—and how. Yards and yards of deep red spirals whirled behind her in the stiff breeze like a celebration of streamers at a New Year's Eve party. She raised a hand and ran her fingers through it.

He exhaled slowly, his blood hammering hot and fast through his veins. He clenched his suddenly tight jaw. His first thought was to avoid her at all costs. He should just turn and walk away. Go home. Take a cold shower. He didn't want the distraction of that image keeping him awake tonight. Or any night.

More disturbing, the sight of Diane had never stirred his body the way Abigail Seymour was doing.

While his feet were still getting the message from his brain, which had suddenly seized up, she flirted with the water's edge again. Her skirt had soaked water up to her knees. Did she even care that other beach-goers enjoying their sunset stroll were slowing down to witness the spectacle of an almost six-foot redhead darting in and out of the waves as if she were performing some kind of dance?

She was a natural. A stunning contrast of curves and colours against the stark linear skyscrapers behind her, her shoulders catching the afterglow of sunset.

A light-bulb moment.

He barely noticed he'd started walking again. Capricorn had a face. It had a body. No model the agency could throw at him would come close. He was prepared to do whatever it took to get her. And that included getting his expensive Italian shoes wet.

In his mind's eye he could already picture her long slim body reclining on the bed in one of his centre's deluxe suites, that spectacular hair spread out on the pillow. A silk negligee clinging to her curves… Even from several steps away he could smell her scent mingling with the tang of salt and sand.

Abby let the sand squish between her toes as she walked along the ocean's edge. Water always relieved her stress; the sign of a true Piscean. She'd wasted time in an Internet café trying to trace a false name and her money. She'd also looked up Forrester Building Restorations and Capricorn Centre to satisfy herself that Zak was who he claimed to be at the same time.

He was. And, from the glowing reports of satisfied

clients and the photos of his work, he was very successful. And she'd found a place to stay within her tight budget,
so it hadn't all been a wasted effort.

But another interesting tidbit she'd discovered was that
Capricorn Centre had business premises to rent, a topic she
intended bringing up when she saw him again.

'Abby, wait up!'

Her breath caught in her throat at the familiar sound
of that deep-timbred voice. How long had Zak Forrester
been watching her cavort in the waves like a regular sea
nymph? She turned to see him striding across the sand
towards her. In his pressed charcoal trousers and shiny
shoes he looked like the self-made success her research
had uncovered.

She almost smiled as she watched the lacy edge of the
sea foam splash those shiny shoes. If she'd been worried
about what he'd make of her little dance, she needn't be;
he looked as out of his depth as she.

'Abby.' He stopped a few feet away. 'First up, have you
been to the cops?'

'Yes. I gave them a statement.' *For all the good it will
do.*

He nodded, then said, 'I have a proposition for you.'

Her face and neck prickled. *'Proposition?'*

'How would you like to make up the money you've
lost? Give yourself some breathing space till you find
something suitable.' So he'd witnessed her few moments
of impulsive abandon—she should be much more concerned that the Hunk was a Sleaze. But his eyes weren't
sleazy—just a hot lightning blue that zinged through her
body like an electric current.

Shocked at her response, she took a step back. 'And that
would be dependent on…?'

'A favour.'

A laugh scraped up her dry throat and escaped. 'Is that one step up or down from a proposition?'

'You can tell me.' Intense blue eyes assessed her, from the tips of her flyaway hair to her purple lacquered toenails, then back to her eyes. 'Let's negotiate something over coffee or a snack. Have you had dinner?'

Her stomach rumbled on cue. 'No.'

'Okay. I know a place.'

Still unsure whether his so-called proposition was a good idea, she asked, 'Is this dinner strictly business or is it personal?'

His gaze wavered a moment before he said, 'Call it an interview in casual surroundings. You can think about my suggestion and maybe I can help you find other premises afterwards. I'll explain my idea and you could explain your Mission Statement.' He stared down at her. 'You do have one, don't you?'

Was that a hint of humour in his eyes? She couldn't be sure. 'Doesn't everyone?'

Of course she had a…Mission Statement. Somewhere. If only she knew what the heck hers was. If only she knew whether he was serious.

She strode past him and across the sand, collected her bag and towel. When she began securing her scrunchie around her hair, he stopped her with a hand on her wrist. Heat zinged up her arm and through her body.

'Leave it.' Then as suddenly as he touched her, his hand dropped away as if he instantly regretted it and his jaw tightened.

'Fine, if you want to share a table with Miz Frizz,' she said, rubbing the spot on her hand that still tingled. Had she imagined the sparks? She shoved the scrunchie into her bag, her taste buds dancing in anticipation of sustenance. 'You promised food.'

'I did,' Zak said, behind her. 'Simon Says has the best-value steaks in town.'

'Oh, before we go any further…' She spun around, her arm brushing against the smooth body-warmed fabric of his shirt in the process, and held up a hand '…so there's no misunderstanding, is there a Mrs Forrester, or someone of the female gender you need to call and explain why you're going to be late?'

She saw the flicker in the depths of his eyes, heard the hesitation in his voice before he said, 'No.'

His shuttered expression forestalled any elaboration. She hadn't had lunch and the offer of a free meal was too tempting to resist. She nodded and headed for the line of parked cars.

'Only one small problem,' he said when they reached the kerb. 'I walked to the beach. Can you give me a lift?'

She couldn't resist a certain smugness. 'Would that be in my beat-up van that's brought me all the way across the country?'

His dimples creased as he smiled. 'That's the one.'

Her heart skipped a beat. Oh, boy. Dimples did it for her every time. But how well did she know this guy? This sexy *single* guy.

Sometimes you had to go with your gut feeling—she felt safe with Zak Forrester. If you didn't count the dangerous spark of excitement in her bloodstream whenever she looked at him. But she was at the wheel and in control and she didn't have to go anywhere she didn't want.

'No out-of-the-way restaurants,' she warned. Unlocking the door, she tossed her stuff in the back, cleared off the passenger seat and wound down the window. The van still smelled of last night's less-than-healthy but quick chicken burger and fries.

As he climbed in he cast a questioning glance at her precious supplies on the backseat and rear. Boxes stacked on boxes, a couple of cases and a mountain of bulging plastic garbage bags.

Ignoring his curiosity, she strapped in and turned on the ignition. Her bare foot tapped the accelerator. 'All in good time, Mr Forrester.'

Zak directed Abby to his favourite eatery overlooking the esplanade where the food came fast, was well prepared and inexpensive.

But it wasn't the ocean view that had Zak's attention tonight. It was Abby. The damp hem of her skirt and bare feet suited the casual atmosphere. His wife would have been appalled, hence he'd never come here unless he'd been alone. Diane had never stepped outside without high heels and make-up, but on Abby it looked right.

Diners lingered over their ice-cream sundaes or mango delights in shorts and beach wraps. In his blinding white shirt sleeves and formal trousers, *he* was the one out of dress code.

'What appeals to your taste buds?' he asked when Paul appeared at their table. He knew what appealed to his own right now and it wasn't on the menu. Had he made a mistake bringing her out to eat, when a nice safe coffee at the office would have served the same purpose?

She looked up at him with those luminous grey eyes. *Yeah, big mistake.*

'I'll have the seafood linguini, please,' she said.

'Wine?'

'Just a glass of hot water with a teaspoon of apple cider

vinegar and one of honey…You can do that, right?' she asked Paul.

'Of course,' he said, without a flicker of surprise, while Zak felt his own eyebrows lift. 'I'll have the fillet steak, rare, with a side serve of vegetables, please, and a beer.' He set the menu aside. 'An interesting choice of beverage.'

'A natural feel-good tonic. After today I need an extra boost. I take it twice a day, that's how I stay balanced.'

He toyed with the salt and pepper shakers. Balanced: two perfect eyes, perfectly aligned shoulders… But that was symmetrical, not balanced… A pair of firm breasts resting like half moons on her folded arms as she studied the decor. She was in perfect shape…ah…balance.

She turned her head and caught him looking. In the long pause he was aware of the muted sounds of a CD playing a Hawaiian love song, the ocean's roll, snatches of other diners' conversations.

'Whereas you…' She stared at him. Not *at* him, but around him. He had to force himself not to turn his head. 'You need to change the colour of your bedroom,' she said, without a glimmer of humour. 'You suffer from insomnia and recurring lower back pain.'

A tingle sprinted down his spine. Only his physician knew about the pain he'd suffered since the accident and the nightmares that plagued him. He wanted to test Abby's theory. He wanted to take her to his bedroom and ask her decorating advice. See if she could give him some personal help with his insomnia. And his lower back.

Hell. He shifted on his chair, cracked his knuckles. What was happening to him? 'That's not caused by my choice of interior decorating. It's the stress of renovating my home while splitting my time between two businesses. And I lift heavy equipment for a living.'

Her gaze dropped to the open neck of his shirt. 'Tell me about it.'

His skin tightened at her intimate invitation and a spike of adrenaline stabbed through his body.

'Conferences and tourism, wasn't it?' she said, grinding his wrongly interpreted thoughts to dust. 'Where do I fit in?'

Their drinks came at that moment with a basket of fragrant hot rolls. He took a gulp of beer to moisten his mouth. 'Okay. Here's what I'm offering. The centre needs a promotion to really get it up and running. I'd like to use you.'

She took a long sip of her beverage, her eyes wary. 'How do you propose to do that?'

'We'd employ a professional photographer. Some shots of you on the beach in—' his gaze slid to her visible top half '—something like what you're wearing now.' He forced his eyes to hers. 'And maybe a bathing costume, another of you in conference mode... A business suit...?'

She didn't smile as he'd hoped. 'I don't own one.'

'Not a problem, we'll get you one. I'll pay for the necessary clothes. Think about it, Abby. I'm offering to recompense you for your loss in exchange for a couple of hours of easy work.'

Her brows lowered, and he could almost hear her mind working over his suggestion.

He pressed on. 'We'll take a look at where I intend to shoot it and you can give it some thought. Throw in a beauty makeover, new wardrobe, whatever you want—'

'I'm comfortable with the way I look, thanks.' Her eyes cooled, her lips pursed. 'And dress.'

'Of course. You look great the way you are, which is why I want you. For the promotion.' Crikey, he was negotiating a high beam here with one foot in his mouth.

She lifted her glass again. 'I don't want payment. I want first option on the empty retail space you're advertising.'

He jerked upright. Out of the question. He knew next to nothing about her or her business. And how the devil did she know?

She tipped her glass towards him. 'I saw it on the Internet.'

'I'm considering another tenant,' he lied. 'And since you haven't mentioned the nature of your business—'

'I'm a remedial massage therapist. Just the thing your centre needs. I look forward to seeing it.' She settled back comfortably. 'Ever had your horoscope charted?' she asked suddenly, jerking his attention in another direction. 'By the way, your star sign's Taurus.' She opened her roll and buttered it.

His own bread lodged behind his Adam's apple. 'You believe in that stuff?' The fact that she had him pegged so neatly was as unnerving as it was fluky.

She smiled that knowing smile that raised the hairs on the back of his neck and tapped a finger on the table. 'You're grounded, Zak, and you don't like change. You like the sensual things in life. The massage thing appeals to you, I saw it in your eyes. You're also practical so you're wondering if you should take a chance on an unknown girl who's a little too alternative for you.' She paused. 'How am I doing so far?'

You're a good people-reader, that's all. 'That doesn't mean I fit into a mould created by the position of a bunch of stars in the sky.'

'You own a house and a centre named after a zodiacal sign—keep an open mind.' She licked a smidgen of butter off her thumb. 'But I'll forgive you, because a Taurean is also a fixed sign and stubborn into the bargain.'

'You could be right. Because I'll tell you now, this stubborn Taurean doesn't give up easily.'

'Good for you.' She pinned him with an equally obstinate gaze. 'But if you don't agree to my suggestion, it's a moot trait.'

Their meal came, a rather silent affair because Abby seemed more interested in food right now and he had to wonder when she'd last had a decent meal, given her circumstances.

He waited until she'd scraped the last morsel from her plate, then said, 'Tell me more about your business.'

'Ah, that would mean my, um...*Mission Statement*, I assume?' Her brow wrinkled in thought. 'Good Vibrations offers a holistic approach. A balm for body, mind and spirit. To this end, I also include aromatherapy and music in my sessions. Because I believe the whole experience is governed by the mood created by the surroundings, I'd also like to have the final say in the colour scheme.'

What? 'Wait up—'

'Let me finish.' She tapped a purple fingernail on the table between them. 'Colour affects the environment and our moods.' She looked about her. 'This café, for instance. The red cloths and warm honey wood give a feeling of welcome. The windows, open to the green of the palms and the blue of the sea, invite relaxation. Agreed?'

He leaned back in his chair, prepared to listen, at least. 'Go on.'

'Colour's invisible vibrations help us in our lives. Good Vibrations will treat clients to all aspects of relaxation and incorporate services which indulge or soothe the senses, such as aromatherapy and massage.' She smiled as she rolled her napkin between her fingers, excitement dancing over her features. 'I'm told my massage technique is magic. Just think, I could cater to tourists and conference attendees after a long hard day of playing or conferring.'

He *was* thinking, but for a moment he was lost in the way her eyes lit up as she talked, the sparkle of enthusiasm in her voice. He was thinking how her oiled hands would feel sliding over his scarred lower back... He shifted inside his shirt. And he couldn't avoid the clench of his body whenever she lifted a shoulder in that fascinating way she had.

But guests would take advantage of a service like massage or aromatherapy, particularly if it was right in the centre itself. 'It could work. But the rental on a place like this doesn't come cheap.'

'Neither do my massages.' Her smile was wicked as she leaned down to collect her bag. 'Let's go.'

Heat smoked and curled deep in his gut. The air in his lungs thickened. He clenched his hands into fists on his knees, willing his reaction away. *No*. But denial laughed at him and the aching loneliness of losing Diane, the absence of a woman's touch in over a year, blazed to hot and hungry life.

By the time he shook away the red haze from his vision he realised she'd hitched her bag onto her shoulder and without a backward glance was walking to the door.

He watched her while he dug out his wallet. This meal had been *business*, he reminded himself. As was his relationship with Miss Abigail Seymour.

So why was he still sitting here with his eyes glued to the sway of her backside, the long, long length of her legs silhouetted against the sheer fabric of her skirt, and wondering what colour negligee would suit her best?

Damnation. He dragged his gaze away, pulled out his credit card and slapped it against his palm. He should have gone for a professional model as he'd intended. Now he had to be on hand for the photographs. He had to make decisions about how best to clothe—or unclothe—that body.

His mouth dried and his body spiked with a sexual energy that jolted him from head to toe. What the hell had he got himself into?

CHAPTER THREE

ZAK'S voice turned all clipped and businesslike as he directed her to the centre. Abby didn't spare him a glance; she didn't need the distraction. With the van's windows down, the breeze caught her hair, tossing it every which way.

To ease the tension that had sprung up between them, she flicked the radio on to a local station and concentrated on the scenery. It was full dark and an old gold moon was rising over the Pacific. Architecturally diverse skyscrapers she'd never seen the likes of in her part of the world slid by. A fairy-tale land of twinkling lights and holiday-makers.

But this was no fairy tale, Zak was no prince and she needed these premises.

'This is it.' Zak indicated a white building with jutting balconies on the upper floors. Lights shone through a few windows.

'Wow.' She braked in the driveway for a better look as excitement buzzed through her veins.

'The centre's open but we're just getting started,' he explained.

Setting the van into motion again, she continued up the circular drive lined with pandanus and bright hibiscus bushes and, at his direction, parked under a covered portico, then gazed up at the shiny bronze lettering. 'Capricorn Centre.' Its unique angles and architectural charm were as clear as day in the floodlights illuminating the building.

A row of old pines separated the centre from an expanse of sand covered in sea grasses, and beyond she could see the white scrolls of surf glittering in the moonlight.

They climbed out at the same time and walked to the glassed entrance. A chandelier's light flooded the lobby. She instantly approved the colour scheme: a basic warm cream with splashes of emerald green and rose in the upholstery and furnishings, the gleaming wooden floor and banisters on the staircase that led upstairs. Mirrors reflected the lights and added a sense of space.

She caught a whiff of Zak's cologne—something cool and green—as they crossed the marbled floor. She was going to smell that scent in her sleep—if she got any sleep. Her mind was ticking over at a hundred miles an hour.

'The ground floor's admin and shopping, conference rooms and dining. The upper two are bedrooms. It's not large, but I didn't want large. I was going for exclusive.'

'So where's the room I'll be most interested in?'

'Over here.' He led her down a wide hallway and unlocked a double-glass door. Through the window on the far side she glimpsed the sea through the pines before he switched on the subtle lighting.

Oh, my… She drank in the pastel-blue walls, the deeper blue flecked with plum in the wall-to-wall carpet. 'Your interior decorator knew what they were doing.' She couldn't have chosen better herself. 'I'll need a privacy screen and maybe a little tabletop fountain there…' She reined in her runaway enthusiasm. She had to fulfil her side of the bargain first. *And* get him to agree to rent it to her.

He walked to the window and stood, shoulders tense, hands on his hips; a lengthy pause while he watched the moon reflecting on the water, obviously grappling with some inner conflict. 'Do you come with any testimonials from satisfied clients?' he said. '*If* I agree to this, I'll need to be able to recommend your services to our guests.'

'I do. But you and your staff will each receive a complimentary session. We can schedule yours as soon as I've set up.'

His hands clenched. 'That won't be necessary.'

'From where I'm standing it sure looks like you could do with one.'

She watched his shoulders hunch further. 'Very well,' he said finally. 'A rent-free three-month trial. In return for a series of professional photographs to be used for promotional purposes only…and all expenses incurred—the outfits you'll wear—to be covered by me.'

Yes! Because he had his back to her, she punched one fist into the air and yelled a silent *hallelujah*! 'You won't be sorry.'

'What about a massage bed?' His voice dropped a notch on the last two words, and he seemed to be having trouble with the imagery because he waved a disconcerted hand, then ran it around the inside of his collar as he turned.

'I don't need one. I prefer working on the floor.' And despite her best professional intentions, she couldn't prevent her own images of a naked Zak Forrester and heat and hands and fragrant oil from creeping into her consciousness. Not professional at all.

His eyes darkened to indigo, and a muscle jumped in his jaw. 'I'll supply shelving, anything else you provide yourself.'

'Fine. Oh, and I want it in writing first.'

He nodded, moved to the middle of the room. 'Pleased

to see you're being careful. I'll have it drawn up and bring it over… You haven't told me where you're staying.'

'No. I didn't.' Nor did she intend to. He didn't quite believe her; she could tell by the crease between his brows. 'I'll be here tomorrow.' She held his gaze. 'Trust me, Zak, I'll be here. It started out such a horrible day, and now…' She crossed the space between them. 'Thank you.' And threw her arms around his neck and planted a purely innocent lip-smacking kiss on his mouth.

But there was nothing pure, or innocent, about the way her body responded. Her lips buzzed, burned. Every internal organ seemed to trade places. Her arms turned as limp as the linguini she'd eaten for dinner, sliding off his shoulders and down his chest, the weave of his shirt soft against her fingers as she leaned back to stare up at him. At that mouth.

As his hands splayed around her waist. As he leaned forward, just a little… To kiss her again?

No. To steady her—she was the one swaying.

His mouth didn't look at all pleased. 'Are you always so enthusiastic about everything?' it said tersely, his hands dropping away to fist at his sides. But the heat in his eyes said something entirely different.

'I'm afraid so. Sorry.' She backed away on wobbly legs. Oh, that mouth was a temptation. 'Let's…um…sleep on it. You look like you could do with some.'

He didn't respond, but his eyes darkened with some unidentifiable emotion as she turned. She could feel those eyes on her as they tracked her progress to the door.

'Try some chamomile tea,' she suggested as she turned to him in the doorway. 'On second thought…your lower-back pain?' She hadn't meant to say it, but a sudden image of her hands working over his back, her thumbs digging into the taut muscles of his buttocks—*without* the clothes—and finding all those secret, sensitive places…' Better make that valerian.'

Abby pulled up at her unpowered site in the caravan park she'd booked earlier in the day. She switched off the ignition. 'Welcome to your new home, Abby,' she said, staring up at the nearby holiday apartments lighting the night sky and wishing she were cosying up in one of those luxury beds.

Instead, she was slap bang in the middle of Surfers without any kind of a bed and no electricity.

But once the deal was signed, she could offload her supplies and sleep in the back of the van. Not an ideal situation but she could make do.

She speed-dialled Aurora's number on her mobile. Guilt niggled at her, but she'd put off calling today hoping she'd have better news or at least some concrete information.

The familiar voice at the other end brought a lump of homesickness to her throat. Aurora meant more to Abby than anyone in the world. When she and her husband, Bill, had fostered the rebellious sixteen-year-old ten years ago, Abby had had no idea how her life would turn around.

She pressed the phone closer to her ear, wishing she were there. Wishing she hadn't rushed into something without discussing it with Aurora first. 'Hi, Rory, it's me.'

'Abby, thank goodness. I've been worried. When you didn't call…'

'I've been busy today. First up, how are you feeling? Is the career working out?'

'Fine to both questions. How's everything at your end? Did you get the job you were hoping for?'

'I did.' She injected a smile into her voice at the small

lie. 'It's in a new conference centre. Get this, Rory, it's called Capricorn. It has loads of potential.'

Abby hadn't told Aurora the truth when she'd left—that she'd wanted to set up her own business. That she'd hoped to be able to bring her here as soon as she had it up and running.

'Capricorn? Well, that's a good sign if ever there was one.' There was a pause, then she said, 'I know you have your own life now, but perhaps I can come up when I'm feeling better, and stay with you a while.'

Abby heard the wistful tone in Aurora's voice. She missed her already. She *hated* letting her think she'd taken a job in Queensland for the fun of it, especially so soon after Aurora's stroke. But if she told her the truth and what a mess she'd made of everything, Aurora would worry and insist on helping her out financially, and Abby refused to allow that to happen. She owed her foster mum, not the other way round.

She dashed the moisture from her eyes. 'It won't be for ever, Rory. Just until I get my feet on the ground, then I'll get you up here.'

'Of course, love. Who's your boss, what's he like and what's his star sign?'

Boss. The nearest she had to a boss was…Zak. Abby's heart skipped a beat as the man who'd put her hormones on alert came to Technicolor life behind her eyes. She could still smell his cologne in the car, could still feel the tingle of his lips on hers. 'His name's Zak Forrester and he's a Taurean.'

'*Ah-h-h…*'

Abby frowned at the tone, as if all the mysteries in the world were solved. '*Ah*…what?'

'Nothing, love. He's a hard worker, that's all-practical, and don't forget obstinate.'

Don't forget tall. Gorgeous. Sex god. 'Obstinate, indeed,' Abby agreed, 'particularly when it comes to alternative beliefs and practices.' And over-enthusiastic redheads.

'Don't let him intimidate you.'

She almost laughed. She'd been the one who'd intimidated *him.* 'I won't. Keep safe, I'll ring you tomorrow.'

Abby didn't see the sun's watery ascent over the sea, but she felt its tentacles as they crept over the dashboard, peeling her eyelids back just when she'd finally managed to snatch a couple of hours' sleep. Her neck ached from being propped against the van's door. Everything ached, she discovered as she dragged the hair out of her eyes and pushed upright. Stretching out the kinks, she took in her new surroundings.

Instead of the sound of eucalypts tossed by winter winds, palm fronds slapped languidly against each other. Children were already splashing in the park's pool. And some sadist was cooking bacon. She sucked the greasy, tantalising aroma into her lungs while she searched out an over-ripe banana, muesli bar and bottled water.

With the unwrapped bar clenched between her teeth, she rifled her suitcase for something that didn't need an iron, pulling out denim shorts and a sleeveless orange top. A reviving shower in the amenities block—

Her mobile buzzed. She leaned over, grabbed the phone and said, 'Hello?' around a mouthful of dry oats.

'Good morning.'

'Uh.' Her bite went down the wrong way at the sound of that deep businesslike voice. She coughed, swallowed. 'Good morning.'

'Am I interrupting your breakfast?'

'Yes. No. I'm nearly done.'

'Have you changed your mind?'

'No. You?'

'No. I've drawn up an agreement. We'll both sign off on it first, then we need to go shopping.'

We? 'Ah…' Of course he wanted to come with her. He'd already made that clear; it was his money, his promotion. His say. But the thought of putting her body on display—in nothing more than a bathing suit—for Zak Forrester's perusal sent hot and cold shivers down her back.

'I told you, I'll cover the cost,' he said, hearing her hesitation.

'You're already letting me have the room rent-free.'

'Part of the deal,' he clipped. 'Where shall I pick you up?'

She almost smiled. He was doing his darnedest to find out where she was staying. Not as long as she could help it, he wasn't. 'I'll meet you. I need to drop my supplies off anyway.'

'The room's locked…it's probably easier to meet at my place—the agreement's here.' He sounded abrupt, as if he didn't want her anywhere near his home. 'Make it one hour. I've got to pick up my car from a friend's place first. We'll get the paperwork out of the way, then unload your gear before we hit the malls.'

He wasn't here. Abby knocked again. No answer. Presumably he was still collecting his car from wherever. She took the opportunity to wander to the rear of the property, absorbing the smell of salty air and the unaccustomed but welcome warmth of the sun on her bare legs.

Along one side she could see floor-to-ceiling windows plastered with yellowed newspaper. The veranda did indeed wrap around the entire house. At the back an old couch and a well-worn wicker rocking chair sat at one end, and there was a tiny table and two chairs beneath what must be the kitchen window—she could see a pot of yellowed parsley on the sill through the pane.

A man who cooked, but not often? She couldn't resist a closer look. Pressed up against the glass with her hands beside her eyes to shut out the light, she saw a surprisingly modernised kitchen. Buttercup-yellow walls, touches of green and terracotta. At the moment a day's worth of crockery was stacked in the sink and the kitchen table looked more like a workman's bench—

She wasn't alone.

The glide of sensation stroked up the length of her legs from ankle to knee to buttocks and she instinctively reached behind to tug the hem of her shorts as she swung around. Heat stung her cheeks for the second time in as many days. She caught at the strands of hair that fluttered across her vision in the breeze. 'Hi…Zak,' she said, as if she hadn't just been peeking uninvited in his window. Invading his privacy.

That was why his jaw must be so rigid, his lips a tight line. He stood at the base of the stairs beside a bush covered in purple flowers, his hands in the pockets of khaki trousers, eyes hidden behind a pair of wrap-around sunglasses. He wore a blindingly white snug-fitting polo shirt and casual shoes.

'Sorry to keep you waiting.' His voice was as tight as his expression. 'You'll see better from inside.' She didn't miss the note of sarcasm as he turned stiffly and began walking to the front of the house.

She didn't catch up with him until he was stabbing the key in the front door. This man's moods changed like the sea. He really needed to loosen up. 'I'm sorry…' She grazed his arm with her fingers, felt the tendons move beneath his bronzed skin, felt him flinch as he turned the key.

She'd always been a toucher and didn't see any reason to stop now. She'd just have to show some restraint with this guy. 'I shouldn't have snooped. It's just that I had such plans for my own little shop… Are you sure you haven't changed your mind…?'

'I haven't. And you were more than welcome to look around.' He seemed to make an effort to relax. Took off his sunglasses and made eye contact.

Wow. Ocean-blue today, and so deep, she wanted to sink in and lose herself in their mystery. Because that was what they were. Mysterious. Sultry one moment, cool the next… She wanted to find out what made the enigma called Zak Forrester. 'We're all set, then…'

'After you.'

She realised he was holding the door open for her. 'Thanks.' Her shoulder barely brushed against his chest, just enough to catch a degree or two of body heat and his freshly showered scent as she stepped into yesterday's mess.

'When this is finished it'll be the living room and family/entertaining area,' he said, scooping up a handful of potential hazards—loose nails on the floor—and popping them in a stack of miniature portable drawers. 'There's also an area that used to be an art studio with its own facilities at the back of the house, but that renovation's down the track a bit.'

Ah, the big windows she'd noticed earlier. 'What do you want to do with it eventually?'

'Haven't decided. Kitchen's this way.' He opened a nearby door and stepped into a hall, its floorboards gleaming but otherwise bare, skipping the two bedrooms and barely allowing her to glimpse more than a blur of colour as they passed. 'I'm just waiting on the deep freezer, but the room's functional.'

She nodded her approval. The kitchen had a sliding glass door that opened out onto the veranda with the table and chairs she'd seen earlier. 'You've made it a room where you can eat and relax.'

His facial muscles relaxed into a semblance of a smile and he picked up the kettle. 'I'm afraid I haven't had much time to relax here yet. Coffee? Or do you avoid caffeine?'

'Coffee'll be fine, thanks.'

While he hunted up a clean mug she explored, running her hand over the satin-smooth cupboards, admiring the terracotta containers precisely arranged against the splashboard, the fragrance of coffee as he spooned granules into the plunger.

She noticed a wedding invitation on the bench. 'Nick and Tina request the pleasure of the company of Zakary Forrester and Friend…' His godson's parents.

Hmm. Who was the lucky Friend? She shook her head. Now she was getting too personal; she didn't need to know.

Then her attention snagged on a pile of cookbooks stashed on a cupboard in a corner. 'You like to cook?' She wandered over and sifted through, pulling out one near the bottom. *Play Food for Lovers.*

A gift from a woman called Diane, she noted from the inscription dated some years ago at the front. Well, surprise, surprise. Zak Forrester had a playful side. She opened a page at random— Oh, my… A very playful side. And immediately wondered whether Zak often entertained. More specifically whether he cooked for two on a regular basis. What he liked to do after those dinners for two…

'Haven't had much time for it…' His eyes stalled on the open page, those long fingers tightening on the milk carton he'd taken from the fridge.

Then his gaze collided with hers, and suddenly the atmosphere in the kitchen, which had seemed light and airy a moment ago, plunged into thick and heavy and filled with a sexual tension that left Abby feeling pleasantly weak all over.

'Obviously you enjoy it when you do have the time.' She traced a fingertip over the erotic picture, smiling at Zak's visible discomfort, delighting in the way his eyes shifted from her to the window to the book, as if they couldn't find a place to settle.

A throat-clearing preceded his terse directive to, 'Take a look around the rest of the place if you want while the coffee brews, and I'll get the paperwork.'

'Sure.' She carefully stood the book upright on the counter-top so that its explicit cover faced Zak, a wasted effort since he was busy watching the kettle boil, and said, 'I look forward to sampling your cooking expertise sometime.'

Zak turned his back on the girl who'd just sent his emotions spinning from one out-of-control direction to another and faced the bench as he set the milk carton down, willing the beat of his pulse to subside, commanding his errant body to return to something approaching normal.

He waited, listening to her footsteps as she walked down the hall, and the tinkle of her anklet with its accompanying image of her sexy ankles faded.

Cool it. This wasn't supposed to happen. It wasn't *going* to happen. His fists tightened at his sides.

It already had.

He was as hard as the granite counter-top. Thank goodness Abby hadn't seen his body's response. He'd thought he'd got rid of that saucy book and its associated memories. 'It'll spice up our sex life,' Diane had told him on their third wedding anniversary.

Just watching Abby poring over the pictures had certainly spiced up his morning. And he could've sworn there was a hint of naughty in her voice when she'd mentioned sampling his cooking.

He snatched it up, slammed it shut. He was tempted to bin it, but that would be like admitting Abby had got to him. Instead, he stuffed it beneath his woodworking manual on the table.

Diane was dead. And the guilt he carried was the price he paid. Guilt, nightmares, regular recurring visions of what had happened and a decision to live the rest of his life alone.

Payment in full.

So this attraction—this damn *inexplicable* attraction—that had sprung to life the moment he'd met the woman claiming to be his tenant must be dealt with swiftly and harshly. He gazed out the window over the sink but he wasn't seeing the view. All he could see was Abby. Even if he was looking for a woman—for whatever reason—Abigail Seymour was all wrong for him. He didn't know if he trusted her. He didn't know if he even liked her.

And he had to take her shopping today. And it had to be today—he couldn't afford to wait until this crazy fever he felt whenever she came within cooee of him dissipated. Now he'd committed to using her as his model, the photo shoot needed to be dealt with regardless of his personal feelings.

So he had to breathe that exotic essence of whatever the hell it was that seemed to cling to his nostrils like a vine. He had to endure the sight of those endless legs in those short denim shorts…

'Hi there, I'm back, and impressed, Zak Forrester.'

Zak closed his eyes, pinched the bridge of his nose. When she said his name in that soft, breathy tone, Abby's voice did things to his body. Remembered, unwanted things. She didn't know the effect she had on him, which was a partial relief. 'Coffee's ready,' he said, grabbing a cloth and wiping spilled coffee grains off the bench. 'How do you take it?'

'White, no sugar. Thanks.'

'Me, too.' He glanced up and met her eyes. 'Now, if we can just agree on clothes.'

'Your money, your photos, your choice.'

He stirred in milk, feeling the tension ease a bit at the no-hassle arrangement. Simple. Brilliant.

CHAPTER FOUR

IT WAS neither simple, nor brilliant.

Why had he taken Abby's words so literally? He should've known no woman was immune when it came to shopping. It was a communicable disease peculiar to females.

In the end they compromised. He chose outfits he considered suitable and tried not to imagine how they'd look on her body. She tried them on for size in private. Then they came back with enough clothing and shoes and accessories on approval to fill the Surfer's Q1 seventy-five-storey apartment building. All on his credit card.

His suggestion that they take them to her hotel to choose was knocked back. She told him it was a mutual decision so they ended up killing two birds with one stone, dropping in at Capricorn Centre with Abby's shop supplies and the outfits to try on.

And the prospect of viewing them on the model loomed closer. Postponing the inevitable, he left Abby sorting clothes in one of the upstairs suites and set himself the task of hauling her cartons and boxes inside before heading into the office.

He found Tina kneeling on the floor, unpacking stationery supplies. She was wearing a pert yellow sundress, her hair a sleek cap of gold. 'Hey, Tina. I thought I told you not to bother coming in today?'

'Zak, hi.' She gave him a quick smile as she slit open a carton with her Stanley knife. 'You know Mum, she insisted on taking Danny, and, as much as I love him, I wanted the break.'

'Yesterday was a great day, Tina, and I'm honoured that you're entrusting me with the godfather role.'

'Hope you'll still feel that way when he's seventeen,' she said, swiping her blond bangs off her forehead with the back of her hand.

'You bet I will.' He leaned a hip on the edge of her desk and tried to imagine where he'd be in his life when Daniel reached those rebellious years. 'I was going to do it myself, but, since you're here, could you ring the photographer, please—name's on my desk—and schedule a time for tomorrow? Arrange for a hairdresser and we'll want a make-up artist on hand. I want those shots as soon as possible so we can upload them to the website. Oh, and organise for the pamphlet to go out as soon as we have the photos.'

'You've got yourself a model, then?' Tina paused with a handful of paper-clip boxes in her hand.

'Yeah…She's not exactly a model, she's more of a… massage therapist…' What did he really know about her except what she'd told him? 'She's going to be renting the empty room. It's a trial run, we'll see how it works out.'

'You don't look too thrilled about it. She giving you a hard time already?'

Ah, her choice of words. *You don't know the half of it.* 'We're still at the negotiation stage—at least we are with the outfits.'

'So what's she like?' Tina rose and began packing stuff in cupboards.

'Tall. Slim. Red hair…' His mind slipped back to last night's vision on the beach, the way her hair streamed behind her, the flash of her legs behind that gossamer skirt. So tall that if she wore heels that perfectly symmetrical mouth would line up against his and…

'Zak. You look…harassed. Is that the word I'm searching for?'

He met Tina's speculative gaze head-on and ran a hand through his hair. 'I've just been *shopping*—I think we cleaned out every mall in town—how do you expect me to look?'

'Okay, I get her visuals. That *is* the reason you selected her, I take it.' She arched her brows. 'But what's she *like* like?'

'Alternative. Vintage clothes.' Although today's shorts had been very modern and casual, he remembered. And short. 'Tinkly jewellery, into astrology and all that.'

'The kind who sprinkles herself with essence of moon drops?'

That's it. 'Yeah. Kind of.'

'And dances naked under the full moon, too, no doubt. So…not your type at all?'

'No,' he said, too quickly, he realised, and probably too forcefully as Tina's word images played through his mind.

'Known her long?'

'Only met her yesterday.'

'Ah.' Tina smiled. 'That explains the perfume I smelled on you at the christening.'

'She slipped—'

'And you came to her rescue. Okay. Tell Tina all.'

But as he explained Abby's problem—now a shared problem—and gave her a brief rundown Tina's expression sobered and a small frown creased her brow.

'Sounds a bit dodgy,' she said, and slid a comforting

hand over his. 'Be careful, Zacky. Innocent eyes and all that.'

An unwelcome thought slid through his mind. While he'd been unloading Abby's sealed boxes, which could be filled with rocks for all he knew, she could have done a flit with thousands of dollars' worth of merchandise.

No. He considered himself a good judge of character.

But his brain had been carpenter's glue since yesterday morning. He could no longer remember the flow of events or figure the logistics of how she might have planned to rob him blind, only that it was possible. It had taken Tina's objectivity to point that out.

'I'll be careful.' He removed his hand from beneath Tina's. 'Excuse me, I've some matters that need my attention.'

Who was that woman in the mirror? Abby studied the professional business image before her. Couldn't go wrong with a navy suit, white blouse and low-heeled navy shoes, she supposed. She pondered her next choice. Bathers, formal gown or negligee?

Zak had told her to choose her favourites from his selections. But how to choose from so many? And in the luxury suite he'd provided this was like a dream and she felt like a movie star.

She stripped down to her skin and picked up a white nightgown with an expensive label. It slid over her skin in a rippling waterfall of silk. 'What do you think, Zak?' she said, gazing at the suite's Pacific-sized bed, imagining him stretched out and naked, head propped on one elbow and watching her with lust in his eyes.

'How do you take a woman's clothes off?' she wondered. 'Do you prefer smooth and slow or fast and frantic?'

Or an erotic striptease? 'Maybe you're the rip and grab kind.' After all, he could afford a few torn garments.

She lay down on the bed, stretched out and stared at the speckled ceiling. 'Which are you, Zak?'

It had been a while since a man had made love with her. Her relationships had been short and not-so-sweet, the men in her life had never lived up to her ideal. She'd wanted so badly to be loved, she'd let the first guy to pay her any attention into her heart and her body.

But he hadn't been interested in her mind or her family history. All he'd wanted was sex as often as he could get it, and in her *naïveté* she'd mistaken that for passion.

She'd never been that trusting again.

But where Zak Forrester of the lake-blue eyes and charming crooked nose was concerned, she had a feeling she could easily forget.

Perhaps once Good Vibrations was up and running and she could afford a place to live, she wouldn't see him so often, wouldn't be tempted to think about him. To imagine all kinds of forbidden scenarios involving him and her and lots of bare, bronzed skin.

For goodness' sake. He had his own life and she'd be working and Aurora would need her to keep her company in the evenings. And it was the best feeling to be needed, wanted. She knew too well what it was like to be alone in foster families who didn't give a damn and were only in it for the money.

A sharp rap on the door had Abby bolting upright and scooting to the edge of the bed. She cast around for something to cover herself, but the knock cut through the room's silence with even more urgency.

'Hang on, I'm coming.' With only one hand in front to shield herself, she dragged the door open. 'Zak?' The lines around his mouth and eyes looked even deeper than usual, his looming stance blotted out the glow of light from the corridor. 'What's wrong?'

His fist was raised to hammer again, but he lowered it the instant he saw her. His eyes swept up her body like a forest fire, making her shiver in their heat, before coming to rest on her face. If you could call the blue-flamed intensity that singed her cheeks restful.

He didn't answer. His breathing was elevated, she noticed a few heart-pumping seconds later, as if he'd taken the stairs two at a time. But now he slowed his pace, aborting eye contact as he stepped inside and closed the door behind him.

'So what's the emergency?' she demanded, when she could speak again.

'I apologise, I shouldn't have overreacted,' he muttered. He walked past her and went to the window.

'Overreacted to what?'

Ignoring her repeated question, he made an all-encompassing gesture behind her. 'You should be very careful about opening doors dressed like that.'

'You made it sound critical. No one knows I'm here, who else would it be but you? And you said you needed to see the clothes on the model, so here I am.' She held her arms out to her sides. 'What do you think of the white?'

He didn't turn around. 'I *think* you need to consider wearing underwear if you're going to model the white.'

A glance in the mirror showed a hair-tumbled woman, her nipples clearly outlined against the fabric, the shadow between her thighs— 'Oh. I see what you mean.' No wonder he looked so uptight. 'I'm sorry. But you chose this garment, Zak, I'm merely the model. In my opinion wearing underwear, even that scrap of string and lace would make it look tacky. We'll have to go with something darker.' She grabbed up a handful of the nearest garments and backed away towards the bathroom. 'I'll try the red—'

Watching his profile, she saw him close his eyes and rub the bridge of his nose. 'Tell you what,' he said in a laboured voice, 'I'll trust your judgement. Be here tomorrow morning at eight o'clock. The photographer's coming at eight-thirty.'

'Fine,' she said. 'Whatever you want…' She saw his fingers clench on the back of the armchair against the window. 'I'll go change and be out of here before you know I've gone.'

But he wasn't waiting for her to leave. As he moved to the door he said, 'Take anything you want to try on and leave the rest here. We can use this room to set up in tomorrow morning.'

She watched him jerk the door open and nodded to his retreating back. 'See you tomorrow, then,' she said into empty air.

A short time later Abby pulled into her spot in the caravan park, her skin clammy, her mood decidedly lacklustre. Late afternoon thunderheads had gathered over the ocean, dark and ominous, but the air was warm and smelled of vegetation and bitumen.

The prospect of sitting in Scrappy for the evening if it rained wasn't good. The prospect of doing it night after night even grimmer. At least she had room in the back now to stretch out for some much-needed sleep.

She called Aurora first to check on her, cutting the call short because her battery was low, then picked up her grocery bag and climbed out of the van. She'd bought a packet of plain crackers, some salad vegetables that she could cut up in the kitchen amenities block and a tin of tuna.

'Now I know why you didn't want me to pick you up.'

She turned at the harsh accusation, clutching her groceries in one hand, shielding her eyes with the other as a final burst of sunshine pierced through the clouds. Zak stood at the back of the van, his face in shadow, one hand on Scrappy's rear windscreen.

A sense of betrayal knifed through her. 'What are you doing here?'

'I wanted to apologise. I was short with you back at the centre.'

'Yes, you were, but that's not it at all. You didn't come to apologise, Zak. You followed me.' She dumped her grocery bag on the car seat. 'You didn't trust me. You think I'm trying to rip you off somehow.' She saw a muscle clench in his jaw and knew she was correct in her assumption. 'I haven't figured *how* you think I'd do it, and maybe you haven't, either.' She shrugged, philosophical, and watched the ice-cream-cone clouds continue to build in the distance. 'I can't say I blame you.'

'I didn't—'

'Admit it, Zak.' She swung her gaze to his. 'If nothing else, I value honesty.'

Something flickered in his gaze, as if he'd suffered some form of deceit in his past. 'We're in total agreement on that point,' he said, stepping away from the van. 'I was *concerned*. Now I'm glad I was. How long were you planning on staying here?' He waved a disparaging hand at her surroundings. 'You don't even have power, for goodness' sake.'

'I thought maybe I could buy a tent—'

'Live in a *tent*? For how long?' He shook his head. 'Forget it, get back in your car.'

'What?'

'Just get in the damn thing. You're coming home with me.'

'To Capricorn? Your house?' She shook her head. 'Thank you for your offer, but it's obvious you don't want me there.'

His blue eyes darkened and for a heartbeat she thought she saw something else lurking in their depths, but then he lifted a shoulder and seemed to make a deliberate effort to remain calm. 'I have a spare room. At least you can boil a kettle, have a decent shower, make a meal.'

'No. I got myself into this, I'll—'

'You come back with me or our deal's off.' The bark was back in his voice.

'Hah. You need me for the photo shoot.' *And I need that rental space.*

He shovelled a hand through his hair. 'Just do it.'

'Not "just do it." Let's make this clear from the outset. I don't *do* charity. If I stay at your house, I work off the rent in some way: cleaning, cooking or painting walls. Whatever. At least until I start pulling in some income. In which case I'll be looking for my own place. She crossed her arms and met his eyes. '*Now* do we have a deal?'

He heaved a resigned sigh. 'We'll come to some arrangement.'

CHAPTER FIVE

ZAK didn't want her in his home—at his kitchen table, between his sheets, using his towels—but what choice did he have? He pulled into the driveway and watched her park behind him in the rear-vision mirror.

Watched her climb out of her van, all long limbs and red hair, and felt the jolt of sexual attraction down to his toes. How long was he going to have to endure a house guest? Especially one built like that.

He must be mad.

He had one bathroom—his bathroom. An *en suite*. Which meant she had to go through his room to use it. Right now the second bathroom's renovation assumed top priority unless he wanted to be forced to shower with the unwanted image of her soaped-up body behind his eyes, the scent of her soap in his nostrils for the next—how long?

Rolling his head back on the padded headrest, he blew out a long slow breath. He hadn't thought it through. He'd taken one look at her living conditions and known he couldn't walk away and pretend he hadn't seen her. It was minimal comfort that she hadn't looked any happier about the arrangement than he. With a shake of his head, he unfolded himself from his SUV and slid out.

She was already rolling a couple of trolley suitcases up the path. She'd left them in the van—another reason he'd had his doubts about her motives. Now he knew why—she'd planned to live out of a suitcase indefinitely. Sleep in a car for crying out loud.

And he knew he'd done the right thing—no, not right, not by a long shot. But he'd had a moral obligation to help her out and he'd done the only *decent* thing.

'I can manage a couple of rolling cases,' she told him when he would have helped.

He shrugged and unlocked the door. 'You know where the room is. I'll let you settle in. There are sheets and towels in the first cupboard. There's a second toilet off the studio but, I'm sorry, we'll have to share the bathroom for now.'

She stopped, momentary indecision etched on her face. 'Oh.'

I don't like the idea, either.

Then her face cleared and she smiled. 'We'll manage, somehow. I take quick showers.'

'If you're uncomfortable with the arrangement, I'll move into the spare room and you can have my bed.'

'No way,' she said quickly. 'But thank you.' She did the little shoulder thing and smiled again. 'Lucky you have a spare room or we'd really have a problem.'

He already did. 'You haven't eaten yet,' he said.

'No. But I've got some makings for salad and a can of fish. I'll just—'

'Okay, you make a salad and I'll throw a couple of steaks on the barbecue.'

They ate at the little table on the veranda while the rain came down in sheets, cooling the steamy air with its scent and mingling with the smoky aroma from the grill. Zak always ate out here, partly because the kitchen table was stacked with stuff, but mostly because he loved being outdoors.

As dusk closed in he lit mosquito candles and placed them on the railing and put one on the table. Purely functional, nothing more, but the soft glow lent mellowness to the atmosphere. 'More wine?'

'Thanks.'

He refilled her glass, then sat back and watched her looking out at the darkened backyard. He'd meant to excuse himself as soon as they'd finished eating to strip the wallpaper in the living room, but the wine's effect had him pushing back in his chair and postponing that moment a little longer.

He'd forgotten how much he'd enjoyed relaxing over a bottle of red at home after dinner with someone to talk to. Even if that someone wasn't a wise choice in dinner companions. Not if he wanted to sleep tonight. For now, though, it was enough to just chill out and appreciate the company.

'It's beautiful here,' Abby murmured. 'Back in Victoria we'd be inside huddled over our heaters.'

'I've lived in Queensland all my life, but I imagine an open fire would be cosy. Do you ever have one?'

'Not in ages.' She stared at one of the candles for a long while, her eyes turning dreamy and reflecting the glow. 'I remember…I was about four…Mum made a picnic for me and my baby sister one night in front of the fire. We toasted bread on a long fork.' Her eyes took on a deeper, misty, faraway quality. 'Thinking back now with the wisdom of age, I'm pretty sure it was because the electricity had been cut off.'

He leaned closer, his interest piqued. This was the first

time she'd volunteered any personal information. 'You live with family?' he asked.

'With my foster-mother.' A smile curved her lips. 'I was hoping to bring her up here to live. She had a stroke a while back and suffers with the cold. I thought a warmer climate would help. When I saw the ad for Capricorn, all I could think was here was our chance. I could work from home and care for her at the same time. Now I'm just hoping I can make a go of this business and bring her up here soon.'

'Who's caring for her now?'

'She's employed a live-in carer since I left.' Thoughtful, Abby leaned her arms on the table, her sensational cleavage shadowed in the candlelight. 'She can afford it, but I don't like leaving her in the care of strangers.'

'You didn't consider asking her to help with your business?'

Her head came up and her eyes flashed a defiant silver. 'I've always paid my own way. And I'm not about to tell her I've failed. Yet.'

As she talked her determination, the love and care she showed for her foster-mother, earned her his growing respect. 'You haven't failed, Abby. Not by a long shot.' And he'd do his darnedest to make sure that didn't happen. 'You said foster-mother?'

'Mum died when I was four. I never knew my father.'

'You mentioned a sister.'

'I haven't seen her since the night Mum died. We were separated when they put us in foster care.' She shook herself as if coming out of a sleep, straightened, ran a hand through her hair. 'And here I am telling you my life history. Sorry.' She pushed up. 'I'll just wash these dishes—'

'I've got them—'

They both reached for the salad bowl at the same time. A long hesitation as they stared at each other. Until Abby's voice washed over him. 'Zak?' She dipped her fingers into the bowl and looked down into his eyes. 'Pucker up.' And pressed something smooth and cool against his lips. 'Can't waste a perfectly good cherry tomato.'

His lips seemed to part of their own accord, her fingers grazing his mouth as she pushed the delicious little morsel inside. He barely tasted it—it rolled around his mouth, then he chewed and swallowed. Hard.

She laughed, her eyes sparkling in the candlelight. 'You look positively stricken. Did you think I was going to…?' That teasing expression in her eyes remained, but her mouth softened, parted just the tiniest bit as she leaned closer. Enough for him to see the tip of her tongue touch her lower lip.

Enough for him to wonder how it would feel against his. How she'd taste…

He wasn't aware of meeting her halfway, he wasn't aware of moving at all, of tilting his head back or lifting his hand to touch her petal smooth cheek, but then she was kissing him.

And he was kissing her back.

Rubbing his lips against hers, absorbing her sweet frivolity. Mating his tongue to hers and savouring the warmth. Reaching behind her neck to pull her closer.

He felt her hands move over his shoulders, her thumbs drawing tight circles below his collarbones.

His own thumb stroked back and forth across her nape, to her neck where her pulse fluttered. Smooth, incredibly smooth.

Stupid. Incredibly stupid.

He reared back, away from the temptation of her lush

mouth. The rain drummed on the roof, or was it the blood pounding in his ears? No, he was sure his blood was nowhere near his ears; it had pooled lower down and was beating like a jackhammer. He grabbed her hands, pushed them away and rose in one jerky movement.

They stared at each other for a taut, charged moment.

'Hey, it was a simple kiss…' She blinked, the soft dreamy light in her eyes dissipating, and he felt like all kinds of an idiot.

'You were the one who turned it into not-so-simple,' she pointed out. 'You really need to lighten up. I'm a physical person—it's part and parcel of my job. Don't take it so personally.'

'Fine.' His skin heated and tightened at the thought of getting physical some more with his house guest. Hard *not* to take it personally with his lips still throbbing with her taste. He turned away and began stacking plates. 'I'll finish up here. You go ahead and use the bathroom before I turn in.'

'Okay.' But she stopped at the kitchen door. 'But I'll say it again now. We share chores.'

'Agreed.'

'And, Zak. About that kiss? If it makes you feel better, forget it happened.'

The instant she'd gone he plunked down onto his chair again. *Forget it?* He blew out a long harried breath. Not flaming likely. But he thought back to the conversation they'd been having *before* the kiss. And he had to admit she wasn't quite the flaky, irresponsible woman he'd thought.

It didn't make her any less dangerous.

Zak knew he was drowning…

Black salty water rushing into his mouth, choking off

his air. Down. Desperate fingers plucking, searching. Find Diane!

Feel her hand through the car window. Explosions of light in front of his eyes. Sound. The low slow beat of thunder. The bottom of the world. Eardrums bursting. Lungs burning. Diane! Fingers slipping away. Alone in the dark. Midnight.

Peace. Floating. Accepting. White light.

Screams. Cold. Diane! No!

He struggled through the miasma of dreams and memories and into a semi-reality. Not his wife's golden hair and honey eyes. An auburn-haired silver-eyed woman floated before him.

Jackknifing upright, his body clammy and shivering, he listened to the pounding of his heart, willing it to slow, willing the tantalising image away.

'Just a dream,' he told himself into the darkness, and slid back onto the pillows, wide-awake now. He had no control over his subconscious, but he'd damn well control his waking hours.

Despite her lack of sleep over the past few nights with the travelling and last night's dismal effort in her van, Abby was awake at dawn. Her sleepy gaze took in the freshly painted room with its cool blue walls, the deeper blue summer quilt and white shabby-chic furniture. Not a bad effort for a guy.

And that guy made her…hot. In places he shouldn't. Such as when he'd looked at her in that negligee…and last night when she'd kissed him, *and* he'd kissed her back. When his fingers had stroked her skin and set her nerve endings sizzling.

Before he'd realised what he was doing and pulled away.

But he'd shown her more kindness than anyone ever had, apart from Rory and Bill. She owed him. She was going to pay him back the best way she knew how. By releasing those inner tensions that were, for whatever reason, holding him back from enjoying life. Even if she had to fight him every step of the way.

'Good morning.' Abby stood on the back veranda with two mugs of blackberry tea spiked with cider vinegar and honey. The rain had long gone, leaving only the smell of damp vegetation. Sometime in the night Zak had dragged his pillow and a sheet outside to the couch.

At the moment he was flat on his back, his morning stubble wildly attractive and making Abby wish she could lean closer and run her fingers over it. Instead, she sat on the rocking chair.

He muttered something and rolled onto his side, dragging a corner of the sheet with him. Too late, she realised he didn't sleep in pyjamas. Only a pair of red boxer shorts, which were currently riding low on his belly, exposing an arrow of dark hair that pointed the way to—

Out of bounds.

'Zak, good morning,' she said again, taking a sip from her mug.

His eyes flickered and she caught a glimpse of vulnerability in their sleepy depths. 'Abby,' he mumbled, his voice thick. Then he blinked twice as he registered her presence, the haze in his blue eyes sharpening. 'Something wrong?'

'No. Are you ready for a walk?'

His eyes slid shut. 'Something's very wrong. A walk. At this time of day. Or should I say night?'

'This is the *best* time of day. The grass looks like

emeralds, the air's as fresh as a song out here, and it's calling our names.'

'Maybe yours. I don't hear mine.' Eyes still closed, he rubbed his chest. 'Why can I smell blackberries?'

'I made tea for us. I find it's a good way to start the day with something warm and herbal.'

Although, with the unfamiliar scent of musky male in her nostrils, she could think of a warmer and more invigorating way than a tea tonic and a walk on the beach...

He muttered something short and terse and undoubtedly rude into his pillow.

'You didn't sleep well,' she told him. 'It might help.'

'Hmph.'

'Okay.' She set a mug on the veranda beside the couch. 'I'll let you get acquainted with the morning.'

Aborting her beach-walk plans, she grabbed a mat from the veranda, walked a short distance down the garden path and set it on a patch of damp grass and sat down facing him.

She wasn't letting Zak off the hook so easily. If she could just get him to take some time out, look at the world around him instead of working twenty-four-seven. She already had him pegged. If it wasn't the centre, it was his house, and he had a construction business chugging along somewhere. Something had turned him into a workaholic.

She reached for the sea-green crystal at her neck, closed her eyes and let her thoughts dissolve like clouds in a summer sky. Let impressions and sensations surround her as the morning sun caressed her eyelids with golden warmth.

Until languid turned to heat and tranquil turned to edginess, prickling her skin with goose bumps.

She opened her eyes and saw Zak glaring at her from the veranda, and every peaceful cell in her body jumped to attention. She hadn't heard him rise and change but he was wearing those itty-bitty shorts that showed off the long, powerful musculature of his legs and a navy T-shirt with the sleeves ripped out, baring equally impressive bulges.

She let herself indulge in the sight of that athletic body. To imagine gliding oil-slick palms over those strong lines. Her hands itched and a bolt of energy powered through her veins.

As she watched him step off the veranda, his eyes on her with single-minded purpose, she wondered if she'd made the right decision in waking him up. Perhaps she should have left him to his dreams. Or his demons, she thought, remembering the haunted look she'd seen in his eyes as he woke.

Then he stopped in front of her and she was glad she hadn't. Looking at Zak with the sun behind him like some sort of halo won hands down over any visualisation she could come up with.

She sifted her hands through the cool grass. 'Hi.'

'What happened to your walk?' Even with his face in shadow, she could see his frown.

'I changed my mind. I decided to meditate here and wait for you to wake up.'

'Aah, meditation.' He let the word slide out slowly between his lips. 'That mystical Eastern pastime.'

'There's nothing mystical about it. Just close your eyes and open your mind, listen to what the universe is telling you. Visualise.'

Except all she could visualise right now when she closed her eyes was Zak lying down beside her. The sun warming his skin to honey-brown as he dragged her against him. The grass's coolness a sharp contrast to the heat of his body on her. In her. She pressed her legs tighter together to ease the tingling. *Try harder.*

He sat down, out of arm's reach, obviously prepared to humour her. 'So what's the universe telling you today?'

'To focus on Good Vibrations and not let distractions get in the way.' *Like you.*

'Ever get mixed signals? Like someone else's messages instead of yours?' He tugged out a blade of grass, threaded it between his fingers.

'Sceptic,' she accused. 'Now you…' She shuffled the metre or so between them on her backside. 'You need to let go of a truckload of baggage.' And recognised his denial. The rolled eyes, the tensed jaw. 'Hey, it'll come— My guess is you're facing difficulties in your life right now.' And for whatever reason, he didn't feel inclined to share them with her.

He looked away, the sun's rays striking off the blue irises, then turned to her. The heat she saw there seared her own eyeballs. *Yeah, difficulties—you're sleeping in my spare room.* If he'd said it aloud, he couldn't have been clearer. He shook his head, looked away again. 'I'm fine.'

'If you say so.' She reached out to soothe his cheek. The pads of her fingers skimmed over the rough texture, sending instant sensation fizzing through her veins.

Before he could flinch or do his pulling-away trick, she dropped her hand, curled her fist around the tingles. 'If my being in your home is going to make your life more difficult, I'll leave. I'm paid up at the caravan park for a week.'

'No. You're staying until you're in a position to find other accommodation *as we agreed*; end of discussion.'

His words, clipped and hard and remote, chased away the warm fuzzies she'd been harbouring since she'd touched his face. 'Okay.'

'Okay.' He underscored her acquiescence, then pushed up without looking at her. 'Breakfast in ten minutes if we're going to make our appointment.'

CHAPTER SIX

ZAK leaned against the conference room's wall and watched the photographer snap a series of pictures, scowling as Carlo's long arty fingers skimmed Abby's neck while he adjusted her blouse, tilted her chin so that she was looking directly into the other man's eyes.

Carlo moved behind the camera. 'A little to the right, honey, and looking at the camera… Perfect.'

Zak's sentiments exactly. Abby's hair was caught in a neat upswept style that exposed her creamy neck, and her earlobes glinted with tiny gold hoops. In the navy suit and crisp white blouse, she looked the epitome of a successful businesswoman.

He mentally nodded his satisfaction with the image that would appear on his website, but his frown remained. A *smiling* businesswoman who looked as if she was enjoying the flirtation coming her way during office hours, and a little too much.

The fact that the man was obviously gay didn't soften Zak's mood any. Especially when Carlo murmured something to Abby that no one else heard and they both shared a laugh, heads almost touching. What was it that women found attractive about gay men?

And it was all going downhill from there.

Jorge, the male model Zak had chosen from the agency's files last week, was the kind of suave, good-looking blond with an ego as big as his chest measurement. The kind of guy women fell for, which, he reminded himself, was why he'd chosen him.

Before he'd met Abby.

Irritated with himself, he pushed off the wall. This was crazy, and not what this morning was all about. This morning's shoot was his opportunity to sell the centre to tourists and conference-goers, nothing more.

'Let's move on to the pool, shall we?' Carlo flapped a hand at the camera crew. 'Abby, darling, the black one-piece.'

Zak watched Abby make her way towards the door that led from the conference room. On a sudden impulse, he followed.

She caught sight of him in the mirrored lobby and turned on the staircase, her brows raised. 'Something wrong?'

He walked right up to her. Imagined burrowing into that sexy curve of neck to breathe in her alluring feminine scent. 'I just wanted to check that you're okay with this. I know you weren't enthusiastic with the idea.'

Her face relaxed, and the smile she gave him was pure sunshine. 'I'm fine.'

She lay her fingers on his arm, a habit of hers, he was beginning to realise, and not one she restricted to him. He'd seen her touch Carlo and Macho Man the same way.

'In fact, I'm kind of enjoying it,' she said with her little shoulder lift. 'It's fun, like playing at being someone else.'

Didn't she like being herself? he wondered. Was she un-happy with who she was? Then he remembered she'd come from a foster-home background, something he had no knowledge or understanding of. Her biological mother was dead; she had no knowledge of her sister's whereabouts.

'Was there anything else?' she asked, already on the third stair.

'Ah…you don't need help with anything, then?' He hadn't meant it the way it sounded, particularly as his gaze had been skimming over the curve of her bottom as he spoke. He struggled to block the image of slipping her jacket off for her and undoing the row of little white buttons down the front of her blouse…

She glanced back over her shoulder. 'I think I can find my own way into a bathing suit.'

Just as well, he thought as he walked away.

An hour later with the pool shoot out of the way, thank goodness—because watching Abby's wet body snuggled up to Jorge's had Zak's teeth on edge—they moved to the dining area to shoot the wine-and-dine scenes.

When Abby entered the room fifteen minutes later, Zak suddenly found it difficult to breathe. She wasn't wearing the red number he'd chosen, but an emerald-green dress that had caught her eye. It complemented her auburn hair, which was pinned up with a green comb.

But it was the tempting deep V zip that could slide all the way to her navel if she chose that had his attention. As she turned the hem teased the backs of her knees and the dip at the back had his hand itching to touch, to see if her skin was as smooth as it looked.

And the way her feet arched over those strappy gold sandals— He had a sudden vision of those stiletto-clad feet arched over his shoulders as she writhed in passion—

'Darling! You look stunning.' Carlo blew an air kiss in the flamboyant way he did everything and shook back the long hair that had dipped over his brow. 'And that colour is *so* you. Now, come and sit.'

Zak ran a tongue around dry lips as she seated herself at the little table. At least her legs were safely hidden behind the tablecloth.

Carlo fussed with the table setting and waved a hand. 'Curtains closed, please. And someone light the candle. Jorge, offer her the rose…'

The session continued before his eyes, but Zak's mind wandered. He could imagine taking her to dinner at some upmarket restaurant. Something outdoors or on top of a building overlooking the ocean where he could watch the evening breezes play with that delicate hairstyle, until it tumbled over her shoulders in an auburn tangle beneath his hand. Or where he could watch the moonlight reflect the silver in her eyes.

He wouldn't go with a rose. No, he'd give her a sunflower. He didn't know what yellow might mean in her colour-conscious mind, but for him, now, watching her, he'd say it symbolised light. Openness. Yes, honesty.

But her lifestyle, her personality, was at odds with his—the woman seemed to bend with the wind, whereas he liked things where he could see them, put his hands on them and understand them. She had a foster-mother, he came from a big family. Loving parents and three siblings; scattered all over the country, but when they got together it was as if they'd never been apart.

'…to the suite upstairs.'

Zak realised Abby had already gone to change for the romantic bedtime scene. He watched the camera crew, Carlo and Jorge head down the corridor, the flurry of noise and activity recede. And knew he couldn't do it. He couldn't watch Abby recline on that bed in nothing but a negligee, no matter how innocent or tastefully done.

The thought alone was enough to have the blood pumping fast and heavy through his veins. A restless primitive beat that he had no right to feel. Didn't *want* to feel.

No. Paperwork awaited his attention. Attention that he'd neglected over the past couple of days. He'd be better served to get it out of the way. Carlo had everything under control. He'd see the shots when he approved them before uploading them to the website.

While Abby slipped out of the cappuccino-coloured negligee and redressed in her own skirt and top, she wondered where Zak had been during the final photo shoot.

At the vanity she reached for cleanser and removed the unfamiliar heavy make-up she'd felt uncomfortable with all morning and reapplied her own moisturiser and a light lipstick. He'd been as distracted as she. His eyes, when they'd met hers, had wiped whatever she'd been thinking clean out of her mind. It had been all she could do to stay focused on Carlo's instructions.

First off she was going to track him down; she had no doubt he was still here somewhere. She'd tell him she'd finished the shoot, then she'd see if the shelves had arrived and do some setting up in the shop. Then she'd walk home—it was only a short distance—and familiarise herself with his place. Maybe do a bit of cleaning and prepare something for tea.

He'd given her a key. The strange feeling she'd had when he'd detached it from a ring in his kitchen drawer and met her eyes with a gaze that blew hot and cold rippled through her again. A look that said having a key to his house would be like living together and way too intimate. But necessary.

The sounds of a fussy baby reached her ears as she

knocked at the open door to a spacious office. A harassed-looking blonde was trying to juggle an infant in one arm and a pile of folders in the other.

'Hi. Sorry to bother you. I was looking for Zak.'

'Next office down.' She flashed a brief smile. 'I'm Tina, by the way.'

'Hi, Tina. So this must be Daniel. Zak told me about the christening. I'm Abby Seymour. I just took the vacant shop.'

'Ah-h-h.' Tina's smile cooled a few degrees. She dumped the files on her desk and switched the wriggling child to her other arm. 'The massage therapist. You turned up out of the blue and into the right place at the right time, didn't you?'

'I did.' Abby bit back the surprise and hurt at Tina's less than cordial welcome. 'And Zak's been more than kind.'

Tina's brown eyes pinned Abby's with a slow I've-got-your-measure perusal. 'Zak's a kind sort of a guy. The sort of guy people might try to take advantage of.'

'Zak strikes me as being far too astute to allow that to happen,' Abby countered.

At that moment Daniel rocked and squirmed, knocking the files Tina had placed on the desk to the floor.

'I've got them.' Abby picked up the paperwork. 'Looks like you've got your hands full.'

'The baby-sitter cancelled at the last minute.' Tina's harried exhalation blew at her bangs as Daniel began wailing. 'I promised I'd have this mess sorted by the end of the day.'

'Let me take him a moment,' Abby offered, tapping her hands gently in Danny's face. 'I love babies, especially ones as cute as this.' Danny quieted, stilled, eyeing Abby with fascination. 'What is he—seven months?'

'Eight.'

'He's probably teething.' Abby stroked the red splotch on his cheek. 'Poor baby. Come to Abby?'

'I'm… Yes, he is.' Tina hesitated, then handed him over somewhat reluctantly. 'Just for a moment, then, while I re-sort this mess.'

Abby set the child on her hip, offering him the teething ring pinned to his bib, but he was more interested in her hair. 'I could take him for a stroll around the centre, give you a break.'

'No.' Tina stopped midway to the filing cabinet. Then nodded, and her swift refusal was tempered with a softer, 'He's not used to strangers.'

'We'll just go to Zak's office,' Abby assured her. 'See if he's there and be right back. How does that sound, Danny? Want to see Uncle Zak?'

'Well, that's a first,' Tina remarked thoughtfully. 'I've never seen him go to someone he doesn't know so readily.' She nodded. 'O-kay. He's right next door.'

Abby found Zak's door open but the man himself was nowhere to be seen. His computer's screensaver scrolled through tropical images. A full mug of coffee steamed be-side the mouse, his reading glasses lay on a folder. So he hadn't gone far and intended returning.

Or maybe not, if he'd heard her talking to Tina. 'What do you think? Is he trying to avoid me?' she asked Danny. Her heart melted when Danny tugged at a strand of her hair and responded with a salivary grin that showed off three stubby teeth.

With Tina's maternal concern in mind, she returned to her office. 'Here we are, all safe and sound.'

Some of the tension eased out of Tina's face and the hint of a smile tipped a corner of her mouth. 'Thanks.'

'No problem.' Abby pulled out her mobile with her free hand, thumbed in Zak's number.

'Forrester.'

'Good afternoon to you, too,' she replied sweetly, smiling at Danny. 'With a bark like that, should I be afraid of your bite?'

In the ensuing silence the ether hummed with all kinds of erotic possibilities; she could almost see him closing his eyes and rubbing the bridge of his nose as he was wont to do when he was harassed.

'Very afraid,' he said finally. 'What can I do for you, Abby?'

'You didn't view the final shots.'

'I've been tied up with the electrician.'

'Sounds kinky.' She glanced at Tina who was hunkered at the bottom drawer of her filing cabinet, ears flapping. 'Is that why there's a hot coffee on your desk going cold?'

Another silence, then a resigned, 'You've got me there.'

She had to smile. 'And *I've* got a little boy *here* who thinks his godfather works too much and needs a break. Right, Tina?' she said, and saw her nod in agreement. 'Perhaps you'd like to help his busy mother out and take me and Danny off her hands for a while—that is, if you're in the vicinity…?'

She disconnected, cast a conspiratorial grin at Tina. 'He'll be along.'

'That'd be great. For me *and* for Zak. Thank you.'

'No problem.'

'Be assured I'll be one of your first customers,' Tina told Abby as Zak relieved her of his hefty godson five minutes later. 'My back could do with some pampering.'

'The first session's on me,' she said, pleased to have won over Tina at least.

Now, if she could just get Zak to trust her… Her gaze swung to the man in question, juggling the child against his white business shirt as if the little guy belonged there.

And something inside her went ping. If ever there was a picture that warmed her heart it was a man prepared to let himself be strangled by his own expensive silk tie with the saliva-wet fingers of an eight-month-old...

'Daniel and I need fresh air and ice cream,' she told him, and cleared a sudden lump from her throat. 'A little ice cream's okay, isn't it, Tina?' Her eyes were still locked on the domestic sight before her.

'He loves it,' she heard Tina say.

'So let's go.' Abby slipped a hand in the crook of Zak's elbow and tugged him towards the door.

Zak felt as if he were skating on thin ice and wondered how he'd got himself into this unsettling situation: a baby and a woman on his arm, neither of whom belonged to him.

'Let's try that place on the corner with the yellow beach umbrellas,' Abby suggested as they exited into the afternoon sunshine.

He nodded, wishing the sensation of Abby's arm in his didn't feel so damn good. He couldn't shrug her off—by her own admission she was a physical person—she didn't mean anything by it.

They must look like any other family out for a stroll. It was the oddest feeling and one not to be probed too deeply because the wounds still bled. His wife was dead, pronounced guilty by him before she could prove her innocence. By his own actions he'd cheated himself of fatherhood.

He was never committing to a woman again, which meant no kids. Ever. His choice, he reminded himself, but the knowledge wrenched soul-deep.

'Stop. Right. Here.' Abby swung in front of him. 'You were supposed to leave your problems at the office. For the next thirty minutes it's time out. Agreed?'

He looked at her eyes, pleading and demanding at the same time, and felt his resolve slip a notch. He was quickly discovering it was her nature to care about others. And this afternoon wasn't about him. She was giving Tina a break, the least he could do was support her... He tried a grin, and found it easier than he'd thought. 'I'm thinking a triple chocolate-chip sundae.'

Her smile was pure summer. 'Vanilla for me. Your shout.'

They found a table outside beneath one of those umbrellas. Abby relieved him of Daniel, setting him on her lap, playing pat-a-cake and cooing maternally as if she was born to the role.

When their order came, she fed Daniel tiny spoonfuls of her vanilla scoop, gently rubbing the cold along his gums, letting his sticky fingers play with her hair, seemingly unconcerned that he was staining her top. The antithesis of Diane, who had hated mess and avoided babies. He found the change refreshing. Endearing. Was he falling for this woman? He shook the thought away and concentrated on his sundae.

Daniel nodded off against her breast. It made Zak wonder how it would feel to rest his own head on that gentle slope and twine those auburn curls around his hand. Watching Abby eat ice cream was almost a more sensuous experience than the treat itself. The way she slid the spoon between her lips, almost closing her eyes in bliss with each mouthful.

'You're an ice-cream junkie,' he said.

'I prefer *devotee*.' Her tongue darted out to lick her lips and she grinned. 'How can you tell?'

'I recognise the symptoms. Or, if you prefer, the traits. I must admit to being guilty of the same myself.'

'One of life's more pleasurable indulgences.' Smiling, she scooped up a parfait-size spoonful, held it to his mouth. 'Swap you.'

He took the spoon between his lips—the spoon straight from her mouth—watching awareness sharpen her eyes as they locked gazes.

'My turn,' she said.

Scant millimetres from her lips, Daniel woke from his brief hiatus, decided he wanted in on the action and batted the spoon Zak was holding out with a fist, toppling the confection onto the front of Abby's neck.

'Here.' Grabbing a paper napkin, he swabbed the chocolate smear. *I could lick it off.* He immediately pulled away, offered Abby the napkin. 'Stick to vanilla, mate,' he told Daniel, glad to have somewhere else to focus his gaze. 'It's colourless. More or less. Sorry, Abby, your top's a mess.'

'It'll wash,' she said. She didn't seem bothered. 'We'd better be going—someone needs a nappy change.'

Five minutes later Zak handed Daniel over to his grateful mum, then walked Abby to the lobby. 'Thanks. Tina appreciates it, and so do I.' He glanced at the stained top—but not too closely. 'Sorry about the mess.'

'It doesn't matter. I had fun.' She smiled that summer smile but didn't touch him.

He felt oddly disappointed. 'So did I,' he said. And realised he meant it.

'I'll see you at home, then.'

Her casual words, the farewell flip of her hand— He felt his muscles tense. Something only a wife or lover would say.

'I'll be late,' he said around the cramp in his gut. He turned abruptly and hurried to the sanctuary of his office.

'Where are you, Zak?' *And what business is it of yours, Abby?* She covered the bowl of dinner she'd put aside for him and slid it in the fridge. Just because she had a room here didn't give her the right to question where he was. He'd said he'd be late, but she hadn't thought he meant *this* late.

She'd cleaned what she could of the kitchen, attempted to sort the mess on the table, then, using what ingredients were to hand, she'd cooked up a batch of chilli con carne and prepared a tossed salad. It was now eleven o'clock. Time to go to bed and *not* think about where he was.

She slipped into her sleep shirt, lay down and stared at the night sky through the open window. This afternoon he'd been so approachable, so smiley, she'd glimpsed another side of him.

Until she'd ruined it when she'd said she'd see him at home. Too intimate. Too fast. Something had happened to him in his past. A woman; she'd bet on it.

Zak set a fast pace along the beach. White fingers of surf curled against the indigo sea, stretching out into the distance along the coastline. Since Diane had died, he often walked here nights to take in the changing moods of the sea and seek the absolution he craved, but tonight he barely noticed the way the moonlight rippled on the water, the ceaseless soughing of the waves on the shore.

Abby had somehow got under his skin; she knew how to make him itch and he had no idea how to relieve it. *Yes. You do,* an inner voice said. Shaking his head, he began jogging, trying to erase the images of a mermaid-like creature who'd danced on this sand a couple of evenings ago.

His bare feet welcomed the cold as the incoming tide washed over his ankles. He was almost tempted to strip off his too-tight trousers and cool his entire body's restless heat in the sea.

But to do that would mean facing his demons and letting the water do its work. His pulse spiked and his heart clenched at the thought. He could almost feel it strangling him, the burst of pain in his ears as he plunged after the doomed car and sank, his instinctive action consigning him to a watery death.

Fighting off the panic that always accompanied the images and clawed without mercy up his throat, he veered from the water's edge towards the softer sand dunes. Dragged in salty air. *Breathe, two, three.* He was alive.

Alive and alone.

And horny as hell.

He pushed on, feeling the sweat trickle over his brow and down his back. He'd never considered himself a man who avoided uncomfortable situations, but he was doing a damn good job of it tonight. The glow of his guest bedroom's light and knowing Abby was there had been enough to slam his car in Reverse and speed back down the road and away from temptation.

But he didn't want her to feel she was intruding or not welcome. She'd lived with foster-families, for heaven's sake. He wanted her to feel his place was relaxed enough that she could call it 'home.' For the time she'd be there.

Except it wasn't a home, was it? A home, by Zak's definition, included laughter, kids, pets. Love. It meant sharing—not simply taking turns in the bathroom and dividing chores. It was opening yourself up to another person, taking the good times with the bad.

He stopped, hands on his knees, to catch his breath and his runaway thoughts. Was he confusing a home with love? Or did the two go hand in hand?

Either way, it wasn't going to happen. Not again.

CHAPTER SEVEN

NEARLY midnight. Abby would be asleep now. Zak breathed a sigh of relief as he parked and looked up at the darkened windows. This was what he wanted, right? To come home to some semblance of solitude?

But she'd left the front porch light on. A 'welcome home' sign.

The fact that she'd thought of it niggled at him as he unlocked the back door and quietly let himself inside. A spicy aroma hung in the air. He followed it to the kitchen, switched on the light and stopped in surprise—the neat-as-a-pin kitchen.

Further inspection revealed the source of the aroma in the fridge. She'd also cooked for him. Bought a bottle of pink champagne, he noted, even though she couldn't afford it. He glanced at the outdoor table and now he noticed the cutlery setting and wineglass reflected in the kitchen's light. She'd probably waited to eat with him, too.

Guilt twitched between his shoulder blades. He'd paid her consideration back by avoiding her. Being the perceptive woman she was, he had little doubt she'd recognise it, making him feel twice the idiot he was.

He reached for a beer as he shut the fridge. Twisted the

top off and chugged half the liquid down. They were going to have to set some ground rules. Simple gestures like
the security light were fine. Probably. Maybe. Anything
that smacked remotely of a couple—wine, dual table
settings—was not.

He yanked out a chair and sat, scowling at his beer bottle as he twisted it round and round in his hands. Who said
she'd been thinking 'couple'? Probably cooked for herself
and had leftovers. Ditto the wine. It was *him* thinking 'couple'. Imagining 'couple'.

Abby stood at the kitchen door, pushed the hair from her
face as she watched Zak frowning at his bottle. His absolute aloneness tugged at her. 'I didn't know you were
home.' His head whipped around, then back to his bottle,
and she watched his jaw bunch as she padded further into
the room. The new slate tiles felt cold beneath her feet, a
stark contrast to the heat blossoming in her cheeks. She
knew she looked sleep-mussed. Knew he'd noticed. 'Or
can't you sleep?' she asked.

He slid another long look her way, then took a pull at
the bottle he was torturing. 'Haven't tried.'

Her heart did a flip as she visualised placing her
masseuse's hands on the tense set of his shoulders. Oh,
he'd feel good. Hard and warm. She'd slide her fingers up
his neck, into his hair, feel its texture, breathe its scent
while her fingertips massaged circles over his scalp and
absorbed the day's stresses. 'It's been a long day for you.'

'It's not over yet.'

His eyes met hers, deep pools of promise, and her heart
did another of those amazing, unsettling flips, but she
blinked and those pools could have been made of glacier ice.

'I've still got some work to do.'

'Surely you could take a break? It's late.'

'I promised myself I'd work at least an hour a day on the house, no matter what.' He tilted his bottle in the direction of the living room. 'And we need somewhere to relax other than the kitchen.'

Or the bedroom. She could feel his rejection, his discomfort from halfway across the room. If she'd tried to act out her massage fantasy, he'd have resisted. The man was an island.

'You made dinner,' he said gruffly. 'I grabbed a burger, I should've let you know. Perhaps it'd be easier if you just cooked for yourself.'

She started to agree, then stopped. No, she wasn't letting him off that easily. 'It *is* easy, Zak,' she said, meeting his eyes. 'All it takes is a phone call.'

She walked back to her bedroom, closed the door. And made a decision. She stripped off her sleep shirt. If he was going to be an idiot and work till he dropped, she was going to be there to catch him.

He was squatting in the middle of the living room mixing paint when she strolled in two minutes later, in shorts and T-shirt chewing on an apple.

His eyes flared when he saw her and his hand stopped mid-stir. 'What are you doing?'

'I'm here to help. Want a bite?'

Ignoring the proffered apple, he shook his head, resumed stirring. 'Go back to bed, Abby.'

She stood over him, chewed a few moments, watching the way the muscles in his forearm moved. The way his T-shirt stretched taut over his back and didn't quite meet the dip in the centre of his shorts, leaving a tantalising wedge of skin…

'Aren't you going to strip first? The rest of the wallpaper,' she added, indicating with her apple when his eyes flickered up at her beneath lowered brows.

'Yes.'

'So why are you mixing the paint?'

He closed his eyes briefly. 'I want to try a patch to make sure the colour's right.' Carefully placing the rod he'd been stirring with on newspaper, he stood, the can of paint in his hand. 'Why can't you do as I ask and go to bed?'

'I'm obstinate, too, when necessary. Let me give you a hand stripping. Just tell me how.'

She hadn't meant it the way it sounded. Really, she hadn't. Until the can he was holding tilted as he stared at her, dribbling paint over his hand.

'I meant…the wall—'

'I know what you—' He tripped on the rod, splattering paint on his feet. 'Damnation!'

She bit her lip. 'Oops.'

He set the paint on the floor. Rubbed a paint-smeared finger between his brows. 'Okay. I'll finish the wallpaper; it needs the ladder. You paint.'

While he hunted up rags to deal with the mess and studiously avoided looking anywhere near her, she found a brush and got started.

They worked in silence for a few minutes, until Abby said, 'Are you going to use a darker shade for the window frames?'

He paused to look at her paint pot, blew out a breath. 'That *is* the shade for the window frames.' He descended the ladder as he said, 'It's a smaller can, see? The paint for the walls is the other one. And you use a roller on the wall, not a brush.'

'Oh.' She shrugged, dipped her brush in the can. 'If you'd

taken a look around instead of focusing on what's in front of your nose and nothing else, you might have noticed.'

'I think… What are you doing?'

'It's called having fun, Zak.' She finished painting her name in large curly letters on the wall, then painted her palm ready for the final touch.

And changed her mind as she felt the heat of a solid masculine presence right behind her. Instead, she turned, planting her hand in the centre of his chest and smiled up at his incredulous expression.

No response. Nothing but silence in the sultry evening air that seemed to have engulfed them. Impossible to tell whether he was angry or amused in the depths of those smoke-dark eyes.

Her smile widened. 'Guess I owe you a T-shirt.'

Wordlessly, he took the brush and can from her hands. Set them firmly on the floor. 'You push a man too far…'

'Question is, how far?' He smelled of sweat and beer, his paint-smeared brow endearingly amusing. Keeping her eyes on his, she inched the fabric of his T-shirt upward, felt a spasm in unyielding muscle beneath her hand.

'…you're going to get burned,' he finished, though it was his voice that sounded singed. Like charred paper.

She watched his eyes turn a smoky blue, saw a single bead of sweat track down his forehead to disappear into his eyebrows. Was it her imagination or was he leaning closer?

One arm came up to rest beside her head, until all she could see was that incendiary blue gaze, all she could feel was his body heat grazing the front of her body.

'I love hot,' she said, and noticed her voice had dropped a notch. 'Chilli pepper. Saunas. Lying naked in front of an open fire till your—'

His mouth crashed down on hers. Fast, scorching. No

patience, no tenderness, just one touch and a fevered need that flared to instant life between them.

Oh, yes. Her blood turned to syrup and her body sagged against the wall. She'd known he'd taste like this. Potent, powerful and hungry as he meshed those luscious lips with hers, carnal pleasure that left her dizzy.

Deeper. She moaned into his mouth, willing more as his lips pried hers apart and demanded entry. His tongue was quick and clever, with dark desire and dangerous delights. Desire for *her*.

The universe shifted, stars collided.

The woman inside her instinctively leaned closer, her pelvis brushing against hard masculine arousal, her fingers twisting in the soft folds of his T-shirt.

His hands slid down, over her waist, to cup her bottom and pull her closer, then immediately rose again to fan out over her ribcage, just below her breasts. Her mind emptied of everything except Zak and how good he felt. How good *she* felt. How good they felt together.

Then his fingers were clenching against her, his body rigid with the strain, his breathing harsh as he lifted his head. Shock darkened his eyes, furrowed his brow, as if he couldn't quite comprehend what had happened.

Hell. Abruptly Zak stepped back, cursing the mind pictures Abby had painted that had pushed him to the edge. Over the edge, he admitted, appalled.

'Why did you stop?'

Her breathless words had him cursing anew. 'One of us had to,' he rasped.

'Why? You liked it. I liked it.'

He took in her glazed eyes, the lush temptation of her mouth still damp from his, the rapid rise and fall of her breasts. Oh, yeah, he liked. Too much. He wanted to do it all over again, and more. To strip away those clothes and fill his hands with that soft female flesh. To lose himself inside that body and forget the pain of the past year.

But it wouldn't be fair. He would *not* use her to drown out the past or for his own lust. 'Believe me, we'd be wrong for each other.' He turned away and swiped up the brush she'd been using. 'I'll say it again: go to bed, Abby. I don't have time for distractions.'

All he could hear in the silence that followed was the sound of the sea matching his body's restless response. A tense silence. Enough time and silence to realise his words had offended, had hurt.

'You're right,' he heard her say at last. 'Workaholics aren't my type.'

Hurt or humiliation—perhaps both—trembled ever so slightly in her voice as she walked out, shutting the door behind her.

His fingers tightened on the brush, then he tossed it on the newspaper as he bent down to slam the lid on the paint tin. Dark emotion tortured him. If Diane had lived, if he knew the truth now about what had been going on behind his back—*or not*—maybe things could have been different between him and Abby.

Maybe.

He sat down on the trestle, resting his forearms on his knees, then remembered he'd not returned a message from Nick earlier in the evening. Probably to see if he'd lined up a date for the wedding yet. Zak could almost hear the conversation…

'Problem?' Nick would ask.

'Could be.'

'Does it have anything to do with a certain auburn-

haired massage therapist who's great with kids and has you
awake at night thinking crazy thoughts?'

Bingo.

'So again, what's the problem? Ask her. It's been over
a year, Zak. An evening with an attractive woman…We
know you and Di had a great marriage. She'd have wanted
you to get out there again, be happy…'

Zak shuddered. Nick didn't know squat about Zak's
marriage. No, he decided, as he dragged his soul-weary
self off the trestle and headed for his room. He was going
to the wedding alone.

The three hours' sleep Zak had managed hadn't improved
his mood any. He pulled out the makings for breakfast.
Abby's sense of fun had been… Okay, he admitted, it
would have been fun…with a guy who appreciated it.
Someone who could give as good as he got.

Once upon a time that man might have been him.

He slapped a pack of bacon on the bench. Yes, he was
attracted to her spontaneity. Her open, caring nature.

The way she kissed.

A bolt of heat shot through his body. Oh, yeah, the sensation of her mouth against his—satin and sun. He
cracked four eggs into a bowl. Scrambled, he decided,
pulling out the whisk. Very scrambled. *Don't think.*
Thoughts were dangerous. He might be tempted to be that
fun guy again.

He glanced up at the ceiling. Hell, did he even remember how? One thing was damn certain: Abby didn't deserve
his shabby dismissal.

He was sliding bacon onto the eggs when Abby appeared at the kitchen door in a fanciful lavender dress with
sparkly bits on the bodice and hem and white knitted

bolero. She looked fresh. Refreshed. How did she manage that on three hours' sleep?

'Good morning,' she said, as if they hadn't kissed each other senseless a few hours earlier.

'Good morning. You want breakfast?'

She nodded. 'Only if you have enough.'

'Coffee? Or would you prefer your witch's brew?'

'Coffee's fine.'

He caught two slices of toast as they popped up. 'Toast?'

'Please.'

The only sounds were the scratch of metal on toast as he buttered them and cut them into triangles. He flicked a switch and filled the silence with cheery breakfast radio, then carried the plates to the veranda.

Abby followed with the coffee. 'I've been thinking,' she said, sitting opposite him and pouring two mugs. She pushed his mug towards him and her gaze was bright and sure. 'And I've decided to focus on practicalities. Right now I need customers on my massage mat more than I need your problems with intimacy.'

His bite of toast lodged behind his Adam's apple. She always saw right through him, but this time she wasn't trying to fix it. He cleared his throat. 'About last night—'

'No.' She shook her head as she cut him off. 'We do not want to talk about last night. I'm going to the shop soon to finish setting up and I don't need the added stress.' Cool and firm and distant.

Understandably so. 'It's Sunday,' he said. She'd told him she was going to spend the day relaxing before opening her shop on Monday. 'And you're not dressed for work.'

She forked up some egg. 'You're a seven-day-a-week

guy, aren't you? And my choice of clothing's none of your concern.'

Her words were clipped, and deep in her soft grey eyes he saw an uncharacteristic melancholy that wrenched at his heart. This morning she wasn't the Abby he'd come to know, and he wanted the old Abby back. 'I'm going to the Numinbah Valley this morning,' he said. 'I'm doing a quote for Forrester Building Restorations. Come with me.'

The words were out before he could call them back. Someone on the radio was singing about being accidentally in love. He gulped down coffee. 'It's okay, you're busy—'

'How far is it?' She picked up a slice of crisp bacon in her fingers and nibbled.

'An easy drive, less than an hour. You'll still have time to do whatever you need this afternoon.'

'In that case, thank you, I'd like to come.'

'It's called "the green behind the gold",' Zak told Abby as they drove into the hinterland west of Surfers Paradise.

Abby could see why. They stopped near Tamborine Mountain's golf course to admire the view. Lush green slopes swept down to the clump of high rises in the distance and the misty Pacific Ocean beyond.

She kept her distance from Zak, kept their conversation light and *not* flirty. Whenever she raised a hand to touch his arm, whenever she was tempted to lean closer, she withdrew. His words came back at her. *We'd be wrong for each other*.

They stopped in a little town and while Zak met with the owner of a small café about some renovations Abby wandered the tourist shops—art galleries, crafts and antiques, souvenirs.

The gentle tinkle of wind chimes and the scent of

incense drew her to a New Age shop. From behind the counter, a woman in a sleeveless gown of crushed white velvet assessed Abby and, obviously recognising a kindred spirit, smiled and pointed to a sign in the window. Readings by Destiny. Sundays 10-4. 'Can I do a reading for you?'

'Oh…' She was so tempted. 'Not today. Thanks, Destiny, I'm waiting for someone.'

'Some crystals, then?' She drew Abby's attention to a multicoloured display.

'They're lovely. I'm afraid I can't afford them.' But she held up a pale amethyst on a silver chain. It didn't cost anything to look.

'Thought I'd find you here.'

Caught unawares by the familiar voice, Abby looked up to see Zak in the middle of the shop, framed by Native-American dream-catchers. She'd seen him less than half an hour ago; there was nothing different about him now. But, oh, her heart spun a giddy circle. Her fanciful Piscean nature spun impossible dreams.

She was falling in love with him.

Falling in love with a man who didn't want love.

'Your man.' She heard the smile in Destiny's voice but it seemed to be coming from a long way away.

'Ah…no,' Abby said, looking away, suddenly unable to hold his gaze. She would *not* let him see what Destiny already knew.

'It's not a question, it's an observation. She likes this amethyst.' Destiny handed Zak the chain. 'Not her birth-stone, but it matches her dress.'

'It does,' Zak agreed.

'Try it on—see how it looks.'

'No.' Abby stepped back, unusually flustered. 'It was just a whim…'

But Zak was already stepping closer. Almost as close as last night. She could smell him. Familiar, enticing. Exciting. He was lifting her hair, sliding warm fingers around her neck to fasten the clasp.

So close that now she had nowhere else to look. But she refused to notice the way his eyes caught the light. Or the way that very clever mouth curved a little at the corners, not even when his dimples came out of hiding for a brief moment.

'Whimsical looks good on you.' The pads of his thumbs soothed the pulse in her neck that was fluttering like the wind chimes in the doorway. 'Whimsical *is* you. We'll take it,' he told Destiny without breaking eye contact. He pressed a thumb against Abby's lips when she would have refused and said, 'Let me, okay?'

'You sure I can't do a reading for you two?' Destiny said. 'I could do you together; two for the price of one.'

'No, thanks,' Zak answered for them both. 'Not today.' He straightened up, drew out his wallet. 'It's time for lunch.'

As if Abby felt like eating now. But she let him escort her to a little outdoor café while they listened to cicadas and soaked sunshine into their skin.

At least it gave her time to settle and decide that her epiphany wasn't going to change their relationship. The glass of wine helped, and the knowledge that tomorrow she'd be too busy to think about it.

'If you don't mind, I'll just finish up that quote…' He produced his laptop from his briefcase.

'I do mind, as a matter of fact.'

Her dress and the crystal glared back at her in his glasses but his lips curved. 'Two minutes. Your nose and shoulders are turning pink.' He leaned down, produced a bottle of sunscreen and set it on the table.

She lifted her brows in surprise as she looked at his sun-kissed neck. His bronzed skin was used to the climate. He'd packed it with her fair complexion in mind.

So let him mind a little more. She uncapped the bottle, rubbed some into her nose and cheeks. 'I can manage my nose. I can probably do my shoulders, too, but I'm going to interrupt you.' She held the bottle over his keyboard. 'You're too work-oriented.'

'A second business, house to renovate.' But he took the bottle from her hand and squeezed a dollop onto his fingertips. 'Turn around.'

She did as he asked, lifting her hair from her nape. And sucked in a breath at the first contact of cold lotion and warm fingers. Ignoring the fact that it was Zak's fingers, and that they were doing crazy things to her libido, she kept her attention on the conversation. 'Agreed, but I have an off switch. Are the rest of your family workaholics?'

'Dad was until he was forced to retire due to ill health. He built Forrester Building Restorations from scratch.'

'And you took over.'

'My brothers didn't want a bar of it—they moved to Sydney, which left me. I couldn't let Dad's life's work be all for nothing.'

'Family's important,' she agreed.

He recapped the bottle, slid it back in his bag, ditto his laptop. 'Was your foster-mother in business, too?'

'You may have heard of Aurora. She had an astrology column in the daily newspaper and regular segments on TV shows. But she guards her privacy. My foster-father had his own remedial-massage business.'

'The reason you got involved in massage therapy?'

'Yes. His dedication inspired me. I did courses, worked as his assistant. He died of a heart attack some years back.'

'I'm sorry,' he said. 'What about your sister? Don't you want to find her?'

'Of course, more than anything. But it takes money, and after all these years…' she shook her head as the age-old loss wrapped around her heart '…I don't think it's even possible.'

'Your foster-mother won't help?'

Abby stiffened at the unintentional slur. 'She would, without hesitation, but I wouldn't expect her to. So I've never told her about wanting to find my roots. I made a promise to myself never to ask for monetary assistance. I stand or fall on my own two feet. Always.'

'What's your sister's name?' His voice was low and tender and it made her ache.

'Hayley.' She shrugged. 'Who knows what name she goes by now? When Good Vibrations is making millions I'll find her.'

'Speaking of Good Vibes, do you have everything you need for the big opening tomorrow?'

Abby nodded. 'Tina's in for a session tomorrow morning. And I have a couple of bookings for the afternoon. Tina says she needs some relaxation therapy before the wedding preparations start.'

He seemed surprised she knew and hesitated before saying, 'Yes, it's getting hectic. The wedding's weekend after next.'

'She tells me it's on a private island north of here.'

'That's right.'

'You're going, of course.'

'Yes.' He reached for his beer, avoiding eye contact.

'Good. That's good,' she said, when what she really wanted to know was if he was taking a Friend. She concentrated on keeping her expression casual and not thinking about Zak with a woman. 'You need a break.' Her voice sounded a bit high, a bit brittle.

His eyes followed a young couple enjoying one of Tamborine Mountain's carriage joy rides. 'Unfortunate timing with the centre just getting started, but it's only overnight.'

'Yes. Overnight.' She decided now was as good a time as any to say, 'I hope you won't mind, but Tina's invited me to the wedding, too.'

CHAPTER EIGHT

IN the run up to the wedding Zak was busy with renovations. He finished the second bathroom for Abby's use, and the living room looked comfortable with the new furniture and wide-screen TV. One day he might even have time to turn it on.

At Tina's invitation, Abby was going to the wedding. Abby's explanation was that there'd been a last-minute cancellation—but Abby didn't know it was his decision not to bring a partner that had resulted in the vacancy.

One of life's little ironies.

Even though he hadn't seen as much of Abby since that night in the living room when he'd all but lost control, reminders were never far away. If she wasn't steaming up his bathroom with enticing feminine scents or concocting delicious-smelling dishes in his kitchen, it was her multi-hued and very brief undergarments drying on the line.

She'd packed a picnic tea complete with candles one evening and they'd eaten it on the beach. He simply hadn't had the heart to say no. On another occasion she'd somehow secured his help applying *rainbow icing*, for heaven's sake, to a batch of chocolate-chip cookies for the office staff.

Since the painting incident, she hadn't pushed him towards anything intimate, but nonetheless something bordering on intimacy came out of their short times together. He felt…connected, in a way he'd never experienced before.

Abby was so different from any other woman he knew. And she seemed to know him, often better than he knew himself. Sometimes when she looked at him with those silver eyes he wanted to lash out at what had gone so horribly wrong with his marriage. He wanted to bury past hurts and mistakes and start over. With Abby.

But that was impossible.

He owed Diane. Some kind of self-sacrifice was her due, and his punishment.

Abby had made the journey to the island with the other guests, first by bus, then on the luxury yacht Nick and Tina had chartered with a scrumptious luncheon while on board. But Zak wasn't amongst them—he'd hired a helicopter to save time and was unloading his bag as they arrived.

Abby broke from the guests to meet him as he stepped from the floating helipad, the down-draught plucking at his hair as the helicopter rose, its blades chopping noisily through the air. His face was set in stern lines, his eyes hidden behind dark glasses. But she knew when he caught sight of her by the way the hairs on her arms lifted and her heart beat that little bit faster. She was practically out of breath when they met up.

The harsh expression softened. 'Good trip?' he asked.

'Wonderful. You?'

'Not bad.'

'Apparently we're going to be neighbours.' She waved to a clump of dwellings surrounded by palms near the water's edge that the wedding planner had indicated. 'We've got the villas closest to the beach, numbers eight and nine.' *Couldn't get much closer without sharing the same oxygen.*

And that thought must have registered in Zak's mind, too, because his smile dimmed a little. 'Better check it out, then.'

Since that kiss in the living room, she'd allowed Zak space while drawing him into simple activities and concentrating on Good Vibrations, which was starting to attract plenty of customers. He'd seemed happier, more at ease in their shared space, but tonight… She shook the thought away. They were here for a wedding, it wasn't a date.

The doors were unlocked and Abby took the first one. *Villa* was a relative term, she discovered. The little huts were constructed with wood and native palm. A panel opened to provide a window and let in air.

She swung her bag onto a simple bed. Mosquito netting suspended from the ceiling was draped to one side.

'If you need anything…' He nodded to a rattan-type door.

'Ah…the bathroom?'

'Afraid not. It's my room.' And he didn't look thrilled about it.

'You've been here before, then?'

He nodded once. 'The ablutions blocks are alongside the house. The island's not a regular tourist resort, and it only caters to twenty people, tops. The rest of the guests are sleeping on the launch tonight.'

'Okay.' Barely a screen separating them. And so small, so close, Abby had no doubt she'd hear him breathing, hear his body sliding over the sheets. If they had come as a couple…

But she told herself again, she was not Zak's wedding date. She was only here at Tina's invitation. She unzipped her bag. Its sharp rasping sound split the silence.

'I hope you'll have a good time while we're here,' Zak said. As stiff and formal as the suit he was about to put on.

'What about you? Are you going to let yourself enjoy a well-deserved break?' Frustrated at his non-reply, she turned away, pulled her slinky green dress out of her bag.

The one with the go-as-low-as-you-dare bodice.

'You're wearing that,' he said slowly into a sudden thick silence. She replayed Zak's reaction to seeing her in her emerald dress at the photo shoot. He'd looked as out of breath as she'd felt when she'd locked eyes with him across the room.

He looked that way again now. Only sterner.

'I am. Loosen up, Zak. It's only a dress.' *A dress designed to be taken off. Slowly. An inch at a time.* She slipped off her sandals, reached for the sparkly stilettos. Her anklet jangled as she stepped into them. 'Should I wear these, do you think? Are we going to be standing in sand?'

He looked down at her feet, his eyes flared a fraction as his gaze lingered on her ankles. 'I think there's a paved area…'

'If I fall, you'll catch me, right?' Her body heated at the memory of the last time she'd overturned an ankle—his hands on her as he'd lifted her to the trestle, the feel of his hard body against her breasts.

'I doubt it will come to that.' Clenching his bag, he crossed the room, wrenched the flimsy door open. 'Let me know when you're ready.'

Zak in a suit. Abby bit back the sigh when she opened her door later and saw him adjusting the cuffs while he waited on the path for her. Its dark fabric with accompanying white shirt accentuated his tanned skin as he watched the wedding party assemble.

'I'm ready.'

He turned at the sound of her voice. The setting sun behind him obscured his features and made him look like
some sort of divine haloed being.

'That dress… The colour suits you.' His face might be
in shadow, but she could feel the hot caress of those eyes
over the fabric. Feminine satisfaction slid through her; she
knew she'd wowed him. She was tempted to touch the zip
between her breasts to check it wasn't too revealing, but
decided it might draw his attention there and now wasn't
the time. Instead she fluffed her hair. She'd left it down
since Zak liked it that way.

He stepped towards her. 'Shall we join the others?'

When he offered his arm the gesture warmed Abby
from the inside out. Even though said arm was as tense as
twined wire across a suspension bridge. 'You mean, like
we're partners?'

He hesitated. 'If that's what you'd like.'

She smiled, encouraged, sure the blush of surprise and
happiness showed in her cheeks. Maybe, just maybe, her
attempts to draw Zak out of himself were starting to pay
off. 'I would.'

He nodded. 'Let's go, then.'

They might have been any two people out for a romantic
sunset stroll. She hugged his arm, her hand brushing
against the fabric of his suit as she inhaled his refreshed
cologne.

The last rays of the sun seemed to surround the bride
and groom and their loved ones. Crimson and orange
painted the clear sky and reflected on the water. Tina
looked radiant in an off-the-shoulder apricot organza gown
shimmering in the gentle breeze, her skin bronzed by the
sunset.

After the simple ceremony, a buffet dinner was served

on the veranda of the main house. The band played as Nick and Tina performed their own interpretation of the bridal waltz over the temporary dance floor. Soon other couples were joining in.

'You want to give it a try?' Abby asked as Zak watched the dancers with a beer bottle in his hand.

'Maybe later.'

Yeah. By the remote look in his eyes he meant much later. When the band packed up, more like. What had happened to the Zak who'd greeted her at the villa not more than two hours ago? 'Let me know if you change your mind.' Determined not to show her disappointment, she walked away to mingle with the other guests and perhaps drum up some business in the process.

Whenever Abby turned she found herself glancing at a familiar pair of blue eyes. More often than not they flicked away, but occasionally they lingered for heart-pounding seconds at a time, as if daring her. Or daring himself. It was like a game in itself.

This time, however, she could see him across the dance floor, grinning at something someone said, but his grin vanished as their gazes met and held, and something powerful seemed to open up between them. The rest of the guests seemed to melt away, leaving only the two of them and a shimmering pool of promise—

'Remember me?' interrupted a smooth, masculine, alcohol-imbued voice beside her.

Reluctantly, she dragged her attention away. 'You're Nick's cousin.' She forced a smile at the guy with poster-boy good looks, trying not to be annoyed at the interruption, trying to remember his name and trying to pinpoint exactly what it was she found disturbing about him.

'Vince.'

'Ah, yes.' She took a sip of her drink, cast a quick glance about, but Zak seemed to have disappeared. 'How's it going, Vince?'

'Couldn't be better.' His perfect smile gleamed as his somewhat glazed eyes travelled over her body. She could almost hear his brain cells figuring how long it would take to get the zip down and the garment off.

He tipped his beer bottle to his lips, took a long draught. 'How about a twirl on the dance floor?'

Abby was tempted, just for a minute, to see if it would coax Zak into some sort of action and enjoying himself a little, but the thought of letting Poster Boy get his hands on her changed her mind. 'What about your partner for the evening?'

For a beat out of time something dark lurked in the depths of his eyes, sending a shiver down Abby's spine, then it was gone and his mouth tilted in a lazy grin. 'I came alone. No attachments.' His bottle glinted in the lights as he raised it above his head. 'Live for the moment, I say.' He downed the remainder of his beer. 'So…what say we seize that moment?'

Without realising it, she'd stepped back. 'Thanks, but I promised Zak the first dance.'

'Zak?' He shook his head. 'Trouble with Forrester is he doesn't know how to have a good time.' He reached for Abby but she slipped away, her fingers clenched around the stem of her wineglass.

'Abby, ready for that dance?' Zak materialised beside her, and before she could react he pried the glass from her fingers, set it on a nearby table, then nodded to Poster Boy. 'Vince.'

With the lightest touch, he set a hand at the small of her back and steered her away from Vince towards the dance floor. Even though his fingertips were only a whisper against her silk dress, her heart danced to its own little steps. Those fingers might be barely touching but the *way* they touched… Protective, possessive. As if he were *jealous*?

Someone was lighting kerosene torches amongst the tables and the band switched to dreamy island music. The men had long since dispensed with jackets and ties and rolled up their sleeves.

Abby looked up and saw the flush rising up Zak's neck and slid a hand over one of his. 'Prove him wrong, Zak. Start enjoying yourself.'

Zak uncurled the hand enclosed in Abby's and rotated it so that their palms met and linked his fingers through hers. *Damn Vince.* No way was he letting him get his hands on Abby. Even if she wasn't Zak's partner. Even if he'd had no intention of dancing.

Abby leaned closer, so that her face was all he could see, so that he could smell the sweet pineapple meringue she'd been eating, and said, 'We can go for a walk along the beach instead if you'd rather.'

Oh, yeah, the possibilities *that* suggestion conjured… But, for now, he set his free hands on the satin-smooth curve of her waist. 'Who says we can't do both?'

He slid his hand behind her, working his way up her spine and under the silky tumble of fragrant hair. Wrong move. With a lurching sense of dread, he knew he'd been deceiving himself. It wasn't just the dance or the fact that he wanted to stake his claim for Vince's—or anyone else's—eyes. It was pure possessiveness.

He had no right to feel its burn, so he had no right to hold her close enough that their legs entwined and her breasts slid against his shirt. Close enough to see the steady pulse above the tempting line of her collarbone.

'It's working.' She nodded to where Vince was watching them with an arm slung round a brunette's shoulders, then turned her gaze to Zak.

And everything in his mind vanished. Falling into her silver eyes hadn't been his intention. The torchlight glowed on her skin, glistened on the tiny beads of perspiration dotting her brow. He'd been right: in her high heels she lined up against him perfectly.

Now the patter of island drums in the background echoed to the beat in his ears, the throb in his groin. Stepping back from the too-close contact, he wished there were a jukebox handy or an upbeat rock band so they could move together without the necessity of touching.

And Vince was still watching.

'Stay clear of Nick's cousin,' he advised. 'He's a serial womaniser.'

Abby's smile dimmed a little. 'It's a smokescreen.'

He choked back a short four-letter word. 'You don't know him.'

'I know him better than you think.' She shook her head, setting her long silver and emerald crystal earrings jangling, and the smile returned. 'And I can take care of myself.'

He reckoned she could, and immediately regretted spilling his thoughts and hoped he didn't sound like a jealous lover. He replaced his hands on Abby's waist, but resisted the instinctive urge to let them roam again.

'Mmm, that's nice.' She slid her arms up his chest and, closing the gap he'd created between them, hooked her arms around his neck and massaged little circles at the base of his skull with her fingers. As if she belonged there.

She was looking at him with such hope, her eyes seemed to say, *You're changing, and I like what I see.* He liked the changes, too. He liked the way she made him feel. Too much.

'I think Tina approves,' she whispered against his cheek.

He glanced about them. She was right, he noted with a scowl of annoyance at the subtle glances being cast their way. Worse, the increasingly obvious desire throbbing low in his body was threatening to become the next topic of conversation.

'So…' Smiling, she lifted a shoulder and shifted, so close all he could see was the glint of mischief in her eyes. 'Shall we give all the women something to really knock their stilettos off?'

He smiled back. Why, he had no idea; shock perhaps— because it wasn't remotely amusing, but damned if his body wasn't tensing up in anticipation.

'Relax…' Her hands slid to cup his jaw, smoothing a thumb over his dimple as her lips curved. Then she surprised the hell out of him by planting her mouth, not on his as he expected, but there, in the hollow on his left cheek. He felt its petal softness, the dab of moisture, the lingering pressure before she pulled back.

And all he could think was how her mouth would feel, how it would taste against his.

An extroverted voice cut across the music and out of the corner of his eye he caught sight of Vince as he twirled his partner, this time a long-legged blonde, onto the dance floor.

Zak didn't spare them a glance. His lips itched with wanting, Abby's scent seeped into every pore of his suddenly very hot, very hard body.

He leaned towards her and her lips met his halfway. Not the same tentative mouth that had grazed his cheek, but hotter, firmer, richer. And that same vibrant energy that always accompanied everything she did flowed from her kiss and into him.

A murmured groan rumbled from deep in his solar

plexus and rose up his throat. He didn't want to feel the heat, the tension, this excruciating awareness that twined like silken ropes around him, binding and confining... He reared back and found himself pinned by her gaze.

Then her lips were on his again and his mind shut down. He couldn't think of anything at all. All he was capable of was feeling. And it felt damned good.

Nothing had felt this good in a very long time.

He absorbed the sensations of warmth, understanding and intimacy, reawakening every dormant desire he'd ever had. Every fantasy he'd imagined about Abby since she'd stormed into his life.

She touched him with the assurance of a long-term lover, letting her hands roam over his face and shoulders, and he yielded to her gentle insistence and the soothing murmur in her throat, opening up and letting go.

Somewhere in the back of his mind his conscience hammered at him, reminding him that he was indulging in the moist warmth of her kiss, the satin smoothness of her skin, and warning him that this pleasure could only be temporary.

Temporary insanity, perhaps, because nothing should feel this right.

When he felt her pulling back he wanted to howl at the star-studded sky, *Not yet!* Tangling his hands in the fruit-fragrant tresses of her hair, he held her head still and deepened the kiss. She tasted sweet yet tart, like ripening apples, a temptation no man could resist.

He couldn't remember why he should. His hands moved to her ears to feel the cool silver jewellery against the warmth of her skin. To her jaw, the pulse in her neck beating beneath his fingertips. To cover her hands, which were moving and flexing against his chest.

His ears registered the change in tempo as the band

switched to some sort of fast salsa. Hot, like the woman pressed against him. Like the lava bubbles crackling through his veins.

Finally, as breathless as if he'd danced the salsa himself, he raised his head, shook it to check if the world had tilted or if it was just him. A giddy carousel of colour and movement gyrated about them, but all he saw was Abby. Her hair tangled around her face like errant flames—his handiwork—and her eyes blazed with the same wildfire.

She let out a deep unsteady breath. 'I think we've made our point. Hardly a stiletto in sight.' She laughed, sounding as out of breath as he.

True, he noted, most women had tossed away their shoes to dance barefoot. Abby's eyes, luminous in the orange glow, melted into his. 'So…what do you suggest now?'

Was it a trick of the flickering torchlight or the buzzing in his ears or was Abby imagining what he was imagining? Two naked and writhing bodies burning up the sheets on a single bed a scant fifty metres away.

'That walk you mentioned earlier.' Taking her hand, he headed away from the party and noise and heat, towards the cooler palm-shadowed path.

But despite his inner plea for the sake of self-preservation, the carnal, earthy image of the two of them continued to smoulder behind his eyes and smoke in his blood. The million-dollar question now was how was he going to keep his lips—and his hands—to himself for the rest of the evening?

Darkness hid a multitude of sins. He was grateful for it as he towed Abby along the path where the edge of the sand was dappled with starlight beneath leafy palms. The front of his trousers felt two sizes too tight; he needed the salty air near the ocean to cool off.

'Wait up,' a breathless voice gasped as they neared the villas.

He felt the tug on his hand. Only then did he realise he'd been so focused on his own predicament and how close he was to the edge of control that he hadn't spared Abby a glance. He came to an immediate halt. 'Sorry.'

'Shoes are rubbing,' she apologised, wrapping her hand around his forearm for balance while she rubbed her toes through the straps.

'Why didn't you take them off?'

'Pure vanity. I've never had such gorgeous sexy shoes and I wanted—'

'Well, take them off now. No one's here to see.'

Her eyes flicked to his. 'You are.' The velvet caress of her voice slid through him, but she leaned down and unstrapped them, slid them off. 'Trouble is I have very sensitive feet. Ticklish as hell and when someone touches my—'

'You're bleeding,' he said, cutting off any images involving her feet and touching before they could take shape in his mind while he frowned at the twin blood-stained blisters on her smallest toes.

'I'm fine.' She picked up her shoes, her voice turning to velvet again as she said, 'What I want to know is where to from here?'

'One thing's for sure, it's not walking on the sand—not with the state of those blisters.'

'No, it's not.'

And his body swelled and hardened with the knowledge.

She stepped in front of him, so close that he could feel her breath on his face. The air between them grew tense and heavy, throbbing in time with the distant band and his thickening pulse.

Her eyes were dark in the leafy dimness but wide and aware as they stroked down his body, over every hard and aching inch, and back to his. Eyes that saw too much, knew too much.

The shoes slipped from her fingers and landed with a thud, like the sound of a door closing. Or another opening… She set her palms against his chest, their heat searing him through the soft weave of his shirt as they travelled up to his shoulders. Then hotter, closer as they dipped beneath his open collar to gently knead and squeeze taut muscles.

'You're as hard as iron,' she murmured.

And he could tell by the awareness that burned in her eyes that she knew exactly how hard he was, and where.

'Let me help you, Zak.'

He inhaled sharply, only to drag in a lungful of her perfume.

Let her help?

Let her put those hands on his neck? His back? Or did she mean on other, more needy places? Was it only hands she meant? As the questions spun through his mind he struggled to contain the renewed tide of something akin to fear surging through him. He'd always prided himself on his control.

Dragging his gaze from her solemn eyes and the tempting sight of those full lips only a sigh away from his, he searched the horizon where a few sparse mainland lights glimmered like tiny jewels. And it occurred to him: over the water was his reality, but here…this island was a time-out. An oasis in the desert that was his emotional life right now. *Just for tonight…*

'Okay, forget I spoke.' Her hands slid away and he heard her resignation as she bent to retrieve her shoes.

Instantly the skin she'd touched turned cold and he wished he could call back the moment, recapture a fleeting fragment of that connection. A connection he knew they'd both felt, and acknowledged.

'Let's go back to the party, then,' he heard her say.

He waited until she straightened, then looked into her eyes and made his decision: *one night*. 'No.'

CHAPTER NINE

BLINKING, Abby did a double-take as she looked up into Zak's eyes. And one swift hard spike of adrenaline spurted along her veins. This was The Look. The look that said he was finally going to act on what had been building between them over the past weeks.

The bunching of muscles along his jaw, the almost imperceptible way his lips softened and parted as he drew in an unsteady breath. And, most telling of all, the hot, hot spark that glittered behind those heavy-lidded eyes.

One spark to turn her into a smouldering mass of need. It had been a long time since she'd experienced anything remotely intimate. Just standing within Zak's sphere of potent masculine energy, breathing in his musky, turned-on scent and sharing this amazing eye contact was more intimate than anything she'd shared with another man.

She'd caught glimmers of that look in his eyes before, but this time he didn't turn away. Her heart pounded in her ears, her whole body turned lethargic and fluid, and she wanted to lean against his body and melt into his skin.

He didn't give her time—ironic since he'd spent the past couple of weeks in slow motion—and, grabbing her hand, he strode along the path to their villas, her sore feet obviously forgotten. Seemed once he'd made up his mind there was no stopping him.

They reached her door first. It was unlocked and he pushed it open. The scents of hibiscus and rattan matting wafted out on the evening air. They stepped inside. The glow from the torches outside painted a gold patina over his skin, deepening the grooves in his face.

His breathing was laboured, his gaze harsh and unforgiving as he turned to look at her.

'Perhaps we need to…' She trailed off as his eyes opened and bored into hers, hot with conflicting emotions that, even with the people skills she prided herself on, she couldn't read. 'You have problems with intimacy. Whoever she was, she really laid one on you, didn't she?'

He flinched but didn't reply.

Her voice softened as she said, 'You don't have to do anything you don't feel ready for.'

His lips twisted in a flash of wry amusement at odds with the tortured eyes. 'Isn't that the guy's line?'

A laugh bubbled up. 'Anyone'd think you're a virgin.' She stared back at those eyes and the laughter died. 'You're not, are you?'

His smile eased the tension a fraction. 'No.'

She let out a quietly relieved breath and lit the lavender-scented candle she'd set by her bed to soothe her to sleep later. 'If you just want to talk about…whatever…we can do that.'

'Talk?' The rough sound that erupted from his throat had her turning. 'No, Abby, I don't want to talk.' He pushed the light-framed rattan door closed, leaned his head against it. His eyes flicked shut then opened almost immediately, his fingers fisting at his sides. 'Damn it.'

She saw the way his shoulders hunched, watched the

rise and fall of his chest as he took a deep breath. 'I'm sorry if I make you uncomfortable.'

'Too flaming right you make me uncomfortable.' He shot a disparaging glance downward then his eyes rocked back to hers. 'In too many ways to count. And here's the thing. All I can see when I shut my eyes is *you*.'

Abby caught the bouquet he'd tossed her, thorns and all. What she saw was a man in emotional turmoil.

'That's a backhanded compliment if ever I heard one. I'll try not to be offended.' She moved to the foot of the bed and unzipped her overnighter. 'Sit on the edge of the bed.'

She unearthed her bottle of body lotion from her toiletry bag. 'Oils are better, but this'll do for now.' When she turned, he hadn't moved from his spot by the door. She tilted the bottle towards him. 'A little relaxation therapy. Free of charge.' She felt her half-smile drop away and her own body tensed as she took in the state of his arousal, the way his eyes darkened to almost cobalt in the candlelight as she lifted her gaze to his. 'You'll sleep better.'

He made a guttural sound in his throat. 'Sleep?'

'Later,' she promised. *Much later.* She crossed the room to close the window's rattan panel and shut the rest of the world out.

By the time she'd double-checked the door, poured a glass of water from her bottle on the bedside table, he'd complied with her request and was sitting on the bed, knuckles white on either side of his tense thighs.

'Have a drink first.' She offered him the water.

'Thanks.'

Her gaze was drawn to the way his mouth touched the glass, the long tendons in his neck as he swallowed, the moisture on his upper lip when he lowered the glass. Her own mouth ached to kiss that moisture away, to elicit a smile at the very least. But Zak wasn't big on smiling right now.

When he'd had enough she took the glass from his hands, and, without breaking eye contact, turned it so that her lips touched the rim where his mouth had been. His eyes dropped to her mouth and he swallowed audibly. In the warm flickering light the atmosphere turned sultry, beating with the desire that pulsed through her body.

She set the glass down, resisted the urge to lick her lips. 'Okay,' she said, striving for a light tone in the heavy silence. 'Work with me here. And don't look so serious; this is supposed to be a pleasant experience.'

She knelt in front of him, began untying his laces. 'I'm just going to remove your shoes…' Her pulse tripped as she slipped off his shoes, then his socks and, oh, his feet— long, long toes that flexed and arched beneath her touch. Like feet in the throes of passion…

She squirted a dollop of lotion onto her palms, rubbed them together. Using the flats of her hands, she worked slowly from his ankles and down the front of his feet. Focusing her gaze on the task rather than the smoky depths of his eyes on hers or the fact that the musky curve of his neck was a tempting nuzzle away…

'Close your eyes and think about the stress flowing out through your feet.'

Relax? Let the stress flow out? Under other circumstances, Zak might have laughed at the sheer impossibility. But he was in no mood for laughter. Or talk, for that matter. How the hell did one relax with one's body tight and hot and so pumped he was all but vaulting out of his skin?

Think? He couldn't think about anything but the silky moist touch of her hands, or the fact that he knew she wasn't wearing a bra beneath that dress. That one tug on her zipper and he could bury his face in that sweet shadowed valley between her breasts.

His body tightened painfully. He closed his eyes as instructed only to have them flash open again when he felt her shift as her hands moved to the front of his shirt and began undoing buttons.

Knuckles grazing his chest as she worked her way lower, spreading the sides of his shirt wide. Warm fingers catching in chest hair, and—he sucked in a taut breath—fingernails wreaking havoc as they scored over his nipples. *Intentionally?* 'What are you doing?'

Her eyes met his, honestly and openly, and he could see she was no longer Abby the professional therapist, but Abby, the woman, and that she was as pumped as he.

'I'm removing your shirt,' she said. The silk-over-sand voice—meant to soothe? Or to seduce. Tugging the shirt free of his trousers, she slid her moisture-slick palms over his shoulders and down his arms, taking the fabric with them. Until he was naked from the waist up.

His exposed skin prickled with heat as her breath fanned his cheek, his neck, his upper chest, her unique fragrance and the underlying almost-forgotten scent of woman whirled through his head till he was dizzy.

'This isn't working,' he said, reeling at the thick, turned-on sound of his own voice.

'You're right.' She rocked back on her heels. 'Maybe some other time.'

'No.' A storm of emotions whipped through him. 'Tonight's all there is.' All he'd let it be.

Her solemn eyes locked with his, shimmering in the candlelight. 'If that's your choice.'

No, a voice inside him yelled. 'It is.'

She nodded, then capped her bottle and rose, turning away to place it on the night-stand.

No! Hell. She didn't understand, this evening, the single solitary one he'd allowed himself—them—wasn't over, it was just beginning. Panic swamped him; the restless, insistent need to finish what they'd started pounded through his blood. He jerked up off the bed. 'Abby…'

He heard her breath catch as he moved behind her. At the touch of his fingers on her nape, over her neck, her throat. Her skin was as smooth as polished stone yet soft, warm.

'I'm too strung out for a massage,' he said, against her ear. He continued to play his fingers over her shoulders and down her arms, imagining them playing in other, more intimate places. Her hair tickled his nose: an orchard in spring with a blend of blossom and fruit.

He wanted to taste her skin, right there on her neck just below her ear. And he didn't want to stop there. He ached to taste all her hidden secrets, to lose himself inside her and just for one night to forget the world outside the two of them existed.

In a way it was a relief she couldn't see him because he had a hunch this hunger for her was inscribed in neon over his face, and that was a vulnerability he could do without. She must never see how deeply she got to him.

'I think you misunderstood.' To demonstrate, he set his open mouth on her shoulder and tilted his pelvis against her spine. And, ah, she tasted as he knew she'd taste: a blend of sweet and tart, the way her lips had when he'd kissed her. A shudder ran through him, or her, he wasn't sure who.

'On the contrary,' he heard her say through the drumming in his ears, 'I understand you very well.' If she hadn't turned in his arms he would have missed seeing the hot flare of molten silver in her eyes because her voice was carefully neutral when she said, 'You need a woman.'

No. He didn't. He'd been doing fine up till a couple of weeks ago. He needed… '*You*, Abby.'

That admission, that open acknowledgement, spun through the air, a mutual aphrodisiac, a mutual acceptance.

Their eyes locked, he sucked in a breath as her fingers busied themselves with his belt buckle. Held that breath as she deftly lowered the zipper in his trousers. Nearly exploded as her knuckles deliberately caressed his erection, and again when she slid her hands down his hips and over his thighs, until his trousers hit the floor.

Her eyes flicked down to the tent in his boxers, then back to his. 'You want me to do the honours?'

Yes— No! If she removed them the way she'd removed his trousers, the main event would be over before he'd got started.

And, 'Hardly equable—I'll be the only one naked.'

Her lips pouted, a sensual pucker as she said, 'That's not a turn-on for you?'

He looked down at himself, back to her. 'It's fair to say I don't need turning on.'

Her gaze slid over his erection. 'You're right.' Her voice lowered. 'What now?'

What now? Keep it slow. You're only going to get one chance at this. 'We'll try it my way.'

Without waiting for a response, he pirouetted her, stepping back until the backs of his thighs hit the bed. And not a moment too soon. He sank down gratefully. His legs felt as if they'd run a marathon.

With hands almost as unsteady he drew her between his legs so that her body was flush against him, her pelvic bones rubbing where he burned for her the most. Her dress a silky whisper against his inner thighs, her heat seeping into his body until he reached flashpoint.

He reached out. A rustle as he untied the bow, another as he tugged the zipper, just a tantalising inch, revealing creamy flesh, lightly freckled, like her face. Natural beauty. She didn't cover it up under a truckload of make-up like other women he knew. What you saw was what you got.

Just Abby. He eased the zip down further—*slowly*—refusing to give in to the urgency pounding through his bloodstream.

Slid his palms between silk and skin. Gliding his hands under the swell of her breasts. Around. And, ah…over the hard little peaks that rose like buds in the sunshine against his palms. Her breath hitched. Scarcely able to breathe himself, he parted the fabric, wanting to see what his hands were touching.

His mouth turned dry, his blood sizzled. More smooth pale skin, large rosy nipples that begged for his attention. 'That dress doesn't do you justice.' He lowered the zip all the way, revealing a compact navel, the dips and valleys of her woman's body, gold and violet in the candlelight.

He couldn't wait. He had to lay his lips against her and taste. Had to slide his tongue over the perfect mounds, to take one of those peaks into his mouth, tug on it with his teeth until she moaned. Until it wasn't enough. He let his teeth scrape over her one more time, then pulled away. 'You're beautiful.'

Shrugging the fabric off her shoulders, she slithered out of the dress and stood before him wearing nothing but a teasing minuscule scrap of green lace and ribbon. Her eyes were watching his when he finally raised them. 'So are you,' she said, and leaned down, cupped his jaw in her hand. Then her lips were on his, cool and firm, soothing their heat, stoking the fire lower down.

Ah, when was the last time he'd felt this primed, this hot, this ready?

'Stand up, Abby.'

She leaned back, her eyes on his, then uncoiled herself in a slow sinuous motion that had his tongue all but hanging out.

'I want to look at you.' He slid his fingers beneath the straps on her hips, then watched the thong slither down the long, long length of her thighs, her calves, over her anklet to the floor.

She was perfect. And he wanted to explore all that perfection, starting at her toes and working his way up. But her feet were too far away. His hand slid between her thighs— much closer—to her warm waiting heat. A slow glide and his thumb found the throbbing nub of her pleasure.

'Zak…' She sighed and arched closer.

When her knees buckled, he dragged her closer with a murmured, 'Come here,' and settled her on his thighs, legs parted, exposing her to his gaze.

Lust hummed like bees as his fingers slid over and over against her wetness. His eyes flicked to hers. Glazed, and passion-bright, they melted into his as she clutched at his shoulders, her inner muscles clenched tight around his fingers, drawing him deep, her rippling climax turning his lust to desperation. 'Abby.'

Shucking his underwear, he pulled her up, and backwards onto the bed, dragging her body over every aching inch of his until she sprawled, gasping, on top of him. Her hair brushed his shoulders, her lips and sighs caressed his face, his eyes, an ear. And the friction of her skin against his was like nothing he'd ever felt before. The tip of his erection rubbed like oiled silk against her still quivering heat—

'Zak…' A hand slid between them in the same instant that he remembered. 'Wait…'

Protection.

His runaway hormones screeched to a halt. Everything inside him howled, *Ignore it*, the driving urge to completion pounded in his groin, thundered through his veins. *'Hell.'* Hell, hell, hell.

Abby's wide-eyed gaze locked with his. 'Oh.'

They stared at each other, heavy breath mingling, sweat-sheened bodies pounding in unison. 'Sex was the last thing on my mind when we left Surfers.' A downright lie. He just hadn't intended acting on it.

A wordless message, an erotic heat, shimmered in her eyes. Then she pushed up, knelt beside him on the narrow bed.

And her gaze drifted down.

The air constricted in his lungs, his throat closed over and anticipation surged through him. He ground his teeth till they ached. Not that. Too personal, too intimate. 'No,' he muttered, clutching the sheet either side of him, but his body had other ideas.

'Let me.' She splayed a hand on his chest.

Everything else faded to black.

All he saw was Abby. All he knew was Abby. The scent of her arousal mingling with the fragrance of her skin, her taste on his lips. Her feminine appreciation shivering through him in hot and cold bursts as she caressed his body with eyes and hands and murmurs. Soft and sweet, slow and seductive.

Then she took him into the wet heat of her mouth and his mind and the world as he knew it spun out of control.

On a groan, his eyes rolled back, his lids fell closed. Yes! The feel of her tongue as it skimmed and swirled— 'No!'

he rasped, reaching down between his thighs, catching her face with trembling hands.

She lingered a moment, her eyes on his, then let him go, replaced her mouth with her hands and soothed, 'Okay.'

His head flopped back onto the pillow as she slithered upward. The world would never be the same again. He and Abby could never be the same again. The woman who was pumping him, holding him as he came, as he spilled into her palms. He gripped her shoulders as the force of his climax shuddered through him.

A husky voice breathed his name near his ear a moment later. He couldn't help it—his hand trailed across the smoothness of her shoulder, a breast, her belly as he slid it down towards hers, but she batted it away.

'I'll take care of it,' she murmured.

He closed his eyes.

'You okay?' she whispered.

'Yeah. Great.' Just great. He forestalled any further communication by angling away from her. Guilt wound through the remnants of his pleasure.

'Good.' She patted his arm.

A few moments later, he felt her slide down beside him again. He kept his eyes closed. Gradually the sensual fog cleared, his senses calmed enough to pick up on his cramped surroundings.

Abby's head nestled in his armpit, her breath streaming over his chest as she settled towards sleep. One of his legs dangled over the edge of the bed. He could smell the lavender candle, hear the languorous lap of the sea outside, the faraway sound of party-goers, the annoying buzz of a mosquito near his head.

What they'd done played once more through his head. Even if they hadn't completed the sexual act, somehow what they'd done seemed more intimate. He didn't know why, couldn't explain it. Nor did he want to explain it. Perhaps it was the fact that she'd obviously enjoyed it as much as he.

He'd have to move in a moment. Couldn't leave a candle burning, and he should drape the mosquito netting around them.

His eyes blinked open. *Them?* Every muscle froze in denial. No! No way was he sleeping in Abby's bed with the physical reminder of what they'd shared. The more emotional—and timely—reminder that this was a one-off.

Then he realised the candle was already extinguished. So he lay still, waiting for the slow deep breathing that would tell him Abby had fallen asleep and he could get up and go to his own room without the necessity of speaking further. Telling her it was the closest he'd felt to another human being in a long time. Years, in fact. Crazy.

Diane was the woman he loved. *Had* loved. Abby wasn't his kind of woman. And the laughter he heard wasn't the demon on his shoulder telling him he was a fool and why couldn't he just admit the fact that Abby not only turned him on, she turned him inside out? With need, desire and a whole lot of other emotions he refused to analyse.

He gritted his teeth and stared at the ceiling in the dimness. No, the noise was some drunken party guest enjoying a walk along the shoreline.

But he could talk to Abby in a way he'd never been able to with his wife. Unlike Diane, Abby's moods didn't swing with the wind and she meant what she said and said what she meant. She understood and cared about other people, even had a charitable word to say for Vince—what was it she sensed about a guy she'd never met before?

What would she have said of Diane? How would she

have interpreted the events leading up to that final night? Would she have seen something that he'd not seen until it was too late?

CHAPTER TEN

BEFORE Abby opened her eyes she knew she was alone. Not that she'd expected anything else, but disappointment flooded through her nonetheless, tarnishing the afterglow.

As she shifted muscles she hadn't used in a long while made their presence felt, bringing back last night's images and sensations. The hairy masculine texture of Zak's skin rubbing against hers, his wickedly clever hands and mouth. The feel of him, hard, hot steel as he came in her hands.

But as she opened her eyes all she saw through the mosquito netting that Zak must have closed around her was the aftermath. The rumpled sheets, her dress and panties a haphazard pile of green silk on the floor, her shoes by the door.

No Zak to cuddle up against and relive the night with. No lovers' intimacy and cosy morning love-in.

No lover, period.

Not even his underwear, which he'd discarded so carelessly, so easily, last night. No, he was a few metres away, behind the *closed* rattan door. And, technically, they weren't lovers in the fullest sense of the word.

Because he hadn't brought condoms with him.

He'd never intended making love with her.

And why would he? He'd come to the wedding alone. She wasn't his partner; it just turned out that way later.

She rubbed a hand over the dull ache in her chest. What was it about him that pulled her heartstrings? He was unlike any man she'd ever known, except for her foster-father, Bill. Both men were genuine, generous and caring, willing to trust a girl they didn't know and give her a chance.

Except, unlike Bill, Zak had erected a barrier around his heart. He didn't show his emotions, lose control.

'Oh, but you did,' she said, her body tingling with remembered passion. He'd lost control—with her. For once he'd let go of that tension. Opened up. To her.

And tomorrow would they go back to business and pretend it never happened?

Hah. She shook her head as she swung her feet over the edge of the bed and padded naked to her bag. Only Zak could carry that off; she'd never look at Zak again and not remember what he looked like in the grip of passion. His gorgeous masculine body in full arousal, the sound of his deep-throated groan, the way he shuddered as he came.

Oh. My. Goodness. She blew out a heated breath as her hormones escalated again, speeding her pulse rate up.

Breakfast. Was it too early? she wondered, slipping on a floral sundress. She winced at the pain as she put on her sandals and slipped them off again. Quietly, so as not to disturb Zak—she did *not* want to face him yet—she opened her door to the moist tropical-scented air, and stepped into the morning. Away from the memories of last night.

It was still too early for most guests, but—*oh, no*—not for Zak, apparently, who had the buffet to himself. Abby almost turned back, but he caught sight of her and pulled out a chair.

'Good morning.' His eyes met hers and the air between them crackled.

'Good morning,' she said, as if she hadn't seen the raw passion in Zak's eyes as she'd opened herself to his gaze, his hands. His shattered control, her mindless moans…

'Juice?'

His voice dragged her attention back to the present and that same pair of eyes. 'Thanks.' She struggled for something to say. 'I'm feeling a little guilty that we didn't say goodbye to the newly-weds last night.'

'I said goodbye for both of us.'

'Oh?'

'I went back to the party…after.' He cleared his throat. 'I gave them your apologies. Said you had a headache.'

'You went back to the party?'

Why did she feel the sharp jab of disappointment? Because he hadn't cared enough to stay with her? Because it was only about sex for him?

So, okay, let it be just about sex. One night of amazing sex. They'd given each other mutual gratification. Even if they hadn't made it all the way.

Deliberately casual, she lifted her glass of juice, took a slow sip then said, 'I thought you were asleep—you seemed so relaxed.'

'I guess I wasn't as relaxed as I thought.'

Reaching for a slice of toast, she peeled open the little jam packet. 'So… What was last night? Do we call it a one-night stand?'

He blinked once, then his eyes narrowed. 'Abby, that's not how it is. Was.' For a long silent moment he said nothing as he stroked the moisture on the outside of his glass and pondered its contents. The same fingers that had stroked her body last night, the same eyes that had devoured every inch of her.

She had the feeling he was reliving it and trying to file it away in some neat little compartment in his mind. And perhaps he had, because he seemed to come to some grim conclusion.

The high she'd woken on deflated like a lead balloon. She felt it drop, felt her heart squeeze tight inside her chest.

'Abby,' he said slowly. 'Last night was good.' And the remnants blazed like blue flames in his eyes.

'Yes, it was good.' But it seemed fate didn't include a man who needed her, just her. Someone who wanted more than sex.

Then, damn him, he reached out, lay a hand on hers. One finger, to be precise. One sensory caress to send her nerve endings into a spin. Her gaze slid to their hands. That finger had touched her most intimate places last night and, oh, so skilfully.

'But I don't want a relationship right now,' he said. 'Better to know that up front. No one gets hurt.'

Too late.

'Excuse me.' She forced a smile that hardly touched her lips. 'I need…I need the bathroom. I'll be right back.'

She hurried to her hut, her eyes stinging with moisture, barely feeling the rough stones beneath her sore feet. She didn't need the bathroom. She needed a swim in the salt water to wash away the reminder of last night. Of losing him. She shook her head. She'd never really had him. In her room, she tossed off her sundress, pulled out her new black swimsuit and dragged it on. Slung her towel over her shoulder and grabbed her water bottle.

She followed the shoreline as it curved around a tiny inlet, lush foliage reaching almost to the water's edge. The sun was invisible, rising behind a bruised haze on the horizon, the water a flawless apricot mirror.

No more, she decided, and headed down to the harder sand. Dumped her towel. If Zak discovered how she felt about him—as a man, as a lover—she'd have to leave his home, leave Surfers. Find another town. She couldn't afford to start again, and she had to consider Aurora—she wanted her up here as soon as she could afford a place of her own, and that meant making Good Vibrations work.

Or had she ruined even that chance by becoming intimate with Zak last night?

A lump rose in her throat. What a mess she'd got herself into—falling for a man who didn't want a woman in his life. Not long-term anyway. Her toes curled at the lacy water's edge, as a storm of protest rose and blew right through her. No. *No, no, no.* Been there, done that. Past scars were imprinted on her heart and right now they were bleeding.

She dived in and started swimming.

Bracing his hands on his knees, Zak stopped running to catch his breath. And stared in horror as Abby plunged into the water. His pulse hammered in his ears till he was dizzy with it. Nausea prickled the back of his throat. 'Abby!'

He yanked off a sneaker as he ran to the water line. He should have known earlier that she didn't need the bathroom. He'd seen it in her eyes—the hurt, the sheen of tears. 'Stingers! In the water!'

She trod water to glance behind her, then, obviously not hearing his warning, turned away and began swimming straight out to sea. Away from him.

Diane all over again.

No! 'Stingers! Come out! Now!' He tried to yell, to shout, to warn her about the marine creatures that lurked in the shallows along the Queensland coast, but his throat was full of sawdust.

In his haste, he stumbled, dragged off his other sneaker, dropped it at the water's edge. Dragged his T-shirt over his head. Sweat broke out all over his body, his arms shook, his shuddering legs barely supported him. He hesitated only a second. Then the familiar sickening panic clawed up his throat as he plunged in after her.

He focused on regulating his erratic breathing, the rhythmic movement of his arms, the burn in his muscles, but the panic was alive inside him, a predator waiting to pounce the instant he gave in.

Finally his head popped up beside her. Relief swamped him. He grabbed her arm, squeezing so tight she winced, catching strands of her hair as he tugged her close. She was warm against the cool of the water, safe, in his arms, even if said arms were trembling like a newborn foal's legs.

'Stop it,' she shouted, thrashing her arms while he tried to hold her. 'What is your problem?'

Through sheer desperation he overpowered her attempts to wriggle out of his grasp. He had her, he wasn't letting her go. 'Stingers.' He swiped water from his eyes. 'Out, now.'

He saw fear widen her eyes and felt her resistance melt away. 'What? Oh, no! Zak!'

Their bodies bumped hard as he pulled her closer, then with the life-saving skills he'd learned years ago, he struck out for the shore with her in tow, long limbs tangling with his.

The instant they reached the shallows, he released her. He grabbed the nearest sneaker off the sand and walked jelly-kneed to where her belongings lay and faced away from her. He couldn't let her see him like this.

'Hey,' she said softly. 'I shouldn't have tried to push you away.' He heard her pick up her towel and rub it over her body. 'Thanks. I thought stingers were only around in sum—'

'And what the *hell* were you doing swimming alone?' Now they were safe, a dark tide of emotion surged and swamped him. He wanted to turn and shake the living daylights out of her. He wanted to plaster her against him and kiss her living, breathing body senseless.

'I didn't… What is it, Zak?'

Damn it. His vision turned grey, the sand spun up to meet him as he sank heavily to the ground. He propped his forearms on his raised knees and watched the water drip off his hair into the sand between his thighs. 'I'll be fine.'

'You're not fine now.' She moved in front of him, knelt and offered him the water bottle.

He tipped his head back and took a long swallow. Drew a deep unsteady breath. Avoided her eyes, which he knew were dark with concern. 'It's nothing.' With quick jerky movements, he grabbed his T-shirt, shoved his wet, sandy feet into his sneakers and started to push up.

But Abby was having none of it. She splayed her hand on his chest and held him there. 'I feel responsible. For heaven's sake, Zak. *Tell. Me.*'

'Water's not my thing, okay?' Disgusted with his weakness, he wrenched himself away from her touch and up.

'How can that be?' she said behind him. 'You swim like a professional.'

He closed his eyes, opened them again because all he could see was the black water beneath the bridge. 'My wife drowned after a car accident last year. I couldn't save her.'

Then he started walking.

* * *

Every organ, every limb in Abby's body turned to liquid as she watched him stride back the way he'd come, shoulders stiff, head bent. Her natural response was to go after him, but a deeper instinct rooted her to the spot. Go after him…to offer him…What? Comfort? Sympathy? An apology for behaving like a petulant child?

She hugged trembling arms around herself, chilled to the soul as his figure receded down the beach. No. The last thing he needed right now was her. In any way.

Wife.

Deceased wife.

Everything fell into place. It all made sickening sense. His problems with intimacy—which she'd all but taunted him about—his obsession with work, the haunted look she'd glimpse in his eyes after a sleepless night.

In heaven's name, why hadn't someone enlightened her? Why hadn't Zak just come out and told her right from the start? Was it so painful he couldn't bear to talk about it? The trauma of not being able to save her…

And she'd just reawakened those horrors by swimming away from him when she'd seen him on the beach.

She picked up her belongings and slowly made her way back along the sand. Obviously he was still mourning his wife. Last night…What had she done? What had *they* done? Because he'd been as willing as she. But *one night*, he'd said.

And that night was over.

When she reached her villa, she packed her stuff quickly and headed straight for the ablutions block. She stepped under the tepid spray. At least there was none of the shared-bathroom routine they'd become accustomed to. Rather than smooth tiles and the fragrance of Zak's toiletries, the experience was concrete floor and the smell of bleach.

Which served to highlight the urgency of finding her own place as soon as possible.

The sound of a chopper reached her ears as she exited. She was in time to see it put down on the helipad, saw Zak dump his belongings and climb in. She caught a glimpse of a gaunt face as he donned headphones, watched the chopper rise into the air and veer away.

Somehow Abby managed to get through the trip back, but she couldn't enjoy the luncheon on board or the beautiful tropical scenery they passed through. Just making conversation with virtual strangers was an effort. Thankfully Vince didn't come near her, otherwise occupied with the blonde she'd seen him with on the dance floor.

The minibus dropped her off at Capricorn Centre. She had no doubt he'd plunged himself into work already and they needed to talk about what had happened.

He wasn't there. The temp who was covering for Tina for the next couple of days told Abby Zak had taken four days' leave interstate on urgent family business.

Business? No way. That emotional island he'd exiled himself to was surrounded with cut glass rather than sand and, until he found his own way off it and was ready to talk, she had no way to reach him.

The indications were that Good Vibrations was going to be very successful if the volume of clientele that passed through Abby's door over the next two days was any indication. Her appointment book was full.

Her nights were lonely.

On the third morning Abby poked her head around Tina's office door. 'Hi, Mrs Langotti. Welcome back.'

The newly-wed woman looked up, the stars still in her eyes. 'Hi, Abby.'

'How was the honeymoon, as if I need to ask? That island is magic.'

'Only two days…and nights.' She grinned. 'Not long enough, but it was nice to come home to Danny.' Tina skirted her desk and came around to hug Abby, then leaned back to look at her. 'You and Zak seemed to be enjoying its magic, too— I couldn't help noticing.'

Abby's heart clenched. 'Oh, that…'

'And I think it's great,' Tina added. 'You're just what Zak needs right now.'

'Zak's not ready for a full-on relationship…'

'Abby. Honey.' Tina shook her head. 'From what I saw on the dance floor, he's well and truly ready. And about time, too.' She waved a well-manicured hand, her wedding ring glinting.

'I didn't know he'd been married.' She walked to the full-length window and breathed in the tropical scent outside. 'Why didn't you tell me, Tina?'

'I left that up to Zak,' she replied, her voice sobering.

'He took me into his home, gave me a place to set up my business. Did everything good and decent and honest. Except he left out that one very important detail.'

'And now everything's changed?' she heard Tina ask behind her.

Yeah. I love him.

Somehow those three little words slipped past her defences and rested like tears in her heart. *Forget falling, I'm in all the way over my head. In love with a man who's incapable of loving me back.*

'How did it happen?' Abby asked.

'Her car went over a bridge. Zak was following in his own car. He dived off the bridge but she was trapped inside.

There was nothing he could have done, but he jumped anyway. We almost lost him, too.'

'The scars on his thigh.'

'Yes. Diane was my best friend. The three of us grew up together. I miss her, too.'

'I'm sorry.'

'So are we all. I have a picture… I was going to put it on my desk… I just haven't got around to it.' Tina walked to a pile of boxes, rummaged a moment, then dusted off a framed photograph of Zak and Diane with her and Nick.

Abby couldn't take her eyes off Diane. She could have been a model or a movie star. Sleek and sophisticated, and that one dress would have cost more than Abby's annual income. Both she and Zak looked every bit the successful cosmopolitan couple that graced the front pages of women's magazines.

'I'm sorry, Tina.' She reached for her hand. 'I wish he'd told me.' *I've made such a fool of myself.*

Back in her shop, Abby blended her oils of cedar wood, jasmine and ylang-ylang and set them in the vaporiser, but instead of focusing on her next client all she could see was Diane's face.

How much Zak must have loved her to risk his life in such a hazardous attempt. Had Diane known how much? Had she appreciated what a diamond of a man she'd married? Of course—they'd been a part of each other's lives since childhood. A love that had lasted decades; it was no wonder he'd exiled himself to shut out the emotional pain. No wonder he never wanted to love again. He might want Abby in a physical way, but that was where it ended.

He was still in love with his wife.

CHAPTER ELEVEN

ZAK buckled into his business-class seat for the flight home, breathing a sigh as he watched Sydney's distinctive skyline of Bridge and Opera House disappear beneath low cloud.

His family had been surprised to see him, especially grubby and dishevelled after two days camping out in the bush. He'd used those two days to come to an important decision. Then he'd called them together to explain why he was selling Forrester Building Restorations.

'A drink from the bar, sir?' asked the flight attendant, already pulling down his tray.

'Bourbon on ice, thanks.' He didn't normally drink before noon but today he had to talk to Abby. The prospect scared him almost as much as his quick and shocking dip in the sea. She deserved so much more than he'd given her and somehow he was going to make it up to her in every way possible, if she'd let him.

He loved her.

The acknowledgement might be four days young, and several weeks late, but it still had the power to grab him by the throat, a surge of emotion that had him clenching his hands around his drink and leaning back breathless in his seat.

But it had taken that moment on the island to realise his guilt over Diane's death was nothing compared to the thought of losing Abby. His life was empty without her.

He missed her sunny laugh, that way she had of lifting her shoulder when she talked. She could raise his spirits with just a look, a touch, a word, even when he did his damnedest to ignore her. He loved her positive outlook on life, never questioning the way he chose to live his.

Except to coax him out of his shell. Which, on reflection, was what he'd needed. She'd turned his life around. Had him looking at things he'd not seen before.

Abigail Seymour, who was all wrong for him, had somehow slipped past his defences.

His hand tightened around his glass as he gazed out at the cotton-wool clouds that stretched on for ever. Diane was gone. He'd loved her, but he'd lost her before she'd driven that car over the bridge. Finally, the truth he'd been too stubborn, too hurt, to admit.

He hadn't neglected his wife; they'd grown apart with the years, both busy with their respective careers. But Diane *had* been different those last months. Unhappy. She'd been drunk when she'd got behind the wheel of her car that night. He'd never forgiven himself for not being close enough to snatch the keys from her hand and stop her leaving.

Was he going to continue to punish himself for that for the rest of his life? Or was he going to start again with a new foundation and build something worthwhile? With Abby.

The knowledge he'd imprisoned ruthlessly behind bars of denial burst free. His heart pounded in his chest and crawled up his throat. Every part of his body flexed and tingled. It was like waking up after a coma—and he knew, all too well, how that felt.

Don't give up on me just yet, baby, he willed her silently.

As soon as the plane touched down at the Gold Coast airport, he picked up his car and went straight to Capricorn Centre. He was still figuring the best way to go about it. He knew he had some explaining to do. Knew Abby would be hurt, probably angry. He hoped what he had to say would change that.

Perhaps a late lunch or early dinner? A stroll along the beach that she loved so much? Then he glanced at the thunderheads building over the sea. Not a walk, then.

'It's her afternoon off,' the hairdresser in the shop next to Abby's told him when he found her door closed. 'She said she was going apartment hunting.'

The information drove a fist square into his solar plexus, knocking the breath from his body and souring the anticipation of seeing her.

It rolled around in his gut like a lead ball all the way home. Why was she rushing into something she obviously knew sweet nothing about? With her track record, he didn't trust her not to get tangled up in some dodgy contract.

His hand rasped across the stubble of his three-day-old beard. He knew why.

He swung into the drive a tad too fast, skidded to a halt at the base of the front stairs rather than detour round the back. Meanwhile, he needed a shower, a shave and a cold beer. He could manage two out of three at the same time.

Thunder rumbled in the distance as he tossed his bag on the bed, stripped down to his skin and turned the ceiling fan on full-blast to cool the sweat of the afternoon on his skin. Went to the kitchen, popped the top on a can, then padded back to the bedroom.

He opened the *en suite* door and took two steps in before he realised the air was filled with fragrant steam—*feminine* fragrant steam—and he wasn't alone.

Abby. On hands and knees scrubbing his shower tiles. Wearing nothing but a doll-sized white thong and a low-cut bra. Leaving her all-but-exposed bottom wiggling in time with music only she could hear through the MP3 player dangling round her neck.

His eyes took all that in for a stunned ten seconds while every muscle in his body locked down. While the blood drained from his head and rushed to another part of his anatomy. Another rapidly growing *exposed* part of his anatomy.

This wasn't the way he'd planned it.

Backtrack before she sees you. The order didn't quite reach his feet before she straightened to reclip the wayward hair escaping from its clasp on top of her head. She must have caught some subtle movement or felt the heat of his presence because her head snapped around. A startled gasp and it was too late.

Her eyes flared in panic, then she mouthed his name around an O of surprise, and that panicked gaze calmed a little, turning wary but aware as her eyes flicked down, then back to his face.

Damn. 'Why in heaven's name are you cleaning in here at this time of day?' he demanded, his breath whistling out between his teeth. 'You know I don't expect you to clean up after me.' Beer sloshed over his hand as he set the can on the vanity.

'What?' She tugged out the earplugs. He heard the MP3 slide onto the tiles with a soft metallic clink as she scrambled up. 'I didn't expect you…' she rushed on before he could repeat his question. She looked to the damp towel she'd left on the vanity, but he needed it more than she did.

He stayed where he was, reached out and slung it around his hips. But the damage was done. He forced himself to speak slowly, calmly over the gravel in his throat. 'What's wrong with the other bathroom?'

'Nothing. It's so much easier to clean the shower straight after you've used it and since I'd left my shower gel in here…'

Her voice trailed off—at least he thought it did because he stopped listening. Her freshly showered skin was a delicate shade of coral pink. Except for dusky rose nipples that puckered beneath the sheer fabric of her bra even as he tried not to notice.

It took another thick and heavy beat that pulsed in the steamy air and echoed low in his body to realise he wasn't the only one *not* noticing.

'I'll just—'

'Tess told me you were apartment hunting.' He couldn't help that it sounded like an accusation. And why the blazes were they holding a conversation as if they were passing the time of day on the back veranda?

Her eyes jerked back to his and something flickered in their depths that scared the living daylights out of him. 'I did… I was… I finished. Zak…' A soft feminine sound erupted from her throat. 'This is awkward.'

He remained rooted to the spot. Had she found somewhere else? His heart thundered like the approaching storm. Something like pain tightened his jaw, had his hands curling into fists. He wouldn't ask her about that now.

'I'm sorry,' she whispered. 'I'll get out of your way.'

His stomach muscles bunched as he sucked in a breath,

his groin heating, hardening to the point of pain as she took the necessary steps towards him to reach the door and escape.

The scent of her body, its cool satin smoothness as her arm brushed his, snatched away reason and snapped his tenuous hold on control.

'Don't go.' He heard the rawness in his voice as he turned into her closeness on a soft oath, curling his hands around her upper arms and spinning her to face him. He slammed his mouth down on hers before she could respond. The primitive hunger beat in his blood as he dragged her flush against him until her mouth opened beneath his.

He drank in the dark honeyed taste like a dying man— its sweetness, its promise. He wanted her with tongue and lips and hands, from her mouth to her toes and every place between.

And he wanted it now.

He rushed his hands over the taut, firm lines of her body, sprang open her bra clasp and groaned as he filled his palms with her flesh, her nipples hard against his chest. Not enough.

With his mouth still fused to hers, grasping her buttocks, he swung her around and set her on the vanity. Watched her eyes darken as he spread her legs wide, saw his own eyes glaze over in the mirror's reflection above her head. His arm knocked his beer can; it tipped and rolled, spilling amber liquid over the counter and onto the floor.

Her hips were curved, cool, taut. The inside of her thighs were smooth, deliciously hot. When he ran his knuckles over the tiny triangle of fabric he found it damp and steamy with desire. His knees turned weak, his vision hazed, but he saw her eyes erupt like silver lava and fuse with his.

Watching him, she took the clasp from her hair, freeing her auburn curls, a riot of red streaming over her shoulders. Then, leaning back on her palms, she arched her hips, offering herself to him.

The only answer he needed.

Snap. One firm tug on the strap at her side and her thong was history. He shoved it to one side, pulled her forward until she teetered on the edge of the vanity and set his mouth on the soft skin of her neck.

Sweet, everywhere sweet. He moved lower, over the erotic ridge of collarbone, nuzzling, tasting, teeth and tongue scraping over her flesh while her fingers twined in his hair and tugged on his ears. Her heart beat a fast and frantic rhythm against his hand when he kneaded her breasts.

Lower. At last he was where he wanted to be—close to her heart. Taking one pebble-hard nipple into his mouth, he suckled her, drawing it out with his teeth while he pinched the other between finger and thumb, rolled his hand over it to feel its hardness against his tingling palm.

No thought, just aching, endless need.

'Yes,' she moaned, a strangled sound at the first touch of his fingers on her woman's flesh. Where he burned to touch her again.

Her breath puffed in short serrated gasps against his ear as he plunged his fingers into her wetness and heat, drawing the dewy moisture out and over, up and over until she bucked against him and cried out his name.

His name. Possessiveness lanced through him like a flaming arrow.

A flash of lightning freeze-framed the abandon on her face, an earthy enchantress bathed in silver as she threw her head back, her hair spiralling out of control in the moist air, fingernails digging half-moons in his shoulders while the thunder rumbled nearer.

Alive, so alive. Impossibly high, as if she soared on the wings of angels. The world was still spinning when Abby blinked the haze from her eyes to focus on the wild-eyed, hungry male in front of her. 'Zak.' Her voice sounded hoarse, not like hers at all. 'Please…say…you have condoms…'

'In here.' His breath came out harsh, his eyes never left her face as he tugged open the vanity drawer. He pulled out an unopened packet.

'Hurry.' Her heart seemed to grow too big for her chest, her blood speeding too fast through her veins as he fought the packaging with clumsy fingers.

'Quick.' Finally. She held her breath as he ripped the foil open. 'Now, Zak.' *Before you think about it.*

Before I can think that this is a bad idea.

Almost before he'd finished protecting himself she shimmied forward, wrapped her legs around him, dragging him closer, catching his face between her hands until all she could see was the laser-blue intensity of his eyes.

Hers. Just for this moment he was utterly hers.

No patience for either of them, just need, frantic and fevered. And, oh, he was so hot, so huge, so hungry as he pushed inside her, ruthlessly filling her with his steel-hard strength, learning the most intimate secrets of her body as she learned his.

It was like the storm, all sparks and noise and energy. A cacophony of sensations battering her as she matched her pace to his. Heat where his body drove into hers, where chest abraded breasts. Power in the arms that bound her against him like chains.

His demand, its dark turbulence, pounded her, swept her up again, lifting her higher, higher, and she grabbed hold of his neck and bit his shoulder, afraid she might spin off the face of the earth. 'Hold me.' She almost sobbed. 'Don't let me go.'

'I've got you, baby.'

The thread of gentleness in his harsh tone undid her, but he drove into her until there wasn't room for reason or thought or breath. Until passion exploded and consumed her whole.

She remembered collapsing against him, his sweat-covered chest against her cheek as he lifted her and carried her to his bed. Rain falling, its green drift of scent over cooling skin. His heart beating heavy beneath her ear as he tucked her head against his armpit.

Thundery late afternoon sun filled the room with a murky orange glow. Abby lay skin to sticky skin with a hot-bodied Zak. Her mind was mud. What had just happened? A few moments later, she rose carefully on one elbow to watch him. His eyes were closed, and for once in his life his body looked relaxed.

Her chest both tightened and expanded with love. Oh, this was a heartbreak in waiting. She let her gaze roam over his naked body. Long, lean and hard with a dusting of dark masculine hair that arrowed down to…a very impressive package. His legs were entwined with hers, the skin dark gold against her fair ones.

But it was his face that drew her. She'd see that face in her dreams as long as she lived. His eyes, a burning blue in the throes of passion. Eyes that could turn as remote as a New Zealand glacier, or as mysterious as the deepest ocean with one blink.

And now she knew why. A secret that, for reasons of his own, he'd chosen not to share with her.

She didn't want to disturb him quite yet. She needed another moment to watch him.

She'd seen Diane's photo; she knew Abby with the frizzy hair and freckles would never fit into his life. Nor would she change the woman she was, for anyone. She was comfortable with who she was. That didn't alter the fact that she loved him—for who *he* was. Very slowly she freed her legs from his.

'Where're you going?' a sleepy voice drawled, the sound sliding over her like dark chocolate. He rolled over, and, with one large calloused hand beneath her breasts, scooted her close so that he lay hot—and already hard again—against her. Temptation never sounded so good. Never felt so good.

No, no, no. Abby extricated herself, her skin gliding over the expensive cotton sheets as she moved to the edge of the mattress and sat up. There were three people in this bed. 'You need that shower now,' she said. 'I'll be in the kitchen when you're ready to talk.'

So hard to leave his room naked, knowing he tracked her every step to the door, to escape to her own room and drag on shorts and top with trembling fingers. To tame the nest of hair the steam—and Zak—had rendered feral. And try very very hard not to cry.

She heard his shower running and chopped salad vegetables for something to do with her hands while she waited.

His eyes clashed with hers the moment he entered the kitchen, but they held firm, unwilling to let her go, and for a moment she was spellbound, her whole body aching and tense, remembering how those eyes had burned with passion not thirty minutes ago.

They burned now, but with a different emotion. Did she see regret or self-recrimination in their depths? Hell, she couldn't read him with her own emotions churning inside her like a blender.

He was wearing jeans and his navy knit shirt. His hair was damp and the thick stubble that had felt so good against her face and breasts was gone.

The knife she was gripping skated off the carrot and skidded over her finger. Damn! She walked to the sink and wrenched on the tap as blood welled over her fingers.

'Let me look at that,' he said, behind her.

'It's only a scratch. All it needs is a Band-Aid.' Shrugging him off, she moved to a nearby cupboard and reached for the packet in the first-aid box. She sealed the dressing, flexed her finger. If only emotions could be mended as easily.

'Stop it,' he said, and took the knife from her hand, set it on the bench with a clatter. 'I'm sorry.' He gripped her chin, forced her to look at him. 'I should've told you.'

'Yes, you should have. Why didn't you? You must have known how I felt about you.'

Acknowledgement burned in his gaze. 'I didn't want to see the sympathy—not in your eyes, Abby. I've had a gut-ful of sympathy over the past year. No more.'

'Not sympathy. Understanding.'

'I don't want that either, because no one really understands.'

'Okay. Help me understand. Tell me about Diane.'

He rubbed his chest, as if to ease an ache. 'What do you want to know?'

Everything. Nothing. Did you love her? Stupid question. Stick to the mundane. 'Was she involved in your business, too?'

'No.'

Something in his voice prompted Abby to say, 'I'm not the only one who thought you worked too hard, then. Did she work?'

'She was a fashion buyer for a department-store chain.'

'So…she travelled?'

'Sydney, Melbourne. The occasional trip to Asia.'

'She went alone?'

One hand fisted on the counter-top. 'I had the business.'
Ah.

'The night she died, I accused her of having an affair,'
he said, and the fist curled tighter. 'I'll never know if that
was true or not. She died before we could thrash it out.'

The information was a surprise to Abby. Yet…on reflection, perhaps not. 'You blame yourself.'

He let out a slow sigh and his whole body seemed to
implode.

'How long are you going to hold onto that guilt, Zak?
Because until you free yourself you'll never move on.
You're not ready for a new relationship. You've demonstrated that over and over. Have you forgotten that only a
few days ago you told me you're not looking for a relationship?'

His jaw clenched, and something flickered in his eyes.
'That was before—'

'You went AWOL for four days,' she interrupted. 'Not a
word from you, Zak. I only found out when the temp at
Capricorn Centre told me. Is that the sign of a healthy relationship? If what we have can even be termed a relationship.'

And because she didn't want to hear excuses, even legitimate ones, she picked up the knife again, and tapped
it firmly on the counter. Looked into the eyes of the man
who'd held her body and her heart in his hands and steeled
herself. 'You know how I feel about you, but I'm through
with the emotional merry-go-round.'

He shook his head. 'Damn it, Abby,' he said softly. 'Don't give up on me now.'

God knew she didn't want to, but could she trust him not to reject her again? 'We need some space. Which is handy because I arranged to go over to Tina's tonight. I can't cancel now. Nick's gone to Brisbane and in return for a traditional roast-lamb dinner I'm giving her a massage—if Daniel allows it. And since I'm in the mood to drink to excess tonight I promised to sleep over.'

'I can pick you up.'

'No,' she said firmly. 'I need this for me. Use the time to catch up on work. Your businesses must be falling apart without you.' She heard the sarcasm in her voice and wasn't sorry for it.

'I'm selling Forrester Building Restorations. Already have some interested parties.'

A glimmer of hope lit inside Abby. 'Well, that's…a start.' She nodded. 'That's good. But how does your dad feel about it?'

'I flew down to Sydney, talked to Dad and the rest of the family. They understand, and they're okay with it.'

'Great. I hope it works out for you.' And before she could change her mind, she slipped past him and headed for her room to pack her overnight gear.

He was already gone before she left.

CHAPTER TWELVE

AT CAPRICORN CENTRE Zak shut down his computer at 2:00 a.m. Because he'd seen the determination in Abby's eyes, because she'd already made plans and he had no right to make demands after pulling his own disappearing act, he'd used the evening as she'd suggested, but he hadn't achieved much. He closed his door, and instead of heading out he found himself walking down the now-empty corridor to Abby's shop.

Using his master key, he let himself inside. Light from the lobby filtered through the large shop window so he left the shop's lighting off. The cool air that greeted his nostrils was tinged with the fragrance of the essences she used, the ones he smelled on her when they were in the same room at home.

He ran his fingers through the dish of tumbled crystals she kept by the cash register, listening to the clacking sound they made and feeling their smooth surfaces against his skin. What would she say if he booked himself in for that promised massage? The scenario of him lying on her massage mat and letting her fingers work his stiff neck muscles skated through his veins like quicksilver. He flicked through her appointment book and saw tomorrow's schedule was full.

His gaze snagged on the hat-stand and the white jersey leggings and top she wore while working. He couldn't help himself. He walked over to feel its texture and breathe in that familiar scent some more.

He wanted to be with her again. Connected. The way they'd been together this afternoon.

The house was dark when he pulled up ten minutes later, another reminder that Abby wasn't there—no porch light illuminated his way.

He walked down the hall to his room, but paused at her door. It was open, the curtains drawn back. 'Abby,' he murmured into the darkness, his pulse gearing up in hopeful anticipation of touching his mouth to her sleep-soft lips even though he knew she wasn't there.

He waded through the semi-darkness to her bed. His hand slid over the quilt. No warm bumps, the way it should feel with a curvaceous body beneath it. He could still smell her fragrance mingled with sunshine-fresh linen.

'Come back,' he said into the silence.

He walked on to his own room. The sheets were still rumpled from their afternoon. Then he saw the note on the pillow.

Dear Zak,
I hope you didn't work too late. Get some sleep tonight and I'll see you at work. A. X

He glared at her trademark flamboyant A and that simple kiss. He wanted that kiss delivered in person.

His hand halted midway through his furrowed hair. A gem of an idea glimmered in his mind. He flipped open his planner, checked some numbers and started making a list.

* * *

'Can't sleep?'

Abby turned, her teacup in her hand rather than the alcohol she'd promised herself. A sleep-deprived Tina was jostling a fussy Daniel on her hip. At least they'd squeezed in a massage before he'd woken up.

'Not yet. I just made some valerian tea and honey. Want some?'

Tina's nose wrinkled as she reached for a baby bottle she'd prepared earlier. 'I'll pass, thanks, although perhaps I should put some in Danny's bottle; give us both some peace.'

'Let me take him for a few moments.' Setting her cup on the table, she clapped her hands and reached for the child. 'Come to Auntie Abby?' Sucking on two fingers, Danny regarded her with wide dark eyes.

'That'd be great, I need to go to the bathroom. Won't be a minute.' And without waiting for his lordship's approval, Tina delivered Danny into Abby's arms.

'Take your time.' Maternal instincts Abby didn't know she had swirled to life inside her at the contact of petal-soft flesh against hers. 'Hello, sweetie, you giving your mummy a hard time?' Abby cuddled the restless child, rubbed her cheek over the soft fuzzy head, inhaling his sweet baby-powder scent. 'You know, I don't get the opportunity to do this very often,' she told him softly.

For a dreamy moment, as she rocked from side to side, she was immersed in a daydream of holding her own child. A little boy with blue eyes like his dad and the cutest dimples you ever saw. Her womb tightened at the image, and she shivered.

'I've got him,' she told Tina when she returned, unwilling to give him up just yet. 'I think he's settling.'

Tina smiled. 'Another first. At night he usually turns

into a real mummy's boy.' She sat down at the table and watched Abby. 'Motherhood would look good on you.'

'Only in a safe and secure marriage, thanks.'

'No marriage is totally safe and secure,' Tina said.

Abby knew Tina was thinking of Diane. How even the happiest marriage could be over in the blink of an eye. Abby was thinking of her own mother and Hayley and the tough times they'd lived through.

She touched her lips to Danny's head. 'That makes it all the more important to cherish what you have while you can.'

'Speaking of which, I wonder whether Zak's still burning the midnight oil.'

Abby beat back the image of Zak burning the midnight oil with her not so many nights ago. 'It's not that serious between us, Tina.'

Tina cocked her head. 'You try looking in the mirror and telling yourself that, girl, because I see a different view from this side.'

Abby sighed. 'Until Zak's over Diane…'

'He needs a gentle push, or even a shove, and you're the one to give it to him. I saw the way he watched you at the wedding. And I know it wasn't a headache you had on our wedding night.' She leaned back in her chair. 'So what's your next move?'

Abby shook her head. 'The next move is his.'

Zak missed her arrival the following morning, but he knew Abby was already in the building because he'd smelled her perfume waft past his door while he was on a conference call.

The instant he put down the phone, he left his office and headed for Good Vibrations. She'd already changed into that sexy white uniform that moulded to her shape—he could see the generous globes of her breasts and the distinct jut of her nipples against the fabric.

At the moment she was mixing a potpourri of scented oils. Mood music, which reminded him of a tranquil lake, played softly in the background.

She looked up when she saw him, her smile clouding a smidgen as she poured the oil into a vaporiser and lit the candle. 'Good morning, Mr Forrester.'

'I'm glad you think so. What—?'

'I'll be right with you, Mrs Dexter,' she called, jerking her head towards the screen behind her and spoke softly. 'You'll scare your guests away. I can't talk now, I have a client.'

He grasped her forearm, registered the familiar contours of bone and flesh, of heat and strength. Looked into those clear grey eyes that told him sweet nothing about what she was thinking. But he lowered his voice. 'When are you free?'

She slipped out of his grasp, only because he let her go. 'I'm booked right through today.'

Of course, he already knew that. 'Lunch—'

'Sorry, meeting with a sales rep about some coloured essences I'm interested in trialling. I plan to eat here while she talks.'

He snapped his palms firmly on the counter, squared his gaze, spoke through his teeth so only she could hear. 'Make time for me.'

He saw the tiny flinch as she set her own jaw. 'Okay…' She reached for a pen. 'Since you're the boss.' Her eyes flashed up at him, then she made a formal note in her planner. *Zak Forrester*. 'Your appointment's for six-thirty.'

Patience was not his strong suit, but he'd take what he could get. He nodded. 'I'll meet you here. Six-thirty.'

* * *

At six twenty-five, he shut down his computer. At six twenty-seven Tina poked her head in the doorway as he was packing his briefcase. 'Zak, can you sign some cheques before you go?'

He checked his watch. 'Leave them on my desk. I'll do it in the morning.'

'I really need them signed now, if you wouldn't mind. I have to—'

'Okay, okay. Where are they?'

'In my office.'

He closed his eyes briefly and prayed for restraint. 'Right behind you.' Why in heaven's name couldn't she have brought them with her?

He cast only a cursory glance as he scrawled his signature on the line. 'Have a good evening, Tina.'

By the time he made it to Good Vibrations it was six thirty-three and her door was shut.

As his fist curled in frustration against the glass panel the door slid open a fraction. As he tapped lightly to alert her to his presence he caught a glimmer of something. A flicker of light, on the ceiling behind the privacy screen where Abby did her massage.

He stepped inside, cleared his throat, watching the flicker on the ceiling blossom into a glow, dancing as a distorted shadow formed, grew and receded. 'I can come back if you're still busy,' he called.

'No, I'm ready for you.'

Her words, spoken in that low, melodic voice, were like a torch to dry grass. But as she appeared from behind the screen Abby in work-mode was a different woman from the one he knew—or thought he knew. Still in her whites, she looked as fresh as she would at 9:00 a.m. The exuberance was still there, but hidden behind a professional demeanour.

'Hi, Zak. Come on in.'

She stepped behind him and closed the door. The air eddied around her, a mix of musky feminine sweat and the exotic fragrances he'd come to associate with her.

He heard the lock click and his pulse spiked. But he stayed where he was—in unfamiliar territory. An empty shop bore no resemblance to this intimate room with its Bolivian lounge music and candles that spread shadows and smelled like orange blossoms.

'How's your day been?' she asked, a hand lifted, indicating he should precede her to the other side of the screen. Pleasant and polite, the way she'd ask any client.

'Good, busy. Abby—' He made a move towards her but she sidestepped out of his reach and rounded the screen.

'Come on through. I'm just warming the oil.'

'Oil?'

'For your massage. It's a blend of lavender, orange and sandalwood—good for insomnia.'

'We need to clear up a few things.' He came to an abrupt halt at the foot of her massage mat. 'That's why I'm here.' His gaze took in the scene. A dozen scented candles—violet, a couple of pink, a red. The sound of water trickled over the tabletop fountain in the corner. 'I'm not one of your clients.'

'You asked, *demanded*—' she sweetened the word with a quick smile as she took a folded towel from her stack '—me to make a time for you.'

'Not an appointment.'

She smiled again. 'It's on the house. I promised you a massage, remember?'

Vividly.

That same hot, needy tension knotted at the base of his spine and worked its way up, only now it was tangled with other, more volatile and deeper emotions he struggled to control.

'I'll wait out front while you remove your clothing,' she said. 'You can leave your underwear on. Lie on your stomach and cover yourself with this.' She handed him the towel, then moved to the screen. 'Let me know when you're ready. Zak. Trust me, you'll enjoy it and it'll help you sleep tonight.'

He pierced her with a telling look. 'What if I don't want to sleep tonight?'

He saw something infinitely sad cloud her eyes that cooled his blood a few degrees and put his hormones on hold. 'Tonight's not about seduction,' she said. 'And it's not about sex.'

While he tried to come to terms with that plainly stated fact, she waited, her arms crossed beneath her breasts. 'I want to give you something back. I *need* to give you something back. Can you understand that?'

And in a sudden flash of insight, he grasped her meaning, understood that need. Give and take. Sometimes you had to take from someone, accept their gift, in order to give. He'd never allowed Abby that self-satisfaction or given her that validation.

He would have spoken but his throat was clogged with emotion, so he nodded and slipped open the first button of his shirt.

Drawing a breath as soon as he was alone, he tossed his clothes on a stool, lay on the mat as instructed and closed his eyes. At his muttered 'ready,' she returned.

She adjusted the towel over his body and he heard her rubbing oil into the palms of her hands as she knelt at the crown of his head. The heat from her body carried her scent with it, reminding him of the last time she'd been this close… *Tonight's not about sex.* He repeated the mantra as she leaned over him. If he opened his eyes… No.

With the first warm glide of her hands over his back, he tensed, the pressure in his groin skyrocketing. This was never going to work. 'I don't—'

But she placed one soothing, almost impersonal hand on the base of his spine, the other at his neck. 'Draw in the breath slowly, imagine a peach-coloured mist. Think of some place peaceful.' Then she continued with long, slow sweeps up the spine, around his ribcage, over his shoulders.

Not about sex. Not about sex. He slowly relaxed as the comforting warmth seeped through skin and muscle as she worked over his back, drawing away the tension, easing him into a state of semi-bliss, semi-sleep, semi-arousal.

She worked with skill. Magic. Whether her fingers were being playful, passionate or professional he could honestly say no one had ever touched him the way Abby did. She was the most giving person he'd ever met. She understood him better than anyone.

And he'd pushed her away too many times.

Abby felt him tense just then and wondered what he thought of, but kept her mind focused on the task and her strokes smooth, applying more pressure to the knots of tension in his shoulders. Refusing to think about the last time she'd touched him and how he'd taste if she leaned down.

The healing energy in her hands burned and tingled as she worked around the ugly scar tissue that puckered his left buttock, reminding her of what he'd risked to earn it and why.

She ended with a deep massage to his thighs, worked her way to his feet. Finally, she closed her eyes, drew her hands slowly up his spine, wrapping him in a healing pink mist. As she replaced the towel over his body, and pulled back to rest her bottom on her heels, she offered up a silent prayer of thanks that she'd had him in her life, even if it was for a short time.

'I want you in my life, Abigail Seymour.'

The softly slurred words pierced her soul. She wanted that, too. She wanted it all—his name, his love, his babies. But she couldn't be with that man until he came to terms with his loss and made changes.

She lay a light hand on his back, to simply feel him. 'Lie a moment, let your body come to slowly.'

He rolled over, dragging the towel with him. 'You've changed me. You're one of a kind, Abby, and very special. So special I—'

'If you're happy with the changes, then I've done my job.' She pushed up on unsteady legs, moved to the tiny basin and washed the feel of his skin, his scent, from her hands.

He sat up. His blue eyes captured hers, dark with old emotion.

And Abby's heart plunged into those murky depths with his. She wanted to kneel down beside him, to touch him again, as a therapist or a friend. But if she touched him now she might never let go. 'You came to talk. So talk.'

He heaved a big sigh and seemed resigned. 'You were right yesterday. I blame myself. I didn't take the time to find out what was bothering Diane.' His hand rasped over his evening stubble and his gaze lingered on a candle's flickering flame. 'If I hadn't known she was drunk, if I hadn't followed her to make sure she didn't get herself in trouble, she might not have skidded off that bridge.'

'No, but she might have killed someone else, as well as herself.'

His gaze swung back to her. It seemed to absorb her inside him, as if she had no will of her own. 'I'm through with the guilt trip, Abby. I just want to get on with my life.'

And he wanted her in it? No mention of love and ever after. So he wanted her for what? Sex? Friendship? *Not enough. Not nearly enough.* She tore her eyes away. She couldn't be only a friend to Zak any more. She loved him but until he felt the same way…

She wiped her hands, flung the towel over the basin and hugged her arms. 'You have your conference centre, and I have to concentrate on Good Vibrations and bringing Aurora here.' She switched on the main light and blew out the candles; so not the way to end a session. But then, she hadn't thought about that.

She'd come in early tomorrow and clean up—for two reasons. One: if she stayed a minute longer she'd lose it and she was *not* going to cry in front of him. Reason number two: if she left now, she could be out of the car park and away before he'd finished dressing. He wouldn't dare leave the centre in nothing but a towel. 'Close up when you're done, will you?' she said, and headed for the door.

'Wait. We're not finished.'

Behind the screen she heard a thump and the sound of clothes being tossed about. Grabbing her purse, she whisked out of the door with a quick, 'See you in the morning.'

She was wrong. As she pulled out of her parking spot she caught sight of a bare-chested Zak in her rear-vision mirror, trousers low on his hips, half running, half stumbling barefoot across the car park.

CHAPTER THIRTEEN

ABBY lay in her moon-drenched room, gazing up at the ceiling. The evening songs of insects filled the air. Pushing the sheet away, she closed her eyes and willed herself to sleep. Impossible.

There was an ache in her heart that no amount of sleep medication could dull. She wanted Zak in her life. He'd told her the same thing. Why couldn't it be that simple? An extended fling—wouldn't that work? Until they called it a day. Correction: until Zak called it a day. And, no, it wouldn't work, because for her love was for keeps. Good with the bad.

'You know I could have you evicted for unprofessional conduct. Leaving a client dangling…'

Abby's eyes slammed open at the sound of Zak's voice. He closed the door quietly behind him. He was still bare-chested, his bare feet soundless on the polished boards as he crossed the room. At least she imagined they were soundless because all she could hear was the boom of her suddenly wildly out-of-control heart beating in her ears.

His face was in silhouette, except for the glinting eyes, which held a hint of jest beneath the gravity. Moonlight painted silver over the hard planes and angles of the rest of him, inky black flowed into the little dip that was his navel. He looked like a superhero from some future world. A superhero with a sense of humour.

'You weren't exactly *dangling*.' And despite her inner turmoil she couldn't help a grin. 'Isn't there something in your employees' handbook about a dress code? The manager seen running through the centre half naked…'

'You. You make me do things I'd never do under normal circumstances.' He shook his head. 'Okay, I think we're even.' He sat down beside her on the bed, his face coming into view as the moonlight struck it. His palm cupped her face, warm and calloused, his eyes filled with promised pleasures. 'Come to my room.'

The smile hovering on her lips faded as her heart clenched. 'No, Zak.'

'Suit yourself, then, but it'll be a little crowded.'

Still sitting on the bed, he unzipped his trousers, shoved them down with his boxers and stretched out beside her.

She didn't argue. Couldn't seem to get her voice to work, to tell him to go. The hard strength of his thigh abraded her sensitive inner skin as he tangled it with hers, his hand searing her belly through her oversize T-shirt. Could he hear her heart thudding against his as she could hear his against her own?

'Abby,' he murmured.

Then his lips slid over hers and settled and she melted into him with a murmur of surrender. Just this once. One more time to sip at the taste of his lips, to explore the velvet of his mouth and swirl her tongue over his. One more chance to feel the weight of his body covering hers and listen to his voice hoarse with passion against her ear.

His hand found the hem of her T-shirt and glided beneath it; hot fingers seeking out her nipple, rolling, pinching, squeezing. Gently, so gently. Then up, taking the fabric with him so that he could lay his lips and tongue on the aching points he'd aroused while his hand slid along the underside of her upper arm, pushing it up and over her head.

She arched a foot, slid it along his calf to feel the texture of hairy skin against her sensitive sole. Tilted her pelvis and rubbed up against the hard, hot ridge of silken steel between them. Moisture formed a delicious friction, and she reached down to touch him there, her fingers reacquainting themselves with his shape and size.

Zak rocked against her, loving the way she stroked him, her little noises of approval and enjoyment. So responsive, so willing. He had to keep her in his life; he wanted her more than he'd wanted anything. He needed her more than his next breath. Couldn't she see that?

He leaned up on his arms to look down on her. Moonlight threaded through her hair, glistened like tiny diamonds on her dewy skin. He trailed one hand from the ridge of collarbone, over a breast, the curve of her waist, till he covered her fingers with his.

Leaning over the side of the bed, he grabbed his trousers and withdrew a condom from his pocket. She nodded, her pewter eyes turning slumberous as he slid the protection on. Then he pushed inside slowly, drawing out the sensations—smooth and tight and hot—every centimetre pure pleasure.

She moaned and writhed beneath him and the sound of her passion was the sweetest music he'd ever heard. He didn't need her words, didn't offer any. Hands that had massaged him with such skill earlier turned intimate, tensing and flexing and slipping over his back in a sinuous rhythm that echoed his movements.

They moved in sync, fitted together as if they'd been constructed as a single unit and forced apart until they found each other again. Pleasure built on pleasure, taking them higher with each thrust, with every breath, until he was poised on the brink of the world. And she was right there with him.

He reared up to watch her passion as he raced with her over the edge. Then he was exploding, splintering, free-falling into the warmth and sanctuary of her waiting embrace.

He didn't want to move. He wanted to stay right here on this crazy single bed with Abby and—he felt her leg slide against his—maybe he could move…if it involved making love with her again. Or they could continue on his comfortable king-size bed.

He levered himself up on one elbow and stroked a finger down her nose, then followed up with a light kiss. 'My bed's bigger.'

She blinked up at him and what he saw in her eyes chilled him to the core. 'I told you. I'm not sleeping in your bed.'

He touched her cheek. So soft, as delicate as an angel's in the moonlight. 'We don't have to sleep.'

'I'm not coming with you.'

Slowly he sat up, propped his arms on his bent knees and looked straight ahead at the wardrobe. Right now it was preferable to looking at Abby and seeing her denial. 'I thought we just shared something incredible. What *was* it to you, then?'

Silence hung thick in the evening air. 'It was good, Zak,' she said at last. There was a waver in her voice. 'The best. But I'm not changing my mind.'

Oh, yes, you will, he said silently as he slid off the bed, and hoped to God he was right.

* * *

For once, Abby didn't look forward to opening Good Vibrations. Facing the clean-up in the shop on too little sleep for one. When she arrived the first things she saw were Zak's shirt and shoes still on the stool where he'd left them. His cologne hung in the air.

She turned the air-conditioner onto High Fan and fully spritzed the area with a room freshener she'd made with a blend of lemon, juniper and peppermint essences.

She didn't see Zak all day.

He turned up as she was shutting the shop at the end of the day. 'Hi. How was your day?'

'Great. Tiring, but that's what I want—lots of clients. How about yours?'

'I've missed you.'

She looked at those blue eyes and yearned with all her heart. 'Zak, don't do this.'

'I'll keep doing this. Until I know it's over.' He closed the space between them until he was within touching distance. 'But it's not over, is it? Not after last night.'

'Zak…'

'Didn't you once tell me I was a stubborn Taurean?' He was standing too close, smelling too enticing… New aftershave? He was also wearing a shirt she hadn't seen before.

'I'm renovating my wardrobe,' he said when he caught her looking. 'What do you think?'

Blue-grey stripe with a maroon silk tie. Different. 'It suits you.'

'Ah. Tomorrow…' his voice switched to business '…we have an important guest visiting Capricorn. I'd like you to schedule two hours free from noon if you would, for an official meet and greet.'

She perked up at the news. 'Who is it?'

'Someone who's looking to retire up here. They seemed

very interested in your Good Vibrations. Maybe they can offer something we may have overlooked. It's good for business. You'll meet them tomorrow. Oh, and dress for a business luncheon.'

'Okay.' She paused. 'About dinner, I'm not—'

'I won't be home till late tonight. I want to make sure everything's right for tomorrow.'

'See you at noon, then.'

Because she couldn't settle that evening, she strolled through the weekly night market along the beachside boardwalk at the top of Cavill Street. A mishmash of colour and light and movement, the sound and smell of the ocean. Holiday-makers and locals alike sauntered past the stalls, eating ice creams and hamburgers.

Not long ago she'd been a visitor. Now she felt like a local. And she was in love with a local, damn his Taurean hide.

She could take Good Vibrations down the coast and start again, without Zak in her life. But she didn't have the money and right now she simply didn't have the energy. It would mean leaving Aurora alone longer than ever.

So she had to find her own apartment, keep her business in Surfers and learn to work alongside Zak. It also meant shutting off her heart.

'Hi.'

Abby felt the familiar adrenaline rush as she looked up from her account book at ten minutes to noon and saw Zak poking his head around the door. And looking good enough to eat in another new shirt and tie.

'Hi. You're not supposed to be here for ten minutes.' She was glad she'd already changed into her business suit. Dragging her hungry gaze away, she shook her head and frowned back at the columns of numbers in front of her. 'I can't get these figures to add up. I'm just not the accountant type.'

Wrong thing to say. Wrong, wrong, wrong, because he came in and stood right behind her. She could feel his body heat burning into her neck. His aftershave teasing her sinuses. Then he leaned down and placed his palms flat on the desk on either side of hers. His breath tickled her ear as he said, 'I'll send Tina down for a couple of hours later.'

She wanted to turn around and kiss that mouth senseless. 'That'd be great. Thanks.'

'So, let's see.' A hairy forearm brushed hers as he reached for her appointment book. 'You've got a good two-hour break.'

His head was so close to hers she swore she could hear him thinking. Then he angled towards her and his eyes fused with hers and she *knew* she'd heard him thinking.

Yeah, what they could have done with a good two hours.

She pushed up and away. 'I'll get my purse. Is your guest here yet?'

'They're running a little behind schedule.' He ushered her down the corridor and into the car park. 'There's something I need to take care of first, and I need you with me.' He opened the passenger door before rounding the hood and buckling up beside her.

'What's going on?'

'Wait and see.' Zak's expression gave nothing away but when she glanced at him Abby saw a slight tension in his jaw and his hands on the steering wheel.

A moment later as they neared Capricorn house Abby frowned, suspicious. 'Why are we going home?'

'Just for a moment…' he said, and turned into the driveway.

And what she saw had her heart rate soaring.

Splashes of potted sunflowers lined the front fence and edged the driveway as he pulled in and came to a stop at the back of the house. Bright yellow ribbons were twined around the veranda posts, their ends fluttering in the breeze.

'Zak. What is all this?' But she thought she knew and…she was afraid to know. Afraid to be right. Afraid to be wrong.

'Abby, look at me.' Infinitely soft words.

Words that scrambled her pulse and turned her legs to jelly. *Think blue*. He tilted her face up with a finger beneath her chin. She was trying to hold the pieces of her heart together but they were slipping away. *Ice-blue. Sky-blue. Lake-blue.* Like his eyes.

Eyes that pierced right through her and saw too much.

'Don't say no to me.' His gaze darkened and never wavered. 'I want you to step out of the car when I open the door and come with me.'

Her mouth must have opened because he pressed a finger to her lips. 'Don't. Say. No.'

She nodded, her nose prickling while she waited for him to come round and open the door. When he did, he placed a simple bouquet of yellow daisies in her arms. She'd never seen anything so beautiful. 'Oh…Zak…'

'Come on, there's more.'

'You've thought of everything,' Abby murmured as they made their way to the veranda.

He yanked his tie so that it hung loose around his neck. 'I hope so, Abby. I damn well hope so.'

She climbed the steps, placed the flowers gently on the table, then walked to the far end to give herself some space. And wait. Zak remained on the top step with his hands in his pockets. The air smelled of flowers and cut grass. Over the fence somewhere she could hear jazz music. She glanced back along the veranda. 'You've bought another rocking chair.'

'One for each of us.'

Her heart stopped, then restarted at double time. Her gaze cut to his. Then it was impossible for her to look away even though his image blurred with unshed moisture. 'You're too busy to sit on a rocking chair for more than two minutes.'

'That's going to change.'

His words stripped her heart bare. But she shook her head. 'I won't leave Aurora alone.'

He nodded. 'We'll get her a rocking chair, too, if you want. She's your family. I'm used to family. When we were kids our great-grandma lived with us till she passed away. There were always relatives staying over. I miss it.

'I miss you. I miss you crowding my space, I miss your laugh, I miss you in my bed.' He was coming towards her with the breeze in his hair and his heart in his eyes. He didn't try to hide his emotion. It was there, in the rigidity of his jaw, the thin line of his lips, the hoarseness of his voice. 'I want to grow old with you, Abby. I want us to sit in those rockers and hold hands when we're ninety and watch our grandchildren play.'

To stop her hands trembling, she curled them into fists and pressed them to her waist. 'You say you miss me. You say you want me in your life. But I have to keep myself safe.' She rushed on. 'I've lived without love for most of my life. I can't…'

'Abby. Baby.' He reached her, took her fists and enclosed them in the rock-solid warmth of his grasp. 'I was getting to that part.' His dimple came out of extended hibernation as he pried her locked fingers apart and entwined them with his. 'As usual, you're one step ahead of me.' He lifted their joined hands to her lips, cutting the rest of her words off. 'Just let me try and get the words out right.'

She waited with her heart beating its way out of her chest as he stepped back and looked into her eyes, and she felt their intensity clear to her soul.

'I love you, Abigail Seymour. When I saw you in the sea that morning I went a little crazy. A lot crazy. I realised I was living in the past, a half-life at best. That the guilt I felt over the circumstances of Diane's death was nothing to what I feel for you. That losing someone you love, losing *you*, is worse than dying.'

Emotion pounded in her heart like the surf she could hear in the distance. It rolled through her veins, crashed in her ears. He loved her? She replayed his words to make sure she'd got it right. *He loved her.*

'I couldn't deal with it,' he continued. 'I had to get away and knock some sanity into myself before I saw you again. I'm sorry it took so damn long. I knew you were hurting. It killed me to see that pain in your eyes, when I left you there on the island, baby. You don't know how I ached to sweep you up and take you back in the chopper with me.' He stroked her cheek with the knuckles of one fist, strength tempered with gentleness. 'But I couldn't. I needed to be whole again.

'You did that for me. You took the pieces and put me back together. You made me look inside myself when I didn't want to see, confronted me at every turn. And you told *me* I was stubborn!' The corners of his mouth curved into a brief smile, then sobered again.

'I don't just want you in my life, Abby. That's not enough. I want to *make* a life with you, to share my life. With you. I made mistakes with Diane. I didn't always put her before work. But you will *always* come first, that I promise you. We can build Capricorn together. Heaven knows, I don't deserve it. I don't deserve you after what I've put you through, but I want a second chance. I'll beg for a second chance if I have to.' He clutched her hands to his chest so she could feel his heart beating a mile a minute beneath. 'Will you marry me, Abby? Will you be the mother of my babies and spend the rest of your life with me?'

'Oh…oh…' She blinked, giving him her wordless answer through blurred eyes, happiness seeping through her body. 'That's perfect. Absolutely perfect.'

'So…' He raised their hands, pressed a kiss to her knuckles. 'What do you say?'

'Kiss me, already.'

'With pleasure.'

And his kiss was filled with all the love she'd seen in his eyes. Warming her lips, filling her heart. Finally, breathless, he drew back. 'Do you have an answer for me?'

She sniffed, smiling through her tears, and reached out to creep her fingers over his chest. 'Do you really need one?'

'I do. I want to hear the words. One word, to be precise.'

'Then the answer's yes. In triplicate. I love you, Zak. I've loved you for so long.' She sniffed. 'No tissue.'

He grinned. 'Go ahead and use my tie.'

'But we have an important luncheon appointment.'

'And I have a stack of new ties.'

A short time later, he ushered her past the poolside café with a light touch at her back. 'We're eating at the Capricorn Bistro.'

'Ooh, flashy,' she murmured, wondering if she was walking on air. She was still reeling with the events of the past half-hour.

'Important,' he told her.

She straightened her lapels again. Tucked a stray hair behind her ear. 'Do I look all right? You still haven't told me what to expect.'

'You look perfect. Wait and see.'

They were met and greeted at the restaurant's reservation desk like— Well, to the wait staff, Zak *was* royalty, she supposed.

Light from the central chandelier glinted off crystal and silver. Tables looked inviting in maroon cloths with snowy-white napkins. Something violin and classical played in the background. Abby's feet sank into the plush cream carpet as they made their way towards the view of the ocean.

An elderly woman with vivid pink hair in flowing tangerine pants and lime-green top was already studying the menu at the table by the window. Her back was towards them but only one woman Abby knew dressed that way…

She slowed, then stopped, surprise and anticipation beating a fast rhythm through her veins. 'Rory?'

The woman turned, her lined face creasing into a smile, and Abby's breath caught, released, caught again. 'It *is* you.' Happiness burst like bubbles as she rushed towards Rory's open arms and held on tight. 'Oh, Rory, it's so, so good to see you.'

'You, too, Abby dearest.' Rory's words were muffled against Abby's cheek.

Still clutching Aurora's hands Abby leaned back. 'You're looking so much better than the last time I saw you! Where's Maddie? When did you get in? Why didn't you let me pick you up at the airport?'

'Your young man picked me up yesterday.'

'My…oh…' Her gaze switched between the two of

them. 'Zak arranged all this?' She felt perilously close to tears again.

'We spent a very pleasant evening getting properly acquainted. He put me up in a luxury suite with twenty-four-hour room service and my own maid on call.' Her face puckered as she smiled up at him. 'I let Maddie go. I don't need a carer with you and—'

'I didn't know you were coming!' Abby almost wailed. 'You never said a word.'

'Zak swore me to secrecy. We've had a couple of long talks by phone.'

'Long talks…' Aurora and Zak had been having long talks and not telling her? If she wasn't so happy she'd have felt left out. 'And did he let you chart his horoscope?' She heard the tinge of sarcasm in her voice.

Aurora squeezed Abby's hand, her smile widening, her eyes twinkling up at him. 'Yes, as a matter of fact he did.'

He hadn't let *Abby* chart his horoscope. No, not quite true. She'd never asked him because she *knew* he thought it was a crock. Her nose prickled ominously. Oh, she was going to tear up again. *Think blue, think blue.*

He'd brought Aurora here to surprise Abby. He knew what she wanted, what she needed. Knew her better than anyone else. 'I need another tissue,' she muttered, fumbling in her pocket. 'Never have a darn tissue when I need one.'

'Come here, baby.' Zak wrapped his arms around her, drew her against his warm masculine body and just held her. 'Use my tie again,' he whispered against her ear. 'The shirt, too, if you need it.'

A wet, sobbing laugh bubbled up as she clutched fistfuls of the crisp new fabric. Dabbed at her eyes with the soft silk tie. Sniffing, she flapped a hand behind her for Aurora.

'Join the party.' And gathered them into a three-way clinch.
'Sorry. Emotional overload.'

Aurora was the first to break away. 'Well, you two can
stand there and canoodle all you want, but I'm going to sit
right down here and wait for this calorie-laden meal Zak's
ordered. The man's positively wicked.'

Oh, yes. Abby knew. Wicked, and tempting and… She
hiccupped… Hers. 'Oh, Rory. That man you're accusing
of wickedness is my fiancé.'

It was Rory's turn to look wicked as she sat down. 'I
know, dear. He's the Taurean I saw in your horoscope.'

Somehow Abby managed to make it through the meal,
though she couldn't remember what she'd eaten, or if she'd
eaten anything at all. Aurora and Zak talked like old
friends. It warmed Abby's heart to see her more animated,
more cheery than she'd been in a long time. And Zak,
well…for the first time in her experience, he looked alive.

When the two hours were up, and Abby reluctantly
excused herself to get back to work, Zak informed her
he'd employed another massage therapist for the rest of the
day.

Then Zak drove them back home. He walked Aurora
inside, outlining his plans for the house, Abby following
more slowly.

She passed Zak's bedroom door. And didn't realise
she'd stopped moving. Stopped breathing. There was
Abby's photo—on his nightstand in her green cocktail
dress. The one he'd taken off her that first night they'd
made love.

Aurora and Zak were admiring the tropical garden
through the back door, but they turned when Abby reached
the kitchen. 'Ah, there you are,' Aurora said, and tapped
her cane lightly on the floor. 'I'm going to take a nap.'

Zak straightened away from the door frame, walked to the table and unrolled a long sheet of paper. 'If you wouldn't mind, Aurora, before you do, Abby hasn't seen the renovation plans for the studio yet and I'd like to show both of you while you're here.'

Abby looked up in surprise. 'I thought you were turning it into a gym?'

His eyes met hers. 'My plans changed.'

The studio was now officially going to be turned into a bedsit with its own tiny kitchenette and it didn't seem as if anything had been overlooked.

'I'm employing the instant kitchen renovations crew. No more additional working hours.' He pulled Abby to him. 'I've got better things to do with my time.' His eyes were laser-bright and full of promises. 'And Aurora can stay whenever she likes, as long as she likes. Permanently, if she wishes.'

'And until then, Rory, you can sleep in my room.' Abby looked up at the man she loved, who loved her back. 'I've officially moved out.'

It was another half hour before Zak could finally seduce his fiancée into bed to celebrate in private. They decided to keep it secret a few days until they had a ring to show off. Aurora was the only one privy to the happy news. But then she already knew—she'd charted both their horoscopes weeks ago.

Zak played with the ends of Abby's hair as she kissed her way over his chest in the languid aftermath of lovemaking. He couldn't get enough of her hair.

'I want a garden wedding,' she said, between kisses. 'Here, at Capricorn.'

'You can have whatever you want, as long as it's soon.'

She looked up at him and a smile spread over her face. 'Whatever I want, really?' She settled in beside him. 'The truth, then. When was the first time you knew you loved me?'

'Easy. The first night I came home and you'd left the porch light on for me. I realised I'd been marking time, that my life had been on hold, not for the reasons I'd clung to but because I'd been waiting for you. Of course, I didn't know it at the time.'

'I'll always wait for you, Zak.' And her kiss warmed him all the way to his toes.

'No more waiting. You won't need to leave the light on again,' he murmured against her mouth, absorbing the sweet taste of her love. 'We'll drive home together from this day forward.'

Smiling, Abby rose up on one elbow to look at him. His eyes, warm with wanting and full of love, smiled back at her.

He was home, he was whole, and, best of all, he was hers. She sighed with satisfaction and kissed him again.

Mission accomplished.

* * * * *

BOUGHT: DAMSEL IN DISTRESS

BY
LUCY KING

Lucy King spent her formative years lost in the world of romance novels when she really ought to have been paying attention to her teachers. Up against sparkling heroines, gorgeous heroes and the magic of falling in love, trigonometry and absolute ablatives didn't stand a chance.

But, as she couldn't live in a dreamworld forever, she eventually acquired a degree in languages and an eclectic collection of jobs. A stroll to the river Thames one Saturday morning led her to her very own hero. The minute she laid eyes on the hunky rower getting out of a boat, clad only in Lycra® and carrying a three-meter oar as if it were a toothpick, she knew she'd met the man she was going to marry. Luckily the rower thought the same.

She will always be grateful to whatever it was that made her stop dithering and actually sit down to type Chapter One, because dreaming up her own sparkling heroines and gorgeous heroes is pretty much her idea of the perfect job.

Originally a Londoner, Lucy now lives in Spain, where she spends much of her time reading, failing to finish cryptic crosswords and trying to convince herself that lying on the beach really is the best way to work.

To my family, for their unfailing support.

CHAPTER ONE

'YOU must be wondering what sort of girl ends up for auction on the internet,' said Emily, picking up her glass of champagne and taking a quick sip. If she'd known such a course of action would lead to being swept off to the south of France by a gorgeous man in his private jet she'd have done it years ago, and to hell with what sort of girl it made her.

'The thought had crossed my mind,' Luke replied. He reached for his briefcase and flicked open the catches.

Emily settled back into the beige leather seat and looked out of the window, down at the fields and towns outside London as they blurred into ever smaller smudges of grey and green. 'What conclusions did you draw?' she said distractedly.

'I couldn't possibly comment.'

'That bad?' Was he being serious? Emily stifled a tiny sigh of defeat. Trying not to stare at the handsome face, broad shoulders and lean body of the man sitting diagonally opposite her, trying not to ogle the big tanned hands extracting a report from a folder, wasn't working. It was like struggling to ignore the pull of a very strong magnet. Impossible. Her eyes swivelled to the dark head bent over the papers.

'Unrepeatable,' he replied, glancing up at her.

There went her stomach again. Slowly flipping over at the combination of eyes the colour of the Mediterranean in summer, the sexy half-smile and the deep, rumbling voice. Swooping in a way that had nothing to do with the flight.

Emily wrinkled her nose. 'I can imagine. I'd have run through Lonely to Loopy with a stop-off at Desperate on the way. Not that I am any of those, of course,' she added hastily.

'Of course not,' he said, in a tone that suggested he thought just that. 'How did you guess?'

Ooooh, *ouch.* 'I simply imagined what sort of person would respond to an ad like that,' she replied sweetly.

Luke sat back and fixed her with a coolly amused stare. 'I see you've regained the power of speech. It's back with a bite.'

Emily fought the urge to squirm under his penetrating gaze and gave him what she thought might look like an apologetic smile. 'Today has taken on an unexpectedly surreal quality. I'm only just getting my head round it.'

The moment they'd met, the instant she'd put her hand in his to shake it, she'd been struck uncharacteristically dumb. Her body had felt as though it had received a thousand-volt charge. Her heart had jumped and she'd gone momentarily dizzy, the blood racing to parts of her body that had been out of action for so long she'd forgotten she had them. She'd never experienced sexual attraction like it, and it was making her feel slightly unhinged.

'You don't invite strange men to transport you to foreign countries often?' he asked, tilting his head to one side.

'I don't invite strange men to transport me anywhere ever.'

'In that case why are you here?'

Emily shuddered. 'You met my sister.'

He nodded. 'A formidable woman.'

He sounded as if he thought this was an admirable quality. Emily frowned and pinched the bridge of her nose. 'You have *no* idea.'

Four hours earlier

'You did *what*?' Emily nearly dropped her muffin into her cappuccino as her head snapped up and she gaped at her sister.

'I said I sold you. On the internet.' Anna glanced at her watch and then wiped her sons' faces.

Emily felt a sliver of concern and raked her gaze over her sister's immaculate exterior. Had she gone mad? Anna certainly looked normal, but who knew what could be lurking beneath the surface? If this was what motherhood did to a previously perfectly intelligent, clear-thinking woman then she was glad she'd made the decision never to have children herself.

She nodded as if in understanding. 'Right. You sold me. On the internet. Aren't there laws against things like that?'

'Apparently not. It was surprisingly easy,' replied Anna, calmly folding the tissue and placing it on her empty plate.

'You are joking, aren't you?'

Anna fixed Emily with a stern stare. 'Not at all. I'm deadly serious.'

It was a look Emily was very familiar with. As realisation dawned, her smile slipped from her face. 'Oh, my God. You *are* serious.'

'Of course. I wouldn't joke about a thing like this.'

Emily began to hyperventilate.

'Now, don't get hysterical,' said Anna, thrusting a glass of water into her hand. 'Deep breaths… If it makes you feel any better, I didn't exactly sell *you.*'

Emily flapped her other hand in front of her face and fought for breath. 'So what did you sell?' she said, when she was finally able to speak.

Anna shrugged. 'A once-in-a-lifetime opportunity. In this age of equality, a chance to be chivalrous. The rescue of a damsel in distress.'

What? Since when had her sister developed a romantic streak? 'And I'm the damsel?'

Anna nodded.

'But why would you do that?' Emily asked, utterly bewildered. 'I'm not in distress.'

'You are. The French baggage handlers are on strike.'

Oh, no, not this again.

'Don't look at me like that,' said Anna indignantly. 'Your obstinate refusal to go to Tom's wedding is not healthy. You haven't been out for so much as a drink with anyone since you split up. That's not a single date in over a year. You need closure, and you're not going to get it until you see the rat safely hitched to some other poor woman. Then you'll be able to move on.'

'He may have dumped me and got engaged to an aristocratic French floozy two months later, but he's not a rat,' said Emily wearily, ignoring the sceptical look Anna threw her. 'And for the millionth time I *have* moved on.'

Anna glanced at her watch. 'Talking of moving on, we need to go home.' She turned, and with an imperceptible nod of her head signalled for the bill.

'Why?' Emily said carefully, tendrils of suspicion winding round her nerves.

'Because the person who won the auction is turning up at any minute.'

Emily gaped in horror. 'What? *Now*?'

'Of course,' Anna replied, standing up and brushing a crumb off her front. 'The wedding is tomorrow, isn't it?'

Emily could only nod in dumb stupefaction.

'Well, then. You leave this afternoon.' Anna marched to the bar to pay, leaving Emily to unravel the chaos of the last five minutes. But it was all too much. Where did she start?

'Who won?' she managed eventually as they started along the path that led across the common to Anna's house.

'A man called Luke Harrison. He was very determined. The bidding went right to the wire. It was gripping stuff, I can tell you.'

'I'm so glad.' Emily's sarcastic tone went unnoticed.

'So was I. *greatsexguaranteed* was also extremely persistent, but I had a funny feeling about him.'

'Can't think why. So how is this Luke Harrison going to

help me get to France?' Emily panted, struggling to keep up with Anna's brutal pace.

'Private jet. Rather inspired, I thought.'

'But I have plans this weekend. I can't just drop everything.'

Anna shot her a sceptical look. 'A pot that urgently needs glazing?'

Emily bit her lip and nodded.

'You're twenty-eight. You should be Out There. Meeting men. Not hunched over a wheel with clay under your nails. Pots won't keep you warm at night.'

Emily glared at Anna mutinously. 'I have an electric blanket.'

Anna marched on, undeterred.

Emily tried again. 'How do you know he's got a plane? How do you know he's going to turn up? He might be a lunatic. I mean, what sort of person bids for a woman in an internet auction? He could be a kidnapper, a murderer—anyone.' Her voice was rising, becoming more desperate. Anna merely looked at her witheringly and Emily threw her hands up in exasperation. 'You're insane.'

'I'm a genius. Don't be so melodramatic. I spoke to his mother on the phone and discovered that we have friends in common.'

Emily's jaw dropped. 'His mother?'

'I had to get references,' said Anna defensively. 'You don't think I'd send you off with just anyone, do you?'

'I am suddenly at a complete loss as to *what* you would do.'

'I've arranged for him to pick you up here so that we can check him out first. Just in case.'

Emily ground her teeth. 'It'll be a wasted journey. I'm not going.'

Anna stopped at the bottom of the steps leading up to her front door and rummaged in her bag for the keys. 'Think of the charity.'

Emily's eyes narrowed. 'What charity?'

'The money Mr Harrison paid is going to a charity that in-vestigates and helps prevent maternal mortality.'

Emily gasped. A familiar dull pain clenched her heart and she felt the blood drain from her face. 'That's a low blow, Anna,' she said quietly.

'It's not meant to be, darling. But I spent years bringing you up and I hate to see you wasting your life over that loser. Will you do it for me?'

Emily wavered. She owed her sister so much. Anna had made huge sacrifices on her behalf. When their father had died, fourteen years after their mother, it had been left to Anna to raise her. And she knew she hadn't been the easiest of teen-agers to handle. Besides, her sister in this mode was unstop-pable, and there was only so much battering she could take. Her resistance crumbled and she let out a resigned sigh. 'OK. Assuming he's not crazy, or worse, I'll go. Can I take David with me?'

'No husband borrowing. Besides, he's at a conference in New York.'

Emily straightened her spine. 'Fine. I'll just have to enter the lion's den single and strong and shod in killer heels.'

'They're already packed.'

Emily raised an eyebrow. 'How ruthlessly efficient.'

Anna inclined her head. 'Thank you.'

'It's not a compliment.'

But Anna wasn't paying attention. She was staring over Emily's shoulder, and her expression became dreamy. 'I think this might be him. Bang on time too.'

Emily turned to look at the man striding towards them. He was tall, broad-shouldered and very good-looking, and a dart of awareness shivered through her. 'If it is,' she murmured, watching the sun glinting off his dark hair, 'I may just forgive you.'

After that her composure had taken such a hammering she couldn't really remember what had happened. Her sensible court-shoe-wearing sister had batted her eyelashes and giggled her way through some very rudimentary questions about his integrity and his intentions, had established that Luke Harrison was single, solvent, and in possession of a plane, and had then bundled Emily into his car without so much as a backward glance. Was it any wonder that she'd been unable to formulate a sensible sentence throughout the journey to the airport?

'So, why are you here?'

Luke's voice jerked her out of her reverie. 'Oh, er—' She stopped. She could hardly tell him the truth. Revealing that she was heading to her ex-fiancé's wedding to another woman would rather negate her earlier declaration that she was neither lonely nor desperate. 'A friend's getting married near Nice, and Anna was under the misapprehension that I wanted to go to the wedding.'

'Scheduled airlines a little pedestrian?'

Emily bristled. 'Of course a man who has a private plane wouldn't know about anything as trivial as industrial action, but for us mere mortals a baggage handlers' strike does tend to put a spanner in the works.'

Luke had the grace to look a little apologetic. Only fleetingly, but it was enough to mollify her. 'The only flights that weren't cancelled were full. Which suited me fine.' Emily twiddled a lock of hair around her finger. 'I have better things to do with my weekend than go to a wedding I don't want to attend.'

'Why didn't you say so earlier? I could have dropped you home on the way to the airport.'

'I did think about it, but Anna probably has her spies ready and waiting in France, primed to report back on my every move from the moment I arrive. You saw her earlier. She'd broken into my house to pack and pick up my passport. She didn't tell me that she'd put me up for auction until about half an hour before you showed up, and even then she deliberately waited until we were in a public place so I couldn't throttle her.' Not to mention the emotional blackmail that Anna had deployed with such success. Emily sighed. 'She's utterly devious. It's not worth the grief. I'll just have to grin and bear it and count down the hours until you take me back.'

'She went to a hell of an effort so that you could attend this wedding. Why would she do that if she knew you didn't want to go?'

Emily shrugged evasively. Those blue eyes of his were far too probing for her comfort. 'Beats me. Before she went on maternity leave she used to troubleshoot for one of the big accountancy firms. I think she's been missing the challenge. Do you have siblings?'

'No. I do, however, have relatives with an over-zealous interest in my well-being, so I can sympathise.'

'Perhaps they should meet. We could cast them into a parallel universe where they're forced to watch reality TV on a ten-minute loop for all eternity.'

One corner of Luke's mouth lifted and Emily was instantly transfixed by the movement. What did his lips feel like? she wondered. Soft or firm? What would they feel like moving over hers? Her own mouth tingled at the thought and her pulse leapt. An image of him tugging her into his arms, plastering her up against that hard body, kissing her senseless slammed into her head, making her dizzy and breathless. Then she noticed his smile fading. When she looked up his face was blank, but his eyes had darkened to indigo.

Something resembling irritation flashed across his face. Emily swallowed and tried to get a grip. 'So, what exactly did the advert say?'

'It offered a once-in-a-lifetime opportunity to be a knight in shining armour. The chance to rescue a damsel in distress. And mentioned the more prosaic need for a plane, a passport and a free weekend.'

Emily bit her lip and nodded. Then she frowned. 'That's it?'

'There was a photo.'

She went cold. 'A photo?' Oh, God. 'Which one?'

'You were on a beach.'

Emily went even colder. Please, no. She took a deep breath. 'Green bikini?'

'That's the one.'

Freezing to red hot in under a second. It had to be a record, she thought, as her cheeks burned. If it was the picture she was thinking of, she was wearing a green rather-on-the-small-side bikini. In fact, she wasn't so much wearing it as falling out of it. 'I'm going to kill her,' she muttered.

'Why?'

'Why?' she spluttered. Oh, the humiliation.

'You had over a hundred people bidding for you.'

'Really?' Emily's pride swelled for a moment, before mortification squashed it. She dropped her head in her hands. 'How could she do that?' she mumbled. 'Of all the photos… I don't know why she didn't just put a flyer in a phone box and be done with it.'

Luke laughed and the sound rumbled right through her, scrambling her brain momentarily.

'Dare I ask which category she put me in?'

'Are you sure you want to know?'

'Not entirely. But you might as well complete my humiliation.'

'Collectibles. Decorative Objects.'

Emily groaned. It went from bad to worse. How long could she stay there with her head buried in her hands? For ever? At some point she'd have to look up. Denial, that was the thing. Generally she wasn't a fan of denial, but this was an exceptional circumstance.

Fixing a neutral expression on her face, Emily lifted her head and shot him a curious glance. 'Why did you bid?'

Luke went still and his gaze dropped to his papers. Then he shrugged. 'To be honest, I'm not sure.'

A flicker of something that Emily couldn't identify passed over his face. Whatever his motives had been, like her, he wasn't sharing. 'A rash impulse?' she suggested helpfully, when no further answer seemed forthcoming.

Luke sat back and looked at her, that faint smile still playing around his mouth and doing all sorts of strange, fluttery things to her stomach.

'Maybe it appealed to my adventurous side.'

Emily considered this. Adventurous? For a man who must regularly fly by private jet? She shook her head. 'Nope, sorry, I'm sticking with the rash impulse.'

'Maybe I was intrigued by the idea of being a knight in shining armour.'

Right. Sure. She didn't believe that for a second either. 'With a plane instead of a horse?'

'A suit instead of the armour.'

'Same thing sometimes,' she batted back.

He tilted his head and regarded her thoughtfully. 'Very true,' he said finally.

'With a laptop instead of a lance,' she added, tapping a finger against her mouth. 'Of course, no real knight would be anything without a castle.'

Luke rubbed his jaw. 'A castle?'

'At the very least. A palace would be ideal.'

'Would a penthouse in Mayfair do instead?'

She pretended to give it some consideration. 'Lots of chrome and steel and glass and thoroughly pointless gadgets?'

Luke nodded. 'Goes without saying.'

'In that case, congratulations. You're really rather well-qualified for the role of knight.'

'Thank you. How well-suited are you to being a damsel in distress?'

'Not well at all, I'm afraid,' she said with a rueful smile. 'No flowing locks and no ivory tower.'

'No evil father and wicked stepmother either, I hope.' Amusement glinted in his eyes.

'No parents at all,' she said evenly.

The amusement faded. 'I'm sorry.'

Emily shrugged. 'Don't be. They died a long time ago.' The lightness of her tone belied the clench of her heart. She knew it did. She'd spent years perfecting it. Swallowing down the lump that had lodged in her throat, she gave him a bright smile. 'So, knights in shining armour aside, do you often look for women on the internet?'

From the scowl that appeared on his face, Emily deduced that he didn't appreciate what she was implying. 'Sorry,' she said, flushing slightly. 'That didn't come out quite the way I expected.'

Luke picked up his pen and uncapped it. 'It's an inevitable assumption. But, no, I don't trawl the internet looking for women.'

Of course he didn't, she mused. He probably had women tripping over themselves to appear on his arm. He clearly hadn't entered into the bidding war because he'd been overwhelmed by her curves.

'A friend of mine e-mailed me the link. I was going to Nice anyway. I was curious.'

Bizarre. It was bizarre enough to be true. She hardly knew him. It might be exactly the sort of thing he would do. How did she know?

'Just out of interest, how much did I fetch?'

He smiled suddenly at her, and her breath caught. 'Do you want it in dollars, euros or pounds? It's a global market out there, you know.'

She couldn't help smiling back. 'An estimate will do.'

'Around six figures.'

Emily nearly knocked over her glass.

'Are you mad?'

His jaw tightened. 'Very possibly.'

A tiny trickle of ice shivered down her spine at his tone. He wasn't joking. Emily stared at him as he raked a hand through his hair and yanked open the top button of his shirt. On a plane with a madman, however gorgeous, was not top of her list of ideal scenarios and if he'd said 'yes' instead of 'possibly' she'd be reaching for the nearest parachute. 'At least it's tax deductible.'

'There is that,' he agreed.

'Why are you going to Nice?'

'Meetings in Monte Carlo.'

She tilted her head. 'Convenient.'

'You don't believe me.'

Emily shot him an assessing glance. 'I'm not sure.'

He clutched his chest as if in pain. 'I'm wounded.'

'I'm devastated that you're wounded.'

'You should be. Your sister accepted my reasons without question.'

Did she? Emily's eyes narrowed. 'My sister's brain has been pulverised by motherhood,' she said darkly.

'You're more wary?'

'Maybe,' she murmured, wrenching her eyes from his and looking down at where her fingers were playing with the ends of the scarf tied round her head.

That particular avenue of conversation was not one she wanted to pursue. Weaving the strands between her fingers, she found herself wondering whether it was true. She'd spent hours analysing her relationship with Tom and what had gone wrong, but she hadn't looked at the effects it had left behind.

She probably had become more wary since breaking up with him, she acknowledged, her brow creasing. Five years with the same man was a long time, even if the last year had been pretty rocky, and her dating skills were rusty. Plus, she thought she'd known her ex-fiancé inside out, and it turned out she hadn't known him at all.

Perhaps Anna was right. Perhaps she did need closure. It wasn't normal for a girl of twenty-eight to hang up her dating shoes. She did need to get Out There.

At least her reaction to Luke proved that she was still capable of feeling sexual desire. Emily stole a peek at him from beneath her lashes just to make sure that it was still there. He was reading a report with amazing speed, underlining sections, writing notes, his long fingers flicking though the pages, almost *caressing* the paper. Oh, yes, sexual desire was definitely still there, if the bolt of fire that spread through her was any proof. Her gaze slid up to where a wedge of chest was exposed by the open collar of his shirt. Her focus zoomed in on the fine dark hairs that emerged from the bottom of the V, and she had to ball her hands into fists to stop her fingers whipping up and ripping open another couple of buttons.

'I can't concentrate on my report if you keep staring at me like that.'

Emily froze. Oh, God. He was watching her watching him! Had she been caught in the act? How excruciating. She tentatively lifted her gaze further, fully expecting to see a mocking glint in his eyes, but he was still looking down. That was even worse: he'd been able to *feel* her eyes devouring him. She went crimson and clapped her hands to her cheeks, turning an involuntary groan of shame into a lengthy cough.

'Would you like some water?' he enquired mildly, still apparently absorbed.

She cleared her throat. 'Yes, but don't worry. I'll get it.' Standing up and moving around would do her good. It might even give her body the opportunity to redistribute her blood away from her face. 'I wouldn't want your concentration to be disturbed any further,' she added, levering herself out of the seat.

She wandered across the cream carpet towards the drinks cabinet where Luke had poured her champagne when they'd boarded. What a way to travel. No interminable check-in queues, no stuffing your case into an overfilled overhead locker and yourself into an uncomfortable seat. And a travelling companion that looked like Luke. Her skin prickled and she went warm.

'Would you like anything?' she asked, taking a bottle of water out of the fridge and filling a glass. She pressed the cold bottle against her cheek and felt it cool her overheated body.

Sticking a hand in the back pocket of her jeans, she took a sip and bent down to look out of the window at the great expanse of azure sky.

'No, thanks. And you're disturbing me.'

Emily blinked, instantly aware that her skin had prickled, was still tingling, because his eyes had been burning into her back. 'No, I'm not,' she said calmly. 'You're watching me.'

A pause, and then, 'Like I said, you're disturbing me.'

CHAPTER TWO

EMILY went still while her body temperature rocketed. Had he really just said that? Did it mean what she thought it meant? She straightened and turned, eyes wide, not quite sure what to say next.

Luke wasn't in his seat. He'd moved to the fax machine and was shuffling the pages into the feeder. What with the hum of the engines and the thickness of the carpet she hadn't heard him move.

She took a deep breath. 'Am I?' she said.

Luke didn't break from what he was doing. 'Are you what?'

'Disturbing you?'

'Not at all,' he said, whipping round and flashing her a brief smile. 'Make yourself at home. Help yourself to anything you like.'

What?

Then she shrugged. She must have misunderstood, she decided, following his movements over the rim of her glass as he strode back to the chair. He picked up his own glass and tossed the contents down his throat. Emily slid back into her seat and watched him as he leaned and twisted over to pull out another report. The muscles in his torso were clearly defined beneath his shirt. He pushed up his sleeves to reveal strong, tanned forearms and her mouth went dry.

Emily didn't generally have a thing about forearms, but

Luke's were—well, they were making her reconsider. Tanned, muscled, lightly sprinkled with rough hair. She felt a fierce urge to run her hands over them. Her eyes fell to the long brown fingers idly twirling the pen as he concentrated on the report. Compared to the speed with which he'd read the last document, this one seemed hard going. In fact, he hadn't turned the page once, and he hadn't underlined a single word or made any notes whatsoever. If pressed, she'd have sworn he was distracted.

She would do the decent thing and rescue him from his torturous report by dazzling him with her conversational skills. But before she could make a start on finding out what made this enticingly enigmatic man tick, Luke shot to his feet and went to pour himself some more water.

'Don't you drink?' she asked when he returned. She'd been merrily sipping away at her champagne since take-off, but he hadn't touched a drop.

'Not on a Friday when I've got meetings in the afternoon.'

She nodded sagely. 'Very wise. On the other hand, who arranges meetings on a Friday afternoon? It's practically the weekend.'

'I have clients in Monte Carlo. And it's not the weekend.'

Mmm. 'What do you do?'

'I'm a fund manager.'

'Ah, interesting.'

Luke smiled. 'Not really. Unless you happen to have an obsession with derivatives and index futures.'

'Which you do?'

'I seem to have a knack for making money out of them.'

And didn't that neatly avoid the question? She nodded in what she hoped was a knowledgeable fashion. 'I should imagine there are quite a few high net worth individuals in Monte Carlo.'

Luke's eyebrows shot up. 'You know about high net worth individuals?'

'Don't sound so surprised. I know a little about lots of things.'

'Like what?' He linked his hands together and leaned forward.

'Like how City boys like you can spend ten thousand pounds on a gold leaf cocktail,' she said, giving him a small smile to show she was half joking.

Luke frowned. 'A few do. I don't. And nor do any of my staff. They don't have time. Plus, they know they'd be fired if they did.'

She shuddered. Ruthless as well as gorgeous. A dangerously attractive combination.

He shot her a sudden killer smile that had her blood racing round her body. 'Besides, I prefer to spend my money on rescuing damsels.'

'You mean there are others?' she said, trying not to sound too curious.

'Not at the moment. It's very distressing.'

Emily let out a burst of laughter.

'What about you? What do you do?'

'A bit of this, a bit of that.' Emily smiled at the quizzical look on his face. 'I'm a professional temp, currently resting.' She waited. This was the moment when people usually scoffed at her, or told her what an idiot she was for not pursuing a proper career.

Luke leaned back. 'What made you choose to be a temp?'

Emily was taken aback. He sounded genuinely interested. Most people assumed that she was temping until she could find a proper job. Whereas she'd made a deliberate decision to make it a career. 'I like the flexibility. Days off when I want. It's perfect. It gives me time to do the things I love doing.'

He was looking at her as though she was speaking in a foreign language. 'Such as?'

'Spending time with my sister and her twins. Seeing friends, potting, that kind of thing.'

'Potting?'

'Potting. Making pots.'

'Are you any good?'

'No idea. But I don't have to be. It's a hobby. I do it for fun.' That wasn't strictly true. She'd love to make a living out of it, but she suspected she wasn't much good. 'Temping is really just a way of paying the bills. Funnily enough, I once worked at a fund manager's.'

'Oh? Which one?'

'JT Investments. Do you know it?'

Luke nodded. 'I know the CEO.'

'Jack Taylor? I never met him, but the work was interesting. Challenging.' She shrugged. 'That's what I mean. I like the variety of the work. Meeting new people, discovering new gossip without any need to get involved in office politics. And then, just when you start thinking it's getting a tad monotonous—which, let's face it, most jobs are—you get to leave and try something else. It's great.' She grinned at him. He still wasn't getting it, but that was all right, most people didn't. She leaned forward. 'Are you sure you don't want to give me a lecture on the folly of my decision? About how unstable temping is, and how my brain must be atrophying, and that at my age I really should be sprinting up a career ladder?'

'Why would I do that? You clearly enjoy what you do.' He frowned slightly at this, as if it was an unfamiliar concept to him. 'And it's none of my business.'

Emily sniffed. 'That doesn't stop most people.'

He looked at her thoughtfully. 'I know… I've been on the receiving end of something similar.'

'Really?'

Something in his voice—bitterness, weariness, maybe—had her senses leaping to attention. 'What would people lecture you about, I wonder?' she said.

In the long silent seconds while he regarded her, Emily's heart began to beat faster.

'Apparently I need more fun in my life,' he said eventually, his tone leaving her in no doubt about what he thought of that piece of advice. 'Apparently I work too hard.'

'Do you?'

'Perhaps.'

'Why?' she asked, suddenly feeling that she was entering into choppy water.

'Habit,' he said flatly.

'What do you do to relax?'

'Relax?' His brows snapped together.

'Yes, you know. Relax. Chill out, unwind.'

'I don't have time to relax.'

Okaaayyy. 'What about the fun part?'

His eyes glittered. 'If I needed fun in my life,' he said, his voice rumbling over her, 'I'd be perfectly capable of finding it.'

The way he was looking at her, his gaze scorching over her face before resting on her mouth, set her blood to boiling. His eyes had turned the colour of the sky at midnight and his expression shifted, darkened, intensified—as if there was only one thing on his mind. Then it vanished and his face was impassive once again.

But Emily had caught it. She *hadn't* been mistaken about what exactly it was that had been disturbing him earlier.

For that brief moment Luke had considered finding fun with *her.*

Her heart pounded and her ears popped. The problem was, she mused, as the pilot's voice advised them they were starting their descent, that once they'd landed and gone their separate ways there wasn't anything that could be done about it.

He should have left her at the bloody airport, thought Luke grimly, handing the porter a crisp note and watching him disappear with Emily's suitcase.

That would have been the sensible, logical, rational thing to do. It was a shame, then, that sense, logic and reason had taken a hike hours ago.

'Are you sure this is the right place?' Emily was squinting up at the hotel and rocking on her heels.

'Yes,' he said curtly. Her sister had booked her into the one of the oldest, most exclusive hotels on the coast.

'But look at the place,' she wailed. 'And look at me.'

Against his better judgement, he did as she suggested. He ran his gaze over her profile. Wavy fair hair was held back in a wide scarf, the ends of which dangled down her back. She was wearing a close fitting pink T-shirt and well-worn jeans that hugged the curve of her bottom. He felt a savage kick of desire in the pit of his stomach as he followed the long line of her legs to where fuchsia-painted toenails were peeping out of some sort of high-heeled shoe.

'They'll never let me in in jeans—and non-designer ones at that.'

'You have a room booked for two nights at five hundred euros a night,' Luke said tersely. 'They're not going to question what you're wearing.'

Emily swivelled to face him, her jaw dropping. 'Five hundred euros? A night?'

'A night,' he confirmed, grabbing her elbow and leading her into the lobby. 'You'd better make the most of it.'

'I shall,' she said, flashing him a wicked smile. The sooner he got out of here the better. 'I'll raid the mini bar and download dozens of saucy films, and then Anna will rue the day she decided to auction me off to the highest bidder.'

Saucy films? Luke's jaw clenched. His fingers tightened and he quickened his pace. He needed to leave. Now. Before he succumbed to the demands his body had been making since the moment he'd laid eyes on her.

He propelled her across the lobby, deposited her at the reception desk, and took a step back. For a second he just stared at her, his mind suddenly blank. Then he noticed that her mouth, that highly distracting mouth, was moving. He forced his attention to what she was saying.

'Thank you for the lift,' she said, smiling faintly.

'You're welcome. It was on my way anyway. Have a good weekend.'

A shadow flickered across her face, clouding her eyes. 'I'll try. You too.'

Luke gave her a brief nod, turned on his heel and strode towards the door. With every step he felt the return of his focus. Hell, not just his focus. His sanity. Ever since he'd clicked on that damn link that Jack had sent him and seen her photo he'd been steadily losing it. Lusting over her picture as if he was a hormonal adolescent instead of the cool, disciplined, rock-steady man he had made himself become. For a man who liked to be in control, the last few hours had been a harrowing experience.

'Luke?'

Her voice reached him when he was halfway to the door. You didn't hear that, he muttered to himself. Don't stop. Nearly there.

'Luke?'

This time her voice was closer and huskier, wrapping round the sound of his name like velvet, and it slammed him to a halt. He turned to find Emily standing a foot away from him, looking at him warily. 'Yes?'

'Would you come to this wedding with me?'

When Luke went rigid, and paled beneath his tan, Emily instantly regretted the impulse that had made her run after him. She shouldn't have asked. She knew that. It was just that as he'd walked away she'd had the oddest feeling that she'd never see him again. That somehow he'd arrange not to have to accompany her back to London on Sunday. And that she'd have to endure the torture of Tom's wedding with nothing whatsoever to look forward to.

But maybe he had plans for the weekend. She'd seen how busy he was from the endless string of phone calls that he'd juggled during the journey from the airport to the hotel. He must have piles of work to do. Why on earth would he want to waste his valuable time on her?

* * *

No. That was Luke's answer to her question. He had a stack of analyst reports and stockmarket data to get through before the weekend was over. Even if he hadn't had that excuse, he hadn't been to a wedding or inside a church in years, and he certainly wasn't about to start now. So if that was what she'd been planning all along, she'd got landed with the wrong man.

His eyes narrowed as he watched her, standing there waiting for his answer, fiddling with her hair, her green eyes shining steadily at him. She was nibbling on her lower lip again. An arrow of heat fired through him, tightening and stiffening his body, just as it had done on the plane. He fought back a surge of desire. Emily was resourceful and confident. She'd manage fine on her own.

At the precise moment when Luke opened his mouth to tell her that he had other plans Emily jammed her hands in the back pockets of her jeans. The movement thrust her breasts forward and he lost what little sense he'd had left.

'Forget it. I—' she began.

'Sure—why not?' He cut her off, his voice thick and distant. His head throbbed with a sudden desperate urge to haul her up against him and see if she was as soft and yielding as she looked.

'Really?' Emily let out a breath and her shoulders relaxed, while Luke shoved a hand through his hair, nodded, and called himself all kinds of bloody idiot.

'Great,' she said, beaming at him. 'It might even be fun. It's at six tomorrow evening, at a château near Valensole. There's a reception and a dinner afterwards.'

Luke was looking shell-shocked. Emily was just beginning to wonder whether he'd heard her when he said, 'I'll pick you up at three.'

She looked up at him in surprise. 'Is it that far?'

'A couple of hours.'

Emily frowned. That changed things. She couldn't expect him to give up such a large chunk of his weekend. 'Are you sure you don't mind?' she asked.

He lifted an eyebrow. 'I may even be able to dig out a morning suit.'

Emily smiled, feeling happier and more settled than she had in hours. 'Thank you, Luke.'

And then, because she really was grateful, and because it seemed the natural thing to do, she reached up and planted a light kiss at the corner of his mouth.

But there was nothing natural about her reaction. The moment her mouth grazed his skin the world wobbled. Her lips tingled and his smell—clean, masculine and untainted by after-shave—swirled into her head. Sensation washed over her. Emily swayed and then jerked back, unable to stifle a tiny gasp of shock.

She saw her own surprise and confusion and something else reflected in his eyes. Her breath caught in her throat and suddenly she couldn't breathe. She was too close. The heat radiating off his body was scorching her. She stumbled back, but his hands shot out, and before she'd realised what was happening he was pulling her back against him, wrapping his arms around her and crashing his mouth down on hers.

He took advantage of her parted lips instantly, his tongue darting into her mouth and exploring her with a thoroughness that turned her bones to water. His fingers tangled in her hair, angling her head, and he deepened the kiss. Emily's heart banged around her chest and her blood raced around her body like a stream of fire.

Her own hands found their way to his back and her fingers bunched the fabric of his jacket, itching to delve underneath and touch his skin everywhere. The hard length of his erection pressed against her stomach. His hand curved round to brush the side of her breast and she moaned into his mouth.

She froze. The sound of her own desperate longing brought her thundering back to reality. What on earth were they doing? Locked together, kissing frantically, about to rip each other's clothes off. In the lobby of a five-star hotel.

An identical thought had obviously occurred to Luke at

exactly the same time. His hands stilled and he pulled back, staring down at her, his eyes so dark they were almost black, his breathing ragged as he struggled to get his body back under control.

'Oh, dear,' he said huskily, letting her go, turning on his heel and striding out of the hotel.

'That's all he said? "Oh, dear"?'

'Yes, for the tenth time, that's all he said.' Emily closed her eyes and flopped back on the bed, seriously doubting the wisdom of calling her sister in the hope that she'd be able to shed some light on the situation.

'How did he say it?'

An image of Luke's face just before he marched off floated into her head. 'Kind of neutral. Expressionless. Blank. What do you think he meant?'

'Who knows? It could be anything from *That was fantastic and I'm in danger of falling head over heels in love with this woman—*'

Emily's heart lurched for a second. 'Rather unlikely, don't you think?'

'—to *God, I pity you. Your kissing technique is diabolical.*'

Emily groaned and clapped a hand over her eyes. As far as she could remember—and she'd relived the experience a hundred times in the past hour or so—his technique had been perfect. Whether hers had been any good was anyone's guess. She'd lost her mind and any finesse the moment their mouths had met. 'I'm rather hoping it was *What the hell are we thinking of, two grown adults kissing like frenzied teenagers in a hotel lobby in full view of a dozen people?*'

'Perhaps we'll never know. How is the hotel, by the way?'

Emily sat up and surveyed her room. 'Amazing. Forget a cat, you could swing a pride of lions in here. Thank you for booking it.'

'You're welcome.'

'Guess what's on the balcony.'

'Hmm, let me think. A table? Chairs? A couple of wilting pot plants?'

'A hot tub.'

'Big enough for two?'

'Oh, yes.' Her imagination had come up with some pretty racy scenarios involving her and Luke, with little clothing and lots of bubbles. She closed her eyes and lost herself in the memory of Luke's mouth moving over hers, warm and firm, his taste, his smell, the feel of his body crushing hers…

'Remember that at the wedding. You're clearly on a roll. You might get lucky.'

'What wedding?' asked Emily dreamily.

'Er, tomorrow?' Anna's tone sharpened. 'Don't even *think* about not going. If you do, I'll cancel my credit card and you'll be landed with the hotel bill.'

Emily sat up. 'Oh, I'm going. I'm definitely going. Luke's coming with me.'

She had to hold her mobile away from her ear as her sister let out a very unlike-Anna squeal.

She frowned. 'At least that was the plan. After the "Oh, dear" episode I'm not sure whether he'll turn up.'

'Of course he will. He's a man of his word.'

'How on earth do you figure that?'

'He turned up to take you to France, didn't he? He'll be there tomorrow. And when he is, you can ask him what he meant.'

But did she want to know? That was the question that had been swirling around Emily's head for the past twenty-four hours. Their kiss had replayed in her mind all night. Her response to Luke was overwhelming. How could she react like this to a man she'd only just met and barely knew? For the first time in her life she was at the mercy of an extraordinary attraction that was as unsettling as it was exciting. This, plus the steamy thoughts generated by the discovery of a complimentary box of condoms in a bathroom cupboard, had made her toss and

turn until she'd finally given up and gone to pound her rest-
lessness out in the pool.

At least the hotel beautician had managed to cover up the
worst of the grey circles under her eyes, and the hairdresser had
sorted her hair out so that her feather fascinator looked as
though it did actually belong where it was.

Her sister had packed well, thought Emily, slipping into the
dress she'd worn to Anna and David's wedding. A dress which
had earned compliments from everyone except Tom. She
should have realised something wasn't quite right between the
two of them way back then.

She thrust her feet into gold strappy sandals and glanced at
her watch. Quarter to three. Her hands were trembling as they
fumbled with the straps. The butterflies in her stomach were
clamouring to escape. She wasn't sure quite what her nerves
were for. The wedding, or coming face to face with Luke? Both
probably.

After the way he'd walked out yesterday evening she
wouldn't be at all surprised if he didn't show up this afternoon,
despite Anna's assurances. Anna hadn't seen the stunned expression on his face when he'd agreed to go with her, as if he'd
been as startled by his answer as she was. Nor had she seen
his face darken in a way that suggested he'd regretted his
decision the moment he'd made it. So if he *was* waiting for her
downstairs, what mood would he be in?

Oh, well, thought Emily, there was only one way to find out.
She picked up her clutch bag, pulled her shoulders back and
glanced at herself in the mirror. If there was one thing she was
certain of, she told herself, taking a series of deep, steadying
breaths and checking her teeth for lipstick, the next few hours
were going to be anything but boring.

CHAPTER THREE

FUN. Was that what this was supposed to be? Luke asked himself grimly, pushing through the hotel's revolving door and stalking across the gleaming marble floor. Fun was supposed to be light, nothing more than a passing diversion. It was not supposed to knock him for six, and it was not supposed to derail his focus to such an extent that his clients had asked him if he was all right in the middle of the meeting.

Luke scowled as he scanned the lobby in case Emily was early, and then flung himself onto the sofa, picked up the first magazine his fingers found and flicked to an article on interest rate forecasts in south-east Asia.

He didn't need to look up to know that Emily had walked into the lobby. He hadn't heard the lift ping, he hadn't heard the swish of a door drawing back, yet he knew. By the way the tiny hairs at the back of his neck leapt up. The words blurred on the page. The tapping of her heels on the marble echoed louder and louder as they came towards him. Deliberately taking his time, Luke closed the magazine, looked up, and his mouth went dry.

She was standing on the very spot where they'd kissed yesterday, wearing some kind of green wraparound dress the exact colour of her eyes. It fell to her knees and clung just about everywhere. His gaze roamed up, taking in the elegant sweep of hair that was caught up with an arrangement of feathers and

tumbled in glossy waves over her shoulders, and then he continued his appraisal down over her curves to the very high
sandals that made her long legs even longer.

Running a finger around the inside of the collar of a shirt
that was suddenly choking him, Luke got to his feet. Her scent
threaded towards him, and he was gripped by a lust so strong
that he had to jam his hands in his pockets to stop himself from
throwing her over his shoulder, bundling her back into that lift
and locking them both in her room for the rest of the weekend.

'You look beautiful,' he managed hoarsely, giving her a
tense smile and then clearing his throat.

Emily returned his smile with a sunnier one of her own and
he was struck by a deep sense of foreboding. Telling him to
get out of here now. Head straight back to Monte Carlo as fast
as Pierre could get him there.

'Thank you,' said Emily, giddy with relief that he'd turned
up to meet her and buzzing at his compliment. 'So do you.'

Luke Harrison dressed for a wedding was devastating. The
fact that he looked tired and drawn did nothing to detract from
his dark good looks, and did nothing to diminish the effect he
was having on her pulse.

But, although he was staring at her as if he wanted to devour
her, he didn't offer her a kiss on the cheek and she suddenly
felt uncharacteristically awkward. He had an edge about him
today that made her feel as if she could be walking on eggshells, and she couldn't bring herself to ask him what the 'Oh
dear' had meant. If she did, it would stir up memories of that
kiss, and Luke didn't look as if he was in the mood to discuss
it. Much better to pretend it had never happened.

'Would you like a drink before we go?'

God, no, thought Emily. Who knew how long it would be
before she stepped too heavily on those eggshells? Two hours
in a confined space with him would be bad enough as it was.
Why prolong the agony? 'Would you mind if we just went
straight there?'

'Not at all.' Luke put a hand on her elbow to lead her out to his car. His chauffeur-driven car, if the well-built man dressed in a dark uniform and cap and standing by the rear door was anything to go by. 'Give the address to Pierre and he'll put it into the navigation system.'

Emily fished the invitation out of her bag and presented it to Pierre with a flourish. '*Voilà*,' she said, smiling up at the driver, who took it with an inclination of his head and then held the door open for her. Emily swung into the car as if she never travelled any other way, while Luke stalked round to the other side and folded himself onto the back seat beside her.

The Provence countryside had been whizzing by for about an hour before Emily had finally had enough of the crackling silence. Wasn't *she* the one who was supposed to be on edge and tense? Her ex-fiancé was, after all, within a hair's breadth of marrying another woman. To add insult to injury, she was bound to bump into people who'd taken his side after the split and whom she hadn't seen or spoken to since. Yes, *she* was the one who should be trembling in trepidation. But, bizarrely, she felt fine. Amazingly calm and collected and ready to face whatever the afternoon held in store for her.

Luke, however, who should be relaxed and looking forward to spending the afternoon drinking champagne at someone else's expense, was radiating unease and sitting unnaturally still. He was staring into the distance, probably totally unaware of the quaint towns and swathes of fields zipping past.

What on earth was the matter with him? Yesterday, for the most part, he'd been charming. Today he was decidedly unsociable and it was unsettling her. To hell with the eggshells. This silence was driving her nuts and the thought of another minute of it was unbearable.

Emily swivelled round and studied his profile. 'How were your meetings?'

Luke barely blinked before replying. 'Productive.'

Hmm, not a promising start. She tried a different topic. 'Where do you stay when you're here?'

'I have offices in Monaco.'

'Handy. But that's not what I asked.'

'One of the rooms has been converted into a bedroom. It has an *en-suite* bathroom and a dressing room.'

'You sleep in your office?' Emily couldn't keep the incredulity out of her voice.

'It makes for an easy commute,' said Luke, twisting round and shooting her a humourless smile.

'You have a chauffeur. Commuting should be a cinch.'

'He's on loan for this evening. I have a feeling I'm going to need a drink.' His face hardened and his jaw set as if in preparation for something unpleasant.

She could sympathise. 'I know what you mean.'

'I doubt it,' he said harshly.

Emily frowned. 'Don't you like weddings?'

'Not particularly.'

'Not even the church part?'

'Especially not the church part,' he said, with a vehemence that made Emily flinch.

'Why not?'

'I just don't.'

Which was one way of saying mind your own business, she supposed. 'When was the last time you were in a church?'

'Three years ago.'

'That's a long time.'

'Too long.' His voice was bleak, and she wasn't sure she wanted to know any more. Invisible barriers were springing up all around him, warning her to back off, not to pry any further.

So she sat back and contemplated what might cause such a strong dislike of churches and weddings. According to one of her girlfriends, the mere mention of either had a tendency to cause most men to break into a sweat. It certainly had with Tom, even after he'd proposed. Although he'd managed to get over that particular fear with unflattering speed.

Perhaps Luke Harrison was a commitment phobe. That might explain why he was still single when he was handsome, wealthy and intelligent.

'How on earth did you slip through the net?' she murmured, and then gasped in horror when she realised she'd said the words aloud.

'What net?'

There was no way she could pretend she didn't understand what he was talking about. Not when his eyes had narrowed and were trained on her face.

Emily gulped nervously. 'The marriage net. I'd have thought someone would have snapped you up years ago.' Why, oh, why hadn't she kept quiet? Eggshells were beginning to shatter all over the place.

A muscle started ticking in his jaw. 'Marriage isn't for me,' he bit out.

Something about his stillness, the flash of desolation in his eyes, made Emily yearn to find out why he was so against marriage. But she'd already gone way too far.

Desperately seeking to lighten the atmosphere, she gave him what she hoped was a conspiratorial smile. 'I agree. Commitment, responsibility, a relationship…' She shuddered. 'I can't think of anything worse.'

After several minutes of more thundering silence Luke rubbed a hand over his face, and when he looked at her again something seemed to have shifted inside him. The tension ebbed from his frame and his eyes cleared. 'Talking of commitment, you'd better fill me in on this wedding we're going to.'

Emily swallowed and looked out of the window. 'I know the groom. Tom's a—er…a friend of mine.' Quite why she was reluctant to reveal the nature of their relationship to Luke was a mystery. He'd find out soon enough. With any luck after she'd had a glass or two of champagne.

'Why didn't you want to go?'

'Oh, well, I—er—haven't seen him for a while. There didn't seem much point.'

'Why was Anna so keen for you to come?'

Emily stifled a sigh of exasperation. Couldn't he just let it

go? 'She thinks I need to get out more,' she said firmly. And
that was as much as she was willing to say on the matter.

Luke acknowledged her determination to change the subject
with a tiny nod. 'Who's he marrying?'

'A woman called Marianne du Champs,' she replied, adding
'perceptive' to the long list of his attributes. 'I believe she may
be a countess.'

She leaned towards the window as Pierre pulled the car up
opposite a huge looming church. Everywhere she looked
guests were milling around, the women dressed up to the nines
in the latest designer outfits, the men elegant in traditional
wedding attire.

'Ah, look,' said Emily, 'a nice, small, intimate wedding.'

She spied two of Tom's friends, who up until a year ago had
been her friends too. A tremor shook through her and her confidence wobbled. She brushed her palms against her dress and
fought back a sudden attack of nerves. Perhaps this was going
to be more gruelling than she'd imagined.

Luke climbed out of the car, walked round the bonnet and
opened the door for her. Emily swung her knees round, put her
hand in his, and in one fluid movement she was on her feet.

'That was beautifully done,' he said, offering her his arm.

'Thank you,' she replied, taking it. 'If you're trying to boost
my confidence, you're doing a good job.'

'Does your confidence need boosting?'

'Ask me in an hour.'

Some people would gossip about her presence at the
wedding of her ex-fiancé, and the grapevine would no doubt
tremble violently. But she'd just stepped out of a chauffeur-
driven car and was now on the arm of the sexiest, best-looking
man on the face of the earth. As they crossed the road, Emily
took a deep breath and rallied her strength.

'Are you all right?' asked Luke.

'Absolutely fine,' she said firmly. 'You?'

'Absolutely fine.' But he wasn't. The tension was back and

he was staring up at the church, his eyes icy blue and his face frozen.

'If it helps,' she murmured, 'there should be plenty of extraordinary headwear and stained glass to focus on.'

A glimmer of a smile hovered over his mouth for a second before his lips tightened. 'Do you want to wait out here or shall we go in?'

Emily glanced round and saw that they were attracting considerable attention. Or rather Luke was. But he seemed unaware of the appreciative looks being shot in his direction. She scanned the crowd to see if she could spot anyone she could say hello to, but there were no friendly faces among the guests. She doubted there'd be many inside either, but there was no going back now. 'Let's go in.'

He walked up the steps stiffly, and she had the impression that it was only sheer will-power that was moving him forwards and up and through the huge oak doors. As she followed him inside and her vision adjusted to the gloom she noticed that he'd gone alarmingly pale. His fingers tightened around hers and she realised that this wedding wasn't only going to be an ordeal for her.

But what could be the reason for Luke's unease? she wondered, taking one of the orders of service that were being held out by an usher. Was a fear of weddings a medical condition? Matrimoniphobia, perhaps? He didn't strike her as the sort of man who would tolerate a fear, yet he was clutching her hand as if his life depended on it.

He let her go so she could shuffle along an empty pew. Had he been dropped in the font as a baby? Had he too once been to the wedding of someone he'd cared about? A funeral, perhaps? The possibilities were endless, but it was hardly the sort of thing she could ask.

'I was right,' said Emily, glancing around before putting her handbag on the floor.

'About what?' muttered Luke.

'Hats and glass.' She tried to settle herself on the uncomfortable pew.

When Luke didn't answer she stole a quick peek at him. He was studying the church's architecture with an almost fierce intensity, but at least some colour had returned to his face. It was as if he'd gone into some sort of zone, she thought, running her fingers over the engraved front of the order of service. She was willing to bet that he was totally unaware of her presence. Or anyone else's, for that matter.

'Emily?' A voice behind her and a tap on her shoulder made her jump. She twisted round and found herself face to face with one of the few people who had stayed in touch when she and Tom split up.

'Felicity, how lovely to see you,' she said.

'Likewise. How are you? It's been ages.'

'Too long.'

'Isn't this fantastic?' Felicity waved a hand around to indicate the magnificence of the church. 'I don't think I've ever been to a wedding like it. I can't wait for the reception. Marianne's lovely, and doesn't Tom look great?' There was an awkward pause as Felicity's expression of delight turned to one of horror. She clapped both hands to her face. 'Oh, God, I'm sorry. Sometimes I only open my mouth to change feet.'

'Sorry about what?'

Felicity looked bewildered for a second. 'Well, you know. Banging on about the wedding. When Tom is marrying Marianne.'

Emily glanced at Luke, but he didn't appear to be listening. 'Don't worry about it,' she assured Felicity, who was staring at her with concern.

'Are you all right with it?'

'Heavens, yes.' She could feel herself going red. She'd been so wrapped up in what was going on with Luke that she had barely given Tom a second's thought. 'I'm happy for him. Truly,' she added at the sceptical look that crossed Felicity's face.

'I can well believe that,' she said, leaning forward. She nodded in Luke's direction and asked, 'Who's your friend?'

Emily caught the appreciative note in her voice and felt a stab of irritation. Whatever Luke was going through, he didn't need to be subjected to a barrage of questions by an over-flirtatious female.

A rustling behind them saved her from having to answer Felicity's question. 'Oh, look, I think the bride's arrived,' she said brightly, as the organ boomed the opening bars of the 'Bridal Chorus' and everyone stood and turned to watch the entrance of Marianne du Champs.

The organist then launched into the first hymn, and Emily took the opportunity to survey the congregation. As she'd sus-pected, she didn't spy many allies among the glamorous throng. Mainly she encountered expressions of surprise. One or two glimmers of sympathy, which she could have done without. And there was enough eyeing up of the man beside her to have her inching towards him in a distinctly proprieto-rial fashion.

She was just debating whether or not it would be a bit much to thread her arm through his when Tom's voice poured through the speakers and jerked her head back. Had they got to that part already?

For the first time since the ceremony had begun, and with a faint sense of shame, she turned her attention to what was happening in front of her. Her gaze rested on the man with whom at one point she'd been planning to spend her future. Tall, blond, good-looking and familiar, he was smiling down at the woman in white—the woman who at one time could have been her.

She waited for her heart to lurch, for a stab of pain, perhaps, or regret, but as she watched and heard him say his vows all she could think of was Luke and that kiss.

Which wasn't right, surely? Even if she was over Tom, shouldn't she be experiencing some sort of inner turmoil at seeing him standing up there at the altar about to marry another woman, instead of lusting after another man? She frowned. Perhaps her mind had sent her into denial without her knowledge.

Emily emptied her head of all thoughts and forced herself to focus on Tom. He was looking proud, happy and relaxed. Unlike Luke. Oh, no. How could she examine her emotions for turmoil if Luke clouded the issue? She blinked and pushed him to one side.

Now, where was she? Oh, yes. Tom. He was sliding a ring onto Marianne's finger and staring down at her with an awed expression on his face. Hang on, she thought with a frown. Did her heart just ping? And was that another one? Yes, it was definitely pinging. Thank God for that. Two tugs on her heartstrings was perfect. Just enough to reassure herself that she cared, not enough to cause her pain. What a relief. Now she could dally with Luke without any nasty insecurities popping up at inconvenient times.

And she did want to dally with him. Very much. She looked up at him. He was glowering at a window and a muscle was ticking in his jaw. Desire mingled with curiosity. Whatever the reason for Luke's phobia of churches, it clearly went a great deal deeper than a simple fear of commitment.

Luke barely heard the music and words echoing through the church, and he wasn't concentrating on the stained glass. No. He was far too busy gritting his teeth and fighting for control of his mind.

It had been three years since Grace's funeral. Three years since he'd last stepped inside a church. Of all the things that should be going through his head, skin-prickling awareness of the woman beside him was not one of them.

Yet every time they stood or sat a fresh wave of her intoxicating scent hit his perplexed brain. The memory of her in his arms, her mouth and body moving against his, rolled back into his head and he had to clench his fists to stop himself from reaching for her.

Luke sat down and studied the painting above the altar. Exhaustion. That was it. That was why his mind hadn't been working properly in the meeting yesterday and wasn't working properly now. That was why his attraction to Emily was hitting him quite so hard. He should take a break—ease up on his insane workload before he burned out. And maybe he should indulge in the 'fun' that Jack kept banging on about.

Luke heard the rustle of people standing and automatically got to his feet. He had the feeling Emily could be a lot of fun. Emily was warm and vibrant and attracted to him. Her response to his kiss had been hotter than he could have imagined.

Her arm brushed against his, making him jump as if he'd been poked with a cattle prod. That was it. He'd had enough of only half existing. It was about time he had some fun. He tore his gaze from the cherub he'd been focusing on and turned his head to look down at her. At the same time she looked up. Their gazes collided, and the leap of desire he saw in Emily's eyes decimated any remnant of doubt he might have had.

Emily nearly collapsed back down on the pew from the scorching heat of Luke's gaze, but she couldn't drag her eyes away. Her heart raced. If she combusted on the spot would it be hailed as a miracle? Her head went fuzzy. A flash of white cut across her vision. Didn't some people see a bright light before passing out? She had to get out of there before she found out.

How much longer would this blasted service go on for? Summoning every ounce of strength she possessed, she wrenched her eyes away from Luke's. And blinked in astonishment. Everyone was moving. The ceremony was over? Already? That look must have frozen them in time. And that flash of white must have been the new Mrs Thomas Green gliding back down the aisle. Nice to know Luke didn't, after all, have the power to send her into a swoon.

But the dramatic change in his demeanour was odd. From tense and edgy to carnal and predatory. It wasn't normal. Before she could analyse this any further, Luke took her arm, clamped her against him, and starting pushing them through the crush of people in the aisle.

'Would you like to go in the car, or shall we walk?' he asked when they finally managed to get out of the church.

'Let's walk,' she replied. 'It's not far, and I love the smell of Provence in summer.'

Luke's gaze slid down her body. 'Will you be able to walk in those shoes?'

'Nope. But I won't have to.' She pulled a pair of sparkly flats out of her bag.

'Practical,' said Luke, sliding a pair of sunglasses onto his nose.

'Not a fan of blisters,' she said with a rueful smile. 'Can I borrow you?'

Without waiting for an answer, she grabbed his arm and quickly switched shoes. When she was back on her feet, sandals dangling from one hand, there was no reason for her other hand to still be on his arm. But for some strange reason she was reluctant to let him go. He was so warm and hard under her fingers, and she had to force herself to break the contact before her hand started doing something inappropriate—like creeping up his arm to his shoulder, to see if his muscles were as defined as she remembered.

Reluctantly she dropped her hand and lifted her face to smile her thanks. Without the added height of her heels, Luke towered over her. Now that she thought about it, yesterday she'd been wearing three-inch wedges and earlier today the sandals. She hadn't realised quite how tall and broad he really was. It made her feel dainty and feminine—which, at a generously proportioned five foot seven, didn't happen often.

'Let me take your shoes,' he offered.

She was hit by an image of those big hands holding her delicate shoes, and maybe offering to put them back on when they arrived at the château, his fingers circling her ankle, trailing up over her calf… She swallowed and blinked rapidly. 'They wouldn't suit you.'

A hint of a smile curved his mouth and he took her shoes gently from her. 'Ready?'

'Lead on.'

She brushed down her skirt and checked herself for dust, and then looked up to find him watching her, his expression dark and serious, the sunglasses lending him a sinister air. 'What?' she asked, her heart thumping. 'Is something wrong?'

'Very wrong.' His voice had softened, deepened, and it slithered over her like silk.

'Do I have lavender in my hair?' Her hands flew up to check. 'Fluff on my dress?'

He gave his head a quick shake, hooked a finger under the bridge of his sunglasses to slide them off and took a slow step towards her.

Emily's mouth dried at the look in his eye.

'It's occurred to me that I've been somewhat remiss,' he said.

'You have?' she said, her voice suddenly hoarse.

'Mmm-hmm. I forgot to kiss you hello earlier. That wasn't very gallant.'

'It wasn't,' she agreed breathlessly, backing up against the tree and lifting her chin.

'But fortunately easily remedied.' Luke placed his hands either side of her head and leisurely scanned her face, as if deciding where to begin.

Emily's heart raced and she began to fizz with anticipation. His head came down, blotting out the sun. Her mouth tingled. But at the last minute he turned his head a fraction and his lips brushed her cheek. He stopped and drew back an inch, leaving her screaming inside with frustration.

'Now *that* wasn't very gallant,' she murmured, her eyes fixed on his mouth.

'I haven't finished yet.'

His hand found the curve of her neck and he pulled it forward so that her head tipped back and her lips parted. As his mouth closed over hers and he started to kiss her properly

Emily's head swam. Hot excitement darted through her and pooled deep inside her. She was melting…

He broke away, breathing hard. 'Better?' His eyes glittered down at her, his pupils so dilated that she could hardly see any blue.

'I'm not sure,' she said hazily, her mouth still on fire. 'I might need another demonstration just to double-check.'

'If we stay here any longer we might not get to the reception at all.'

'Fine by me,' murmured Emily. As far as she was concerned she could stay pinned up against that tree kissing Luke for ever.

'What about Anna and her spies?'

Emily felt as if a bucket of cold water had been thrown over her. Summoning strength into her watery limbs, she pushed herself off the tree and checked that her feathers were still in place. 'You're right,' she said, stifling a sigh and joining him in a stroll along the avenue.

As the magnificent château standing at the far end of the road came into focus Emily's breath caught. Duck-egg-blue shutters framed three storeys of windows set in weathered grey stone. Golden light spilled out of the windows, casting a fairytale-like glow over the darkening evening. Elegant cypress trees surrounded the house, allowing only a tantalising glimpse of the grounds.

They followed a stream of guests through an arch in a wall that led down onto a wide balcony overlooking immaculate formal gardens. Torches blazed along the gravel paths. The fountain in the centre gushed, droplets of water twinkling in the firelight like diamonds. The effect was magical.

'You see,' said Emily, sweeping an arm around to encompass all she saw. 'This is the sort of place a knight should have.'

'I'll bear it in mind,' said Luke dryly, his eyes scanning the throng. 'There's no pleasing some people. I thought I'd gone above and beyond the call of duty with the shoe thing.'

'You did. It was unexpected and very noble.'

'And I did rectify the remiss kiss,' he pointed out.

Emily laughed and gave an apologetic shrug. 'What can I say? I'm a demanding damsel.'

'Would the demanding damsel like a drink?'

'She certainly would.'

He ran a finger down her cheek. 'I'll be back in a second. Don't go anywhere.'

With Luke weaving his way through the crowds towards a waiter bearing a tray laden with bubbling glasses, and Tom heading purposefully towards her, Emily realised she couldn't move even if she'd wanted to.

CHAPTER FOUR

'EMILY.'

Emily dragged her gaze from Luke's back and her heart flip-flopped as she stared up at her ex-fiancé. Into the face she'd once thought would be the first thing she looked at in the morning and the last thing she saw at night. A face that she hadn't seen for a year, but she still remembered every contour of it. A lock of fair hair had fallen over his forehead, and she had to clench her fists to prevent her hand from automatically reaching out and pushing it back. That right belonged to someone else now.

Tom was looking at her as if he wasn't sure whether to kiss her on the cheek or not, and her heart twinged. To spare him any further awkwardness, she reached up and gave him a quick peck instead. Her eyes closed for a second and she inhaled, expecting to feel the warm familiar smell of him waft through her and steeling herself to deal with it. But instead of familiar he smelled weird. Spicy, woody, musky. Different.

'Tom,' she said, drawing back and blinking to hide her confusion.

'It's good to see you, Em. Thank you for coming.' He shifted his weight from one foot to the other. 'I wasn't sure you would.'

'Oh, well—you know,' she said with a shrug. 'I was at a loose end this weekend.'

He smiled and his shoulders relaxed. 'You look well.'

'I am well,' she replied. 'Thank you for inviting me. Congratulations. Marianne seems lovely.'

'She is.' The pride in his voice was unmistakable.

There was a brief silence. Emily watched as Tom's eyes flickered everywhere but at her, and marvelled at how relaxed she felt now that she was actually seeing him again and in these circumstances. Yes, her heart had hurt a little earlier, and still felt a bit on the tender side, but every twinge lessened in intensity. The past year, with her sister providing a shoulder to cry on and a steady stream of white wine, had obviously healed more of her wounds than she'd realised.

Now, thinking about it, all she felt for him was a sort of fond nostalgia. Nostalgia that was rapidly turning to impatience. Surely he had *something* to say to her? They'd been together for five years, for heaven's sake. At the very least he owed her some sort of effort at small talk. Had he always been so useless at making conversation?

When the silence became excruciating Emily couldn't bear it any longer. 'It was a beautiful service,' she said. 'Sublime flowers.'

'Yes, they're all from the estate.'

'It's a magnificent house. Will you be living here?'

'Nearby.'

'How lovely.'

Five years of going out, and this was what they were reduced to? A handful of awkward platitudes? Emily inwardly sighed. Tom had done the polite thing. They'd navigated successfully through the most delicate of situations, and he'd done his duty, so what was he doing still here? 'I'm sure you must have lots of other people to greet, Tom. Please do go ahead.'

He shifted again and his eyes slid from hers. 'I just wanted to say I'm sorry for the way things turned out between us.'

Emily's heart skipped a beat. Surely he wasn't going to rake all over this again? On his wedding day?

'Honestly, Tom, it's fine. It was for the best. We wanted dif-

ferent things. You know that, I know that. We've both moved
on. Haven't we?'

Emily heard a steely edge creep into her voice and watched
him straighten.

'I guess we have. Who's the chap you've brought along?
New boyfriend?'

'My plus one,' she said. An image of Luke flashed into her
head and Emily found herself assessing Tom's features critically. Was there a hint of fleshiness at his jawline? The beginnings of a receding hairline? Her eyes flickered over his tall
frame. Had he been indulging in a little too much fine French
food?

Wishing that Luke would hurry up with that drink, Emily
decided she'd wasted quite enough time on Tom. Somewhere
in the throng was a god of a man whose kisses promised a
heaven she'd quite like to explore.

'I really ought to go and find him,' she said, looking around
until she spied Luke a few feet away, a glass in each hand,
talking to someone obscured by a towering flower arrangement. Who was it? Who had made him laugh like that? Emily
used the excuse of a guest bumping into her to slide across
enough to see Felicity curling a hand on Luke's arm and
reaching up to whisper in his ear.

'Wait, Em. Before you do, there's something I need to tell
you.'

'Hmm?' she murmured, stifling the urge to race over to the
pair of them, grab one of the glasses Luke was holding and hurl
it down Felicity's cleavage.

'Marianne's pregnant.'

Emily's attention whipped back to Tom. Her vision blurred
for a second. 'Congratulations again,' she said, her voice
sounding steady but distant. It was, after all, what Tom had
always wanted.

No, she amended tartly, not always. When they'd first
started going out they'd been in perfect agreement about not
having children. But shortly after they'd got engaged Tom had

revealed that he did in fact want a family, and had done for quite some time. He'd thought he'd be able to change her mind, especially after proposing. Emily, shell-shocked first by the revelation and then by the realisation that the person who should have known her best of all had assumed her position on the subject was negotiable, had felt betrayed. She knew that some people might consider her decision unnatural, but she had her reasons and she'd always thought she'd had an ally in Tom. But apparently not. In the end the unexpected deadlock had meant the end of their relationship.

'I didn't want you to hear it from anyone else.'

'I appreciate it.' She gave him a brittle smile. 'Thank you for telling me. Now, go and circulate. Find your wife.'

'Thanks, Em,' said Tom. 'Enjoy the party.' He dropped a kiss on her cheek and gave her arm a quick squeeze before moving off to shake the hand of another guest.

'So, Luke, how did you meet Emily?'

Luke was struggling to pay attention to Felicity. Ever since she'd cornered him on his way back to Emily he'd only really been half listening to her anyway. He'd laughed at what he'd imagined were the appropriate times, and responded to her chatter automatically, while wondering how he could extricate himself from the hand on his arm without seeming too offensive.

'A mutual friend,' he muttered, glancing over at Emily. He was finding it hard to concentrate on anything other than a long-forgotten urge drumming through him to have her hot and naked and beneath him. Which was why he'd kept one eye on Emily's exchange with the groom. He hadn't liked what he'd seen. Whatever the details of their relationship, Tom was without doubt more than merely a work colleague.

Luke had watched the expressions flit across her face as they spoke. Bewilderment, regret, maybe, detachment, a flash of impatience, and then something that had made his jaw clench. The sparkle faltered in the depths of her eyes and the colour drained from her face.

His eyes narrowed as he realised that he wasn't the only one who was interested in what was happening between Emily and Tom.

'I ought to deliver this,' said Luke abruptly, indicating the glass in his left hand, vaguely aware that he'd interrupted Felicity's stream of chatter.

'She must be needing it,' said Felicity. 'Poor girl.'

The pitying tone of Felicity's voice as much as her words snagged his attention quicker than any amount of eyelash-fluttering and coy smiles had. 'Oh, really? Why's that?'

Felicity leaned forward conspiratorially. 'Well, it can't be easy for her. I mean, the *humiliation*. She's so brave.'

He raised an eyebrow calculated to encourage Felicity to gossip as she so clearly wanted to do.

'Tom and Emily used to be engaged.'

Luke went still. 'I didn't know that,' he murmured, his brain rapidly processing the information. No wonder she hadn't wanted to attend the wedding.

'No one really knows why they split. I think it was because Tom's mother is a crashing snob and never thought Emily was good enough for her only son. Others say it's because Emily has a fear of commitment and responsibility.'

Luke's brows snapped together as he watched Tom leave Emily alone in the crowd and oblivious to the sidelong glances and whispers. She needed an ally and a drink. He muttered an apology to Felicity and made his way to where Emily was standing frozen to the spot.

'Are you all right?' he asked, putting the glass in her hand.

'Couldn't be better,' she said, with a brightness that sounded strained.

'Good,' he said. He planted a hard swift kiss on her mouth. 'That should give people something else to talk about,' he murmured, noting with some satisfaction that her eyes were sparkling again and her cheeks had more colour.

He wound an arm around her waist and directed her towards a gate he'd spied in the wall. He pushed it open and led her down the steps into a sunken patio. Light filtered through the entrance, illuminating the path but leaving the rest of the patio in shadow. Honeysuckle tumbled down the walls, permeating the warm air with a sweet, heady fragrance.

'Why did you bring me down here?' asked Emily, her gaze sweeping over the patio.

'So we can have this conversation in private.'

'What conversation?'

'The one where you tell me why you didn't happen to mention that you were once engaged to the groom.'

'Ah, that one.'

'Yes, that one.'

'How did you find out?'

'Your friend Felicity.'

The way Emily was studiously not looking at him was beginning to irritate him, so he put his fingers under her chin and gently turned her head, lifting her face until she had no option *but* to look at him. 'So?' he asked softly, when it became obvious that she was stalling.

'Does it really matter?'

'You tell me.'

Emily let out a little sigh and he saw the tension drain from her body. He dropped his hand before it could curve round the back of her neck and pull her to him.

'I guess that's only fair, seeing as I did drag you all the way out here.' She took a sip of champagne. 'I went out with Tom for five years, lived with him for the last two, got engaged to him and then disengaged.'

'What happened?'

She chewed on her lip and her gaze slid to the lion's head spouting water from the wall. 'Nothing spectacular.' She shrugged. 'We simply drifted apart.'

Just like that? thought Luke sceptically as she set her glass down on the stone bench. Five years condensed into a dozen or so words? The flatness of her tone almost disguised the hurt and pain, but not quite, and Luke felt his stomach clench. His head went fuzzy for a second and he had to shake it to clear it. He blinked and focused back on the woman standing in front of him, staring at him with mesmerising green eyes. His mouth went dry and he cleared his throat. 'Not just a work colleague, then?'

'Oh, well, yes—in the beginning. That's how we met. I was temping at the company where he worked. IT consulting. Very tedious.' She stuck up her chin. 'I'm sure you don't really want to know all the gory details.'

He did. For some unfathomable reason he did. 'Not particularly.' His fingers tightened around the champagne flute and he downed what was left in the glass.

'If he hadn't ended it,' Emily was saying, her jaw set and a glint in her eye, 'I would have. I'm totally over it. I didn't need to come here to know that, but Anna had this idea that if I didn't come people would think I was so prostrate with grief that I was unable to lever myself out of bed.'

'Do you care what people think?'

'Not in the slightest.' She gave him a small mischievous smile. 'But I must admit I was a bit curious.'

'Why didn't you say anything?'

Emily stared at him as if he was mad. 'Hmm, let me see. Telling a complete stranger that my ex-fiancé's invited me to his wedding to the woman he left me for. Doesn't exactly do much for a girl's image, does it? And then rashly asking said complete stranger to go with me to the wedding, because the idea of going with a very good-looking man was more appealing than going alone?' She shook her head ruefully. 'Pathetic.'

She crossed her arms over her chest. Luke's gaze dropped to the deepening V of her cleavage and a bolt of desire shot straight down to his groin.

'If it's any consolation,' he said hoarsely, 'I think the man's a fool.'

'Thank you.'

Luke couldn't resist any longer. He wrapped his arms around her and lowered his mouth to hers. He felt her melt against him, and as they kissed a tremor ran through him. The glass slipped from his fingers and shattered on the stone, making them both jump.

'Oops,' she said shakily.

'I'll buy them a dozen more as a wedding present.'

He drew back, breathing hard, and stared down into her eyes, glazed with desire, her lips wet and parted.

'What was that for?' she said huskily, drawing back to unfold her arms.

'I'm finding it increasingly hard to keep my hands off you.'

'Oh,' she murmured, sliding her hands up over his chest. 'In that case, don't let me stop you.'

Her touch burned through the layers of clothing to scorch his skin. He traced the line of her lower lip with his thumb until her breathing became ragged and her eyelids fluttered down. The tip of her tongue darted out to touch his thumb, sending fire twisting through him. With a groan his lips met hers and the rhythmic beat of desire flared between them as their tongues tangled. What the hell was it about her that sent his temperature into the stratosphere? His brain fogged. Had someone spiked his champagne with absinthe?

Deciding to find fun with Emily was definitely one of his better ideas, he thought with satisfaction as he broke off the kiss and dragged in a shaky breath. His gaze fixed on her mouth—red, swollen, luscious—and the primal need to taste her again surged in him.

'I'm definitely over it,' muttered Emily, her eyes still closed and her voice low and breathy.

'It doesn't do much for a man's ego when the woman in his arms is picturing someone else.' Luke's mouth hovered millimetres over hers. 'I must be losing my touch.' He could feel her heart hammering against his, although with desire or mortification that she'd been caught out he couldn't tell.

A sexy smile curved her mouth, and suddenly he didn't

really care. 'If you are,' she breathed against his mouth, 'I'd be very happy to help you find it.'

'So selfless.'

Emily laughed, and Luke covered her mouth with his and kissed her until her laugh turned to moans of pleasure.

She suddenly stilled in his arms. Luke jerked back and looked down at her in the flickering darkness.

'What is it now?'

Emily smiled. 'Just something I remembered. What was that "Oh, dear" all about?'

'What?'

'Yesterday afternoon,' she prompted, 'after we kissed in the lobby. You said "Oh, dear" before marching out of the hotel.'

Luke frowned. 'Did I say that out loud?'

'You did. What did you mean?'

Luke rubbed a brown hand along his jaw as the image of them locked together flashed into his head. That kiss had blown him away, hurled him off balance and nearly shattered his control. If she hadn't hesitated for that instant who knew where they'd have ended up? 'You've turned out to be rather more than I expected. When I won that auction, I didn't anticipate being quite so attracted to the lot.'

'Oh.' There was a pause as this sank in. 'But that's a good thing, right?'

He hesitated before answering, his gaze transfixed by the feathers dancing around her head in the light. 'I'm not sure.'

She let out a little indignant huff. 'How flattering.'

Luke tilted his head. Then he pulled her hips against him, so she could feel just what she was doing to him. He leaned down and murmured in her ear, 'Is that flattering enough for you?'

He felt her shiver. 'It all depends what you're going to do about it,' she murmured back, the warmth of her breath making his skin contract.

Luke went still. Was she really saying what he thought she

was saying? He drew back to check her face, and the seductive smile curving her mouth had his blood pounding along his veins.

'Well?' she said.

The demands of his body were telling him exactly what he was going to do about it. To hell with this bloody reception. 'The way I see it, we have two options. We can either stay here and provide fodder for the gossips…'

'Or?'

His pulse was racing. 'Or we can go.'

Her eyes darkened. 'Go where?'

'Somewhere we can continue this in private. Which is it to be?'

A tremble shuddered though her. He saw it, and had to hold himself back from making the decision for her.

'Stay or go?' he said, the desire throbbing inside him making him sound harsh.

'Go.'

'Sure?'

'Never more so.'

Luke grabbed her hand and practically dragged her back through the guests, who were drifting towards the colonnaded courtyard where dinner was taking place.

'Shouldn't we say goodbye? Or at least apologise for missing dinner?' she said breathlessly.

'We should,' he said, without breaking his stride.

Emily's pace quickened and her fingers wound more tightly round his. 'I'll write a letter.'

Emily jammed herself into the corner of the car, pressing herself into the leather. They were halfway back to the hotel and the atmosphere inside the car was electric with desire. Luke's kisses on the patio had obliterated everything except the need to have his hands and mouth roaming all over her. Her body was trembling, overwhelmed with such longing that she was incapable of thought. She glanced over at Luke, who was staring at her with eyes that were navy. His face was tight. A muscle ticked in his jaw.

'Come here,' he said.

'No,' she breathed. One touch and she'd lose control. She'd be on his lap, purring into his ear and pulling his clothes off, and probably frightening the life out of Pierre.

'Then I'll just have to come over to you.'

'Why?' She clutched the door handle, trying to make herself smaller.

'Because I want to tell you all the things I'm going to do to you and I don't want Pierre to hear.'

Emily shook her head. Her pulse raced. The dragging magnetism was getting harder and harder to resist. 'It's all right. I can imagine,' she said weakly.

Luke's eyes gleamed. 'I don't think you can possibly imagine the plans I have for those feathers.'

Her heart jumped and her skin prickled. 'What sort of plans?' Her voice was hoarse.

'Unwind yourself and I'll tell you.' He unknotted his tie and pulled it off. Emily watched the red silk slowly slither around his neck, teasing her, taunting her—the beginning of something they'd have to wait hours to complete.

Helpless to resist, she let go of the door handle, uncrossed her legs and slid over the leather until their thighs touched from hip to knee.

Luke reached his arm over the back of the seat, taking her hand in his as he bent his head towards her ear and started to tell her exactly what he was intending to do with the feathers.

In the inky darkness of the car Luke's words, full of sensual promise, and the feel of his thumb stroking relentlessly over her wrist, her palm, her fingers, gradually dissolved Emily into a quivering puddle of lust. Every cell in her body hummed with a desire so strong it was almost painful. She trembled and throbbed and ached. She had to bite hard on her lip to stop whimpers pouring from her mouth.

Oh, God, thought Emily, as embarrassment filtered though

her desire. She ventured a glance at Pierre through the rearview mirror, but, like the true professional he was, his attention was fixed firmly on the road ahead. What must he be thinking?

By the time they arrived at the hotel Emily was beyond caring. At one point when Pierre had gone round a corner her hand had accidentally on purpose brushed over Luke's erection. She'd heard his sharp inhalation and so she'd done it again and again—until his fingers had snapped round her wrist and stopped her.

Now all she wanted to do was wrap herself around him and have him sink into her and satisfy this insane craving. Her heart was about to burst from her chest. Bidding a hasty goodnight to Pierre, she tumbled out of the car.

They didn't speak as they crossed the lobby towards the lift, and yet awareness crackled between them. The arrow showed that the lift was at the top floor and Emily let out a tiny groan of frustration. Luke jabbed the button and then thrust his hands into his pockets. Emily fixed her gaze on the arrow as it began to move in an agonisingly slow arc. Seconds had never felt so long. Every part of her body was tight with anticipation.

Once in the lift, Luke leaned against one side and Emily against the other, and for the interminable journey back up to her floor they just stared at each other. Emily saw naked desire in his eyes and knew that he'd see the same in hers. Then his gaze travelled over her, slowly, lazily, stripping her bare from head to toe, and her knees nearly gave way. The lift was going so damned slowly. The frustration was making her demented. *Come on, come on,* she willed, and finally, finally it pinged and the doors swept back.

'What number?' he grated.

'Two-one-six.'

Which way was it? She couldn't remember. Luke's hand gripped her arm and he propelled her in the right direction.

Emily's fingers shook as she tried to insert her card into the door. Luke took it from her and a second later they were in the room and she was in Luke's arms, his mouth slamming down on hers. She threw her arms round his neck and wound her legs round his waist. He backed her against the door, pinning her against it, not taking his mouth from hers for a second. Emily threw her handbag down and pulled off her feathers. She ran her hands over his shoulders, frantically pushing aside his jacket and waistcoat and yanking his shirt up. Hands shaking, she undid his buttons and pushed the shirt off, first down one arm and then the other, and finally her hands were on his bare flesh.

She was desperate to feel all of him and her fingers took over, sweeping up the muscles of his arms to his broad shoulders, while his mouth continued its devastating assault on her senses.

Luke broke away, eyes glittering, breathing raspy. Emily let out a groan of disappointment. 'No,' she mumbled in protest, clinging to him.

'I need to get you out of that dress.'

He stepped back, taking her with him, cupping her bottom against him as he walked her over to the bed. He dropped her onto the sheets and for a moment just stared at her. Emily caught sight of herself in the mirror. Lying knees bent, her dress rucked up around her hips, eyes glittering and mouth red and swollen. With her hair tousled round her face she looked wild and wanton, and almost pulsating with desire.

But instead of joining her, he froze, his face twisting as if he was in actual physical pain.

Her heart stopped. 'What is it?'

Luke raked a hand through his hair. 'I didn't plan this,' he said hoarsely. 'I don't have anything.'

Relief poured through her. 'Bathroom cupboard.'

She didn't have the chance to worry about the fact that protection hadn't crossed her mind. Luke was back in the blink of an eye, dropping a handful of condoms on the bedside table, kicking off his shoes and stripping off the rest of his clothes. Emily swallowed as she drank in the sight of him before he sank down onto the bed with her. He was all lean, tanned muscle, his chest sprinkled with hair that narrowed down to his erection, thick and hard and straining.

He pushed a lock of hair off her face and rubbed a thumb over her trembling lip.

And then he was undoing the ties of her dress and she was wriggling, lying back in her bra and knickers and pulling him with her.

Finally his hands were on her, sliding over the skin of her shoulders, burning a trail over her collarbone, reaching down to cup her breast though the lace of her bra. Emily moaned as sparks of desire shot through the centre of her. She arched against his hand and squirmed as his hand moved lower, tracing the outline of her knickers and down over her thigh. As his fingers trailed back up, skimming over her sex, her heart slammed in her chest.

'Shoes,' he muttered.

'No time,' she groaned, as Luke reached a hand behind her and undid her bra. Quickly dispensing with the flimsy fabric, he skimmed a hand over her breasts, her stomach, her hip. Quivering, Emily felt herself spiralling out of control. 'Don't make me wait,' she moaned against his mouth, and lifted her hips to help him as he pulled her knickers down her legs and threw them aside.

'I won't,' he rasped, and he took her nipple in his mouth. Emily nearly fainted with desire. She could feel the waves of pleasure building, such intense ripples of delight that she didn't think she could take much more.

'Please,' she whimpered.

He leaned away from her and she heard the tear of the condom packet. He swung back over her, staring down at her with such fierce intensity that she nearly came then and there. Then he was nudging her knees apart and lowering himself on his elbows. He entered her with one smooth thrust. Emily gasped as he filled her, pressing inside her, swelling, pulsating. Her hands on his back felt his muscles straining as he fought for control. He withdrew and plunged again, slamming into her over and over, until with a tiny scream she hurtled over the edge, shattering into a million pieces, gasping for air as the waves of pleasure thundered through her. Luke's mouth came down on hers, swallowing her gasps, and with a harsh groan he thrust deep inside her and followed her into blissful oblivion.

Emily woke with a lazy, satisfied smile on her face. She just knew she did. She squinted at the sliver of bright morning light that squeezed through the gap in the curtains and rubbed her eyes. What a night! Who could have imagined that a hot tub would be so much fun? Or that Luke would turn out to be quite so creative with room service? And the feathers… Well, all she could think was that Anna had been right: Luke *was* a man of his word. Every single one of them…

All sorts of muscles she'd never known she had tingled. Her body seemed to be *made* for sex. At least sex with Luke. No one else had ever given her multiple orgasms or taken her to such heights of ecstasy. And to think if she'd married Tom she'd never have known.

Luke must be exhausted. She'd woken in the middle of the night to find him standing on the balcony, staring out to sea. She'd got out of bed, wrapped herself in a towel still damp from the hot tub, and padded over to see if he was all right. He'd turned, the moonlight casting silvery shadows across his face. Emily had scoured his expression but it had been blank, reawakening desire the only sign of emotion in his eyes as they'd raked over her scantily clad form. Then he'd taken her back to bed for another bout of sex that had left her utterly shattered.

She stretched languidly and rolled over. To an empty space on the other side of the bed. Frowning, Emily listened for sounds that Luke might be in the shower or out on the balcony. But the only thing she could hear in the still silence of the early Sunday morning was the sound of her heart thumping away. She was alone.

Her skin prickled with foreboding as she sat up, clutching the sheet to her chest, and ran a hand through her hair. She looked round the room. His clothes had disappeared. Perhaps he'd gone for a swim, a workout in the gym, a run along the beach? Emily's heart lifted before sinking once more. Sure. In his morning suit? It was more likely he'd taken one look at her tangled mess of hair, smudged eye make-up and less-than-perfect figure and done a runner.

Her heart drooped and she flopped back onto the pillows. Whichever way she looked at it, it wasn't good. An image of his shocked expression when he'd agreed to take her to the wedding flashed into her head. He hadn't wanted to go in the first place. That much had been obvious.

And then look at the way she'd behaved. Leaping into bed with him, practically begging him to ravish her having only just met him. She clapped a hand over her eyes. Oh, he might have been equally keen, but there were different rules for men, weren't there? In the cold light of day he might well have decided she was a complete tart and regretted the whole thing.

She was still lying there half an hour later, struggling to justify his absence against the fairly compelling evidence that she'd been abandoned, when the phone rang. Emily jumped and scooted over to the phone, nearly falling out of bed in the process.

'Hello?' she said, snatching up the receiver.

'It's Luke.'

Emily's heart quickened at the sound of his voice. The same voice that only hours ago had told her how incredible she was and how amazing she felt. She shivered. Maybe he was ringing to find out what she wanted for breakfast. Oh, for goodness' sake. How many more straws could she clutch at? A more key question was how was she going to play this? She bit her lip. Breezy. That would be good. Breezy and relaxed. Not clingy and desperate. She was definitely not going to ask where he was and what he was doing.

'Good morning,' she said, perfectly breezily. 'Um, where are you?' Oops.

'I'm at the office.'

The office? On a Sunday morning? He must have been desperate to get away. 'What are you doing there?'

'There's a crisis on the Dubai markets. I'm sorry.'

She shut her eyes tight. Even the most over-active imagination wouldn't have dreamed up that excuse. And it *was* an excuse, wasn't it? Because had she heard his mobile ring? No. The beep of a text? No. The whine of a television? No. So how had he *known* about a so-called crisis in Dubai? 'Oh, right.'

'I didn't want to wake you.'

'Sure.' If there was a crisis, wouldn't people be shouting in the background, frantically buying and selling and generally panicking?

'I'm not sure when I'll be finished here. The plane's available all day, so why don't you have a lie-in or hit the beach, and I'll come and find you when I'm done.'

'I may just do that.' To her ears her voice sounded brittle, a little too bright.

There was a heavy silence. 'Look, Emily, I have to go. But we'll talk later.' He sounded as if his attention was on other things—as if the phone call he'd made to her was an irritation he could do without. Something snapped inside her. Dignity was pretty much the only thing she could cling to at that moment. Dignity and the bedsheet.

'Don't worry about it,' she said, injecting her voice with a breezy lack of concern she didn't feel. 'Thank you, Luke, for ferrying me to France and accompanying me to the wedding and…er…things. It was fun. I hope your crisis sorts itself out. Goodbye.'

Without waiting for him to answer, and fearing that she might not be able to disguise the disappointment in her voice, she replaced the receiver gently in the cradle.

Sighing deeply, she got up and went into the bathroom. She stared at herself in the mirror—at the messy hair, smudged mascara and flushed cheeks—an image which was worse than she could have envisaged. She smiled ruefully at her reflection. *Well, Emily, it looks like you've just had your first one-night stand.*

CHAPTER FIVE

LUKE slammed the ball against the wall and took grim pleasure from the stinging in his muscles from the force with which he'd hit it.

Jack lunged and ducked, shoes thudding and squeaking on the floor of the squash court as he removed himself from the path of the ball whizzing towards him. Breathing heavily, he bent over with his hands on his knees. 'Right. That's enough,' he said. 'I concede.'

'We're in the middle of a game,' said Luke.

Jack straightened. 'Yeah, well, I'd quite like to come out of it alive, and the way you're playing I'm not sure that's going to happen. So, if you don't mind, I'll quit while I'm still more or less standing.'

Luke frowned and lifted his arm to wipe his brow with the towelling band on his wrist. 'You're out of shape.'

'Nope. You're out of control.'

'I'm never out of control.'

'That's the trouble. Tell you what,' said Jack, slapping him on the back and slinging his towel round his neck, 'buy me a beer, tell me what's put you in this mood, and I'll let it slide.'

Twenty minutes later Luke set a pint of beer on the table in front of Jack. He probably owed him more than that, he thought grudgingly. It wasn't the first time he'd thrashed his frustration out during a squash game. It was one of the reasons he enjoyed playing against Jack, who could usually give as good as he got, sometimes even better. He hadn't meant to annihilate Jack out there on the squash court. He hadn't even realised he'd been playing with such ferocity. No point in wondering what had caused it. He knew full well. And he wasn't about to divulge it to anyone—least of all Jack.

'So what's up?' said Jack, taking a long slurp of beer and sighing in appreciation.

Luke shrugged. 'The usual. Stress.'

'Work?'

'What else?'

Jack raised his eyebrows. 'You need to let up. By the way, how was Nice?'

Now, there was a question. Luke's mind whipped back to Saturday night. It didn't take much effort. The long, hot night had been replaying in his head in Technicolor with surround sound. The incredible way Emily had exploded in his arms again and again, the feel of her convulsing around him, her smooth satiny skin and her warm, wet mouth creating devastation on his body.

And then the way she'd upped and left.

'Busy.'

'What was she like?'

Hot, amazing, mind-blowingly sexy… Luke shifted as his jeans tightened uncomfortably.

'What was who like?'

'The green-bikinied damsel in distress. Was she as desperate as I thought?'

Luke clamped down on the urge to thump the smile off Jack's face. He sat back, adopted a bored expression and studied his beer. 'She was fine.'

Jack's jaw dropped. '*Fine*? That's all? I should have known you wouldn't take advantage of such a God-given opportunity. You never have with any of the women I've introduced you to.' He shook his head in despair. 'I should never have let you win.'

A red mist descended into Luke's head at the thought of

Jack laying a finger on Emily. He might be his best friend, but Jack's reputation was devilish.

However, his observation was startlingly accurate. Luke *hadn't* ever been tempted by any of the women Jack had thrown in his path. And some of them had been stunning. More beautiful than Emily. So what was it about her that had him prowling around in alternating states of arousal and irritation? The image of Emily writhing in his arms, smiling seductively, had been burning in his head ever since he'd gone back to the hotel and found she'd already left. He'd tried to ignore it for days, but it was not going away.

'What did you expect me to do, Jack?' he said blandly.

'Have a bit of fun.'

'Like you, you mean?'

'And like you used to.'

'Not any more.'

'You could do worse. Losing yourself in the arms of a beautiful woman is better than killing a friend on a squash court.'

Luke let out a hollow laugh. How ironic. Jack thought sex would relieve his stress, when it was sex that was causing it in the first place.

'She wasn't my type,' he muttered. In the past, when he'd been single and out with Jack, he'd always gone for brunettes. Which was another reason for wondering what Emily's appeal was. Perhaps he was further along the road to burnout than he'd originally thought.

'It doesn't have to be for ever, Luke,' said Jack. 'You don't have to marry any of them.'

'Thanks for the advice,' said Luke tightly, deciding that the conversation was well and truly over. 'On a different note,' he said, 'what's the name of the temping agency you use?'

'No idea, but I can find out if you like. What do you need doing?'

'Just some bits and pieces round the office.'

'What's wrong with the agency you use?'

'Going downhill.' Much like his integrity.

* * *

Emily toyed with her wine glass. She'd been feeling strange ever since she'd got back from France. Edgy, restless, unsettled. Much as she tried—and she'd tried extremely hard over the past week—she couldn't stop remembering the night with Luke. When she'd first got back to London she'd secretly hoped he'd get in touch, but as the days passed the likelihood of him picking up the phone became more and more remote. Her head had reluctantly come to terms with it. Her body, on the other hand, was slow in catching up.

Daytime wasn't a problem. She'd spent the week temping at an advertising agency and the work had been fun and stimulating. But the nights… The nights were terrible. In the dark solitude of her bedroom the memories descended and any hope of sleep vanished. As a result, she was walking around like a zombie.

'So you left?' said Anna.

Emily rubbed her eyes and nodded. 'What else could I do? I was hardly going to wait around for Luke like some desperate clingy female. He might never have shown up.'

Anna pursed her lips thoughtfully. 'I suppose the Dubai emergency could have been genuine.'

Emily shrugged. 'Possibly. Hard to check when you don't know what sort of emergency.'

She heard the front door slam and the thud of a briefcase in the hall. She saw a smile light up her sister's face and experienced a brief pang of envy. What was it like to feel that way about someone? She'd certainly never felt like that about Tom, except maybe in the beginning. But Anna and David had been married for four years and they were still mad about each other.

She watched her brother-in-law drop a light kiss on his wife's mouth and smile into her eyes, and she realised that it was only her presence that was stopping him from hauling Anna to her feet and kissing her more fiercely.

Something stabbed at her heart. Loneliness? No, that was ridiculous. She was the least lonely person she knew. She had an extremely full life. Lots of friends, great jobs… She fixed a smile to her face as David bent to kiss her cheek.

'Hello, Em,' he said, straightening and surveying the scene. He nodded thoughtfully and rubbed his jaw. 'Hmm, a Monday evening, two women—sisters at that—and a bottle of wine. Do you mind if I retreat?'

Anna nodded. 'Good idea, darling. You may not want to hear us ripping Luke Harrison to shreds.'

David stopped in the doorway. 'Luke Harrison?'

'Yes.'

'What's he done to deserve dismemberment?'

'Never mind that,' said Anna, eyeing her husband closely. 'Do you know him?'

David looked at them warily. 'Only by reputation.'

Anna rose and pulled her husband back to the table. 'Just a few details, darling,' she said sweetly, 'and then you can retreat.'

Emily smiled at the panic that flitted across David's face and hoped that her burning curiosity wasn't too obvious. 'What do you know about him?' she said casually.

'He's some kind of genius. Very successful, very shrewd, very driven, very competitive. Private. And apparently a work-aholic.' Tell me something I don't already know, Emily thought as David paused. 'Actually, it's a coincidence you mentioning him…' he said, frowning.

Emily felt a trickle of trepidation run down her spine. 'Why's that?' she asked, not at all sure she wanted to hear.

'There's a strange rumour whipping round the City.'

'There always is,' said Anna.

'Something about an internet auction. A bet with a friend over some girl. I heard Luke won. Crazy money, apparently,' he added, pouring himself a glass of wine. 'Anyway, why are *you* interested in him?'

Emily's blood ran cold and her head spun. A bet? A *bet*? What sort of a bet? 'I'm not the slightest bit interested in him,' she said, reaching for the bottle with a trembling hand. 'Luke who?'

David looked bemused. 'I'm afraid you've lost me.'

'Female logic, darling,' said Anna, standing up and ushering her husband out of the room. 'You wouldn't understand.'

So much for all that rubbish about being curious, wanting adventure and having meetings in Monte Carlo anyway. She'd thought that had sounded flaky at the time. A bet was much more likely for a couple of testosterone-driven playboys. She could see it now. Two men, too many beers, an irresistible challenge. Just how far had it gone? *Hey, I bet you can't get this girl into bed. I bet I can.* Was that why Luke had accompanied her to the church, despite his obvious reluctance? All those smouldering kisses and steamy looks? Had it really been nothing more than determination to win a bet? Had he had to produce *evidence*?

Oh, God. If she let it, her imagination would run wild. She dismissed the voice in her head that was saying Luke wasn't like that, wouldn't do something like that. Look at the way Tom had behaved. And how well had she really known Luke, after all?

Anna came back into the kitchen, extracted the bottle from Emily's fingers and filled her glass. 'I'm sorry, darling.'

Emily stuck her chin in her hand and shrugged. 'Doesn't matter. Luke and this so-called friend of his are obviously jerks of the highest order. I shall just move on. Isn't that what you're always telling me to do?'

'Yes, but…' Anna trailed off, anguish twisting her features.

'But nothing.' Emily forced herself to give her sister a brave smile. 'A one-night stand is hardly something to fuss about. I'll get over it. In fact, you know something? I think I already have.'

A shrill ring tone shattered the silence. For one insane moment Emily imagined it was Luke, calling to see how she was. It happened every time her phone rang and she was sick of it.

'Hang on,' she said, instructing her heart to resume normal behaviour as she rummaged around in her bag for her mobile. If she banged her head on the solid wood table, would it knock some sense into her? 'Hello?'

'Emily? It's Sarah.'

See? she told herself. Not Luke. Sarah. Her manager.

'Listen, I know you wanted this week off, but I've got a last-minute urgent need for a temp. Great money and good hours. It's only for the remainder of the week. Apparently the girl they had today was worse than useless. Say you'll do it. Pretty please?'

Emily sighed. What else was she going to do? Sit around and mope, and analyse her night with Luke and fume? 'OK, sure. Where and when?'

'Thank you, sweetie, you're a star. It's a fund manager in the West End. Be at 86 St James's Street at nine. You're to report to a Mr Luke Harrison.'

Emily's heart lurched. Her blood went cold and her palms were damp. 'No—wait, Sarah. You know something? I was really looking forward to this week off. Lots of drawers to tidy, windows to clean, that kind of thing…'

'He specifically requested you.'

'Did he just?' said Emily tersely.

'Is there a problem?' asked Sarah.

She closed her eyes briefly and took a deep breath. She was professional. She was an adult. She could handle this. 'Not in the slightest. I'll be there.'

'I knew I could count on you. Bye.'

Emily closed her phone and tapped it against her mouth, a frown creasing her brow.

Anna stared at her in concern. 'You've gone very pale. What is it?'

Emily picked up her glass and took a sip. 'What's with this man?' she said. 'He won me, seduced me, abandoned me—'

'He seduced you?' Anna's voice cut her off like whiplash.

Emily waved a distracted arm. 'Well, not really. Technically,

I suppose I might have seduced him. But that's irrelevant. I don't know what's he's playing at, but it seems I'm to spend the rest of the week temping at Luke's company.'

When Anna recovered from her surprise she shot Emily a conspiratorial smile. 'Interesting… Whatever he's playing at, we'd better draw up a battle plan.'

Professional, polite, detached. Professional, polite, detached.

The words reverberated around Emily's head as the lift zoomed her up to the top floor. But how on earth was she going to be able to do professional, polite and detached when her stomach was churning and her hands were shaking? Any minute now she'd see him again. That thrill currently rippling through her could stop right now. She needed to focus and get a grip. Cool and dignified. That was what she was aiming for. She'd done nothing wrong. He was the rotten coward. She straightened her spine and smoothed her chignon. The lift pinged and Emily fixed a pleasantly neutral expression to her face that she hoped disguised the turmoil that was whooshing around inside her.

Her heels sank into thick cream carpet as she walked to the reception desk. 'Emily Marchmont to see Luke Harrison.'

'I'll tell him you're here,' said the receptionist.

Emily wandered over to the window and stared down at London sprawled out below. Grey streets, teeming with tiny people and mini cars. The hairs on the back of her neck told her he was behind her even before he said her name. Her heart crashed against her ribs.

'Emily.'

She steeled herself and turned slowly round. 'Luke. A delight to see you again.' Thank God her voice sounded steady. He was wearing a beautifully cut navy suit and a pale blue shirt open at the neck, and he was just as gorgeous as she remembered. And, pleasingly, he looked even more tired than she did.

He wasn't smiling. In fact he was looking positively stony. There was a tension in him that made her think of an animal about to pounce. All lean hard muscle beneath that fine wool suit. An image of the two of them entwined on the bed flew unwittingly into her head and for a second she went dizzy.

'Are you all right?' he said coolly.

'Of course,' she replied pleasantly. 'I'm just not too good with heights.'

'You'd better keep away from the windows, then.'

'Ah, yes. Good idea.'

'Thank you for coming at such short notice.' He took her elbow and it was all she could do not to snatch it back. His hand burned through the thin material of her jacket.

'Not a problem. Especially when you're paying so handsomely for my services. Again.'

Luke's eyes narrowed at her saccharine tone. 'How are you?'

'Never felt better. You?'

'The same.' He nodded curtly and led her down the corridor and past a trading room, where a dozen men and women stared at computer screens and talked quietly into phones at each ear. Not for the first time Emily congratulated herself on her chosen career path. Imagine having to work permanently with someone as distracting as Luke.

He opened the door of his office and she went in, taking care not to touch him. Emily looked around the large room, taking in the mahogany table, the ultra-modern cream leather sofa that looked as uncomfortable as it did elegant, and the glass and chrome desk upon which sat a bank of computer screens.

'Nice place. So. Where shall I set up and what would you like me to do?'

Luke walked over and leaned against the edge of the desk while his eyes followed her every movement. 'You can leave your bag there,' he said indicating the sofa. 'There's a pile of filing, and when you've finished that there's some photocopying.'

Emily's spirits sank. If it was any other job she'd be out the door and straight on the phone to Sarah. But if she was honest with herself she didn't want to leave. Despite Luke's filthy mood, it was too good to see him. And it was proving hard to be cool, professional and detached when all she really wanted to do was race over to him and—

Emily swallowed. The bet. Remember the bet, she told herself, fixing a haughty smile to her face. 'I'll get right to it.'

He folded his arms over his chest. 'Aren't you forgetting something?'

Emily raised a quizzical eyebrow.

'My coffee?'

Emily swelled with indignation. How dared he? Of all the outrageous, and probably discriminatory demands... 'Of course,' she purred. 'How do you take it?'

'Black, no sugar. And do have one yourself. The kitchen's down the corridor on the left.'

Emily gave him another hollow smile. 'I'll be right back.'

She turned on her heel and stalked to the door. She could feel Luke's eyes burning into her back as she marched out. She'd give him coffee, she decided, striding down the corridor and swinging into the kitchen. Filing! she thought, as she thrust the kettle under the tap and then switched it on. She hadn't done filing for years. Most of her employers had her putting together presentations, co-ordinating marketing campaigns and managing clients. If he'd bothered to read her CV he'd have known that. By the time she'd finished his filing he'd be sorry he ever asked. He'd never be able to locate anything ever again.

Emily poured boiling water into a cafetière and plucked two cups from the cupboard. And as for photocopying—well, she'd make sure that he'd be recycling paper for years. She pushed the plunger down hard. How was it he wanted his coffee? Black, no sugar? She filled the cups and liberally added milk and sugar to both.

Moving to the other side of his desk to check on his screens, Luke heard the sound of crockery crashing and doors slamming coming from the kitchen. He couldn't prevent a smile spreading over his face. He could almost see the steam coming from her ears. Her expression when he'd mentioned coffee and filing had been priceless.

God, it was good to see her again. Her severe suit, rigid hair-style and bolshy attitude only strengthened his memory of the softness of her body, the tickle of her hair brushing against his skin, and the incredible way she'd responded to him. Images flooded into his head and he felt himself stiffening.

He frowned and switched his focus to the screens. She looked as though she hadn't been sleeping well, which gave him a sort of grim satisfaction. The need to know why she'd left smouldered in him like an ember. By the end of the day he'd have his answers, and she'd be curling up around him, all sweetness and purring for real, begging for his forgiveness.

Emily carried the two cups of steaming coffee back to the office, where Luke was sitting behind the desk, twirling a pen between his fingers as he watched her. She nearly stumbled under the force of his scowl. What did he have to scowl about? *He* was the one who'd casually seduced her and abandoned her in that hotel in France, and all because of some pathetic macho bet.

She handed him a cup and threw him a challenging glare. 'Your coffee.'

Their fingers brushed and sent sparks of electricity running up her arm. Being in close proximity to this man was danger-ous. Especially since the last time she'd seen him he'd been sprawled next to her, naked and all warm hard muscle. Emily swallowed and gave herself a mental kick.

Luke stared down at the cup. 'Thank you,' he muttered with a frown.

'Right. I'd better get on with your filing.'

'Sit down and have your coffee first.'

Emily shrugged and sat on the sofa, which was as unfor-giving as she'd thought. If he wanted to pay her for drinking coffee that was his business. She'd drink it extremely slowly, she decided, wrapping her hands round her cup and blowing on the steaming liquid.

Luke's phone rang and he twisted round to answer it. As he rattled off a string of orders to buy and sell various products at various prices at various times, Emily took the opportunity to study him. From the top of his gorgeous head to the soles of those very expensive-looking shoes just visible beneath the desk he was every inch the financial hotshot. Actually, he was just hot, full-stop. He'd look good in anything. Even better in nothing… Emily felt desire start to wind its way through her and bit on her tongue.

Luke put the receiver down and she managed to avert her eyes before he caught her staring at him. *Focus, you fool. Focus.* She blinked and took a gulp of coffee. 'How much money did you just make?'

'About a hundred thousand pounds.'

Emily nodded. The sum was so mind-boggling that she couldn't even begin to get her head round it. 'In around one minute? That's six million pounds an hour. I should raise my rates.' The ghost of a smile played at his lips and then vanished. 'Talking of which, why me?' she said.

'Why you, what?'

'The sudden urgent need for a temp. Me, in particular.'

Luke's expression was unreadable. 'Why do you think?'

Because you wanted to see me again? Emily felt her cheeks flush and cursed the fact that she blushed so easily. 'I have no idea. How did you know where to find me?'

Giving her a searing glance, Luke got up and moved to the window. He thrust his hands in his pockets and stared down at whatever was below the expanse of plate glass. 'Word of mouth. You're very good at what you do. I heard you were the best.'

Emily rose to put her cup on the table. 'I believe that about as much as I believe the reasons you gave for bidding for me in that auction. Remind me again. What were they?'

'Curiosity and the appeal of gallantry.'

'And nothing whatsoever to do with a bet?'

Emily saw him tense. 'Ah,' he said, after a long silence.

She bristled. Was that all he had to say? No apology? No hint of shame? 'Gossip travels fast in the City.'

'And tends to get distorted along the way.'

He could at least look at her. 'So it wasn't a bet?'

Luke turned round slowly. His eyes locked with hers and Emily had to lean against the table to steady herself. It would have been better if he'd stayed staring out of the window.

'You've already discounted the reasons I gave you, and I'm not the type to lust over a photo, so what other reason would I have had?'

Emily went red again. 'I can't imagine.'

Luke flashed her a quick grin that lit up his features and flipped her stomach. 'Did you know that your face is extremely expressive?'

'So I've been told,' she said grumpily.

'I think you're piqued because I didn't bid for you out of some overwhelming desire for your body.'

'Of course I'm not piqued,' she said, injecting as much withering scorn into her voice as she could. 'I'd be utterly horrified if you had.'

'Admit it—your vanity's stung.'

'I'll have you know my vanity is very much unstung. I just don't appreciate being batted back and forward like a commodity between two bored bankers.'

'We're not bankers.'

She arched an eyebrow. 'Rhyming slang.'

Luke registered her jibe with the flicker of a smile. 'It may have escaped your notice,' he said smoothly, 'but that's how an auction works.'

There wasn't much she could say to that. He was right. Her outrage drained away, try as she might to cling on to it. 'You haven't drunk your coffee.'

He walked over to the desk, picked up the cup, took a sip and grimaced.

'How is it?'

'Milky and sweet—just as you intended.'

'Can you blame me?'

Luke continued moving, closing the distance between them, and put the cup down on the table next to hers. He was so close that Emily could smell the soap he used.

'Don't you think you're slightly overreacting?' he said, drawing back a little but still far too close for her comfort.

Probably. 'No.'

'There wasn't a bet.'

'Right.'

'It was more of a competition.'

'That makes me feel so much better.'

'Jack and I have always been competitive, and I like to win. He sent me the link and needled me until I opened it.'

'Poor you.'

For a few seconds they simply stared at each other. The air thickened, crackled, and every inch of Emily's body became aware of his. Luke's eyes bored right through her. 'Actually,' he murmured, 'when I said that your picture had nothing to do with it, I was lying.'

Emily's heart lurched at the look in his eye. 'Oh?' she breathed.

'I'll admit part of it was competitive drive, but the greater part of it was you. I wanted to meet you. I didn't want Jack to have you. And just for once I felt like doing something completely irrational.'

'Why?'

'Too long playing safe,' he murmured.

She wanted to ask him what he meant, but the blaze in his eyes was scrambling her mind. By the time she'd retrieved it he was staring at her mouth and all she could think of was having his mouth on hers. 'Was it part of the competition to sleep with me too?'

There was a long pause, and then Luke sighed. 'Of course not. I slept with you, and you slept with me back, because of this.' He reached out and ran his thumb over her lower lip. Tingles flickered through her.

'You left without even saying goodbye.'

'You hung up on me. I would have said goodbye if you'd bothered to hang around.'

'How was the "emergency" in Dubai?' she said.

Luke raised an eyebrow at her tone and dropped his hand. 'Bad. A new development partially collapsed.'

Emily frowned. 'Was anyone hurt?'

'Only the investors. It wasn't finished. The construction company's share price plummeted. We lost a lot of money.'

'Oh… How did you find out about it?'

'The office called.'

Emily looked at him sceptically. 'I didn't hear your mobile ring.'

'It didn't. It was on vibrate.'

'And that woke you up?'

'I was already awake. I don't sleep much.'

'You obviously have more stamina than I do,' said Emily, thinking how thoroughly he'd worn her out.

'I went back to the hotel as soon as I'd sorted the mess out, but you'd already gone.'

Emily went hot all over. Heart thudding, she stared at him. He sounded genuinely annoyed. Had she got it all wrong? Had she been guilty of assuming that Luke had behaved like a stereotypical male when everything she'd seen of him pretty much indicated the opposite?

Emily suddenly felt rather small. 'Well, of course I'd gone,' she said, folding her arms over her chest. 'I thought it was an excuse. You know—so you wouldn't have to face me in the morning.'

'Why wouldn't I want to face you? I was rather looking forward to a repeat performance.'

'Really?' Emily's eyes widened and her pulse jumped.

'Really,' he said. And then his expression changed, turned harder. 'But you couldn't wait to leave, could you?' His eyes narrowed. 'Why did you leave so hastily? What was it? Did the night we spent together remind you of what you'd lost with Tom?'

'What?' She gaped at him. 'How can you even think that?'

'You were on a plane pretty much the moment you put the phone down.'

'Believe me, Tom was the last thing on my mind.'

'So why did you leave?'

Emily chewed on her lip. 'I told you. I thought it was an excuse. I was having an irrational moment brought on by lack of experience. I've never slept with someone I've only just met. I thought it was a one-night stand and I didn't feel all that great about it.'

Luke's gaze pierced through her. 'I don't do one-night stands.'

'Neither do I.'

He stared at her, and time seemed to shudder to a halt.

'You know what stops it being a one-night stand?'

All she could hear was the sound of her heart thudding in her ears. 'A time-travelling machine?'

Luke shook his head. 'A second night.'

At those words, fire spread through her. 'That would solve it.'

'It would.'

'When?'

'Soon. Very soon.'

She had to bite on her lip to stop herself from trying to persuade him to bring the night forward to right now. 'I'm sorry about the coffee,' she said instead.

Luke tilted his head. 'What other plans did you have for me?'

'Put it this way: you're lucky I didn't get my hands on your diary or your client contact details.'

'You'd better go home before you wreck my business. You'll be paid until the end of the week anyway.'

Emily shook her head. 'I can't let you do that.'

'Yes, you can.'

'Surely there's something I could do to be useful?'

'Actually, there is something…' He took a step towards her. His eyes took on a predatory gleam.

Emily's pulse began to thud. 'Um, no. I don't really think that's such a good idea. We're in your office, for goodness' sake, and I'd never do something like that in return for *payment*.'

'What?' Luke looked bemused, and then grinned. 'What I was actually thinking of was you coming with me to something tomorrow night. But now you mention it…' He stroked his hands up her arms. 'Your idea is much better.' He backed her up against the mahogany table. His hard thighs pressed against hers. His arms slid round her back and moulded her against him.

'You see,' he murmured. 'Incomprehensible though this might be, ignoring it is pointless. And why would we want to deny ourselves the pleasure?'

'Luke…' she breathed, staring at his mouth.

'But you're quite right. We are in my office. My secretary is just the other side of the door. Anyone could come in at any minute.'

Emily gave a little gasp.

'Does that turn you on?' he said softly.

More than he could possibly imagine. But all she could do was give her head a quick shake.

He bent his head and her heart rate tripled. He brushed her mouth with his and then kissed his way to her ear. 'Liar,' he whispered.

Emily was beyond the point of caring.

'I like you all buttoned up like this. Hair tied back, tight little suit. It makes me want to undo you.'

'Undo away,' she breathed, her hands creeping up his chest. The table looked solid enough…

'Unfortunately I have a meeting in ten minutes.'

'So? Plenty of time.'

Luke chuckled and pulled back. 'Not nearly enough. We'll just have to wait. Think of the anticipation.'

'Highly overrated,' Emily grumbled.

'Then think of the rewards.'

'I am. That's the problem.' She picked up her handbag.

Luke laughed. 'I'll pick you up tomorrow at six.'

'Where are we going?'

'It's a charity gala. Black tie.' He paused. 'And afterwards we'll see about eradicating that one-night stand.'

'Is that a promise?' she said coyly.

'I'd say it's non-negotiable in any way.'

She looked up at him from beneath her eyelashes, well aware that her eyes reflected what was going through her mind. Luke wrenched the door open with an obvious effort of will. 'You'd better go, before you make me miss my meeting.'

'You don't know where I live.'

'Yes, I do. Your address is on your CV.'

'So you did read it?'

'Every word.'

'Then the coffee and the filing…?'

His eyes glittered down at her. 'I don't like people walking out on me.'

Emily stared at his mouth and resisted the urge to reach up and kiss him. 'Are you sure there isn't anything I can do now that I'm here? Buy some gold? Exercise an option? Bring down the stockmarket?'

'You're not authorised, and you're too distracting. Besides, you make terrible coffee.'

She sighed and turned to leave. 'Don't tell anyone, but I'm fairly terrible at filing too.'

'I wouldn't worry,' he said, his eyes raking over her so thoroughly she thought she'd go up in flames. 'There are plenty of other things you're good at.'

CHAPTER SIX

EMILY lifted her face to the breeze and the feeling that the evening was going to be magical washed over her. Everything was perfect. She'd found a stunning dress and matching shoes in the first shop she'd gone into and she'd had her hair professionally dried so that it fell in sculpted waves over her shoulders. She'd been transformed into a nineteen-forties siren, and the look in Luke's eyes when she'd opened her door to him had made her feel amazing. Her whole body was buzzing with anticipation and desire.

They were standing with other elegantly dressed guests on the rear deck of a boat that was gliding along the Thames. The buildings on either bank of the river were bathed in warm sunlight and the water sparkled. At least if she did spontaneously combust with desire they could hurl her overboard.

Luke was staring into the distance, his arms resting on the guardrail and his face inscrutable. Emily glanced at him. The wind was ruffling his dark hair. His profile stole her breath for a second. She wished she could read his mind. There were moments like now, when he was deep in thought and his face took on such a bleakness, that her heart clenched. The need to wipe it away pounded through her.

'What's this gala in aid of?'

He twisted round and leaned against the rail. 'Children,' he replied, regarding her blankly.

'What? All of them?'

He gave her a brief smile. 'A number of different charities. It happens once a year.'

'Do you come to things like this often?'

'Often enough.'

The sun lit up his face and Emily shivered with longing.

'Cold?' he asked, shrugging off his jacket and draping it over her shoulders.

The jacket was warm from him, and it was all she could do not to pull it tightly around her and bury her nose in it. 'No, I—' She stopped as she wobbled on her heel. Luke's hands reached out to steady her.

'I would lend you my shoes too, but they might be a bit big.'

'Thank you, but I should be able to manage. I was momentarily blinded by all these jewels on board. I don't suppose they're paste.'

'I'd be surprised if they were.' His eyes roamed over her and she began to burn. 'By the way, did I mention how spectacular you look in that dress?'

'You did.' Emily's inner siren sprang to life. She shot him a smouldering glance. 'Did I mention how easy it is to take off?'

Luke's jaw clenched and his pupils began to dilate. 'Funnily enough, no,' he said.

She moved closer to him. Luke didn't move a muscle. 'I was getting dressed earlier, sliding little lacy knickers up my legs and then slipping my dress over my head and feeling it slithering over me, and do you know what was going through my mind?'

'Advanced calculus?' His voice was taut.

'How you would soon be taking it all off.' Her voice dropped. 'Sliding down the zip, peeling it off me, your hands on my skin.' Luke was staring at her as if he was about to ravish her. No hint of desolation now. 'You know what I really want?'

He gave his head a quick shake.

'I want you to be thinking about undressing me every time you look at me.'

'Shouldn't be a problem,' said Luke, looking as if someone had hit him across the back of the knees with a lead pipe.

'Fair's fair, after all,' she said, running her gaze over him slowly and deliberately, as if she was imagining what lay beneath his dinner suit.

Luke stared at her, his eyes glittering with desire. 'You are pure evil,' he said softly.

'I know,' she said with a smug grin. 'It's great, isn't it?'

'Are you two getting off?'

At the voice of the boat driver they both jumped. Emily swivelled round, and to her embarrassment saw that she and Luke were the only people left on the boat.

The sounds of music and chatter drifted towards them. Emily reluctantly gave Luke back his jacket, and he went ahead of her along the gangplank. When he was on dry land, he held out his hand to help her off. His fingers tightened around hers as they walked up the path towards the huge cream Georgian building spreading out before them. Acrobats leapt and tumbled on the grass to their left. On the right jugglers tossed flaming torches high into the air. A string quartet was playing at the bottom of the marble steps that led up to the building.

'Luke!'

He jerked to a stop. Emily nearly went crashing into him. A man was bearing down on them, smiling widely, and Luke wasn't looking too happy about it.

'I thought it was you. What the hell are you doing here? You haven't been to this for years.'

'Jack,' said Luke coolly. He shook his hand. 'I didn't think this was your sort of thing.'

'I'm broadening my horizons. What's your excuse?' Jack's gaze swivelled to Emily. 'Ah, I see.'

As he looked her up and down in a blatantly appreciative way, Emily decided she really ought to muster up a degree of outrage. But the wicked glint in his eye made it impossible. A slow smile spread across his face.

'Well, well, well—Miss Green Bikini.'

Emily's first instinct was to turn on her heel and take herself and her mortification somewhere they could hide until the boat came to take them back. But she shot a quick glance at Luke, whose jaw had tightened and who very definitely wasn't smiling, and suddenly the whole scenario was intriguing. Undercurrents swirling. Tension crackling. No way was she going to miss any of it.

'I assume you're *greatsexguaranteed*?' She raised a querying eyebrow.

'Who else?'

She tilted her head to one side. 'Modest.'

Jack grinned. 'Talented.'

Emily laughed. 'Outrageous.'

'Thank you.' He gave a little bow. 'Are you going to introduce us?' said Jack, turning to Luke.

'No,' replied Luke.

'Didn't think so,' he said easily. 'Jack Taylor.' He held out his hand and Emily took it.

'Emily Marchmont.'

'You have no idea how delighted I am to meet you.' He gave a theatrical sigh. 'I wish I'd been more persistent.'

'Jack Taylor? As in JT Investments?'

Jack nodded.

'I once worked at your company.'

Jack frowned, as if he was riffling through the bank of women in his head to recall her and failing. 'Really?'

'A year or so ago. I did some temping. You were away on business.'

'You temp?'

Emily nodded. 'I do.'

Jack's gaze flickered to Luke. 'Interesting.'

'Is it?'

'More than you could possibly know.'

He was still holding her hand, and Luke was watching them with narrowed eyes. Smoothly she extracted it and flashed

Jack a wide smile. Even if he was just being polite, he was irresistible.

'Tell me, is there a special place where only beautiful, charming people come from?'

Jack let out a laugh, and Luke's face turned even harder. 'Don't worry about her,' he said curtly. 'She's delusional. Probably dehydrated,' he added pointedly, looking at Jack.

'In that case why don't I look after the very lovely Emily while you go and find some champagne?' said Jack, his eyes gleaming.

The sound of Luke's teeth grinding could probably be heard the other side of the river. 'You're more likely to know where to find it, given the frequency with which you drink it.'

Jack didn't even flinch, just grinned even more widely. 'When I last passed the drinks table,' he said, 'I overheard a couple of people discussing the disappointing performance of their funds and wondering if they shouldn't switch. On your way, Luke, perhaps you could see if you could persuade them to transfer their assets to you.'

'I was under the impression that this was a social event.' The words were spoken smoothly enough, but Emily could hear the trace of steel in his voice.

'When has that ever stopped you? Don't worry. Emily will be in good hands.'

She'd been watching this mini drama unfold with secret delight, but the way Luke was clenching his fists was slightly worrying and the situation needed defusing. She flashed Jack her best smile. 'Would you mind?' she said, batting her eyelids at him winsomely. 'Luke and I were just in the middle of going over our arrangements for after the gala and there are a couple of details we need to clarify.'

Luke went still, and his gaze snapped round to tangle with hers. For a second everything faded, and all she was aware of was the two of them trapped in a bubble of heat, connected by a thread of passion, tightening, drawing them together.

'Isn't that right?' she said softly.

'Absolutely,' he murmured. Tension eased from his shoulders as his eyes darkened.

Jack looked from one to the other and nodded slowly. 'Of course,' he said smoothly. 'In fact, why don't I leave you to discuss your…er…arrangements, and see you at dinner. I'll get someone to revise the seating plan.'

'That would be lovely,' purred Emily.

'See you later.'

Wow, she thought, watching Jack lope off.

'You enjoyed that, didn't you?' said Luke.

Emily nodded. 'Very much. I could get used to being fought over. Especially if the combatants look as good as you two do. Who is he? Besides your partner in internet auction crime.'

'One of my oldest friends.'

Obviously. 'It was quite some display. A bit like stags locking antlers.'

'I'm glad you found it entertaining,' he said dryly.

'I'll probably send thousands of feminists spinning in their graves, but I must admit the whole "woman is mine" thing is very attractive.'

Luke tensed. 'You're not mine.'

Ouch. Emily sensed him withdraw and kicked herself. 'Oh, no—sorry, I forgot,' she said brightly. 'In that case you won't mind if I practise my flirting skills on Jack. He looks like he might appreciate them. He might even be able to give me some tips.'

He shot her a searing glance. 'OK, you're mine for tonight.'

Luke took her arm and they continued up the path. He knew his expression gave nothing away. It was an expression he'd perfected over the last few years. Blank, neutral, shuttered, inviting neither comment nor conversation. And not showing any hint of the storm raging inside him. A myriad of emotions churning around, all so tangled up that he couldn't have identified any one of them even if he'd wanted to.

Going from feeling nothing to this was like leaping from a freezer into a fire. In fact, years of clamping down on his emotions was probably what was making them attack him so strongly now. He felt like a pressure cooker that had been simmering for too long; the lid had sprung open in that damn church and it was going to be hard to push it back down.

He breathed deeply and was struck by a wave of coconut scent from Emily's hair, mingling with her perfume. Bringing her here had not been one of his better ideas. He hadn't thought it through properly. It had been a stupidly rash mistake. The sort of impulsive decision he'd have made five years ago but would never normally make now. He should have taken her out to dinner and sent the organisers of the gala a cheque. Somewhere loud and bright. Somewhere which wouldn't have required her to wear a midnight-blue dress that gave her an hourglass figure and a dangerous attitude.

That would have been the safe thing to do. Emily in that incredible dress and her current frame of mind was not safe at all. On the boat he'd been remembering the last time he'd attended this gala, with Grace, and then Emily had decided to unleash her inner fox and his mind had gone blank.

Then, just when he was dragging his sanity back, Jack—damn him—had shown up, flirting outrageously and no doubt jumping to all sorts of incorrect conclusions. Luke's jaw tightened. It didn't matter what Jack thought. All that mattered was that he kept a clear head and remained in control.

By reminding Emily what tonight was all about, he knew exactly what he was doing, and he was definitely in control.

As they entered the building, Emily could feel Luke trying to steer her straight on, but the women were flowing to a room on the right, whose door was flanked by two burly security guards, and the pressure of his hand on her elbow was no match for her curiosity.

'My goodness,' she breathed, once they'd gone through the doorway. The room had been set up like the jewellery section of a department store. Beneath ancient tapestries stood randomly placed glass cabinets. Each held necklaces, earrings, bracelets, in diamonds, sapphires, emeralds and rubies. Barely aware of Luke, who'd had little option but to follow her, she moved from cabinet to cabinet, peering over shoulders and around bodies in an effort to sneak a peek at pieces that were quite simply breathtaking.

'Another impressive display,' she said, her fingers automatically fiddling with a diamond pendant that hung around her neck from a fine white-gold chain. Beautiful and simple and of highly sentimental value though her necklace was, she couldn't help but drool at what she saw.

She glanced up and saw that Luke's eyes were watching her fingers, so she trailed them slowly over her skin and along her collarbone.

Luke dragged his gaze back up to her eyes. 'Do you see anything you like?'

Emily smiled. 'I like all sparkly things. What woman doesn't?'

'What about those?' He pointed to a pair of huge diamond earrings. Three carats each at least.

She wrinkled her nose. 'A bit on the small side, I think.'

One corner of Luke's mouth twitched. 'Then the sapphires,' he said, taking her elbow and bending over a display cabinet which held a beautiful necklace of intricate white-gold and dark stones. 'They match your dress.'

'So they do,' said Emily. 'Why not? They're quite dazzling.'

Luke nodded at the man standing quietly behind the cabinet, who moved forward, unlocked the door and removed the piece. 'Luke,' she said urgently. 'I was joking.'

He laid it out on a rectangle of velvet and Luke ran his fingers gently over the stones. Emily swallowed.

'Don't worry. We're only borrowing it. The idea is that you wear the necklace, and then when some fool with more money than sense sees how amazing the sapphires are he won't be able to resist buying them.'

'But this must be worth a fortune.'

'Approximately two hundred thousand pounds,' said the salesman.

Emily had to bite back a squeal. 'I can't possibly wear it. What if the catch breaks?'

He shot her a withering glance. 'Our catches don't break,' he said.

'What if I forget and take it home?'

'Believe me, madam,' said the salesman, flickering a glance in the direction of the security guards, 'that won't happen.'

She was running out of protests. And not before time, she thought weakly. One last attempt. 'I'm already wearing a necklace.'

'Take it off.' Luke's voice was low in her ear.

'Undressing me already?' she murmured.

'Yes. I'll look after it.'

Emily reached up to undo the necklace. It was probably safer with him than in the tiny handbag that she was clutching. As she dropped it into Luke's palm, she lifted serious eyes to his.

'Don't lose it,' she said quietly. 'It belonged to my mother. It's very precious.'

'I won't,' replied Luke, slipping it into the inside pocket of his jacket.

'I'm still not sure that this is a good idea.'

'Shut up,' said Luke gently, picking up the necklace and draping it around her neck.

His fingers brushing against her skin as he did it up were warm in contrast to the cold piece of jewellery.

'I feel like a fraud.' His fingers rested on the pulse in her neck and she was sure he must be able to feel it hammering.

'You look like a goddess.'

'More like Cinderella.'

'You'll be leaving before midnight.'

'With Prince Charming?'

'I'm afraid you'll have to make do with me.'

Emily sighed dramatically. 'I suppose I might just manage.'

And then she frowned. 'How will people know it's for sale and not my own?'

'The show starts in fifteen minutes. There are eight other ladies before you, so if I may take your name…?'

Emily's jaw dropped. 'Show?'

'You'll be modelling the necklace on our behalf.'

'In front of all these people? Please tell me you're joking.'

The salesman's expression told her exactly what he thought of that suggestion. 'If madam isn't happy to model the necklace, I'm afraid she'll have to return it.'

Emily ran her fingers over the necklace. To have to give it back now would be unbearable. She nibbled on her lower lip. All she'd have to do, surely, was parade and pose for a couple of minutes. How hard could it be?

'Madam could probably manage a bit of modelling,' she said. 'After all, it *is* for charity.'

'It is indeed.'

She gave her name to the salesman and then threaded her hand through Luke's arm.

'You're dazzling,' he murmured into her ear, with a low voice that turned her knees to water.

Emily shivered. If she wasn't careful all this would start going to her head, and she might start thinking it was for real—the sapphires, the occasion, Luke. And that would never do. This was one night. Maybe a string of one nights. But definitely only a fling. This wasn't real.

As they moved across the marble floor, Luke introduced her to people he knew and brushed off comments about how good it was to see him there. Despite Emily's best efforts, Luke didn't stop to engage in anything other than the barest minimum of small talk. She didn't often find herself surrounded by rich, beautiful people, and she wanted to absorb as much as possible. All the chatter, the exotic scents, the glamour. Even the disdain of a regal silver-haired lady by the pillar, who she could see watching them intently over the rim of her glass.

Emily continued chatting brightly, but could feel the lady's gaze—hostile, frigid, disapproving—and wondered what she'd done to cause it. Could she tell that Emily's dress wasn't designer? Did she know that Emily's bank balance was several zeroes short of a million?

She was just about to ask Luke whether he knew her when he put his hand on the bare skin at the small of her back. She inhaled sharply and all thoughts of the lady by the pillar were wiped from her mind. All she could focus on were the sparks dashing over her skin.

'How long do you think we'll have to wait before we can get round to the non-negotiable part of the evening?' she said, her voice low and husky.

Luke's gaze trapped hers, and she saw her own longing reflected briefly in his.

'Patience,' he replied softly.

'Unfortunately that's never been one of my virtues. Along with abstinence, permanence and prudence.'

'What about endurance?'

'That's something I have in abundance.'

'I think you're going to need it. Off you go.'

She pouted. 'Fed up with me already?'

Luke's gaze dropped to her mouth, just as she'd intended. 'You're being beckoned. Time to strut your stuff.'

Emily was assailed by a sudden attack of nerves. 'Oh, God, I hope I don't do something awful like trip and land in the trifle.'

Luke backed her into a shadowy corner, away from the main group of people heading into the dining hall.

'What are you doing?' she asked, her heart leaping into her throat when she saw the intent in his eyes.

'You've gone a little pale. Not a good look for sapphires.' He slid his hand round her neck and lowered his mouth to hers. Heat poured through her as she melted against him, winding one arm around his waist to keep her upright. His tongue explored her mouth, languidly at first, and then became more and more demanding as the heat built between them. Emily pressed herself closer, greedily taking everything he was offering until he reluctantly broke off the kiss.

'I've been wanting to do that all evening,' he said, drawing in a ragged breath.

'What kept you?'

'Exhibitionism has never been my thing.' He drew back, checked her face and straightened the necklace. 'That's better.'

Emily knew her eyes were sparkling and her cheeks were rosy. But she felt sluggish. Drugged with desire. How in heaven's name was she going to be able to work her legs?

Luke ran a thumb over her lower lip and her breath hitched. He swallowed hard and pulled back.

'Go. Now. I'll see you at the table. Make sure you don't talk to any strange men.'

Emily blinked rapidly to calm her thudding heart and caught the flapping of an arm from a woman with a clipboard and earpiece. 'I promise I'll only talk to normal ones,' she said gravely, flashing him a sexy little smile before heading off to join the group of women decked out in jewellery for sale.

CHAPTER SEVEN

IT WAS all about control, thought Luke, congratulating himself as he twisted away and strode into the dining hall. When he'd drawn back from that sizzling kiss he could have dragged her off outside and bundled her into the nearest taxi, as his body had urged him to. Alternatively he could have ripped her clothes off right then and there and probably got them both arrested. Or he could have watched her cross the floor and allowed himself to be hypnotised by the sight of her smooth brown back.

But, no, he thought, catching Jack's eye on the other side of the room and making his way to their table. He'd resisted. Fought his instincts. Summoned his strength. Demonstrated to himself that he still had the iron-hard discipline he'd developed.

He was in control. No doubt about it.

'Where's Emily?'

Luke's hackles didn't even quiver at the undisguised interest in Jack's voice. 'Part of the jewellery display.'

'I see you took my advice after all,' said Jack conversationally.

'What advice would that be?' Luke nodded and smiled briefly at the other people at the table.

'To have some fun. You've slept with her.'

Luke frowned and his gut clenched. 'Nobody's business but ours,' he said evenly.

'Aha! I knew it,' Jack said, grinning and clapping him on the shoulder. 'And about time too. Welcome back.'

'I'm not back,' said Luke, his face darkening.

'Of course you aren't,' said Jack soberly. 'But it's good to see you with a smile on your face again. Some of the time at least.'

He turned to head round to the other side of the table, a knowing grin twitching at his lips, but stopped suddenly. 'By the way,' he said, tapping the corner of his mouth. 'Lipstick. Not really your colour.'

Luke scowled, picked up his napkin and rubbed. Dropping the napkin back on the table, he pulled out a chair for the lady on his right—the wife of a client—and then sat down as the lights dimmed and music flooded through the room.

As further proof of just how in control he was, he wasn't even going to watch the jewellery parade. No. Instead he was going to focus on the flower arrangement in the centre of the table and mentally go through the list of companies which were due to report their profits over the next couple of days. Then he'd work out how the results would affect the holdings his funds had.

By the time he'd worked out a variety of permutations for his positions the following day, seven women had sauntered past him. Not that he'd been counting.

'Miss Emily Marchmont,' boomed the voice from the speakers, 'is wearing a sapphire and diamond necklace from Cartier. This exquisite piece features thirty sapphires from Sri Lanka, totalling two hundred carats. Their deep blue colour contrasts brilliantly with a sparkling sea of four hundred and thirty diamonds, weighing eighty-four carats.'

Luke took a gulp of wine, sat back, and focused on the flowers. Right. How would his funds perform the day after? His heart slowed and his vision blurred. He rubbed his face and shook his head. And out of the corner of his eye saw her weaving between the tables, shoulders loose, hands on hips as she struck a pose. The spotlight illuminated her skin and the

sapphires sparkled against the creaminess. He couldn't drag his
eyes away.

His gaze followed her as she came to a stop in front of him
and flashed him a haughty, sultry smile that sent a kick of pure
lust shooting through him. Her eyes held a challenge, as if she
knew exactly how much he'd been trying not to look at her,
and then with a toss of her head she continued to the next table.

By the time the lights came up the only positions on Luke's
mind were the ones that had featured in that hotel room in
France. A light ripple of applause around the table alerted him
to the fact that Emily was standing behind him. That and the
way the back of his neck prickled.

'How did I do?' she asked.

'Great.' Luke could barely speak, and certainly couldn't
stand.

'You were magnificent,' said Jack smoothly, whipping
round from his side of the table. 'Let me introduce you to
everyone.'

Emily nodded politely and murmured greetings, but inside
she was bewildered. She thought she'd done pretty well, all
things considered. She'd coped with having all eyes on her
when generally she hated being the centre of attention. Even
when she'd encountered the silver-haired lady's icy gaze she'd
managed not to stumble. So what was Luke glaring about? And
why hadn't he got up, the rude man?

'At least I didn't land in the trifle,' she said.

Luke gave her a terse smile, and then turned to respond to
something the lady on his other side had said.

His rejection was like a slap in the face, and hurt spiked
through her. 'What have I done wrong?' murmured Emily to
Jack.

'Nothing at all. In fact you're doing something incredibly
right.' Which only added to her bewilderment. 'I've known
Luke a long time, and I'd say he's struggling with some serious
personal issues.'

Emily frowned. 'He's certainly struggling with manners. What sort of personal issues?'

'Control, among other things.'

'Control over what?'

'You'd have to ask him.'

She glanced down at Luke, who was continuing to ignore her, and allowed pique to swallow up the hurt. 'It doesn't look like he particularly wants to talk to me right now.' Which was fine—because she wasn't at all sure she wanted to speak to him either. She might not be able to stop herself from telling him exactly what she thought of his behaviour.

'No. But that's because I rather think talking is the last thing he wants to do to you right now.'

Luke's shoulders tensed, and then he shot her a quick look so full of desire and promise that it nearly melted her on the spot. Her attention snapped back to Jack and she caught the knowing look in his eyes. 'Right. I see.' And she did. Just as she'd seen the look on his face when she'd posed at the table.

The amused glint vanished from Jack's eyes. 'Make him lose it, Emily. If anyone can, you can.'

She was just about to ask him what he meant when she saw the fierce glare that Luke flashed at Jack. It held a warning that Jack acknowledged with a tiny nod.

'Wine?'

'Yes, please,' she said, resisting the urge to ask him to fill every one of the four beautiful crystal glasses on the table in front of her.

By the time Emily sat down Luke was still so engrossed in conversation that she turned to the man on her left, who was looking at her with admiration. 'You were fantastic,' he said.

'Thank you.'

'I'm Andrew.'

'Emily. Are you in finance too?' she asked.

'I deal in stamps.'

'How fascinating,' she said. 'Do tell me more.'

She'd managed five minutes of conversation on the subject

of philately, which she reckoned was something of a personal best, and had just started on an exquisite plate of tiny squid and truffles when Luke's knee first brushed hers. She nearly jumped out of her seat.

'Are you all right?' said Andrew.

Emily coughed. 'Bit of squid going down the wrong way. Please do go on with what you were saying about the Moroccan Post Office.'

'The Mauritius "Post Office". The world's rarest stamps.'

'Oh, yes—so sorry.'

The continuing pressure of Luke's knee against hers made it almost impossible to concentrate any more. She barely noticed the waiters whipping away the starter and delivering the main course of black cod. Or the champagne ice cream. She couldn't taste a thing.

At one point Luke reached down, ostensibly to pick his napkin up from beneath the table. But his hand landed on her foot and then caressed its way up her calf, creating devastation on her composure. She had to shove a handmade chocolate into her mouth to block the whimper rushing to escape. And then he did it again. He was messing with her equilibrium, her concentration and her mind. Well, two could play at that game.

'Excuse me,' she said to Andrew, waiting until Luke had lifted his wine glass to his lips before putting a hand on his thigh beneath the tablecloth. The hard muscles contracted and Luke nearly choked on the mouthful of wine he'd taken. He swallowed hard and looked at her from beneath hooded lids.

'What?' he said hoarsely.

Emily let her expression collapse into one of irritation. 'Lord, I'm sorry, I can't remember what I was going to say. My mind's gone blank. Don't you hate it when that happens?' she added.

'I think the auction's about to start,' said Tamsin, a beautiful girl who was sitting across the table next to Jack.

'Oh, yes, that was it.' Emily gave her head a quick shake,

as if to say *silly me*, and trailed her fingers higher up Luke's thigh towards his hip and then round. She was itching to see if he was still in the same state that had prevented him from getting to his feet earlier.

His eyes narrowed and his hand tightened around his napkin—beneath which were her fingers.

'Rumour has it you like auctions, Luke,' Tamsin said, shooting him a smouldering glance.

She'd been sending him smouldering glances throughout dinner, thought Emily, as she reclaimed her hand. Pretty much every time they'd exchanged words and even when they hadn't. Totally unnecessary and highly inappropriate, in her opinion.

'Depends on what's up for sale,' he said.

'You can pick up some unexpected bargains,' said Jack with a grin.

'Although I guess you can never be sure that what you end up with will live up to expectations,' said Tamsin.

'I've yet to be disappointed,' Luke said lazily, toying with his coffee spoon.

Emily's heart rocked, and then jumped when the sound of a gavel hitting a table ricocheted around the room. A man was standing at a podium in the centre of the hall and all eyes swivelled in his direction as the lights dimmed.

'Ladies and gentlemen.' His smooth, persuasive tones rang out through the speakers. 'I do hope everyone enjoyed the dinner.' A murmur of agreement rippled through the assembled throng. 'Now we move on to the part of the evening where I encourage you to part with vast sums of money. This evening we have some fantastic lots on offer, which I'm sure will generate huge interest. So, without further ado, let's start with lot number one—a bronze sculpture by one of our leading artists. Who'll start me at a thousand?'

Emily tuned out. The next half an hour or so in semi-darkness would give her much needed time to regroup her thoughts and give her heart a chance to slow to its usual steady self.

What was it about Luke Harrison that reduced her to such a frenzied state? OK, so he was incredibly good-looking and sexy, but so was Jack, and he didn't turn her into a puddle with just a touch. Was it that haunted look in his eyes that she'd caught on a couple of occasions? The hint of mystery? The dry humour? Inner strength?

Who the hell knew? she thought, stifling a sigh. And frankly did it matter? Surely all that was important about this evening was what happened after this interminable gala ended. Emily went warm. Where would they go from here? Her house or his flat? His flat was closer. She closed her eyes. His flat would be modern, she mused. He'd said he had a penthouse, so the views would be spectacular.

She'd kick off her shoes and wander over to take a look. And then maybe he'd walk up behind her and run his hands over her shoulders. He'd slowly slide the zip of her dress down, nudge the straps down her arms and let it slither into a pool of midnight silk around her feet. He'd turn her in his arms and he'd tell her she looked like Botticelli's *Venus*. She'd undo his buttons and push off his shirt and jacket, so that he'd be standing there in just his trousers. She'd run her hands over his chest, maybe grazing his nipple, and then he'd be hauling her against him, kissing her hard and deep, tumbling them to a sheepskin rug, desire taking over, losing control, slick heat, skin, tongues, hands…

Emily's eyes snapped open and she let out a breath. Ohhhh, not good for the heart rate. Not good at all.

She hoped to God no one at the table had noticed she'd drifted off into a fantasy of X-rated proportions. Thank goodness. No sign that anyone noticed anything amiss. She glanced at Tamsin, whose gaze was fixed on Luke. Yet again. She'd better not be having similar thoughts to those that *she'd* just been having, thought Emily. But then Tamsin's eyes flickered to Jack, and Emily's little daydream bubble burst.

She looked at Luke, who was focusing on the man at the podium. He nodded almost imperceptibly. Was he bidding?

Her gaze switched over to Jack. His face was set too. Oh, crikey, she thought, not again. What were they bidding for this time? She craned her neck to see what was on offer, and saw with horror that it was a giant painting of a scorpion.

'What are you doing?' she whispered.

'What does it look like?' Luke murmured, his lips barely moving.

'Sixty thousand. Thank you, sir,' said the auctioneer, pointing his gavel in Jack's direction.

Luke nodded again.

'Are you mad?' she said, trying to keep her voice down.

'I have a lot of white walls that need filling.'

'You can't hang *that* on one. It's awful.'

Luke nodded again.

'You're bidding for it solely to stop Jack getting it, aren't you?'

'Not at all. I wouldn't do anything so childish. It's by a highly sought-after artist and a good investment. Not to mention for a good cause.'

'It's still hideous.'

'I'm feeling reckless.'

'So am I. But, Luke, there's reckless and then there's reckless. If you want something to cover your walls, I'll come and scribble on them. I'd do a damn sight better job than that scorpion.'

'It's not just a scorpion. It's a representation of man's fight against the injustice of capitalism.'

'Hypocrite,' she murmured. 'You're a fund manager. You make your living out of capitalism.'

'I'm a liberal capitalist.'

Emily sniffed. 'Do you like it?'

'It's thought-provoking.'

'It's eye-wateringly ugly. Do you really want it?'

A muscle was ticking in his jaw. She could almost see the battle raging in his head. The auctioneer was looking at Luke expectantly and the room was hushed. After what seemed like hours Luke gave his head a quick shake, and Emily let out the breath that had got caught in her throat.

'Sold,' declared the auctioneer, banging his gavel on the table. 'To the gentleman at table six. Ladies and gentlemen, that wraps up the auction. Many thanks to all of you who bid. Thousands of underprivileged and sick children all over the world will benefit from your generosity.' There was a brief round of clapping and then the auctioneer added, 'The dancing and the casino are now underway.'

Emily was feeling rather stunned. He'd *listened* to her. Luke had listened to her and taken her advice.

'I can't believe you let me have it,' said Jack with a raised eyebrow. You and me both, thought Emily, a bubble of delight fizzing around inside her. 'Too much for you?'

Luke pushed his chair back and languidly got to his feet. 'If you want to hang eye-wateringly ugly art on your walls, Jack, be my guest.'

He put his hand on Emily's arm and bent down. 'Dance with me,' he said softly.

Emily suppressed a tiny shiver. She was a truly terrible dancer, and usually had to be dragged onto a dance floor kicking and screaming, but Luke's voice and his hand had her feeling like Ginger Rogers.

'Excuse me,' she said to Andrew. 'You'd better warn people to steer clear.'

Luke took her elbow and led her off in the direction of the music. Luckily the dance floor was filling up, so there was little room to do anything other than shuffle. Even she should be able to manage that, she thought—until Luke drew her into his arms and her heart began to thunder. The brief respite that the auction had provided was over. He put one hand on her back, the other on her shoulderblade, and need poured through her. Her own hands itched to re-enact her daydream and rip his buttons off, so she planted them safely on his shoulders, well out of reach of buttons.

His eyes raked her face, and then fixed on her mouth in such a disconcerting way that she thought she might have a bit of rocket in her teeth.

'What?' she said.

'Nothing.'

'Ah, no,' she said, wagging a finger gently at him. 'You don't get away with that. Only women can get away with the "nothing" card.'

'You saved me eighty thousand pounds.'

'I saved you from having to look at that awful daub every day and from a lifetime of regret at buying it. But that wasn't what you were going to say.'

A smile curved his lips and Emily was transfixed. His arm tightened around her waist even though his tone was mild. 'You seem to be very taken with Jack and Andrew.'

'They're handsome and charming. Who wouldn't be?' The expression on his face darkened. 'Tamsin's a lovely girl, isn't she?' she mused. 'Know her well?'

Luke laughed. Just for a second. But he laughed so rarely, and the sound of it seemed to surprise him as much as her. 'She's a friend of Jack's.'

'She may indeed be a friend of Jack's, but it doesn't answer my question.'

'We went out for dinner once.'

'Just dinner?'

'Just dinner. I may have kissed her goodnight.'

Emily nodded thoughtfully, unable to stop her arms creeping over his shoulders until her fingers slid through his hair and linked together at the back of his neck. 'That would have been the gentlemanly thing to do.'

'I thought so at the time.'

'Just the one kiss?'

'I don't sleep with women on the first date.'

Emily nibbled on her lip. 'So you don't sleep with women on the first date, and you don't do one-night stands. It seems you broke a few rules with me.'

'One, technically the wedding wasn't a date, and two, we've

already established that there is to be a second night. No rules broken at all.'

'Any other rules I should know about?' She arched an eyebrow.

The expression on Luke's face turned serious. 'Only that whatever happens between us can only be short-term. If you remember, I can't offer commitment.'

'Why not?'

'Too messy.'

'You've tried it before?'

'Once.'

'What happened?'

'Not here.'

That wasn't really fair. He'd asked her about her relationship with Tom and she'd told him. Most of it. But the look in his eye prevented her from asking further questions. Emily nodded. 'Well, if you remember, I don't do commitment either.' The last thing she wanted was to go through all the hassle of a relationship again. 'Don't worry, Luke, you've made it perfectly clear on numerous occasions, and I get the picture—really, I do.'

Their discussion was turning so businesslike, and so at odds with the dim lighting and throbbing music, Emily would have stuck her hand out to seal the deal had her hands not been otherwise occupied.

'That's settled, then,' she said, mesmerised by the way his eyes were roaming over her face. 'It's just sex. Pure and simple.'

'There's nothing pure and simple about what happens when we have sex.'

'It's been so long,' she said with a little pout, 'I can barely remember.' She tightened her arms and pulled herself closer, loving the feel of his hardness against her softness.

'You do realise that only one more night isn't going to be enough, don't you?'

Emily nodded. 'How many nights do we have before things become long-term and therefore unacceptable?'

'I've no idea. We'll just have to play it by ear.'

That sounded like a recipe for disaster, thought Emily. How could she stick to the rules if the rules were arbitrary? But it was so lovely moving against him and having his arms around her that she didn't want to break the spell.

'You know what people say about dancing, don't you?' she murmured.

'What do people say?'

'That it's a metaphor for sex. All this closeness. Moving. Touching.'

His hand moved over her back, sliding over naked skin and leaving scorching trails in its wake. 'Is that right?'

Emily bit her lip and nodded. His hand moved lower, his fingers spreading over the top of her bottom, and he pulled her hips to his. 'Like this?'

Emily moaned softly. 'Do you have a sheepskin rug in your flat?'

Luke looked at her in surprise. 'How did you know?'

'This gets better and better,' she said.

The music segued into something more upbeat. 'Now it's getting dangerous,' he said, ducking out of the way of an energetic elbow. He wound an arm around her shoulders and pulled her into his side as they made their way off the dance floor. She could feel the need in her echoing in him and she trembled.

'I'll be back in a second,' she said, extracting herself. 'I think I need to calm down.'

'Then we'll go.'

'So early?' she said, with mock despondency.

The look he fired at her nearly winded her with its intensity. 'It's nearly midnight, Cinders. You and I have a long-awaited appointment with a bed, and I want to get you into it before you turn into a pumpkin.'

Emily felt a beat start up deep within her, obliterating everything except this insane desperate ache. 'Well, in that case I'll be as quick as I can.'

CHAPTER EIGHT

EMILY stared at her reflection. Was that woman with flushed cheeks and eyes that were sparkling as much as the sapphires around her neck really *her*? Her entire body was almost shuddering in longing, and she had to bite down hard on her lip to stop herself moaning out loud at the thought of what she and Luke would soon be up to. She didn't think she'd ever been so turned on in her life. The intensity of what she was feeling, the desire that he whipped up inside her, was slightly scary. She barely recognised herself. Was sex with Luke really such a good idea? She dismissed the rogue thought the moment it entered her head. It was the best idea in the world.

With trembling fingers she unclipped her handbag and extracted her lipstick.

'Excuse me?'

Emily's attention swivelled to the woman who'd appeared in the mirror, standing behind her, and she went still. It was the lady who'd been staring at her earlier. A pearl choker at her throat and heavy diamond studs in her ears, she looked regal and aloof.

'Yes?' said Emily, suppressing an odd flicker of fear and turning round.

'I couldn't help noticing…are you with Luke Harrison?'

Now, there was a million-dollar question. 'I am here with him, yes. Why?' Perhaps this lady was a friend of his mother's. Perhaps this lady *was* his mother.

'Are you stepping out with him?'

'Oh, no, we're just—' Emily broke off and felt her cheeks redden. What could she say? She could hardly tell this *grande dame* that they were planning a long night of hot sex.

'I understand perfectly.'

I really, *really* hope you don't, thought Emily.

'How long have you known him?'

Emily lifted a shoulder. 'Around a couple of weeks.'

'Is it serious?'

Emily resisted the urge to snap that it was none of her business. Anna had spent years instilling in her manners that prevented her from being rude to a woman who was twice her age. 'I don't know. I'm not sure. It's too early to say,' she hedged. The idea of denying it outright was oddly unpleasant.

'He's quite a catch.'

'Er…yes, I guess he is. Do you know him well?

'Very well.'

The lady didn't say anything further, just carried on staring at Emily with a look that she couldn't make out but that skewered her against the marble.

'Can I help you in some way? Pass on a message? He's out there somewhere if you'd like to say hello.'

The lady shook her head briskly. 'It was you I wanted to talk to.'

Emily frowned. This was becoming perturbing. She glanced round. The ladies' room was now deserted. 'Well, it's been delightful to meet you, Mrs…?'

'Pearson.'

Phew, not his mother. 'Mrs Pearson. But I should probably get back to him. He must be wondering where I am.'

She'd released her grip on the vanity unit and moved to pass when a hand clasped her elbow with surprising strength. 'You know he'll never fall in love with you.'

Emily froze as she felt a shiver trickle down her spine. She wasn't hoping or expecting Luke to fall in love with her, but there was something steely in this woman's eyes that was making her uneasy. 'Why not?' she said carefully.

'Because he'll always love my daughter.'

Emily went cold, and stared down at the huge diamond solitaire on one of the fingers that dug into her arm. Luke was in love with this woman's daughter? So what was he doing flirting and sleeping with *her*? Her brain struggled to make sense of it. He didn't seem the type. From what little time she'd spent with him, she imagined that once in love he'd give everything he had to that one woman. He wouldn't play around with someone else. So that must mean that Mrs Pearson was either mistaken or psychotic and deluded. But psychotic and deluded people didn't usually dress up in pink silk and drip with pearls, did they?

The look in Mrs Pearson's eyes had changed, softened, saddened, and Emily was now filled with foreboding and trepidation. 'Who is your daughter and who are you?' she said quietly.

'My daughter is Luke's wife, and I'm his mother-in-law.'

Emily felt the blood drain from her face. Luke was *married*? Nausea reared up in her stomach. No, that was impossible. He'd said he was single. Had he lied? Emily's brain went into overdrive. No, that didn't make sense either.

'Luke's told me he's single and I believe him,' she said.

'Technically that's true. But he's still married to my daughter. In here,' Mrs Pearson said, patting her chest where her heart was.

Emily frowned. 'I'm sorry, I really don't understand.'

'My daughter died three years ago.'

Emily's legs nearly gave way. Luke was a widower?

'He was devastated. We all were.' For a moment Mrs Pearson crumpled, the fight draining out of her. The lines on her face seemed to deepen, shadows of sadness rushed through her eyes and she looked twenty years older.

'I'm sorry.'

Mrs Pearson pulled her shoulders back. 'I don't need your

sympathy. I just wanted to find out if you knew. Grace was heavily involved in this charity. She was a paediatrician. They used to come to this event together. He hasn't been since she died. I come instead.' She gave Emily a piercing look. 'You can see why I was curious.'

'Yes.'

'Has he mentioned her?'

'No.'

'Well, it's probably a good thing that you know.'

Mrs Pearson left the room and Emily felt as if her world had tilted on its axis. Her heart was pounding and she was trembling. She could forgive the older woman's rudeness. Of course she'd want to know who had taken her daughter's place. Except she wasn't taking anyone's place. Part of Emily wanted to race after her and reassure her that she was no threat. The other part of her was still reeling from shock and she couldn't get her legs to work.

How was she going to be able to go out and face Luke now? How was she going to go up to him and flirt and sizzle and leap into bed with him as he'd be expecting? She just couldn't do it. Her insides twisted. All desire had vanished. What remained was a seething morass of doubt and confusion, tinged with an inexplicable sense of hurt.

Luke broke off his conversation with an acquaintance, glanced at his watch and frowned. Where the hell was she? She'd been in the bathroom for twenty minutes and it was way past midnight. Surely the queue couldn't be that long.

He spied Jack emerging from the casino and excused himself. 'Have you seen Emily?'

Jack raised his eyebrows in surprise. 'Yes, a couple of minutes ago. She was heading over there.' He waved an arm in the direction of the huge doors that led to the hall.

'Thanks,' muttered Luke, shoving a hand through his hair and striding towards the exit. He scanned the hall but there was no sign of her.

'How many times do I have to tell you? I wasn't trying to steal it. I simply forgot I had it on.'

Her voice came from his left, and he strode into the room where the jewellery had been displayed.

Emily was standing in the middle of the room, flanked by security guards—one of whom was gripping her arm. The salesman was punching numbers into a mobile phone.

'What's going on?' Luke's voice was amazingly calm, given the urge he had to yank that security guard off her.

He saw her tense and he frowned. Her face was white, but he couldn't see what was going on in her eyes as she didn't look at him.

'I'm calling my manager,' said the salesman curtly. 'The young lady tried to leave with the necklace.'

'By accident,' she protested. 'It was a simple mistake.'

'We treat all thieves the same. Prosecution is something we vigorously pursue.'

Emily gasped. 'I'm not a thief. If I was I would hardly be trying to make my getaway in a tight dress and three-inch heels.'

'Is there any real harm done?' enquired Luke.

'I suppose not,' replied the salesman grudgingly.

'So she could take it off and give it back to you and you could forget all about it.'

'I have to follow procedure…'

'Will your manager appreciate being woken up at midnight when nothing has really happened?' Luke fixed him with a steely look.

The salesman's face twisted briefly as he assessed the tall, very determined man in front of him. 'I suppose we could make an exception in this case…?'

Luke nodded. 'That would be appreciated.'

The salesman nodded and the security guard released Emily. Her hands shot up to the clasp of the necklace, but she was shaking and her fingers couldn't undo it. Luke stepped forward.

'Let me help you with that,' he said, his fingers brushing

over her skin. She went still, and then flinched at his touch. Luke's jaw clenched as he undid the clasp and handed the necklace back to the salesman.

Then he drew her out of the room. His concern at how much she was shaking mounted.

'You look very pale. What's the matter?'

'I don't feel that great. I might head off. But you stay.'

He frowned. 'If you were so desperate to leave, why didn't you tell me? We were going to go anyway.'

'I'm tired, I have a headache, and I didn't want to interrupt your conversation.'

Luke couldn't fathom what on earth was going on. Why was she avoiding his eyes? And why had she been so desperate to leave that she'd forgotten to give the necklace back? What the hell had happened in the twenty minutes she'd been gone? One minute she'd been shooting him sexy smiles full of promise that had had him wondering whether the venue had bedrooms, and now here she was icy cold. 'I'll take you home.'

'No,' said Emily sharply. 'I just need some air. I'll be fine.'

Luke flinched at the faint note of desperation in her voice. He didn't like it. His expression turned grim and he gripped her arm and pulled her outside. Torches flared down the steps. 'Then we'll talk here.'

'We have nothing to talk about.'

'Non-negotiable, remember?' he said coolly.

'I'm not in the mood.'

'I can see that. But I'm not letting you out of my sight until you tell me what this is all about.'

'I'm tired and I have a headache.'

'I don't believe you.' He noticed the moment the fight drained out of her, and that concerned him more than her coolness did.

'Fine.' She whirled round. 'I've just met your mother-in-law.'

Luke went very still and his face tightened. 'Elizabeth? Where?'

'She cornered me in the Ladies'.'

The pieces of the puzzle slammed into place. 'I didn't know she was here.' How had he not spotted her? He'd always been on good terms with Grace's mother, and still saw her occasionally, so why hadn't she come over and said hello?

'She knew we were. She's been giving me odd looks all evening. Now I know why.'

'What did she say to you?'

'That you were married to her daughter. And that she died.'

'That's right.' Luke raked a hand through his hair and braced himself against the wrecking ball of pain that was about to crash through him.

'What happened?'

'Grace was killed three years ago in car accident. She was driving too fast. It was wet. She skidded and went into a tree.' He switched his attention to one of the torches so that he wouldn't have to see the pity and sympathy in her eyes. He'd had enough of both long ago.

There was a tiny pause, and then her voice came, softer than before. 'I'm so sorry.'

'Yeah, well, it was a while ago now,' he muttered distractedly. Where was the pain? The deluge of memories? The burning anger at the injustice of it all?

'Is that why you were so strange in the church?

'Strange?' He was feeling rather strange now.

'White-faced, tense, shaking.'

He shoved his hands through his hair. 'I hadn't been inside a church since Grace's funeral. I was expecting it to be grim.'

'And was it?'

'Yes.' But not in the way she probably thought. What had really been grim was the overwhelming guilt that his awareness of Emily had been far stronger than his memories of Grace.

'Why didn't you tell me?'

'I hardly knew you. It wasn't relevant to us.' His gaze swivelled back to hers and he moved towards her. 'It still isn't.'

Emily took a step back and it was like a slap in his face. 'It changes things.'

'Why?' He jammed his hands into his pockets.

'I don't know. It just does.'

'I see.' Luke nodded and felt the shutters slam down over his features. This was precisely what he'd wanted to avoid. Personal stuff getting in the way. *His* personal stuff. 'I'm not surprised you decided to disappear.'

'I wasn't going to disappear.'

'That's what it looked like to me.' His jaw clenched.

'I'm sorry for not coming and finding you. I just wanted some time to process it all. It's quite a lot to take in.'

'You know how I feel about people running out on me.'

'This time you can't give me filing.'

Luke sighed and pushed a hand though his hair. 'No, but I can give you time to think it over.'

Emily nodded. 'I'd appreciate that.'

'Let me know when you've decided what you want,' he said, cursing himself and Elizabeth and coincidence under his breath. 'I'll find you a taxi.'

CHAPTER NINE

EMILY staggered out of bed the next day as dawn was breaking. If things had gone according to plan she and Luke would now be winding themselves around each other and waking up in the slowest, steamiest, most heavenly way possible. Instead she was alone. Her eyes were gritty through lack of sleep, her nerves were jumpy, and she was all tangled up inside.

As she stumbled downstairs she ran through the end of the night before. At last she knew the reason for the haunted look in Luke's eyes, the desolation in his expression, the moments where he seemed to be far away. The death of a beloved wife. Something deep inside her clenched and twisted.

She switched on the kettle and leaned back against the counter while the water boiled. Questions streamed into her head. What had she been like? What had *Luke* been like? How long had they been married? And most of all why hadn't he thought that the fact he'd been married was relevant? That hurt. There was no reason why it should, but it did. Was what they had really so inconsequential?

Well, yes, she supposed it was. What did they really have anyway? she wondered, chewing on her lip. They were simply about sex. Hot, steamy sex. For as little or as long as it took for either of them to get bored. His past didn't need to get in the way any more than hers did. There was no need to torture herself over this.

* * *

Emily sat at her kitchen table, staring at her laptop. She moved it an inch to the right. Now it was bang in the centre of the table. Or was it? No, hang on, it was a little bit too close to the far side.

Oh, come on, she castigated herself. Don't be such an idiot. Just send the damn thing. She'd spent the last two days dithering over whether to phone or to e-mail him. And then, after finally deciding that e-mail was less embarrassing, less intrusive and generally the easier way out, she'd spent hours trying to compose one. She was aiming for brief and businesslike and at long last she thought she had it. She reread what she'd written for the thousandth time.

Dear Luke

I hope you are well. As you must be busy, I'll get straight to the point. I've been thinking about recent revelations and after due consideration, given that neither of us is interested in anything long-term, I don't see any reason why we shouldn't continue as planned. We do, after all, still owe each other one night. If you're still interested, please feel free to get in touch any time.

Emily

All those other incoherent steamy messages into which she'd poured her yearning were safely tucked away in the draft folder and would never see the light of day. She hit the 'send' button before she could back out and got up.

Heavens, it was hot, she thought, fanning herself vigorously with a magazine. Her body temperature was sky high. She'd spent the morning on a lounger in the garden, which in hindsight had been a mistake. The warm sun on her skin had made her think of Luke's hands roaming over her and she'd got all flustered. The heat and the hum of desire coupled with severe sexual frustration were making her restless and edgy.

There was only one place to be when she was in this sort of state. Her shed.

Emily was sitting at her bench when the doorbell rang on the extension. She was in the middle of painting a particularly intricate design onto a huge oval plate, which luckily required every ounce of her concentration. The harder the work the better, she thought. One momentary lapse of concentration and she found herself absently grabbing any stray lump of clay and moulding it into a shape that looked suspiciously like Luke's head.

The heat was unbearable. She'd hoped that the dark, cool shed might have a calming effect on the buzzing inside her. But it wasn't. If anything she was feeling even more feverish.

The bell rang again. She wasn't moving. If it was important they'd come back.

Suddenly a shadow passed across the window, momentarily blocking out the sunlight. There was a quick tap on the door and Luke was standing there, looking big and gorgeous.

Emily gave a quick squeal of shock and leapt to her feet, her paintbrush clattering to the floor and her heart thumping wildly. 'How did you get into the garden?'

'It's nice to see you too. You should lock your gate.'

'Anna said she might pop round later. What are you doing here?'

'You didn't really think you could leave me in limbo for two days, e-mail me like that and not expect me to respond?'

'I only sent it about ten minutes ago.'

Luke held up his BlackBerry. 'I was in a taxi on my way to a meeting. Hardly any traffic.'

He was wearing jeans and a white shirt and had a jacket slung over his shoulder. Despite it being the hottest day of the year, he looked cool, if tired and rumpled. His eyes were glittering dangerously.

'You were going to a meeting in jeans?'

'I've instigated a dress-down Friday policy.'

She had to make a conscious effort not to let her mouth drop open in surprise.

'Aren't they waiting for you?'

'I delegated.'

This, from a workaholic? Perhaps she wasn't the only one being affected by the heat.

'I didn't realise that my e-mail would inspire such haste.'

'You sent me two.'

Emily's heart rate picked up. 'Two? No, I definitely sent only one.'

'I definitely received two.'

Emily went cold. Two? Impossible. Wasn't it? Could she really have been so stupid? Oh, God. What with her nervous energy and the heat, she could easily have clicked on the 'send' button instead of the 'save' button. There it would have sat, innocently lined up and waiting, until she hit the button that actually sent all the messages in the queue.

'There's the one about hoping I'm well, due consideration and recent revelations, etcetera, etcetera,' he said, scrolling down his phone. 'All very promising and interesting, of course—and I *am* well, if you ignore the uncomfortable state of unfulfilled desire. But it was the second one that had me calling one of my team and diverting my taxi. Let me read it to you.'

Emily's cheeks went red. It could be any one of about six…

'No, there's really no need.'

'I'd like to.' He scrolled down further and clicked. 'Here we are… I'll add my own punctuation, as you didn't bother with it.'

'I probably wasn't thinking about punctuation,' she muttered.

'I don't imagine you were,' he said, taking a step forward and bending down slightly, so that he filled every corner of her vision. When he spoke his voice was low and husky, and it grated along her nerve endings. '"This heat, this need, this desire is making me demented. I want to feel you. I want your hands on me. Here. Now. I want you inside me. I need you inside me. I want you to—"'

'Yes, that's quite enough,' she said, burning up inside and out. 'Any good pretending it wasn't intended for you?'

'Wasn't it?'

'Of course it wasn't. It wasn't intended for anyone. I was just…extemping.' Wait, that didn't sound right.

'Extemporising?' One corner of his mouth lifted.

Emily nodded. 'Right, that's what I meant.'

'Whatever you were doing, you can't go round sending e-mails like that unless you're prepared to deal with the consequences.'

He leaned a little closer and the shed suddenly felt far too small. Luke's broad frame took up much needed air, and Emily found herself struggling for breath. She was so hot and flustered. So jumpy inside. Her head went fuzzy and her vision went grey, and then, with a tiny groan, she sank into nothingness.

When she came round she was lying on the sun lounger in the garden beneath a tree. Luke was sitting on the edge of the lounger, staring down at her, concern etched on his face.

'What happened?' she said, blinking up at him.

'You fainted.'

'Odd. I never faint.'

'When did you last eat?'

Emily tried to gather her very woolly thoughts. 'A couple of hours ago.'

Luke gave her a wry smile. 'So I can only assume that it was the shock of seeing me.'

'Probably mortification and heatstroke. Too much time in the sun. Getting all hot and bothered and dehydrated.'

'I must admit you had me worried for a moment. The grey look doesn't suit you.'

Luke was worried about her. Emily tried the thought on for

size and decided she rather liked being worried about. Especially by him.

He was leaning over her, his hands planted either side of her on the lounger. The leaves of the tree rustled and the dappled sun had a kaleidoscopic effect on his face. Light and dark. Colour and shade. The shadows racing over him were making her head swim.

'I'd have thought you'd have women falling at your feet on a regular basis.'

'You're delirious.' The smile playing at the corner of his mouth made her pulse leap.

'Deliciously delirious.' Lord, maybe the sun really had gone to her head. 'How did I get out here?'

'I caught you as you collapsed and carried you out.'

'Anything to get me horizontal?'

'I'd prefer you fully functioning when we finally do get horizontal. How are you feeling?'

'Fine.' Actually, she wasn't. She was feeling rather peculiar—as if someone was slowly replacing her insides with cotton wool.

'You know the cure for heatstroke?'

'Staying in the shade?'

'Removal of clothing.' His eyes glinted at her. 'To encourage heat loss.'

A pulse began to beat deep inside her. 'That would make sense.'

'So we really ought to get you out of those clothes.'

Her gaze flickered over his torso, and she noted with horror that he was smeared in clay. Great splatters and swathes of earthy red all across that white shirt. 'How did you get covered in clay?' she murmured in dismay. How had she not noticed it before? Oh, yes—too busy staring at his face and into those mesmerising eyes.

'You fell at an angle. I landed on your wheel.'

'Did you hurt yourself?'

'No.'

'Clay stains.'

'I have other shirts.'

Emily closed her eyes briefly and pictured him shirtless. Then she shot him a smouldering glance and fluttered her eyelashes. 'It's only fair that if I'm to get out of my clothing you do too.'

'I'm not suffering from heatstroke.'

'Yet,' she said, lowering her eyelids and giving him a slow smile. Her hands reached up and began to undo the buttons of his shirt. 'This really should go into the dishwasher right now.'

Luke grabbed them, putting a stop to her movements. The smile on his face faded. 'You really are delirious.'

'No, I'm not. Just a little fuzzy-headed—and so hot.' She writhed for a moment on the lounger to get some air beneath her.

Luke put his hand on her forehead and frowned. Then he scooped her up as if she weighed no more than a feather and strode into the house. Emily hardly had time to register what was happening, but her arms wound themselves around his neck of their own accord and her head dropped against his chest. He carried her up the stairs, backed into her bedroom and deposited her on the bed.

Oh, yes! she thought, feeling the heat rippling through her. This was what she'd been waiting for, yearning for, ever since she'd woken up alone in that hotel room.

'Stay there,' he said.

'Not planning on going anywhere,' she said, and thought it strange how thick and slurred her voice sounded. Through the haze in her head Emily heard the sounds of taps being turned on in the bathroom and footsteps thundering down the stairs.

He returned with a glass of water and thrust it into her hand. 'Drink this.'

Luke in authoritative, demanding mode was irresistible, so she did as he asked, feeling the icy cold water trickle through her and cool her heated body. And then she tasted a nasty mixture of salt and sugar and nearly threw up. She grimaced and her head swam.

'Yuk, what was that?'

'Take your clothes off,' he said tightly.

Ah, thought Emily. At last. At long last. She fluttered her eyelashes at him and lay back against the mountains of pillows. 'Why don't you do it?'

Luke shook his head with what she thought was a rueful smile. He leaned forward, untied her shirt, and unbuttoned her shorts. 'You're going to have to help me. Sit up.'

'No,' she said, stretching her arms over her head and raising her hips.

'Thought you might say that,' he murmured, lifting her into his arms and carrying her through to the bathroom.

When he put her into the bath of cool water Emily let out a shriek. 'What did you do that for?' she squealed, splashing around in an attempt to get out. But once the initial shock had receded, the coolness of the water was heavenly.

'You, my delirious siren, really do seem to be suffering from heatstroke. Ten minutes in here and then you're going to bed.'

'Are you going to join me?'

Luke sighed. 'You have no idea how tempting that is, but no.' He stood up, thrust his hands in his pockets and turned to head for the wicker chair in the corner.

Emily allowed herself to sink into the water. She felt it seeping up her neck, her chin, then over her mouth and nose and eyes until she was completely submerged. How refreshing. How calming.

Then something gripped the back of her neck and hauled her head out of the water. Panic flooded through her and her hands flailed.

'Emily.' Luke's voice lashed her like a whip. 'Open your eyes.'

She wiped the water out of her eyes and blinked rapidly. His face was white.

'Ow,' she spluttered, twisting her head out of his vice-like grip. 'I was enjoying that.'

'Don't do it again,' he grated, his eyes blazing with anger and what she thought looked like fear.

'I won't,' she said, glaring straight back at him. For a few seconds they stared at each other, and then the anger and panic and concern shifted into something altogether more intoxicating. She saw desire seep into his eyes and her body began to respond. Her nipples tightened and pushed against her bikini top and the sodden fabric of her shirt. Luke's eyes flickered down to her breasts and he jerked back.

Emily felt the wet drag of her clothes against her body. The material felt like sandpaper scraping over her sensitive skin, and every tiny move was exquisite agony. 'Would you mind turning around while I get out of my clothes?' she said huskily.

'After that little stunt, not a chance.' Luke backed away his eyes not leaving her for a second.

Emily shrugged. It wasn't as if he hadn't seen it all before anyway. She peeled off her shirt and deposited it in a dripping heap on the floor. She wriggled out of her shorts and did the same. She twisted her wet hair into a thick rope and drew it to one side. Then she lifted her hands to unclip the straps of her bikini top, dropped it over the side of the bath and sighed in relief as the water swirled over her bare breasts. She glanced at Luke and caught the hungry look in his eye before it vanished. Taking care not to splash any more water over the side, she reached down to slide her bikini bottoms off and then she was naked.

She closed her eyes and sighed with pleasure. The fuzziness in her head was clearing. She heard the rustling of movement, the sound of a towel being pulled off the radiator, and clapped a hand to her mouth to disguise a yawn.

'Can you stand up?' said Luke.

Emily opened her eyes to see him staring down at her. He was standing over the bath holding a towel out, determinedly looking at her face, a muscle ticking in his jaw.

'Of course I can,' she said, frowning. 'I'm not some wobbly waif.' She levered herself to her feet, the water sluicing off her, and still Luke was focusing on her face. She swayed and his arms snapped around her, enveloping her in the towel and lifting her out of the bath.

'I have two perfectly functioning legs,' she muttered. 'But they'll seize up if you keep carrying me everywhere. Where do you get the strength?'

'I play a lot of squash.'

His chest rumbled beneath her ear and Emily shivered. 'So you do have a hobby.'

'I suppose I do,' he agreed, setting her down and rubbing her dry before helping her into the bed and drawing the covers over her. 'Now, get some sleep.'

Luke raked a hand through his hair as he stared unseeingly at his computer screen. Since he'd set it up in Emily's kitchen an hour earlier he'd watched the numbers flicker, brooded about not being in the office, and done absolutely nothing. How could he when all he could think about was Emily, lying naked upstairs? He was going out of his mind. Two days of frustrated waiting. Then that e-mail. Having to put her in the bath and then into bed. He wasn't prone to violence, but right now he wanted to hit something very hard. He rested his elbows on the breakfast bar and flexed his fists.

Judging by the results that were coming though, his traders were doing fine without him. And so they should be. But it was still a disconcerting thought. He rubbed his face. Maybe it was time he took his foot off the accelerator every now and then. His business wasn't going to go down the tubes if he wasn't there every second of the day. He had a first-class team and more money than one man could possibly need. And what was the point of all that money if he didn't have time to spend it? Or anyone to spend it on…?

Luke hit a button on his laptop and the screen switched to the New York Stock Exchange. It was going down. Just as he'd predicted. Good. The kick of satisfaction that he'd got it right was enough of a thrill. He'd survived perfectly well for the last three years without anyone to spend his money on. He didn't need anyone now.

'You're still here?'

Luke looked up and took a sharp intake of breath. Emily was standing in the doorway wearing a short red dress, barefoot and brown-legged, her hair a tangle of curls and sleep still in her expression. 'You startled me.'

'Shouldn't you be at work?'

'They're managing without me.'

She smiled and he felt his body tighten. 'That must be disappointing.'

'Very.'

'I'm sure Anna would have come if you'd rung her.'

The thought hadn't even occurred to him. 'How are you feeling?'

'Much better. Thank you for looking after me.'

'No problem.'

'I was an idiot to stay out in the sun so long.'

'Yup.'

She walked over to him, and with every step she took his blood pressure increased a notch. 'The bath and the sugary salty water… How did you know what to do? When you're not storming the financial markets do you moonlight as a doctor?'

'My talents don't extend to nursing victims of heatstroke. I rang the local clinic after you fainted.'

'You certainly have a fabulous bedside manner.'

'I'm now supposed to check your heart rate,' he said hoarsely.

Emily took his hand and put it on her left breast. 'Feel anything?'

Luke frowned and moved his hand up to hold his fingers against the pulse at the base of her throat. He checked it against his watch.

It was racing.

'Normal,' he said curtly.

'I'm sorry for scaring you,' she said softly.

'You didn't scare me.'

'How can I make it up to you?'

'Don't worry about it.'

'I know we're not doing long-term, but would you like to stay for supper?'

'Fine.'

'Why don't I put that shirt in the washing machine?'

'Not necessary.'

Emily smiled that little smile of hers that turned his brain to putty. 'I think it is. I still ache. You read my e-mail. You know what I want. I know you want it too.'

'You're not well,' he said gruffly.

'I'm fine. Honestly. Look—even my legs are working properly.'

She gave a twirl and dropped into a curtsey, to demonstrate just how steady she was on her feet, and then rattled off a couple of tongue-twisters. 'I can even walk in a straight line.'

She walked over to the freezer perfectly balanced. Then she bent down to take what looked like a couple of steaks out. From the lack of lines beneath the flimsy dress it looked as though she wasn't wearing any underwear, and Luke's resistance snapped.

'All right. I'm convinced.'

Emily straightened so slowly that he could see every movement beneath that red silky material. His mouth went dry as she put the steaks on the worktop and turned round. He was so hard he ached. His erection strained against the zip of his jeans and he didn't think he'd ever felt pain like it. The need to feel her body beneath his hands and sink himself inside her nearly floored him.

And then she was walking towards him. No, walking wasn't the right word. Sashaying. That was the only word to describe the way her hips were gently swaying from side to side as she closed the distance between them. Her eyes darkened and her breathing slowed.

'So, we have a couple of hours before the steaks defrost. What are we doing to do with ourselves?'

His jaw clenched. 'I'm sure we can come up with something.'

She stopped just beyond his reach and arched an eyebrow. 'Monopoly? Charades? Read a good book?'

Luke's heart raced. He unfolded his arms and stared at her. 'How about a game for only two? This has been going on long enough. Any longer and I may suffer permanent damage.'

'Well, we can't have that,' she murmured, resuming her sauntering until she was pushing herself between his knees.

'Are you sure about this?' he grated.

'Of course. Everyone has baggage. But ours needn't affect this in any way.'

'I couldn't agree more.'

Then her fingers were fumbling with his shirt buttons and his hands were on her hips, tugging her towards him. His fingers dug into the soft flesh of her buttocks and he pulled her against him to where he ached and throbbed. By the time she got to the last couple of buttons her fingers were shaking so much that she couldn't undo them.

'Oh, sod it,' she muttered. 'It's ruined anyway.' Her hands gripped the thick white cotton at the bottom of his shirt and yanked it open. The buttons spun into the air and bounced off the work surface.

'And I do have plenty of others,' he said, his eyes boring into hers. 'Just not here. You've effectively rendered me captive.'

'So you have to comply with my every whim?'

'It does look that way.'

'Then I demand that you kiss me.'

'I think I might like being held captive by you,' he said. He leaned forward and planted a kiss at the base of her throat, where her pulse was hammering. And then another lighter kiss just above. He carried on until she was whimpering.

'Luke.' It came out as a groan, a plea full of longing. And just when she thought she could bear it no longer his mouth settled on hers. A slow, languid kiss that made Emily's blood start rushing through her veins. Her hands slid over his chest, smoothed over the muscles of his shoulders and then wound around his neck, pulling him closer, deeper, as if yearning to fuse with him.

A pulse began to throb deep in the centre of her, and she moaned beneath the movement of his lips, loving the taste of his mouth and the feel of his tongue lacing with hers. She pushed his shirt off. He deepened the kiss and she shuddered. She couldn't stop her hands running over his back, curling in his hair, gliding over his shoulders, gripping his hips so that she could grind hers against them.

Emily's heart raced. Her body was out of control, and an exquisitely painful pressure was building inside her that only he could assuage. Her fingers fumbled at the button of his trousers. With a groan of frustration she wrenched her mouth from his and looked down to see what she was doing.

As her fingers brushed over his engorged flesh Luke inhaled sharply. He stilled her trembling hands and guided them behind her back. 'No,' she moaned. 'I want you inside me now.'

'Soon.' He stood up and backed her against the breakfast bar. 'We have a lot of making up for lost time to do.'

'No, now,' Emily whimpered, but he took no notice. He lifted her up so she was perched on the edge of the bar, placed her palms on the cool granite behind her and pressed her back. He pushed the straps of her dress down and the bodice slithered to bunch at her waist, exposing her swollen, heavy breasts to his hungry eyes. Luke dropped a trail of kisses along her jaw and down her throat, cupping one breast in his palm and rubbing his thumb over her nipple. Emily went dizzy from the sensation, darts of pleasure shooting through her, and then his mouth continued, caressing down gently over the slope of her breast and closing over her other nipple. Hot and wet, his tongue flicked over the tight bud and she let out a groan of pleasure.

His hand trailed lower, his fingers gliding over the skin of her thigh under the hem of her dress, creeping higher until they found what they were looking for. Emily's hips jerked and she bit on her lip to stop herself crying out when he slipped a finger into her hot wetness and stroked back and forth, finding and rubbing her clitoris. Bursts of pleasure rippled out from her core and she groaned, panting wildly.

She tried to stop the sensations. She wanted to hold on until he was inside her, properly inside her, filling her, swelling, pounding into her. The image was too much. The pressure too great. His fingers too relentless. Demanding too much. Waves of desire rolled through her. She could feel herself tensing. Her breath came quicker, her heart thundered as the coil inside her wound tighter and tighter. And then his lips found hers, his tongue plunging into her mouth, mimicking what she really wanted, and she shuddered, tensed, and splintered into millions of tiny shafts of pleasure.

'So unfair,' muttered Emily when she finally got her breath back. 'Damn you and your control.'

He kissed her hard, setting her on fire all over again, pulling a condom from his back pocket with one hand and drawing her dress up over her head while Emily grappled with his jeans. She was desperate for him to get as naked as she was, so that finally she could feel him, all of him, touching her body from head to toe.

And then he was standing in front of her, all glorious tanned muscle, his erection thick and big. Emily shivered.

'Cold?' Luke murmured, rolling on the condom, his face tightening with the effort of clinging on to his control.

She shook her head quickly. 'Burning up.'

'Me too.'

Locking her ankles around his waist, he slid his hands along her legs, gripped her hips, and entered her with one long smooth thrust. She felt herself stretching to accept him and great bursts of pleasure began to throb deep inside her.

His hands steadied her hips as he set a rhythm that had her pelvis tilting and drawing him in deeper. Emily groaned, slipping one hand behind her to support her and wrapping the other around his neck. He crushed his mouth against hers, their tongues duelling as his pace increased, pushing her closer and closer to the brink.

Emily wrenched her mouth away and drew in great gulps of air. 'Oh, God,' she panted. How was it possible? France had been amazing—unsurpassable, she'd thought. But this—this was something else. She felt she was about to break open. Surely her body couldn't stand so much intense, deliriously mind-blowing pleasure. He withdrew and she moaned with despair. And then he drove into her one last time, hard and up to the hilt, and she came apart, spiralling into blissful oblivion, convulsing around him as waves of delight crashed over her, feeling him climax a second after her, pulsing into her.

Her hand drifted down over his shoulder and she could feel his heart hammering. He ran his hands up her sides, round her back, and cradled her head against his shoulder. They stayed like that, locked together, for a couple of long, hot minutes while their breathing regulated and their heart rates subsided.

Then Luke gently withdrew from her and she missed him immediately. Reality intruded, and the realisation that they were standing in her kitchen naked in the middle of the afternoon made her want to giggle.

Luke picked up her dress and slipped it over her head. She sat there, legs dangling, watching him as he discarded the condom and thrust his feet into his jeans. Was there anything sexier than a man in nothing more than a pair of jeans? She wanted him again. How was it possible? And then he was pulling on his shirt and buttoning up what few buttons there were. Surely he wasn't leaving…

'Where are you going?' Her voice was still husky and unsteady.

He picked up the foil packet and turned it over in his fingers.

'We're going to need more of these. A lot more.'

The relief that flooded through her nearly knocked her off the breakfast bar. 'No need. I have hundreds. Well, maybe not hundreds,' she said, when Luke raised an eyebrow, 'but certainly enough to last until supper—and they should just about be within their use-by date…'

'Good,' said Luke, shooting her a smouldering stare and unbuttoning his shirt. 'Where?'

A broad grin spread across her face. She levered herself off the worktop. 'Come with me,' she said, taking his hand and leading him towards the stairs.

CHAPTER TEN

PULLING a blanket over her shoulders, Emily watched Luke at work at the barbecue. As she regarded him over the rim of her glass of wine she was struck by how very at home he seemed, lighting the coals and blowing on them so that they'd catch. His shirt had long since been abandoned, and she had a glorious view of his back, bending and twisting, the muscles rippling beneath tanned skin. Strong, capable shoulders—the sort of shoulders that could bear a great deal and had no doubt already done so.

She was insanely attracted to him. But there was something else too. Something deeper, entangling her emotions and making her giddy. He flashed her a smile over his shoulder and her heart gave a little lurch, as if to warn her of how much danger it was in.

'While we're waiting for this to get ready will you show me your pottery?'

Emily chuckled. 'Are you asking to see my etchings?'

'I've already seen your etchings quite a few times this afternoon.'

Lord, and didn't she know it? Lethargy had taken hold of her, and she wasn't sure if she could summon the strength to get up and cover the short distance to her shed.

'Right now I'd like to see what you get up to at the end of the garden.'

'OK.' Emily stretched and got up. 'When I'm not communing with the fairies I make all sorts of things. Jugs, bowls, plates, vases. Big ones. Didn't you see them earlier?'

Luke shook his head. 'Too busy making sure you didn't hit your head.'

Generally she didn't allow anyone in her shed. Not even Anna. But Luke had already been in it once, so what harm would there be if he went in again? This time she'd keep a good few metres between them, she resolved, stepping through the door and switching on the light. He bent his head and followed her.

'This is what I do.' She swept an arm wide to indicate the bench cluttered with an assortment of brightly coloured pieces.

Luke surveyed her bench, and then picked up a bowl and turned it slowly in his hands. Emily's throat tightened as she banked down the urge to snatch it back. He was staring at it assessingly and she felt it personally. She hadn't asked for his opinion, but suddenly she found it mattered. Which was not only annoying but also potentially dangerous. If he was critical in any way, she'd jab him with her paintbrushes.

'These are good—very good.'

Pleasure and relief spun through her. 'Thank you.'

'Have you sold any?'

'No. I give them away. Mainly to Anna and to friends.'

'Have you ever had a show?'

'No. Why?'

'You should.'

She let out a resigned sigh. 'Let me guess. You think I should see if I can make money from it.'

'It's really none of my business, but if you can make money doing something you love it does seem the ideal scenario.'

'Hah! I knew you wouldn't be able to resist.'

'What do you mean?'

'Someone who eats, sleeps and thinks work would never understand doing something just for the sheer pleasure of doing it, with no monetary gain.'

'That's rather harsh,' he said, sending her a slow smile.

'I've just spent the entire afternoon—a weekday afternoon, I might add—doing something just for sheer pleasure with no monetary gain.'

'I'm not talking about sex,' she said, feeling herself grow hot. She took a deep breath and a step back.

'Pity.' Luke turned his attention back to the bowl. 'You could sell these for a fortune. All those people with minimalist flats and acres of white walls.'

'That's true. As someone with lots of white walls, what would *you* choose?'

Luke scanned the room. 'The vase,' he said eventually.

Emily followed the direction of his gaze and had to hide her surprise. It wasn't what she would have expected him to choose. She would have thought he'd go for something solid and dark and useful, but the three-foot-high vase he'd chosen was delicate and curvy, and painted in turquoise and green with splashes of red. It had taken her ages to make and then decorate and was one of her favourite pieces. She'd had to hire a kiln specially to fire it.

'Good choice,' she said, nodding.

'Wouldn't you like to sell your work?'

'Not really.' No one she knew would pay good money for an oversized, garishly painted bowl.

'Or simply exhibit it?'

'That's just vanity. And can you imagine how embarrassing it would be if no one came?'

'They would. How could they not?'

Emily felt something unfurl deep inside her and swallowed hard. 'I should tell you that this is a conversation I've had on a regular basis with my sister for a number of years. Whatever you say won't make the slightest difference.'

'There's no reason why it should, but if you don't take risks, you don't get rewards.'

God, if only he knew, she thought. She was reaping rewards with him—but at what risk? 'Do you take risks?'

'Taking risks is part of my job.'

'And personally?' She stared into his eyes and heard her breathing shallow.

'Are you trying to distract me?' Luke murmured.

'Yes. Is it working?'

'No.'

'Should I faint again?'

Luke glowered. 'Don't you dare.'

'I reckon the barbecue should be ready by now,' she said.

While Emily headed into the house to fetch salad and baked potatoes, Luke tossed the steaks onto the grill and watched them sizzling and spitting. She was wasted as a temp. She ought to be creating great vibrant pieces that would shake people like him up. Not that it mattered to him what she did with her life one little bit.

'Hmm, that smells good,' she said brushing against him. 'And the steaks don't smell too bad either.'

Luke grinned. 'How do you like it?'

'Rare, please.'

'In that case they're done.' He put the steaks on a plate that was obviously one that she'd made, and took it to the table on the patio. A candle flickered between them and light spilled out from the kitchen.

'Did Anna show up while I was asleep?' Emily said, helping herself to salad.

'No.'

She dropped the salad servers into the bowl and went red. The way she blushed so easily was oddly captivating. 'What?' he asked, filling her glass.

'I hope she didn't pop by while we were…you know…'

'Testing the strength of your kitchen units?'

'Precisely,' she mumbled, and took a gulp of wine.

'I hope she didn't either.' Luke had a sudden image of a furious Anna bearing down on him with a meat cleaver. 'She's very protective of you.'

Emily nodded. 'She has a right to be. She brought me up.'

'What happened to your parents?'

'My mother died having me, and my father died when I was fourteen.' Luke saw something flicker in her eyes before she averted her gaze. Only briefly, and a different man might have missed it. But he caught the guilt mainly because he recognised it.

'She brought you up on her own?'

Emily nodded. 'There was no one else to do it. Only one set of grandparents, and they lived in Australia.'

'So Anna was what? Eighteen? Nineteen?'

'Twenty. She was at art college, but she dropped out and did accountancy exams instead.'

'That must have been a hard decision,' he said, slicing through his steak but watching her closely.

Emily shrugged, and once again the guilt was written all over her face. 'She had me to look after. So she passed her exams and took a job with regular hours and a steady income.' Then she smiled. 'Luckily she turned out to be really good at her job and loved it.'

'A bonus.'

'I already feel terrible about what I made her sacrifice. Can you imagine how much worse it would be if she'd hated it?' She shuddered.

Luke sat back. 'It must have been tough on you too.'

'I was a brat.'

'Understandable.'

'Unforgivable,' she corrected. 'I owe her a lot. Now she has my gorgeous brother-in-law and the twins and she's equally good at looking after them.'

'They're very lucky.'

Emily nodded and put her fork down. 'I know I moan about her bossiness and interfering, but really I don't know what I'd do without her.'

The admiration, love and respect that she had for her sister and her family was apparent in her voice. Here was a little group of people having life hurl terrible things at them and they'd weathered it all. By leaning on each other. Whereas he'd weathered his own storms alone. By choice. It had started out as the only way to avoid the sympathy and the pity, and it was now a habit. He felt a pang of something that he suspected might be envy and his chest squeezed. His solitariness had never bothered him before. He considered it to be a strength. So why should he doubt it now?

'What do you fancy for dessert?' said Emily, shooting him a smile that had his body tightening in response.

The need to wrap himself around her gripped him, but this house, so warm and inviting, was suddenly stifling. Luke shoved a hand through his hair and got to his feet. 'I should go.'

Emily's heart practically ground to a halt. He was going? Now? After the afternoon they'd had? It was barely nine o'clock. She'd just fed him and he was leaving? Puff went her dreams of the two of them waking up and making slow, leisurely love before breakfast. She could feel his retreat as strongly as if he'd actually vanished. That blank look on his face and the shuttered expression in his eyes was horrible.

'I need the cover of darkness to hide the fact that my shirt is ripped and covered in clay.'

'Of course. I do apologise.'

Had she gone too far, spilling out her relationship with her sister? Had all that been too personal, given the fact that they weren't having a relationship? God, she was hopeless at this sort of thing. It was precisely why she didn't do casual flings. She tended to forget the rules. Could she persuade him to forget the past half an hour and promise not to mention anything personal ever again?

Emily blew out the candle as Luke headed inside and picked up his shirt. He really was leaving, she thought despondently as she watched him do up what few buttons there were. And by the looks of things he couldn't wait.

But just as she was about to let him know exactly what she thought of his behaviour he swung round and strode towards her. He yanked her up against him and gave her a brief searing kiss that left her reeling.

'Go and get your toothbrush. Underwear is optional.'

Absurd delight bloomed in her chest. 'You want me to come with you?'

'Unless you have plans for the weekend?' he said.

Her heart raced and she grinned. 'No, no plans whatsoever. What about you?'

'My plans have just changed. And I still have your necklace at my flat.'

'Oh, wow,' said Emily, crossing the room to the wall of windows that looked over the rooftops of Mayfair.

'I thought you didn't like heights,' said Luke as he went into the kitchen.

Emily flushed. 'That was before,' she murmured. Heavens, was it really less than a week ago that she'd been storming around his office?

'What would you like? Wine or coffee?'

'Coffee, please. I spy a thoroughly pointless gadget over there in the corner that looks far too clean and complex to have ever been used. I'm intrigued.'

'It's not a thoroughly pointless gadget. It's the Rolls-Royce of espresso makers.'

'Have you ever used it?'

'No. I have a kettle.' Luke started searching through his cupboards. 'Somewhere.'

'Have you ever used *anything* in this kitchen?' she said, noticing how shiny everything was.

'The fridge.'

'How long have you lived here?'

'Three years,' he muttered, finding coffee in one of the cupboards.

Since he'd been alone… That made sense, thought Emily, her gaze sweeping around the apartment. It was as modern and sleek as she'd imagined it would be. Open plan, immaculate white walls, angular furniture and glossy wooden flooring. The only hint of Luke's personality were the bookshelves, which were stacked with an eclectic mix of military histories, biographies and well-thumbed thrillers. There was no sign of his wife at all.

'Your coffee's on the table.'

'Thank you,' said Emily, turning around and seeing where he was staring. 'It looks good, doesn't it?'

The turquoise vase was standing in the corner of the room, a splash of colour against the otherwise rather clinical decoration. She'd been about to get in the taxi when she'd acted on an impulse and dashed into the garden to get the vase to give to Luke.

He frowned. 'It does.'

'Much better than a six-foot by four-foot scorpion.'

'But not nearly so worthy.'

'I'll have you know my vase represents the female struggle for emancipation.'

'Aren't you a bit late for that?'

'Not at all,' she declared airily. 'It's an ongoing struggle. And apart from that it was also a very efficient chaperone in the taxi.' The vase had sat between them like a prim maiden aunt.

'Too efficient. But before we set about reversing that, I'd better go and get your necklace.'

Luke disappeared, and Emily caught sight of something that looked like a photo album. She pulled it off the shelf and opened it, half wondering whether she wasn't intruding.

Her heart thumped. It was full of photos of Luke and the woman Emily could only assume had been his wife. She had brown wavy hair and was lovely.

But what struck Emily most were the pictures of Luke. Luke laughing and smiling. Looking relaxed and happy and carefree. The opposite of the cool, controlled man he was now. Her heart twisted. What would it take for him to be like that again?

'Here you are.'

She looked up guiltily, expecting him to be angry that she'd been nosing around, but his expression wasn't giving anything away. He merely handed her her necklace, which she slipped into her bag.

'I hope you don't mind me looking.'

He shook his head sharply.

'What was she like?'

'Beautiful.'

Naturally. 'Did you love her very much?'

'Yes.'

Emily's heart squeezed. It was her own fault for asking.

'Does it still hurt?'

'Sometimes,' he said, not looking at her.

'Does it get any easier?'

There was a long silence. A crease furrowed his brow. 'Slightly,' he said at last.

Emily closed the album and replaced it on the shelf. She walked back to the window and stared out. She pitied the woman who fell in love with Luke. He was clearly still haunted by the memory of his wife. A woman he'd loved deeply and no doubt passionately. Who'd died before age and life had left their mark. What living woman could ever compete with a memory like that?

It was just as well that she was only interested in him for incredible sex and nothing more.

Luke didn't want to think about Grace. He didn't want to think about the fact that he'd stopped thinking about her all the time some time ago. He didn't want to think about the absence of the ache and start wondering when exactly it had gone away.

He hadn't brought Emily here to talk about Grace. He'd brought her here for dessert.

He moved so that he was standing behind her. He swept her hair to one side, bent his head and brushed the back of her neck with his mouth.

'You're trembling,' he said softly.

'Probably,' she murmured.

'What from?'

'Anticipation,' she whispered.

'Of what?'

'The fulfilment of a fantasy.'

'Care to elaborate?' he said, pushing his hands under her T-shirt, sliding them up over her skin and drawing it over her head.

'I should be wearing my blue dress.'

His hands closed over her shoulder, and then he moved one down to cup her breast. It moved lower still, to dip below the waistband of her jeans. Emily leaned back against him and let her head fall back. He ran a trail of kisses up the side of her neck and then turned her round.

'I can't imagine a fantasy that involves you wearing any clothes,' he said against her jaw.

'I wasn't wearing it for long.' She ran her hands over his chest and rubbed her thumb over his nipple. His skin contracted at her touch.

'You said something about a sheepskin rug. Does that feature in the fantasy?'

'It has a key role,' she said solemnly.

'How key?'

'Tell me where it is and I'll show you.'

'It happens to be in my bedroom.'

'That's good. What I have in mind for it would be most uncomfortable in the bathroom.'

'Why would I have a sheepskin rug in the bathroom?'

'Kinky?'

'Do I look like the kinky type?'

She smiled slowly. 'You've just been undressing me and touching me in front of a floor-to-ceiling, wall-to-wall window. You have the potential.'

CHAPTER ELEVEN

EMILY woke from the depths of sleep to the sound of her mobile ringing. 'Hello?' she said groggily.

'Hi.' The panic in Anna's voice wiped the sleepiness from her head and she sat bolt-upright.

'Anna, what's wrong?'

'It's Charlie. He's got a temperature. A high one.'

'What's the matter with him?' She rubbed her eyes and got out of Luke's bed.

'I don't know.' Anna sounded on the verge of tears. 'He's pink, and there are spots on his chest. Oh, God. I need to get him to hospital, but David's away again, damn him, and I don't think I can manage with Peter too.'

'Calm down, Anna.' Emily scooped up her clothes and tiptoed into the sitting room. She had never heard her sister so shaken and her blood turned to ice. 'Have you called an ambulance?' She pulled on her jeans and somehow got herself into the rest of her clothes.

'Yes, it's on its way, but it's going to be at least half an hour.'

She glanced at her watch. One a.m. At this time of night there wouldn't be any traffic.

'I'll be with you in a quarter of an hour. I'll stay with Peter while you go with Charlie to hospital. Try to stay calm. I'll be there as quickly as I can.'

She hung up and dropped her mobile into her bag. She jumped as Luke appeared in the doorway, already in his jeans, running his hands through his hair and dragging a jumper over his bare chest.

'I'm sorry for waking you. What are you doing?'

'Taking you to wherever you need to be.'

'Luke, it's one o'clock in the morning. I can get a taxi.'

'Not happening. Don't even bother trying. Let's go.' He picked up his keys and ushered her out.

Emily was too worried and too grateful to argue. Within minutes they were speeding through the dark empty streets of central London. Cocooned by cream leather seats and glossy wood, Emily tried to imagine the terror that must be going through Anna's mind. She'd never heard such panic in her sister's voice. Anna had always been the strong, reliable one. To hear her crack like that tore at her heart. If something was to happen to Charlie...after all they'd suffered... It didn't bear thinking about. She couldn't imagine what Anna was going through. And no mother of her own to fall back on. As the familiar pang of guilt reared up in her, Emily had to unclench her fists and remind herself that it wasn't her fault.

Luke pulled up outside Anna's house and Emily scrambled out of the car. The front door was flung open and Anna was standing there, white-faced and red-eyed.

When she saw Emily she crumpled into her arms. Emily hugged her sister fiercely and stroked her hair.

'Oh, God, Em. What if it's meningitis?'

'Shh. The ambulance will be here soon. They'll do tests. He'll be fine.'

'He's so tiny. And so red and blotchy.'

'Where's your husband?' said Luke, moving them all into the house and closing the door behind him.

'Milan. I wish he was here. Bloody conferences.'

At that, Emily found herself smiling slightly. That flash of normal Anna was reassuring.

'When's he due back?'

'He's on the next plane over, but it doesn't leave for another six hours.'

'I can get him here quicker than that,' said Luke, pulling his mobile out of his jacket. 'Give me his phone number and I'll sort it. Emily, make tea.'

'What's he doing here?' asked Anna, watching Luke twist away and punch numbers into his phone.

Emily followed Anna into the kitchen. 'It's not important. What's important is that we get Charlie to the hospital.'

'A bit of a distraction wouldn't go amiss right now,' said Anna shakily.

She'd do anything she could to take some of Anna's worry away, and if it meant spilling the beans about what she'd been up to, so be it. 'He was with me when you called.'

'Doing what?'

'Helping me put up curtains.'

Anna gave her a watery smile. 'That's what it looked like when I dropped by on Friday.'

'You didn't!'

'I did. Briefly.'

'When?'

'Just in time to see you rip his shirt off.' *Oh, no.* 'Don't worry, I didn't hang around. Have you been with him since then?'

Emily nodded. The day before they'd woken up late and then gone out for breakfast. They'd strolled up to Hyde Park and Luke had taken her out on the Serpentine in a rowing boat. They'd spent the afternoon window shopping before the crowds of Saturday afternoon shoppers had sent them back to Luke's flat and its huge bed. Where they'd stayed until Anna's phone call.

'Are you in love with him?'

Emily hid her face in the cupboard as she searched for the tea. 'Don't be ridiculous. Of course not. You can't fall in love with someone in a matter of days. It's just sex.'

'I fell in love with David within half an hour of meeting him.'

'That was different. David's heart wasn't encased in ice, and he fell for you too.'

'Yes, but—' Anna broke off when Luke walked into the kitchen.

'The ambulance is outside,' he said. 'Your husband will be here in a couple of hours. A car will meet him at the airport to take him to the hospital. Let me know if there's anything else I can do.'

'Thank you, Luke—for everything.' Anna gave him a peck on the cheek, scooped Charlie up and headed outside. 'Look after my little sister.'

Emily stifled a groan. Didn't she have more pressing things on her mind? She ran after Anna and gave her and Charlie a big hug. 'Good luck.'

'Thank you for coming to my rescue.'

'You know I'd do anything for you, but I really, *really* wish you hadn't told Luke to look after me. It's not that sort of thing.'

'Maybe not, but are you sure it's just sex?' murmured Anna, giving her a brief wan smile before climbing into the ambulance.

Emily watched the ambulance whizz down the street, a deep frown etched on her forehead. Sighing deeply and wrapping her arms round her waist, she turned and headed back to the house.

'Luke, I know this isn't the way you planned to spend the weekend, so please don't feel you have to stay.'

'I don't.'

Her heart twisted. 'OK, that's fine,' she said, nodding numbly and thinking it was anything but.

'Emily, I'm not going anywhere. We'll wait until your sister's husband gets here.' He glanced at his watch. 'He shouldn't be too long.'

'He could be hours.'

'Then that's how long we'll wait. Stop being difficult.'

He put his arm round her shoulders and led her back into the house. Emily had a sudden vision that had her heart thundering and her mind swimming. What if this was her

house? Their house? And it was their baby upstairs asleep? Oh,
God. Where had that image sprung from?

Heading upstairs to check on Peter, she told herself to snap
out of it. She was tired, emotional and vulnerable. This wasn't
like her. She crept into the twins' room and stared down at the
sleeping baby. A wave of something odd swept through her,
and she jerked back before she could give in to the urge to bend
down and inhale the soft sweet smell of him. What on earth
was wrong with her?

She whirled round, and in her haste to grab the baby monitor
knocked it to the floor. She froze. There was a heavy silence,
and then Peter let out a wail. Emily winced at the sound. If she
remained really still and didn't even breathe maybe he'd go
back to sleep. Another scream tore through the air. No such
luck. The wailing continued. Emily stared down at Peter's red,
screwed-up little face, at those little arms and legs kicking, and
covered her ears with her hands.

'What's going on?' Luke's voice next to her made her jump.

'Ugh, that noise. It cuts right through you.'

'Standing there with your hands over your ears won't stop
it.'

'It hurts. Do something. Make it stop.'

'You're a woman.'

'And?' she said challengingly.

'Don't you have an innate knowledge of what to do?'

Emily raised an eyebrow. 'The maternal instinct bypassed
me. And I'd never have pegged *you* as a chauvinist.'

Luke rubbed his eyes. 'I'm not.'

'So you do it. You pick him up. I don't know how to.'

'Have you never picked up your nephews?'

'No.'

Luke bent over the cot and lifted up the screaming child.
'Never babysat?'

'Anna wouldn't trust me to.'

He held the baby awkwardly, but although Peter's legs were
still kicking furiously the volume of his cries went down a

notch. 'Are you sure? You were the person she rang this evening.'

That was true. But still…

'That's enough,' he said firmly. 'Be quiet.'

The child went still, stopped mid-scream and stared at him. Luke stared back.

'You're a natural,' said Emily, watching him put the baby back down and pull a blanket over his now calm little body.

She stood on one side of the cot and Luke stood on the other, both looking down at Peter. Then Emily's eyes met Luke's, and that image of a happy family attacked her again. Her knees trembled and she twisted away, making a great fuss over searching for and picking up the baby monitor.

'Don't you ever want children?' Luke asked as they headed downstairs.

'Not particularly. Not all women do, you know.'

'Why not?'

Emily shrugged. 'Too much responsibility. Too much pain. Can you imagine the terror that Anna's going through right now?'

'Sort of.'

Emily saw him shudder and kicked herself. 'Do *you* want children?'

His eyes narrowed. 'No.'

'Why not?' If he could ask her, she could ask him.

'I've no intention of marrying again, and I'm neither irresponsible nor careless.'

'There are far too many children in the world as it is.'

'Quite.'

'That's what I tried telling Tom, but he wouldn't listen.'

'Is that the real reason why you split up?'

She nodded. 'He couldn't understand it. Initially he didn't want them either, but then he changed his mind and thought he'd be able to change mine.'

'He clearly didn't know you at all.'

Or perhaps he had. Her resolve seemed to have become

strangely unsteady in the last hour or so. 'I'd better see if there's any news on Charlie,' she said, walking into the kitchen to call her sister.

When she hung up Luke was on the sofa in the sitting room, his legs stretched out and his eyes closed. The deep comfortable sofa with Luke at one end was tempting, but she headed for one of the armchairs by the fireplace. God, he was gorgeous, she thought, and then admonished herself for the rather inappropriate timing of her thought. He'd been amazing tonight. He'd stopped Anna and herself turning hysterical. His strength made her heart wobble.

'Come and sit by me.'

'I thought you were asleep.'

'Nearly. How's your nephew?'

'He's going to be fine.' Relief was still whipping round inside her. 'It's a rash. Some sort of allergy, apparently. Anna did tell me what it was called, but it's late and it was a long, complicated name and I've forgotten.'

'Good.' His eyes flickered open. 'Come here,' he said again.

Emily sank onto the sofa and leaned into him, absorbing his strength and his warmth. She breathed in deeply and felt her tension unravel.

Moonlight was streaming in through the patio doors when she jolted awake. For a moment she was disorientated, and then a number of things filtered into her consciousness. The sound of the front door opening. The steady thud of Luke's heart beneath her ear. Her arm thrown over his chest. The feel of his body entwined with hers as they both sprawled on the sofa.

Emily blinked. Gently she unwound her arm from his chest and her legs from his. Luke jerked awake, and she found herself staring into his eyes. What she read in their unguarded depths she couldn't make out. But it was something that made her heart lurch.

After a couple of heartbeats that seemed to last for hours, Emily pushed herself up and straightened her clothing. Luke rotated his shoulders, flexed his arms, and ran his hands through his hair.

Emily was getting to her feet as her brother-in-law entered the sitting room. He looked haggard. 'How's Charlie?' she said, her voice rough with sleep.

'He's absolutely fine,' he said, his gaze flickering over Luke, 'but they're keeping him in for a while longer just to make sure.'

Emily smiled for the first time in what felt like ages. 'I'm so glad. This is Luke Harrison. Luke—David Palmer.'

'I have a lot to thank you for,' David said gruffly, shaking Luke's hand.

'Don't mention it.'

Emily could see the two men sizing each other up and approving of what they saw. It gave her a warm, fuzzy feeling inside that she wasn't sure she wanted to identify.

'How's Peter?'

'Asleep.'

'Any trouble?'

'None whatsoever. He was as good as gold.'

'It's late. You head off. Thanks Em, Luke.'

They stepped out into the dark night. When they got to the car Luke opened the door for her and she got in. 'Let's go back to your house,' he said. 'It's closer and I'm shattered.'

She gazed up at him. 'Thank you for everything you did tonight.'

Luke shrugged. 'I know what it's like to feel helpless and utterly alone. The least I could do was get David back as quickly as possible.'

'Who was there for you when Grace died?' she asked softly.

'No one.' He shut her door and walked round the bonnet to the driver's side.

Emily went dizzy. She wanted to pull him into her arms. She wanted him never to hurt again. She wanted to protect him, look after him, find out everything there was to know about him. She wanted to go to bed with him every night and wake

up with him every morning. She wanted to make love with him
for ever. Oh, Lord, she thought, her heart hammering as he got
into the car. Once again Anna had hit the nail on the head. She
was head over heels in love with him.

CHAPTER TWELVE

'YOU'RE very quiet,' said Luke.

'Just thinking,' Emily murmured, staring out of the passenger window at the dark terraced houses.

'What about?'

'Things.'

'That's almost as bad as "nothing".'

'Mmm.' Things were certainly bad. She was in love with Luke and probably had been from the moment he'd agreed to accompany her to the wedding when he clearly hadn't wanted to. She was in love with a man who'd sworn never to love again. Who was in all likelihood still in love with his dead wife and only saw *her* as an entertaining diversion.

But *was* it just sex? Surely he must feel something else for her, however remote and tentative. Would he have bothered to take her to the gala if it was just about sex? Would he have looked after her when she fainted, and would he have done all he'd just done if it was only about sex? Or was she once again hoping to see something that wasn't there?

Because it was highly unlikely that he'd have changed. If she wasn't going to fall into the futile trap of thinking he would, she should get out now. Thank him for his help, go into her house, lock the door behind her and protect her heart from any further damage. Now was the time to do it. As he was parking the car outside her house. All she had to do was yank the passenger door open, tumble out, race up her path and she'd be safe. The initial agony would be brutal, but brief. She'd get over it. In about a hundred years.

Her heart thudded and her mouth went dry. Her hand reached for the handle. Could she really do it? She glanced over at Luke one last time and her stomach turned itself inside out. He was watching her, his face serious, his eyes gleaming with simmering desire, and Emily realised she had no more chance of resisting him than she had of becoming a world dance champion. She was doomed.

Every step up the path with him was a step towards insanity and probably unimaginable pain, but she couldn't stop. Her body and her heart craved him. It was out of her control. She would take what she could and worry about the consequences later.

'Just how tired are you?' she asked, dropping her keys on the hall table and turning to him.

Luke's eyes darkened. 'Exhausted. You snore.'

'I don't,' she said indignantly. 'Do I?'

'It's more of a snuffle.' He flexed his shoulders and winced.

'A massage might help to ease those muscles.'

'It might.'

'Did I ever tell you I once temped in a massage parlour?'

'That wasn't on your CV.'

'Well, it wouldn't be, would it?' she said softly. 'It might give employers the wrong idea.'

'It's giving *me* wrong ideas,' he said, tugging her into his arms and kissing her deeply.

Somehow they tangoed up the stairs and into her bedroom, still locked in each other's arms. When they parted Emily's breathing was shaky and her whole body was trembling. 'Take off your clothes and lie on the bed face down,' she said.

'All of them?'

'All of them.'

'Be gentle.'

A minute later she'd stripped to her underwear, and Luke was naked and prone, in her hands and at her mercy. God, he was magnificent. Was it because she now realised that she was in love with him that he seemed so much more…*everything*?

She straddled him, put her hands on his shoulders, and felt his muscles clench beneath them.

'Relax,' she whispered, bending down to his ear.

'Impossible,' he muttered.

'You'll see.' She kneaded and pressed her way over his body until she felt the tension ease from him. Then her touch changed, and the kneading and pressing became caressing and stroking.

'How does that feel?'

Luke mumbled something that sounded like 'amazing' into the pillow, but it could well have been 'agonising'.

'Now the front. Turn over.'

'Can't.'

'No need to be embarrassed.'

'I'm not,' he said, lifting his head a fraction. 'You're on top of me.'

So she was. Biting on her lip to stop a giggle escaping, she moved just enough to allow him to turn over, and then she was astride him again. Only now his erection was pressing insistently against her and she nearly lost her mind.

Luke was watching her with a look in his eyes that said *You've got me where you want me, so now what are you going to do with me*? Emily knew exactly what she was going to do with him. He'd said she needed to take risks. Well, she about to take a massive one. She was going to try and make him lose control.

As if he could read her mind, he clenched his jaw and his eyes glittered. She leaned down, laced her fingers with his and kissed him slowly and thoroughly. The low-burning flame inside her burst into life. His fingers tightened around hers and she felt a tremor rush through him. She dragged her mouth from his and trailed a line of hot kisses down his neck and his chest. Her tongue flicked over his nipple and she heard his sharp intake of breath. She disentangled her hands from his as she continued kissing her way down over the muscles of his stomach to where the hard length of him was straining.

'Emily…' he said raggedly.

'Shh.'

Their gazes locked for a second before she lowered her head and took him into the warm wet heat of her mouth.

She heard him groan, and could feel the effort he was making not to thrust upwards. The hand that wasn't tangling in her hair was clutching the sheet. She swirled her tongue around the tip of his erection, licking away the tiny bead that had formed there, and then slowly closed her mouth around the length of him again.

Luke shuddered beneath her as she carried on. His hips were jerking and she sensed he was close. Emily lifted her head and slithered her way back up his body wriggling out of her knickers as she did so. His eyes were almost black, and the eerie silvery light accentuated the strained planes of his face. He dragged her against his chest and kissed her fiercely, igniting the heat deep within her.

'You're very good at that,' he grated.

Emily pushed herself up on her palms and drew her knees up to straddle him. She reached behind her and unclipped her bra. 'I've read a lot of books.'

'I'd love to know the sort of books you read.'

She laughed softly and leaned over to the bedside table. She rolled a condom onto him and lowered herself slowly, until he was entering her inch by incredible inch.

'Oh, God,' he muttered as she began to rock slowly and sensuously, the moonlight outlining her shape as she moved over him. She bent forward to brush her nipple against his lips, and then leaned back before he could take it in his mouth. And all the time she was looking into his eyes. Boring into him, as if trying to get a glimpse of his soul. She was bewitching him. His heart was pounding. His body was getting tight. She was squeezing gently as she moved up and down him and he could feel his control slipping away. He tried to cling on, but his body was clamouring for the ecstasy that only she seemed able to give him.

Emily shook her hair back as she writhed, and it was the most erotic thing he'd ever seen. Barely aware of what he was doing, he moved one hand from her hip to grip her thigh and moved the other to her waist.

In one smooth move he flipped her over, so she was lying on her back and he was rearing over her, still buried deep inside her. Her eyes registered brief shock, and then glazed over with desire. Her lips were swollen and red and wet, and set something off deep within him—something primal. The need to possess was so overwhelming that he felt himself slide under. He felt as though he was drowning. Her eyes held his. He couldn't break away even though he desperately wanted to. He couldn't stop. His arms were shaking with strain as he drove into her over and over again. Her hips came up to meet each thrust. Her breathing was ragged. Her hands roamed over his shoulders, his back, over his buttocks, pulling him deeper into her, driving him closer to an edge that was sharper and higher than anything he'd ever experienced.

What do you want from me?

Let go.

No.

Yes.

She let out a cry and clamped around him. Her back arched off the bed but still her eyes held his. Her abandon, her complete release, wiped out the last vestiges of his control. As she convulsed again and again he thrust harder and faster, his body coiling, tight, the pressure building.

He stared into her eyes.

Yes.

He shattered. His mind went blank as he emptied himself into her.

Luke sat in the armchair in the corner of her room and watched Emily sleeping. He was transfixed by the soft rise and fall of

her chest, the occasional twitch of her mouth, that funny little
snuffle that she made from time to time. He couldn't fool
himself any longer. This game with Emily was becoming more
than a game. If he was being honest with himself it had never
been a game. He'd just chosen not to acknowledge it.

The feelings twisting around inside him were more than
mere lust. He didn't know what they were, but he was very
afraid of what they might become. He'd tried to keep it light
and casual. But this last time something had changed. His
touch had been different. She'd made him lose control. If she'd
asked him to stop he wouldn't have been able to. Her hands,
her mouth, her eyes, had been telling him something he really
didn't want to know.

His chest squeezed. He suddenly felt as though he couldn't
breathe.

He shoved a hand through his hair and his eyebrows
snapped together. They'd spent the last two days together, and
now he couldn't imagine her not being around. It couldn't be
allowed to continue. He wouldn't get himself into the same
situation as before, where he'd cared for someone, loved
someone, only to have them snatched away. The memories of
that time after Grace's death were too hard to bear. The hollow
ache inside him. The wretched desolation and loneliness. The
guilt that he was still alive. He wouldn't be put through that
again, and he wouldn't put himself in a position where it might
happen.

Emily was aware she was being watched long before she
opened her eyes. She could tell by the way her skin tingled and
desire began to awaken inside her. She stretched out an arm
and felt the space beside her cold and empty. Her eyes snapped
open and she saw Luke sitting in the corner, looking far too
big and brooding for the delicate chair. What was he doing over
there and not in her bed? And why was he dressed? That was
something that needed to be remedied right away.

'Hi,' she said, with a wide sleepy grin.

'Hi.'

His tone had her fully awake. She watched him warily, but he didn't move from the chair and his expression didn't alter. The intensity of his gaze made her uneasy. She didn't know why, but she was suddenly scared.

'Last night, did you ask me to stop?'

What an odd question. 'Of course not,' she said, drawing the duvet up to her chin as if it would provide some sort of defence against whatever was happening. 'Why would I have asked you to stop? I wanted it to go on for ever. Come back to bed.' She tried to send him a smouldering smile, but her heart wasn't in it.

His jaw clenched. 'We need to talk.'

The smile slipped from her face and she felt as though someone had stabbed her with an icicle. 'What about?'

'Us. This.'

His eyes were devoid of emotion. This wasn't the Luke she'd come to know over the past few weeks—the Luke who'd protected her from gossips, given her his coat when she was cold, flirted with her and made such magnificent love to her. This Luke was cold, distant, and she didn't like him one little bit. Her insides felt as though they were being torn in two. The massive risk she'd taken had failed. She made him lose control and now he was punishing her for it.

'Is there any point?' she said, shrinking further beneath the duvet. 'I know what you're going to say, Luke.'

'What am I going to say?'

She closed her eyes for a second. 'You think we should stop seeing each other.'

There was a long pause that told her she was right, damn him. Her heart cracked. A tiny part of her had so hoped that she'd be wrong.

She opened her eyes and forced herself to look at him and continue. 'And I agree.'

'You do?'

Thank God she had a thick duvet. If he could see the way she was shaking he'd never have believed her.

'Absolutely. It was only supposed to be temporary, after all, and it's no longer a one-night stand, so it's probably best if we make a clean break of it. Short and sharp.' Like the knife slicing though her.

'Why?'

Because I'm an idiot for thinking you'd change. Because my heart is breaking. Because I love you too much, and to have to listen to your reasons and your excuses would break what's left of me.

'Because it's what you want, isn't it?'

He sighed and raked a hand through his hair. 'Yes.' He levered himself to his feet. 'I have to go.'

It was only though sheer will-power that she managed to keep her face from collapsing. Inside she was splintering. 'OK.'

Luke walked over to the bed. He placed his hands either side of her head, leaned down and gave her a long, drugging kiss. A goodbye kiss. And then he was gone. The front door slammed and Emily knew beyond all doubt that she'd never see him again.

A wave of nausea hit her and she clapped a hand to her mouth. Flinging back the duvet, she raced to the bathroom and retched and retched. When that was over, she splashed water over her face, threw herself onto the bed and promptly burst into tears.

Over the next few days Emily sank into black despair. She cancelled her work on the grounds of sickness, dimly aware that she was letting Sarah down but unable to summon up the effort to care. She felt wretched, mangled, distraught. Luke didn't want her. She'd offered him everything and he'd rejected it. With an aching heart, she went over and over it in her mind, analysing every conversation they'd had, tormenting herself with wondering whether there was anything she could have done differently. But, whatever she'd done or not done, sooner or later the result would have been the same.

The weather had been largely sympathetic. Great heavy, humid clouds hung over London, suiting and fuelling her misery perfectly. But after a thunderstorm the night before the sun was now out, spilling into her room and demanding that she pull herself together.

Sighing heavily, Emily levered herself and her bruised heart out of bed and went into her bathroom. She flung a cursory look at herself in the mirror, did a double take and then shrank back in horror. Her skin was so pale it was almost grey—except where a rash of spots had broken out—her eyes were red, and her hair was lanky and dull.

Well, that was what a week of no vegetables, fruit or sleep but gallons of misery and chocolate ice cream could do to a girl.

Supposing Luke came back and saw her looking like this? Idiot, she berated herself. There was zero chance of that happening. Still, it wouldn't hurt to get dressed and tidy up a bit, would it? Her bedroom carpet was barely visible beneath the blanket of scrunched-up tissues and her bedside table was piled high with empty ice cream cartons. If she carried on like this for much longer, her bedroom would end up as an exhibit at the Tate Modern.

Emily dragged herself into the shower, threw on some clothes and, feeling marginally better, headed down to her shed. It was time to make some changes. She'd make herself forget about Luke. She'd get over him. She wasn't the first girl in history to have a failed love affair and she wouldn't be the last. She'd just have to find some of that inner strength to support her in the days to come. And she'd find it at her wheel, just as she always did. The feel of the clay squeezing through her fingers and the hypnotic whirl of the wheel would soothe her nerves and wipe her mind.

Mind you, she didn't have much space left. If she didn't do something about her pottery soon she'd run the risk of having the whole lot topple on top of her and ending up fossilised beneath the resulting mountain.

She really should have an exhibition, she thought, eyeing her work critically. Some of it *was* good enough. She could easily make more. As excitement began to creep into her head, her mind swam with possibilities. Images of her lovely creations in a beautiful gallery. All the rich and famous gasping in awe over her talent and the sheer impact of her work.

She'd show Luke. She didn't need him. She'd become an overnight success, receive rave reviews and meet a heavenly man with no issues who would fall madly in love with her.

Hmm. Earth calling Emily. How did one go about sorting out something like an exhibition? Maybe Anna could help, she thought, reaching for her diary. She opened the book and ran her eyes over the pages. How long would it take? She tapped her pencil against her teeth. Did galleries have waiting lists? And how much would it cost? Could she really do it? Of course she could. With a bit of backbone.

She flicked over the pages and her heart skipped a beat. Then it slowed right down and a shiver raced down her spine. As if in slow motion she turned the pages back and went cold. Oh, God. There it was. A week ago. The circle around the date.

All thoughts of an exhibition vanished. Her heart hammering, Emily told herself to calm down. Maybe she'd noted the dates down wrong. With fumbling fingers she turned back through the pages to double-check. The dates were accurate.

No need to panic. There could be a thousand and one reasons why she was seven days late. Even if she was usually as regular as clockwork. Stress. That was a good one. The last week had been stressful, to say the least. And what about the fainting episode? Maybe her blood pressure was still out of balance? Maybe it was all that ice cream?

Just please, please let it be *anything* other than… Bells started clanging in her head. The diary fell from her fingers and thudded onto the floor. Oh, Lord, no. It was unthinkable. Impossible. She and Luke had used condoms every time they'd had sex. Every time. There was no way she could be pregnant. There *had* to be some other reason.

As if on cue, the smell of varnish hit the back of her throat and her stomach revolted. Suddenly drenched in an icy sweat, Emily stumbled out of her shed and threw up into a flowerbed.

Trembling violently, she staggered into the house and gulped down a glass of water, fear gripping her whole body at the mounting evidence. Unable to stand the uncertainty any longer, she grabbed her handbag, flew out of the house and raced to the pharmacy at the end of the road.

Three minutes. That was what the box said. The box was wrong. Thirty seconds was all it took for the second blue line to appear and for her life to come crashing down around her ears. She was pregnant. Her head went fuzzy and she collapsed onto the sofa, curling into a shaky, shivery ball.

Terror wound itself round her insides, creeping through her, twisting, wrenching, until it reached her brain and exploded into sheer white blinding panic. She squeezed her eyes tight shut and started shaking even more.

Then, thankfully, her brain shut down and she spun headlong into denial.

CHAPTER THIRTEEN

'You look sickeningly brown,' said Emily, smiling wanly as she bent down to give her sister a hug.

Anna hugged her back. 'You're looking peaky. Are you all right?'

Not really. She felt battered and bruised, like a tiny yacht that had been tossed around on the high seas by a tropical storm. 'Fine. Tired, that's all. How was the holiday?'

'Corfu was heavenly. Just what we needed after the panic with Charlie. But I don't want to talk about my two weeks of glorious sunshine, empty white beaches and delicious food. I want to hear what you've been up to.'

Emily sat down and wondered what Anna would say if she told her the truth. A week of excruciating unhappiness followed by an attack of twenty-eight years' worth of fear and guilt. It was all too raw. 'Potting,' she replied instead, watching the twins crawling on the grass.

Anna raised her eyebrows. 'I wouldn't have thought you'd have time.'

Emily ignored her suggestive tone. 'I'm thinking about having an exhibition. Displaying some of the stuff I've produced.'

'Really? That's amazing.'

'It's no big deal. My shed is getting cluttered, that's all. But I might need your help with sorting a space and things.'

'Whatever you want, darling,' she said, picking up a menu and scanning it. 'What's brought about this change of heart?'

Emily shrugged. 'Nothing important.'

Anna's head snapped up and Emily averted her eyes from her shrewd gaze. 'How is the lovely Luke?'

'I have no idea,' she said, her throat threatening to close up. 'Rotting in hell, with any luck.'

Anna dropped the menu. 'You're not seeing him any more?'

Emily shook her head.

'What happened?'

'I fell in love with him.'

Anna smiled triumphantly. 'I knew it.'

'And so he ended our affair.'

Her smile vanished. 'Why?'

'I don't know. He backed off.'

'Oh, darling, I'm sorry. No wonder you're looking peaky.'

'Today is a good day. I haven't cried for a whole hour.'

Anna squeezed her hand. 'This calls for wine.' She waved at a passing waitress.

'Bit early for me,' said Emily awkwardly. 'I'll have some camomile tea.'

The order given, Anna sat back and fixed her with a penetrating stare.

'What are you looking at me like that for?' said Emily warily.

'You're pregnant.'

Her stomach churned. 'What makes you think that?'

'You have that look about you.'

'The sick-to-the-stomach-and-utterly-shattered look?'

'That's the one.'

'That could be misery.'

Anna shook her head. 'It's not just misery.'

Emily shuddered. 'Is there any point in my denying it?'

'None whatsoever. I'd simply have to try and ply you with alcohol and prawns and brie until you ran out of excuses.'

'In that case, you're right.' She dropped her head into her hands as her chest tightened and a tremor ran though her.

'Oh, my God, this is so exciting! The twins will have a little cousin. How many weeks are you?'

'I'm not sure.'

Anna frowned. 'You have been to see a doctor, haven't you?'

Emily looked up and bit her lip. 'Not yet.'

'But you should be looking after yourself.'

Emily swallowed painfully. 'I only found out a few days ago. Anna, don't judge. Please.' She was on the brink of tears.

'Of course not, darling. How are *you* taking it?'

She was carrying the baby of the man she loved. Her heart skipped. A little girl or boy who'd have dark hair and green eyes. Or maybe blue eyes and fair hair.

A child who might well kill her the same way she'd killed her mother. The spark of delight was swept away by a tidal wave of pure fear. 'Badly. I will go and see a doctor. Just please don't hassle me. Really. I need time to deal with this. I'm not sure if I ever will.'

'Luke will help you. If you tell him.'

'Tricky when we're no longer seeing each other. Besides, he doesn't want children any more than I do.'

'Nonsense. All men do. They have a built-in desire to replicate themselves.'

'Not Luke,' said Emily, miserably shaking her head.

'Did he tell you that?'

'Yes.'

'Well, he was lying. Or else suffering from some sort of internal trauma.'

'Would still being in love with his wife count as internal trauma?'

'His *wife*?'

'That's what his mother-in-law told me.'

'Whoa!' cried Anna, shaking her head and throwing her

hands in the air. 'Luke's *married*? He has a *mother-in-law*? You've *met* her? Backtrack.'

'Only if you promise to stop speaking in italics.'

Anna nodded vigorously.

'Luke was married to a paediatrician called Grace. She died in a car accident three years ago, around six months after they'd married, I think.'

Anna looked horrified. 'How tragic.'

'Yes. Apparently she was beautiful and caring and warm and obviously perfect. His mother-in-law said he was still in love with her.'

'Is he?'

'I don't know. Probably.'

'Haven't you asked?'

Emily's jaw dropped. 'Of course I haven't asked.'

'You should. His mother-in-law doesn't know his inner thoughts, does she? And she's probably still grieving.'

'So is Luke.'

'Are you sure?'

She hesitated. She didn't know what she thought any more. 'I don't know. Maybe not. He bought the flat he lives in after Grace's death, and the only photos of her are in a handful of albums.' She paused. 'I think I might be the first person he's slept with in three years.'

Anna raised an eyebrow. 'It sounds like he's through with grieving.'

'So why did he end our fling?'

'No idea, but you should tell him about the baby.'

'You're right. I know you are.'

'You're not going to do it, are you?'

Emily fiddled with her hair. 'I will.'

'You can't carry on pretending it's not happening for ever.'

'I know. I do realise denial isn't the way to sort this out, but at the moment it's a cosy place to be.'

Anna glared at her. 'I'm warning you—if you don't tell him soon, then I will. Denial is a complete waste of time.'

Emily let out a sceptical laugh. 'How would you know? You tackle everything head-on.'

'I know all about denial.'

'How?'

'My first two years of art college I spent in denial.'

Emily frowned. 'Really? But you loved it.'

'I hated it.' Anna took a sip of wine.

Emily gaped. 'You *hated* it?'

Anna nodded. 'It was something I'd always thought I wanted to do, but when it came down to it I was bored as hell. All that contemplation and light and depth and perspective. I realised about a week after starting that I'd made the wrong decision. But I couldn't admit defeat. Imagine having to admit to yourself, not to mention to friends, that you have a secret hankering to be an accountant.'

Emily could scarcely believe what she was hearing. 'I thought you took up accountancy because of me.'

'Well, that was part of it. Timing, really. It was the push I needed to take the plunge.'

Emily was pole-axed. Why had they never discussed this before?

'I thought you knew.'

She shook her head. 'I always thought I'd made you sacrifice something you loved.'

Anna gave her a gentle smile. 'Silly thing.'

Emily blinked, trying to come to terms with this new, upside-down world in which years of guilt had just been brushed away as 'silly'. She stared at the twins and her heart felt strangely light. Her hand fell to her abdomen. 'Aren't they gorgeous?' she murmured.

'Do you want to hold one?'

'Would you let me?'

Anna's eyes were shimmering. 'Of course. I've been waiting for ages.'

* * *

The insistent ringing of the doorbell dragged Emily from her shed and had her marching into the house with her hands over her ears and a scowl on her face. Why couldn't she just be left alone? Hadn't whoever it was ever heard of patience?

The Luke-shaped shadow on the other side of the glass made her jerk to a halt in the hall. Her pulse leapt and hope rushed through her. Why was he here? Had he changed his mind? Had he come to apologise? Had he come to confess that he'd been on mind-altering medication and that he was in fact utterly besotted by her?

Stupid fool, she told herself, as the pain he'd caused her flooded back. Bastard. If she slunk into the kitchen would he give up and go away?

'Open the door, Emily. I can see you through the glass.'

Damn. She stood there vacillating for a second, then strode forward and flung the door open.

Luke's eyes were cold, and his face was dark and angry, but nevertheless her heart—pathetically weak organ that it was—squeezed at the sight of him.

'What do you want?'

'When were you going to tell me?'

Emily mentally cursed her meddlesome sister with every filthy word she knew. No point in pretending she didn't know what he was talking about. 'I wasn't.' She tried to shut the door, but he jammed his foot in the gap and then pushed his way into her house.

'Nice of you,' he said grimly.

'Do come in.'

He strode into her sitting room and planted himself in front of the bay window, crossing his arms over his chest. 'When did you find out?'

With the evening sun behind him he looked big and dark, and a shiver of longing ripped through her. Silently cursing her treacherous body, she injected some much needed steel into her spine. 'Three days ago.'

'How did it happen?'

She bristled. 'Do you want me to draw you a picture?'

He glowered at her. 'We were careful. We used condoms every time.'

Emily threw up her hands. 'Well, maybe condoms and hot tubs don't go together. Maybe they weren't within their use-by date. Maybe one split. They're not infallible. Who knows?'

'Maybe you do.'

Emily froze. 'What's that supposed to mean?'

'You tell me.'

'You don't honestly think I've been going round sticking pins in them or something, do you?'

He raised an eyebrow and Emily's blood pressure rocketed. 'How dare you? I'm no more thrilled about this than you are. Have you *ever* listened to anything I've said? I don't want babies. Never have, never will.'

Luke's expression turned even colder and Emily's stomach tensed. 'Of course you don't. In fact with your fear of responsibility, of taking a risk, of actually doing something permanent with your life, I'm surprised you're going through with the pregnancy at all.'

Emily gasped. His words had hit her so hard that she was winded. The air thickened.

Luke shoved his hands through his hair. 'I'm sorry,' he said, 'that was uncalled for.'

'I think you'd better leave.'

'No.'

'Yes.'

'I'm not leaving you in this state.'

'It's your fault I'm in this state. Mental and physical,' she said, clenching her fists. 'You have no right to barge in here, hurling accusations around the place. We are over, remember?'

'That's no excuse.'

'I don't need an excuse. Why are you so angry?'

'You're pregnant with my child—'

'What makes you think it's yours?'

Luke's lips thinned into a tight line. His face turned thunderous.

'OK, it's yours,' she said grudgingly. 'Of course it's yours. I haven't slept with anyone else in over a year.'

'I have a right to know, and you denied me that right.'

'What did you expect me to do?' she said scathingly. 'Place an ad in the *Financial Times*? E-mail you? Turn up on your doorstep? Rather outside the boundaries of our terminated commitment-free relationship, don't you think?'

'You could have rung.'

'Would you have answered my calls?'

'Of course I would have. Don't be ridiculous.' But he didn't look at her, and she felt a surge of righteous satisfaction. 'Why weren't you going to tell me?'

Emily ran a hand through her hair and chewed on her lip. The fact that they'd broken up wasn't really a good excuse, and she couldn't avoid answering him indefinitely.

She stuck her chin up. 'I'll tell you why I didn't tell you if you tell me why you decided to end our fling.'

His eyes glittered at her. 'Agreed. You go first.'

She studied the clock on the mantelpiece. 'The reason I wasn't going to tell you was because I can barely admit it to myself. I was in denial. Probably still am. Is that good enough?'

'Getting there. Why are you in denial?'

'That's none of your business.'

'Oh, I think it very much is.'

Luke still hadn't moved. His eyes fixed on her and she fought the urge to squirm.

'Babies have never been part of my life plan.'

'Why not?'

Emily felt her hackles rise. Hadn't she told him enough that night they'd spent at Anna's house? What did he want? The whole gory story? Well, fine. If he was going to stand there all intimidating and dominating, he could have it.

'Why do you think?' she flung at him. 'I was responsible for the death of my mother. And consequently my father. I ruined my sister's life. I destroyed a perfectly good family. I don't deserve to have one of my own.'

Luke went very still. 'Who told you that?'

'No one. I worked it out all by myself a long time ago.'

'Do you really believe it?'

Emily sank onto the sofa and rubbed her eyes. 'Possibly.' For a long time she had, but her convictions had been on shaky ground even before her conversation with Anna. In fact everything she'd ever believed now seemed to be crumbling around her.

'Is that all there is to it?'

'Isn't that enough?'

Luke frowned. 'I don't think so. I think deep down you *know* you're not responsible for what happened to your family.'

Something inside her snapped. She was fed up with his prodding at her psyche. Fed up with her body's reaction, the constant lurching of her heart and rampaging hormones, and utterly fed up with the futility of being in love with him. She jumped to her feet and glared at him. 'Fine. You want to know what really terrifies me about the whole pregnancy thing?'

He met her challenge with steady eyes.

'Suppose having a child kills me too?'

It was as if someone had hit the pause button. Silence echoed around them. His face softened and his eyes lost some of their iciness. 'Is there any reason it would?'

'The doctor says there isn't, but do you think reason comes into this? My mother had no symptoms. Nothing. She just collapsed the day after she had me. Just like that.' She snapped her fingers.

He unfolded his arms and walked towards her. She just knew he was going to wrap his arms around her and she didn't think she could stand it. 'No,' she said sharply, holding up a hand to ward him off. 'Don't touch me. I should never have let you anywhere near me in the first place.'

Luke recoiled as if she'd hit him, and the shutters came down over his features. He stepped back and turned to look out of the window. 'Is that how you really feel about it?'

Emily went silent. How *did* she feel about it? Denial was no longer an option. She forced herself to think about the tiny life she had inside her. Luke's child. Her heart tripped and then something inside her chest blossomed. There it was again. That spark of sheer joy. Stronger than before. Strong enough to keep burning through the fear. She could do it. Especially if she had Luke by her side. He'd keep her safe. Unlike Tom.

Emily's heart skipped a beat. Where had that thought sprung from? Had she never felt truly safe with Tom? Was that why the not-having-children thing had got so big and so out of control in their relationship? Because she hadn't felt safe enough to overcome her fears? Because their relationship hadn't been solid enough? Because, ultimately, she hadn't loved him enough to give him the one thing he'd wanted?

'I don't know,' she managed, as another long-held belief came crashing down. 'How do you feel about it?'

Luke rubbed a hand over his jaw and his face darkened. 'It's not ideal.'

Emily winced as her insides wrenched. How did he have such power to hurt her?

'Did you really think I wouldn't find out?' he said flatly.

'Why would you? You called a halt to our affair and we don't exactly move in the same circles.'

'As I remember it, you broke up with me.'

'I may have said the words, but that was just timing. I wanted to pre-empt your excuses. Now it's your turn. What reasons were you going to give me for why you decided to break us up?'

He sighed and pushed a hand through his hair.

'Please don't tell me you were going to haul out the "it's not you, it's me" line.'

'Actually, I was going to say it was you.'

Emily's stomach churned. 'Gallant.'

'I would have told you that you're a blonde and I go for brunettes.'

He had been going to reduce it to *hair colour*? Emily

flushed. 'I didn't think you'd had a type in the last three years,' she said bitingly.

Luke tensed, but he carried on as if she hadn't spoken. 'And that you were cathartic. You served a purpose.'

She didn't want to know, but couldn't not ask. 'What sort of purpose?'

'Three years is a long time for any man. You were in the right place at the right time.' She gasped. 'That's what I would have said if you'd asked me why.'

Emily swallowed and tried to stop herself from trembling. 'I wouldn't have let you get away with that.'

'I can't imagine you would have. So what would you have done?'

Luke was still staring out of the window, which made his question easier to answer. Emily took a deep breath. 'After probably slapping you, I'd have called you a coward. I'd have reminded you that you hadn't been to a wedding since your wife died but you went to one with me. You hadn't been to that ball in three years but you took me. When I had heatstroke you could easily have called Anna but you didn't. You stayed and looked after me. You didn't have to help when Charlie was ill but you did. You've been on countless dates since Grace died but you slept with me. You lost control with *me*. I would have told you that I didn't believe all that nonsense about catharsis and hair colour.'

By the time she was finished she was breathing hard and almost bursting with emotion. Luke wasn't saying anything, and he hadn't moved a muscle, so she threw caution to the winds, wanting the truth, however much it hurt.

'Are you still in love with her?'

Luke's jaw clenched and for an awful second Emily thought he might not answer. Then, he said, 'I'll always love her. But, no, I'm not in love with her any more. Not in the way you mean.'

Hope began to bubble inside her and she just couldn't get rid of it. 'So what were your real reasons for ending our affair?'

He turned round slowly, his eyes blank and his expression unreadable. 'You made me feel things I didn't want to feel. You asked for too much. You made me lose control.'

'You can't tell yourself not to feel.'

'Yes, you can.'

She took a deep breath. 'I can't.' She saw him tense and nearly crumbled. But this was her last chance. 'You must know how I feel about you.'

He frowned. 'I warned you.'

His withdrawal was palpable and she felt pain rip through her. What had she been expecting? Luke to fall into her arms, tell her she was right and confess that he loved her too?

She sighed. 'I know you did, Luke, but unfortunately my heart seems to have ignored that particular piece of advice. I'm irreversibly in love with you. I apologise wholeheartedly, but there's nothing I can do about it.'

'There's nothing I can do about it either, Emily,' he said flatly.

Suddenly she'd had enough. Frustration and hurt and hope-lessness tangled into one tight ball inside her and she marched up to him.

'You say you're a risk taker. And maybe you are—profes-sionally. But here?' She tapped his chest. 'You're scared.'

His eyes narrowed. 'Quite the psychiatrist.'

His face was hard, empty, and at that moment she hated him. She'd never get through that wall of ice he'd wrapped around his heart. 'Quite the bastard,' she said quietly, backing away on very unsteady legs. She was about to crack open. Her heart was shattering and she was beginning to shake violently.

'You can, of course, see the baby whenever you want, but for the moment I'd like you to go.'

Luke nodded briefly and went.

CHAPTER FOURTEEN

LUKE rubbed a weary hand over his face and stared blankly out of the window. The last two weeks had been horrendous. How long had it been since he'd slept properly? Eaten properly? Functioned properly?

He scowled and raked a hand though his hair. He'd done the right thing, walking away from Emily. Saved himself one hell of a lot of pain. He'd just have to keep reminding himself of the fact. More often than he already was. This strange churning inside him would eventually settle. Memories of her would stop filling every corner of his head. The look on her face just before he'd left would eventually stop haunting him. With time. Everything got better with time.

If only he could get rid of the knowledge that by trying to protect himself he'd badly hurt her. And if only he could get rid of the uncomfortable awareness that he'd left her to deal with her pregnancy alone and terrified. Because what was right about that?

The sharp rap on his door jerked him out of his thoughts. 'Come in.' The words came out more harshly than he'd intended, but that seemed to be the norm lately.

He turned to see his secretary standing there, chin up and an unfamiliar determined glare in her eye.

'What is it?' he snapped, and then frowned as shock at his tone registered in her expression.

'Luke, I've been with you now for—what?—five years?'

He nodded curtly and strode across his office to lean back against the edge of his desk. If his extremely well-paid secretary was about to ask for a rise, she could forget it.

'Do you mind if I speak frankly?' she said, marching over to him.

He crossed his arms. 'Please do.'

'I think you should go home.'

He could feel himself glowering at her but couldn't stop it. 'Do you?'

She nodded. 'Or at least go for a walk. Get some air. You've barely left this office in the last fortnight.'

'The company doesn't run itself.'

'At the moment it's a miracle it's making a profit at all.'

He had to keep his mouth clamped tight shut to stop himself from snapping that it was none of her business.

'The only reason no one's said anything is they're terrified you're going to fire them, and the mood you're in I don't blame them.'

Luke ground his teeth. 'Really?'

'Really. This has always been a great place to work, but right now it's horrible.'

His jaw tightened. He didn't trust himself to speak.

His secretary frowned and her expression turned to one of uncertainty. 'Right, well. It had to be said. I'm going home now. You should too. See you tomorrow.'

Luke nodded and rubbed his jaw, which was now hurting with the effort of keeping himself together. Once she'd closed the door behind her with a soft click he let out a long ragged breath. She was right. He was falling apart. Cracking up. Putting the fear of God into everyone around him. Scaring the living daylights out of himself.

Blocking everything out by burying himself in work might have got him through the aftermath of Grace's death, but it wasn't working this time. Not when Emily was out there, living and breathing.

How much longer could he tell himself that his recent lousy run on the markets was simply a case of rotten luck and bad timing?

How much longer could he blame his foul mood and short temper on lack of sleep?

How much longer could he bear the emptiness and the bleakness and the loneliness that wrapped itself round him like a thin grey blanket?

How much longer could he keep up the pretence that he was better off without her?

The fight drained out of him. The fragile barriers around his heart came crashing down and a hundred different emotions flung themselves at him. He nearly collapsed under the onslaught. The sensations whipping around him were so fierce that he had to grip the edge of the desk to keep himself upright.

What the bloody hell was he doing? Or rather not doing? She was out there—the woman who'd offered him her love. The woman he loved.

An amazing woman who'd taken a risk with her pottery and was at this very moment in the middle of one of the most important nights of her life. And here he was, missing her triumph and very possibly throwing away any chance of happiness he had. On the basis of what? The fear of some minuscule probability that, had it cropped up in his work, he would have discounted instantly.

How much longer was he going to carry on being such an almighty idiot?

His heart pounded. He glanced at his watch. Seven thirty. He might just be able to make it. He grabbed his coat and keys and raced out of the office.

Emily gazed round the gallery and tried to muster some enthusiasm. The opening night of her exhibition was a success. The trendy East London gallery was full of glamorous people drinking champagne, eating canapés and actually buying her work—despite Anna adding a zero to her prices. She ought to be bursting with pride, not wafting about listlessly, with her wretchedness hanging over her like a great black cloud.

Her pots and bowls and vases stood on shelves beneath spotlights, each piece shimmering and alive, a cruelly ironic contrast to the feelings swirling about inside her. She heard the roar of a car outside. Another of Anna's well-heeled friends, no doubt. Her heart sank. She wasn't sure she could manage much more of playing the gracious host. There was only one man she really wanted to see and he wasn't here.

So much for her foolish notion that Luke simply needed more time. That not having her around would make him see what he'd given up. And so much for thinking that he would at least step up to his responsibilities. How many times in the last couple of weeks had she envisaged scenarios in which Luke turned up on her doorstep, offering to look after her and the baby? She was pathetic.

A lump lodged in her throat and her eyes stung. She blinked quickly, took a deep breath and fixed a brittle smile to her face.

'Anna, I can't thank you enough for this.'

Anna shrugged. 'I never apologised for getting you into this mess.'

'It's not your fault.'

'I'd give anything to go back and change things.'

'Yes, well, what doesn't kill you makes you stronger.' Not knowing how Luke was or what he was doing wasn't making her stronger. It was slowly and torturously killing her. But she had to face facts. All the time in the universe wouldn't be enough to break down that wall of ice around his heart. The fact that she might not have been the right woman to break through his defences was not something she was going to consider.

'It's a shame you decided not to exhibit that bust. I understand, of course, but it is amazing.'

Emily had finally been unable to prevent herself from sticking together all those Luke-shaped pieces of clay and creating a model of his head. Her heart had ached as she'd moulded his cheekbones, his jaw, the straight nose. She hadn't had to add much water. Her tears had kept the clay perfectly wet.

'I can't bear it. I'm going to have to get rid—'

'You'd better not be talking about me,' said a smooth, deep voice behind her.

Emily's heart stopped and she dropped her glass. The blood roared into her ears. The colour and noise of the gallery disappeared. Her head went dizzy and she swayed. Then her heart started up again, so hard and fast that she thought it would break free. Was she imagining things? No, the wary expression on Anna's face told her everything. Luke was here. He was actually here. Why?

She held herself firm and turned round slowly. He looked as though he'd come straight from work. His suit was immaculate and his shirt was creaseless. But his face was pale and drawn, even though his eyes blazed. Emily nearly stumbled at the look in their depths. What was it? It looked like… No, she thought fiercely. No more self-delusion. No more hoping to find something that wasn't there.

'Lucky you weren't holding one of your pots.' He glanced round the room. 'This is extraordinary.'

She blinked and gave him a cool smile. 'Yes, well, it turns out extreme emotion is good for the creative spirit. But you wouldn't know much about extreme emotion, would you?'

'You'd be surprised.'

The smile that curved his mouth made her mad. How dared he laugh at her? 'What are you doing here?' she demanded.

'I received an invitation.'

'Did you send him an invitation?' said Emily, swinging round to glare at Anna.

Anna's gaze slid to her left. 'I might have done. God, I don't know. I just sent an e-mail to everyone in my address book.'

'Anna…'

'All right, maybe I did. But as soon as I'd sent it I wished I hadn't. OK?'

'Someone wants one of your little red dots,' said Luke.

He waited until Anna had excused herself and dashed off in the direction of a potential customer, and then he turned his full attention back to Emily. Beautiful, incredible Emily. Who'd shaken him up, made him want to live life again, who had one hell of a talent and who was currently taking an unnaturally intense interest in her shoes.

'What were you planning to get rid of?'

Emily flushed. 'Oh, er… My first kiln. It's falling to pieces.'

'Not the baby?'

Her head shot up and she gasped. 'Of course not. Didn't you get the scans I sent?'

'Yes.' He grabbed her arm and pulled her away from the crowds and into an office at the back.

Emily shook herself free and glared at him. 'Hey, I'm the star of the show. And you don't get to manhandle me any more.'

He took a step back as a mixture of pride, admiration, desire and love walloped him in the chest. How had he ever thought he could live without her? 'For someone who's apparently in love with me, you're not being very friendly.'

Her cheeks went pink and she bit on her lip. 'Yeah, well, I'll get over it.'

Luke's heart began to thud loudly. He probably deserved that. But, God, he hoped he hadn't left it too late. His mouth went dry. 'Don't.'

'Don't what?' She looked at him with wary defiance.

'Get over it.'

'Why not?'

'I don't want you to.'

She crossed her arms and lifted her chin. 'Tough. If you can repress your emotions, I'm sure I can.'

Luke thrust his hands into the pockets of his trousers. 'I can't. And let me tell you I've been trying pretty hard. Nice dress, by the way.' She was wearing the midnight-blue dress she'd worn to the gala.

She plucked at the material and frowned. 'I was going to take the shears to it, but it was expensive.'

'So you cut it off at the knees instead.'

'Symbolic, I thought.'

'Whatever the length, I have a sapphire necklace that would look great with it.'

Her eyebrows shot up. 'You bought it? I thought only a fool would do something like that.'

Luke didn't take his eyes off her. 'I'm a fool.'

She sniffed. 'In so many ways.'

He took a deep breath and his heart pounded. 'In particular for being unable to admit to myself just how much I love you.'

For a moment he didn't think she'd heard him. Then her eyes lit up for a split second, and it made him want to punch the air.

'What took you so long?' she said coolly.

'Stubbornness, mainly. With a dose of idiocy and fear thrown in for good measure.'

She bit on her lip and nodded.

His gaze dipped to her mouth. He wanted to haul her into his arms and kiss her senseless. He'd missed her so much. 'You were right,' he said gruffly.

'About what?'

'Everything. The way you make me feel scares the hell out of me. And the idea of ever losing you terrifies me. But not having you with me is far, far worse.'

'So where have you been?'

'Hell and back.'

'Good.'

'In a Zonda.'

'Am I supposed to be impressed?'

'Yes.'

'Even if I knew what it was, I doubt I would be.'

'It's a very fast sports car. I bought it last week. I used to have one years ago. It's sitting outside.'

'I hope it gets towed.' She studied her nails. 'Most men when they're about to become fathers trade in the sports car.'

'True, but our whole relationship has been the wrong way round.'

'I wasn't aware we *had* a relationship.'

Luke's eyes narrowed. 'You're deliberately making me suffer, aren't you?' Surely this was a good sign. Wasn't it? If she didn't still feel something for him she wouldn't still be here, would she?

'Don't you think I'm entitled to?'

'You said you were irreversibly in love with me.'

Emily frowned. 'Lately I've been reconsidering the irreversible bit.'

A chill ran through him. 'And?'

'I'm still thinking.'

'Well, while you are, let me tell you what made me realise I couldn't carry on denying how I felt about you.'

'What makes you think I'm interested?'

'You will be. It was your vase.'

That captured her attention. She stared at him. 'My vase?'

'Mmm. There it was, lurking in the corner of my sitting room—'

She shot him a furious look. 'My pottery does not lurk.'

'You're quite right. It doesn't. Your pottery is bright and vibrant. In fact it's pretty amazing.'

'My vase brought warmth and colour into an otherwise sterile environment.'

'Exactly. But I quite liked my safe, sterile environment. And I didn't like the vase reminding me of you, so I put it in a cupboard.'

'That's cruel.'

Luke nodded. 'Unfortunately it left a gap where it should have been. And there's a gap here too.' He tapped his chest. 'Where you should be.' Emily went very still. 'I lose control when you're around and I like it. I only sleep well when I sleep with you. I need you, Emily, and I love you.'

'You've made me pretty miserable.'

The look in her eyes made his heart wrench. 'I know.' His gut clenched with regret. 'I'm so very sorry.'

'This pregnancy thing is hard to do alone.'

'You don't have to. I won't let anything happen to you. If you marry me, I'll spend the rest of my life making sure of it.'

She didn't answer, and Luke suddenly knew what real fear felt like. It clawed away at him. Had he blown it? He went very cold at the thought that Emily didn't love him, didn't want him. That he'd killed any feelings she'd had for him. The need to know either way burned inside him. 'How's that thought process coming along?' His voice cracked and he cleared his throat.

'All done.'

He saw the ghost of a smile hover over her mouth and he suddenly remembered how to breathe. 'And?' He scanned her features, but they held no indication of what was going through her mind.

'It seems irreversible is about right,' she said.

What the hell did *that* mean? Luke was about to demand clarification, but then her eyes met his and he felt himself quake.

She walked up to him and wound her arms around his neck. 'I've tried so hard to stop loving you, but I can't.'

His heart lurched violently and relief poured through him. 'Thank God,' he murmured, wrapping his arms around her and crushing her against him. 'Marry me.'

She pulled back and looked up at him, happiness spreading across her face like sunshine. 'Are you sure?'

He was never letting her out of his sight again. 'You're having my baby.'

'Good point,' she said softly.

His eyes blazed down at her. 'How are you feeling about that?'

'I want it with a fierceness that scares me. You?'

'Unexpectedly ecstatic. I love you so very much.' He looked deep into her eyes and his throat clogged.

'I love you too. We're going to be fine, aren't we?' she murmured, putting her hand on his chest where his heart racing.

'We're going to be so much better than fine,' he said, lowering his mouth to hers and kissing her until they were both shaking. 'I promise.'

A sneaky peek at next month…

By Request

RELIVE THE ROMANCE WITH THE BEST OF THE BEST

My wish list for next month's titles…

In stores from 17th January 2014:

☐ Ruthlessly Royal – Robyn Donald, Annie West & Fiona Hood-Stewart

☐ Millionaire Magnates – Katherine Garbera, Brenda Jackson & Charlene Sands

3 stories in each book – only £5.99!

In stores from 7th February 2014:

☐ Australian Quinns – Kate Hoffmann

☐ Pregnancy Surprise – Barbara McMahon, Susan Meier & Jackie Braun

Available at WHSmith, Tesco, Asda, Eason, Amazon and Apple

Just can't wait?

Visit us Online

You can buy our books online a month before they hit the shops! **www.millsandboon.co.uk**